# OPERATION PASTORIUS

*Another Frank Sweeney Adventure*

*Written By*

# WILL PONNER

ISBN | Paperback: 979-8-89692-362-6
ISBN | eBook: 979-8-89692-359-6

Printed in the United States of America

This book is dedicated to Connie Parker, an absolutely amazing and delightful wife, mother, daughter, daughter-in-law, sister, aunt, cousin, niece, athlete, teacher, and friend who is missed every day by her family and friends. She brought so much joy and light to this world, and her memory lives on in her immediate family as well as her extended one. We all love and miss you, Joe, and are so thankful for the joy and privilege of having had you in our lives.

# CONTENTS

# EXCERPT FROM "OPERATION TORCH"

# CHAPTER 1



*October 24ᵗʰ, 1942, 2:00 AM*
*Local Time*

The 220-foot beast broke the surface of the water, bounced for a couple of minutes, and then settled, gently rocking in the light waves. It was a quiet, peaceful night. The fall air was unusually warm, almost as if it was June instead of late October. As one of the sailors lifted the latch, Hans Heinz-Linder, the diminutive 29-year-old commander of the German U-202 submarine, breathed a momentary sigh of relief. More relief came a few moments after the intake of the fresh air, albeit with a saltwater smell. Still, it beat being a few hundred feet underwater with recycled air. The sub and his crew of 48 had arrived at their destination. A man normally wound tight but trained to never let his men see him sweat, Heinz-Linder had expertly maneuvered the ship from its launching point of Brest, France, 16 days earlier. He was tired. Drained, really. Dodging depth charges and torpedo bombs for the last two weeks was no small task. He and his men were ready for a break, but he knew that that was not going to be happening any time soon. Privately, he knew all too well that this was a war that his country had started, and there was no turning back.

Truth be told, he really shouldn't even be on the submarine in the first place. The Versailles Treaty of 1919 that Germany had agreed to at the end of The Great War expressly forbade the Fatherland from manufacturing any submarines. It stipulated that Germany's entire naval force could not exceed 15,000 personnel, and any shipbuilding that was allowed was only if they were replacing an existing ship. This limited Germany to six cruisers, twelve torpedo boats, twelve destroyers, and no aircraft carriers or submarines. Germany more or less adhered to this in the 1920s, mostly because they had no economic means to do anything different. Runaway inflation and what many would argue to be punitive economic policies that came with the Treaty resulted in financial chaos for the country. The currency was essentially worthless. But as the Nazis came into power in 1933, things began to change. Hitler ordered ships and airplanes to be built in large, unheard-of numbers. Men like Heinz-Linder were the beneficiaries (if one could call it that) of these decisions.

Heinz-Linder had eight years of experience with the Kriegsmarine, or German Navy. He had worked his way up over the years to his current role of Commander. He and his crew had been on quite a few missions of late, all in the Atlantic theatre, and his U-boat had several victories to talk about: they had sunk four enemy ships and damaged four more in less than 12 months. The ship - his ship - was only a year in the water. Germany's massive production of naval vessels - especially the U-boats - had proven to be a brilliant strategy. Construction of almost 1,200 subs had taken place in 11 different cities. This strategy had more pros than cons: The pros were that production could be maximized, and new boats could be in the water relatively quickly over a shorter period of time. The cons were that quality and inventory control was more difficult since it took a massive number of people in many cities to produce the same ships to the same specs. With the Fatherland at war with so many countries, mass production and speed trumped nuanced inventory issues. The one problem was that the German Navy ended up with more boats than they had qualified captains. Given the situation, training as a commander was far briefer than under normal circumstances. Heinz-Linder's own U-boat training was less than nine months, and then he was quickly shoved into command of a smaller U-18, about sixty feet shorter than the U-202.

With his brief but flawless record, he was going places in the Kriegsmarine. This very assignment was evidence of that. This mission was the biggest of all thus far, for his cargo was the most important that he would carry during the entire war. Germany was dominating the Atlantic, sinking or hobbling hundreds of merchant ships already. These vessels were carrying military cargo and supplies - and people - to equip the allies in the fight to restore Europe's freedom. The main deterrent to these efforts was the German U-boats and their uncanny success in making sure these ships never made it to their destinations. Heinz-Linder was proud to be contributing to that dominance.

While this was indeed his biggest assignment, it was also the most harrowing. In addition to having to dodge allied destroyers dropping depth charges around him, he had to always keep his crew ready, watching and listening for enemies in the air and on the sea.

This particular mission came directly from one of the most powerful men in the Third Reich, and Linder was one of two men who were handpicked by the head of the German Navy, Admiral Karl Doenitz, for this effort. His cargo, however, was decidedly chosen by someone else.

As some of his officers climbed out of the sub to get their first breath of fresh air in days, they shook their captain's hand and whispered their congratulations to him on his superb leadership and expertise in bringing the sub to its destination. After a few precious moments of fresh air and a cigarette, Heinz-Linder quietly announced, "It's time to bring the cargo up. We need to get back out to sea as soon as possible."

The four men made their way up the steps to the small deck of the sub. To their right was total darkness. They looked to their left and saw fog. A lot of fog. They could barely make out some sort of lights on the port side. At least they knew which way to head. It appeared that the land was as little as 300 meters away. No one spoke for a full minute, letting the silence of the moment allow them to collect their thoughts and determine if they had been detected.

Finally breaking the silence, Captain Heinz-Linder looked at the men and said in a low whisper, "Welcome to New York."

C H A P T E R   2



Walter Kappe looked over his finished products. Before him sat eight men, all of them hand-picked by Kappe himself. They were all at a bucolic estate outside of Berlin with many acres on which to perfect their craft. The men finished their eight-week immersion training for a very special mission. Kappe himself had been handpicked by Wilhelm Canaris, the head of the Abwehr, Germany's powerful Military Intelligence organization.

A smallish, pudgy man of 37, Kappe had what was called "a high forehead," which meant that he would inevitably be short of some hair in a few years. It was already thinning out. He had accepted his fate in this department. To make matters worse, it was readily apparent that his mouth looked to be too small for his large head, giving him a look of smugness to a casual observer. But then again, he was a bit smug. He felt that no one could do his job as well as he could and that he was the perfect man for this (or any) assignment.

Born and raised in Germany, Kappe came to the U.S. after Hitler's failed Beer Hall Putsch in 1923. He was an ardent Hitler and Nazi supporter. After arriving in New York, he quickly moved to Chicago, and then on to Cincinnati, where he became active in forming an organization that was pro-Germany and pro-Hitler, even before the madman had come to power.

Kappe then moved back to New York and helped organize what became known as the German American Bund, which was the American version of the Nazi party. He was the Press and Propaganda Chief, the second in command. Not satisfied with anything but the top seat, he began a whispering campaign against his boss, Fritz Kuhn. Kappe underestimated Kuhn's base of support and overestimated his own base of support, which led to his ouster.

He returned to Germany in 1937. By the middle of 1941, everyone knew that it was only a matter of time before the U.S. entered the war. There was a consensus building that German citizens who had lived in the U.S. could be quite valuable to the Fatherland. Kappe was installed as the head man to form a department that would recruit Germans who had lived in America, with the express purpose of sabotaging and terrorizing American targets.

He had utilized the Ausland Institute for most of the information that told him who might be a fit. The Institute was sort of a national library of information on people, be they German citizens or not. Birth dates, national origin, full names, addresses, relatives - it had it all. In Kappe's case, he was interested in the records of every German citizen who had lived in America for any period of time. The fact that Kappe himself had lived in America for many years and had traveled around the country there helped him in the selection and recruitment process. He was quite familiar with all things American: customs, traditions, clothing styles, slang, and regional accents that he could easily pass for a U.S. citizen himself. In fact, he had, for all intents and purposes, done just that when he lived there.

He looked over the eight men as they were busy reviewing American newspaper articles and eating as if they were in a diner in New York. He watched them for all of the idiosyncrasies that invariably would make them stick out for all of the wrong reasons. Did they cut their meat with the knife in their right hand and then switch the fork from their left hand to the right one before eating? Or did they simply cut the meat and leave the fork in their left hand and immediately eat it with their left hand with the back of the fork facing out? The first method was the American way. The second was purely and obviously European.

The good news was that each of these men had lived in America before coming back to the Fatherland to help fight the war. Two of the men were actually American citizens, and one of them had even served in the U.S. military. Kappe himself was a lieutenant in the German army. His optimal candidates would be men who knew their way around America, spoke the language flawlessly, and wouldn't attract unnecessary attention. In addition, they had to be experienced in everything from explosives to covert assassination techniques. Most of all, they needed to be completely dedicated to the Fatherland and the Fuhrer and the mission of returning Germany to its proper place in the world's standing.

The eight men were the survivors. The group had started with twelve but there were four who just did not have what it took. Two of the men's English wasn't up to par, and the other two drank too much. Actually, most of the remaining eight men drank too much as well. But the eight drank less than the remaining two, so Kappe told the duo that they would be assigned to a different mission. His training ensured that each man knew how to handle all kinds of firearms, from small pistols with silencers to long-range rifles with scopes attached. They had also been trained in covert operations and learned how to kill a man in ways that made it look like anything but murder. Further, they were equipped with bomb-making capabilities. Canaris had wisely told him that their targets would not be shared until Kappe's men had landed safely in America. That's not to say that the targets hadn't been established; to the contrary, there were photos and, in many cases, blueprints of each of the facilities that were on the list of possibilities. All of them resided with the man who would be their main contact in America. While Kappe wasn't sure which or how many of these methods would be employed, he could say with certainty that American citizens on American soil would soon be dying.

# CHAPTER 3

George Parker sat in his cramped office in a non-descript building on E Street in Washington, D.C. His building was the center of the four-building complex. The complex sat on land that was northwest of the Lincoln Memorial on Navy Hill. The area got its name because it was the original site of the Old Navy Observatory, built almost 100 years ago. He glanced out the window and observed the local brewery in town as well as a skating rink that had yet to be flooded for the winter. "I wonder if they'll even bother with the skating rink," he mused. "Besides, this isn't Minnesota, so I wonder how long a rink would last anyway."

Being in a war tends to change priorities. Indeed, the nation's capital was buzzing with constant activity. It felt like the population in the D.C. area had tripled since the war began. And it probably had.

The simple everyday life in America had changed since that day last December. Things like skating rinks are now considered a luxury. Most things were now being rationed. Gasoline, butter, meat, sugar, canned fruit, and even baby food had made the list. "How can you ration baby food?" he asked no one in particular.

Every American - even the kids - was given a rationing book that was designed with a point system in place. Things like meat and sugar required a lot of points, as opposed to fresh fruit, which were allotted no points. The government figured that fresh fruit wouldn't make it all the way overseas anyway. The rationing ensured that all Americans felt like they were united in contributing something to the war effort. In an unprecedented move, FDR had even put into effect pricing laws to ensure that there was no price gouging going on when it came to high- demand goods.

"What an incredible time to be alive," he muttered. "I hope I get to tell my grandchildren about all of this someday." The alternative was not something that he allowed himself to contemplate too often. America was born as a result of its citizens' absolute refusal to be dictated to by any government entity. Less than 200 years later, here she was again, fighting for her freedom.

Parker was one of many citizens who contributed both directly and indirectly to defeating their common enemies. While his family played by the rules regarding the rationing efforts, he was involved in a game of another sort: intelligence.

He glanced down at his desk. The piles of reports that he had to read just kept coming. But he also had a report to finish writing, and he had almost completed it. Just another page or two and it would be given to his secretary, Peg McFarland, to type up, after which it would be sent to the powers that be. He often wondered how many people saw these reports and how many of these same people actually read them. Knowing his boss, the number of eyes on these kinds of things would be very limited. After all, they were in the spy business.

This latest report that he had to author gave color to a recent assignment called "Operation Grab Bag." The top-secret mission involved his godson, Frank Sweeney, an American pilot, being sent into Germany to determine what sort of secret air technology the Nazis were working on that could change the landscape of the war. Frank and the key players had just arrived in the U.S. yesterday after a debriefing in London that lasted for two days. Dr. Edwin Conway, a world-renowned aeronautical engineer from Ireland, was coerced by the Nazis to work for them. Frank managed to miraculously smuggle Conway and his two children, Leigh and Jimmy, out of Germany, much to the outrage of the Nazis.

Wild Bill Donovan, Parker's boss, was so impressed with Sweeney that he pulled some strings and had Frank transferred into the O.S.S., effective immediately. That was less than a week ago. Frank and Hans Ungrodt, an undercover spy from Germany who worked for the British and secretly helped Frank get the Conways out of the country, were due to be in D.C.

in a few days. Frank would be immersed in serious spy training, and Hans would observe for a while before being shipped back to London for his next assignment. Dr. Conway was due to come to D.C. after a brief time of rest and acclimation to the U.S.

Once in D.C., more debriefing would take place with several military and government agencies.

Parker's aforementioned secretary, Peg McFarland, whom he shared with Donovan, showed him no mercy most days, not that he'd ask for any anyway. Peg was an attractive redhead with two huge strengths: an attention to detail and an ability to handle very sensitive information discreetly. Like Parker, she had worked in the F.B.I. but not with George. She had married her husband Fran 15 years earlier, and the two of them had four children, one cuter than the next. Despite all of this, she felt a powerful call to serve her country. Somehow, she made it all work.

George sighed. There was just so much to learn and get up to speed on. Things were happening in the war - both wars. America was fighting two different wars on two different continents in two different ways against two different enemies. Other than that, they were identical. The threats to the country were real, and they seemed to come from each of the 48 states, although Parker knew that that really wasn't true. But based on the number of reports, it sure felt that way. Discerning fact from fiction and prioritizing which potential threat to act upon and feed into his boss took up most of his hours these days. And that was just the defensive part of the job. He also had to look for more opportunities like Grab Bag, where the O.S.S. went on the offensive to do some damage to the enemy.

Six feet tall with the beginnings of gray starting to reach into his sideburns, the 49-year-old Parker took a mental break to assess how he had gotten to this place. After all, working for the man that he was working for was no small feat. Growing up on Westchester Drive in West St. Paul, he played any sport at the moment that the other neighborhood kids wanted to play. A natural leader, the boys looked to him when a squabble broke out about who was out and who was safe. After a stellar athletic career in high school, he was recruited to play baseball at the "U. of M." for the Minnesota Gophers. From there, he signed with the Washington Senators and played in a couple of different leagues around the country.

After baseball, he came back to the Twin Cities and considered what he would do for a career. There were only a small handful of career choices for a man of Irish descent. There was the fire department, manual labor for a construction company, working your way up to running, and eventually owning a bar or becoming a cop. Much like the Italians, the Irish had been labeled and tended to congregate with their own. Even the Catholic churches were set up this way: St. Matthews on St. Paul's west side was the German church; St. Michael's, where Parker attended, located just a few blocks from St. Matt's off of Concord Street, was the Irish church. St. Stanislaw was for the Poles, St. Louis catered to the French, and St. Paul's Cathedral catered to anyone else who really didn't care.

The fire departments weren't hiring and didn't pay anything anyway; the bars - at least the legal ones - had been put out of commission with Prohibition. Parker was convinced that he had some defect in his family that didn't allow him to be mechanically inclined to anything, which left out construction. So, almost by default, he found himself trying to become a cop. St. Paul's police force was made up of a lot of Irishmen, so his last name certainly didn't hurt him.

He started as a patrolman, walking a beat that included downtown St. Paul along Market Street, and worked his way up to Detective after a few years. While a patrolman usually was in the middle of things - breaking up fights, stopping a robbery, or getting a lost child home, a detective dealt with the aftermath of such events. There were lots of violent crimes back then.

His partner ended up being Michael Sweeney, and the two of them solved many cases together. Nicknamed "The Twin Sleuths" by the St. Paul Pioneer Press, the local newspaper for people on the St. Paul side of the river, they invoked fear in the criminal and relief from the public. So close were the two that George ended up being godfather to Frank Sweeney, Michael's son.

After Michael decided to leave the force and dedicate himself full time to the Sweeney Detective Bureau, George had no desire to start over with a new partner. That's when the FBI came calling. J. Edgar Hoover was building a national police force of sorts and having federal money behind him assured Hoover that he could afford the best of the best when it came to manpower. It also ensured that the F.B.I. would have access to some of the finest minds in research, technology, and science.

But Hoover needed a crisis to justify this power grab from the states, and the opportunity came in the form of organized gangsters who did their crime across state lines. Gone would be the days when a cop had to concede a car chase to the criminal as they crossed over into another state. Hoover now held the ultimate trump card, for the "F" in F.B.I. stood for "Federal." That gave him a jurisdiction that had no boundaries. The ineptness - and maybe the underfunding - of the local police forces allowed the public and many corporations who were tired of being robbed to lobby Congress for a national organization that could fight major crime wherever needed. The timing couldn't have been better. You had Hoover, always hungry for more power, and gangsters wreaking havoc in Prohibition and then graduating to bank robberies.

The decision to migrate to bank robbing really came as the result of Prohibition ending. After all, since bootlegging was obsolete, the gangsters had to make a living somehow, and robbing banks became the easiest and fastest method to do so. However, most banks became federally insured in 1933 with the passing of the Banking Act. Enter the Federal Bureau of Investigation. You rob a federally insured bank, and you don't have a two-man police force after you. Meet today's F.B.I.

Parker and his family had sacrificed a lot for the Bureau. After leaving St. Paul to join Hoover's organization in D.C., the family moved to New York. After a stint there, they moved to Chicago, followed by a three-year stay in Miami, before going back to the nation's capital. George had advanced to become a Deputy Director in the Bureau, but he had become more jaded as he observed - and often got dragged into - all of the politics. It was time to make a move.

His new boss couldn't be more different than his old one. William "Wild Bill" Donovan, the head of The Office of Strategic Services, was already a legend. He was one of the most highly decorated men in history, and he had been awarded every major medal, including the Medal of Honor, for his gallantry in the Great War.

He was a man of action who didn't care so much about who got credit for things as opposed to just wanting to get them done.

Hoover, on the other hand, was obsessed with control and a glory hound, among other things. Parker respected what Hoover had built and was continuing to build, but he didn't always care for his methods. J. Edgar had even recently been in talks with The American Broadcasting Company to start a national radio program tentatively titled "This is Your FBI." Hoover himself would approve the release of certain actual cases that could be dramatized for the national radio audience. "Knowing him, he will want to control the script, the actors, and even edit some of the stories himself," Parker mused. Hoover was all about promoting the Bureau and himself, and not always in that order.

Conversely, Donovan secretly hoped that no one would ever figure out that there even was an O.S.S. Make no mistake, Donovan was anything but a pushover. He was not above raiding every other department and military entity around to build his organization with the finest men and women that he could find. Donovan's vision was more of a crusade rooted in protecting and promoting freedom all over the world.

Hoover's vision was first centered on control and power, with the natural result of that being a sense of order and function. "Still," George said to himself, "It's fascinating to see how two different men with two radically different philosophies and agendas could both be so successful."

Of the two, Parker was clearly more drawn to Donovan. Theirs was a freewheeling, give-and-take relationship. Donovan never made him feel like a subordinate. With Hoover, however, there was a clear line drawn that no one dared cross. There was no question as to who was in charge at the FBI, and every employee had better not forget it.

George's walk down memory lane was interrupted by the aforementioned Peg McFarland, who knocked and came in with another couple of stacks of reports for him to review.

She had the ability to knock and enter at the same time and pull it off in such a way that was neither intrusive nor rude. Maybe because she always did both with a smile.

"This stack came in this afternoon, and it highlights the latest information about the Pacific theatre. And this one highlights the latest information from Europe," she said rather matter-of-factly. "Can I get you some coffee, Mr. Parker?"

"No thanks, Peg. And would you please call me George?"

"I doubt I can do that, Mr. Parker."

"And why is that?"

"Protocol."

"Ok, then, Mrs. McFarland." Having grown up at the FBI, Donovan's more informal culture would take some time for Peg - and even George - to adjust to.

Peg looked at him, shrugged, and smiled, and walked out of the office while shutting the door in one smooth motion.

C H A P T E R   4

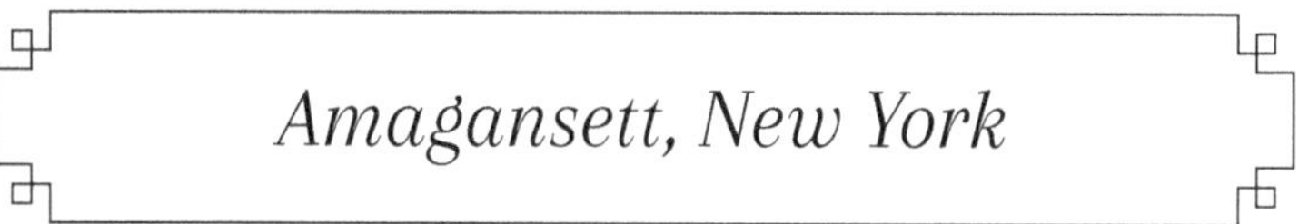

*Amagansett, New York*

The four Germans slipped into a large rubber raft and began to paddle their way toward the shore. They were accompanied by two sailors from the sub, who were in a second raft by themselves, carrying the supplies that were a critical part of the mission. All six men were in German uniforms. They paddled seamlessly through the relatively calm water, maintaining silence throughout the 15-minute voyage. Their silence was met with even more silence. And fog. So dense was the fog that they could barely make out the direction that the few shore lights were coming from.

George Dasch, the leader of the mission, knew exactly where they were. Having lived in New York City for several years before the war, he had ventured outside the city on short furloughs to other areas of New York, particularly Long Island. His work while he lived in New York consisted mostly of waiting tables in upper-class restaurants in and around Manhattan. He hated it. He felt it demeaning to rely on some rich man tipping him for bringing out his food. Dasch had left Germany and came to America in 1922. He had even served in the U.S. Army. At 39, he was the oldest man on the mission. He was a slender man with a long face and a long nose to match. He hardly looked like a spy, and that would work to his advantage.

His time in America was relatively non-descript. He did nothing to stand out. He wasn't unusually successful by any stretch, but he also didn't cause problems. He was not a memorable man and would blend in well. His English was excellent, and New York was full of immigrants anyway. He was actually excited about being back in America.

Dasch turned to the next in command, Ernst "Peter" Burger. "Not much further," he whispered. Burger, 36, had also lived in America for several years, emigrating in 1927 and becoming a U.S. citizen in 1933. Unlike Dasch, Burger joined the Nazi Party at age 17 and, after living in America for several years, decided to return to Germany in 1939 to rejoin the party in order to help fight the war. But the Germany he returned to was not the Germany that he had left. He quickly became disillusioned with what The Fatherland had become and had even been thrown into a concentration camp for 17 months for making critical remarks about the Nazi Party.

In a surprise move, the Abwehr, Germany's military intelligence organization, recruited him into its spy network, and because his English was excellent and he knew his way around America, he soon crossed paths with Kappe, who then recruited him for this assignment. Burger, a stocky man with a no-nonsense face and a striking "don't mess with me" jawline, jumped at the chance when offered the opportunity to return to the U.S., even if it meant sabotaging the American war effort.

The other two men, Richard Quirin and Heinrich Heinck were both in their mid-30s and had also lived in America. Quirin had lived in the states for 12 years, living mostly in Schenectady in upstate New York. He had worked for G.E. as a mechanic. When he and his wife returned to Germany in 1939, he worked at the Volkswagen plant in Braunschweig, a city in north central Germany.

Besides being a key city for manufacturing different armaments for the war, Braunschweig's big claim to fame was that it was the city that granted the Austrian-born Hitler his German citizenship. Strings had been pulled in 1932, so the madman would be eligible to run for office immediately.

It was in Braunschweig that Quirin met Heinck. Like Quirin, Heinck, tall and thin with deep-set blue eyes, took being a member of the Nazi Party seriously. When they were both living in the U.S., Quirin and Heinck were very active in the German American Bund. In addition to being a Nazi front, the organization was made up of German Americans whose mission was to be a public relations entity of sorts that would paint the Nazi party in a positive light to all Americans.

Heinck still spoke English with a noticeable German accent. Like Quirin, Heinck had worked in manufacturing facilities in America. After he returned to Germany, Heinck worked with Quirin at the Volkswagen plant in Braunschweig.

The four men had spent more than enough time together to know each other's strengths and weaknesses, competencies, and quirks.

While they were still waiting for specifics, they knew that their main mission was clear: to disrupt and destroy American installations and infrastructure that contributed to the war effort.

Their secondary mission was equally important: weaken America's resolve to stay in the war by frightening her citizens through random acts of terror.

Finally, Dasch saw some lights off to his left. They would be landing their rafts shortly on Amagansett, a city named by the Indians, meaning "Place of good water." It was a small town on the outskirts of Long Island, about 107 miles from Manhattan.

Thinking that they were almost on shore, he quietly said to the others, "We've made it!" and jumped off the raft and promptly sank well over his head. The other men quickly got him back into the raft, and they paddled for several more minutes. Dasch's second effort was much better. He hopped out of the raft, and the water came up to his waist. The others waited for him to pull them the last few feet to the shore. As they reached the shore, the other three men jumped out and pulled their raft up on the beach. They then began to slowly deflate it. The other raft would be occupied by the German sailors and taken back to the sub, which waited serenely out at sea. The waves gently rolling onto the shoreline helped cover their low whispers. The fog was so thick that none of the men could see exactly where they were going.

The remaining dry men - Dasch's fellow conspirators and the two escorts - quickly unloaded the contents of the second raft and carried them up from the shore to dry land near some woods. They immediately began digging with their shovels to bury the raft and paddles, and much of their supplies. The supplies consisted mainly of explosives, primers, incendiaries, and wire cutters. In addition, they also had fake drivers' licenses, fake social security cards, draft deferment cards, and almost $175,000 in U.S. currency. In short, the Fatherland had removed as many obstacles as possible for them to successfully complete their mission.

Dasch, soaking wet and getting colder by the minute, stripped out of his uniform and grabbed some civilian clothes from one of his sacks. He motioned for the others to do the same. They had purposely come ashore in their German uniforms just in case they were caught immediately. If they were caught while wearing their military uniforms, they would be treated as prisoners of war. But if they were caught in plainclothes, they would be classified as the spies that they were. And spies were treated a lot less leniently than P.O.W.s. Actually, they were treated with no leniency whatsoever. The execution of spies on foreign soil was almost automatic.

Once dry, Dasch began loading some of the U.S. currency into his pockets. Much of the rest would be left in a large sack and a separate briefcase, both of which he and he alone would carry. As the leader, he would have control over the money. He combed his hair as best as he could and then began looking around to try to get his bearings. After a minute, he told Burger that he was going to start walking north on the beach for a couple of minutes just to check things out.

"We'll be finished here in a couple of minutes, then we will follow you," answered Burger.

Dasch nodded and began to move.

The fog was still incredibly thick, and Dasch couldn't see more than a few feet in front of him.

After helping the spies get the holes dug, the two remaining sailors who had escorted them to shore gave them a quick "Heil Hitler!" salute and got back in the remaining raft to hightail it back to the U-boat. Within seconds, they were already out of sight, thanks to the fog. Dasch saw an occasional blinking light coming from the sub that would guide the sailors back to the ship. "That captain has to be anxious to get out of here," thought Dasch. "What news that would be if they were to be caught."

As it turned out, Captain Linder and his crew were in very real danger of being caught. The sub had drifted more toward shore and had run aground, less than 250 yards from Dasch and his men. He reversed engines, but that didn't help. He and his men had to wait over 40 minutes for the tide to rise before they could get off of the sandbar. By the time they were able to escape to sea, they could make out some car headlights driving along the beach. They could only hope that they hadn't been seen.

Dasch continued to walk slowly up the beach toward the lights that they had seen from the raft. He had only gone about 30 yards in about three minutes, so limited was his visibility. He decided to turn around and join the others. "No point in getting separated in this fog," he told himself. He turned around and felt his way back to the other men. All four men met up a couple of minutes later.

"Everything all set?" asked Dasch.

"We're ready," said Burger.

Dasch said, "Good. Show me where you buried the weaponry."

They walked about 40 feet into some high brush. There was a pile of rocks about seven feet from a large tree.

"Everything is right under these rocks," said Heinck. It looked a little obvious to Dasch, so he scattered a couple of the rocks around just to make it look a little more natural.

"That will have to do," he said. "We need to get off this beach and into the city, and it's a pretty long walk to the subway from here."

The men tried to smooth out the ground a little more. After another minute or two, Dasch said, "All right, let's go." They each had flashlights (most Europeans called them torches), but given the fog, they were of little use.

"Burger and I will walk ahead. It's best that the four of us not be seen together. You two stay about 10 meters behind us, just in case. It will probably be a slower pace due to the lack of visibility. And remember, your voice will carry so close to the water, so if you must talk, keep your voices down."

Quirin and Heinck both did the eye roll, somewhat insulted by Dasch's stating of the obvious.

Dasch turned to begin the trek to the train station. The two groups of men began walking further away from the beach, hoping that the fog would lift enough for them to pick up their pace. They continued to keep a reasonable distance between them, per Dasch's order. They walked toward the lights, what little they could see of them. Only ten minutes into their journey, a single light out of nowhere showed several feet away from them. And it was a moving light. Within minutes of landing in America, their entire operation would be threatened before it had even begun.

# CHAPTER 5

It was another late night at the office for George Parker, so much for dinner with the family. He stared a moment at the latest pile of reports that Peg had dropped off. He was trying to get up to speed with all the potential threats to the country. Parker's job was a new role in a new organization. The O.S.S. was the brainchild of Donovan. In addition to his WWI heroics, he was a well-respected attorney and even a former candidate for Governor of New York, among many other things. Donovan also happened to be a former classmate and longtime friend of the current occupant of the house that sat on 1600 Pennsylvania Avenue. Although they had their differences politically - Donovan was a staunch conservative - friendship and the country's safety trumped everything else.

There was a knock on his door, and before he could even say, "Come in," Wild Bill Donovan was in the office pacing in front of him.

"Hello, Georgie," he said to Parker, walking back and forth in Parker's cramped office.

Parker stood immediately and said, "Good evening, Director."

"What are you up to?" asked Donovan as he motioned for George to sit.

"Just trying to get caught up on all of the reports that are coming in from all over the world."

Donovan, clearly distracted, grunted an "I see."

Parker looked at his boss for a moment, trying to determine if he should ask what the problem was or remain silent and let Donovan take the lead on what came next.

It was Donovan's trips to Europe in the late 1930s and in 1940 (at F.D.R.'s request) that had convinced Roosevelt that things over there were bad and about to get worse. Donovan's stops in England were of particular importance. The English made quite a show of things for him. Donovan's reputation as a war hero was known far and wide, and the English spared no expense in wining and dining him. They took him all over the country, showing him their military might and preparedness for what some deemed the inevitable coming war. Most of what he was shown was smoke and mirrors. Despite their attempt to impress Donovan, he saw through their bluff and determined that the Brits were woefully unprepared and lacked the resources necessary to fight a war with Germany. However, he also felt strongly that Britain could prevail in a war with Germany - but only with America's involvement and partnership.

Donovan met with Prime Minister Neville Chamberlain while in England and found the man to be a complete head shaker. "No one can be this naïve," he thought. He even wondered if Chamberlain was a German agent, so bent was he on avoiding a war with Hitler. He reported back to Roosevelt that the man that he came away impressed with was Winston Churchill, a career statesman who had been very outspoken about Hitler himself and saw the madman for who he was.

"I'm telling you, we can work with this man," Donovan told Roosevelt. Churchill himself hosted several tours of the various military bases that Donovan took. The two men took an instant liking to one another.

Donovan was also introduced to Bill Stephenson, a man of Canadian descent who headed up the office of British Security Coordination (B.S.C.) and also oversaw the S.O.E., or Strategic Office Executive Department - their intelligence and spy operations.

After the war began in Europe, Stephenson opened the kimono to Donovan and gave him invaluable insight into organizing and training a spy network, intelligence gathering, and tools of the trade. Stephenson even trained Donovan's first recruits.

The Canadian proved to be a true friend to Donovan and the mutual respect between them was unmatched. The two shared many secrets and confidentialities with one another, with full blessing from both Churchill and Roosevelt. In fact, it was Stephenson who suggested to Roosevelt that he appoint Donovan to head up U.S. spy operations.

As close as Stephenson was to Donovan, he had little time for Parker's old boss. He found J. Edgar to be pompous, secretive, and condescending. Hoover actually did Donovan a favor by behaving this way because it drew Stephenson even closer to his O.S.S. comrade.

Their commitment to work together formed the foundation of a partnership between all British Intelligence and the O.S.S. Parker had yet to meet Stephenson, but he figured it would only be a matter of time.

Parker decided to wait and let Donovan's mouth catch up to his brain. He was clearly preoccupied. Finally, Parker said, "Is there something I can help you with, sir?"

Donovan was staring out to who knows where then finally came back into the conversation.

"First, I told you that my name is Bill." Clearly, Donovan was struggling with what to do next. Finally, he turned to Parker and said, "George, I need to confide a couple of things to you."

"Bill, I hope you know by now that you can trust me with sensitive information of any kind."

Donovan, again staring somewhere: "What?" Then: "Oh, yes. Yes, George. I know that. That's why I'm here."

Parker waited another minute. Then Donovan finally spoke.

"George, we are finally going on the offensive in Europe. As you know, plans have been underway for quite some time between our British friends and us. Debates and downright screaming matches have been going on for weeks and months about how and where we should strike in the European theatre. Our military brass pushed hard for a direct attack somewhere in France. The Brits were just as adamant that we were not ready for such an assault on French soil, even with all of the Allies coming together. They wouldn't budge on this. They are absolutely convinced that we would get slaughtered over there."

Donovan paused again, making sure that George was grasping all of this.

"So, after months of debate, the bottom line here is that we are planning to attack in North Africa. It's by far the safer play, and there are more areas there that are less fortified than in France. Frankly, I hate to admit it, but they're right about this. We have a bunch of untested troops, many of whom have just come through training. Better to ease them into the war if there is such a thing. Regardless, it will be anything but a cake walk."

More silence, as Donovan continued to reflect on all of it. Parker was taking it all in, absorbing this new information, and picturing what an offensive might look like.

"Who's running it?" asked Parker.

"Eisenhower will be heading it up."

That got a raised eyebrow from George. Dwight Eisenhower was a logical choice for the operation, given his background in planning and logistics. He was totally qualified to plan it, but he had no field experience in an actual war. Ever.

Parker, still processing, said, "Well, we'll certainly learn a few things, won't we?"

He went on: "Ike's right-hand man is Mark Clark, a guy who skipped the title of Colonel and went right to Brigadier General. Stellar record and all, but I'm not sure how I feel about him. He is not naïve to the art of politics."

Donovan nodded and said, "Yep, I've met him. And I agree that the jury is out on him."

Donovan continued: "Look, I need to get over there right away before everything starts. This is risky on a lot of fronts. Eisenhower is in Gibraltar right now, and there are variables that really need to be worked through."

Parker, more than a little bit curious, said, "Such as?"

Donovan, not wanting to say much more, said, "Well, for one, there is the Vichy military, which is actually in parts of Casablanca, Algiers, and Oran."

The Vichy was supposed to be the remaining French government that represented the parts of France that hadn't been overrun by the Germans, but it was, in fact, little more than a puppet regime for the Nazis.

Donovan went on: "But we are getting reports that the French citizens in these places might support our troops when we invade. Some of our best people are on the ground there now, talking to the French Resistance leaders in these three areas that I mentioned. I need to get over there and support them and make sure that they are being heard by our military and the Brits. This Intel could affect the whole invasion strategy, and I want to make sure that we have a seat at the table. Eisenhower knows almost nothing about our organization. That's not an indictment on him. Believe me, he's bright. But he just hasn't been exposed at all to the O.S.S."

Parker nodded, seeing the wisdom in Donovan's rationale.

"Your reputation with the French could really be an asset for Eisenhower." Parker was referring to Donovan being awarded the two highest medals of the French Military for his extraordinary bravery on French soil during the Great War. He had also been awarded a third, equally prestigious service medal.

The French revered Donovan, and his influence could prove helpful in greasing the skids with the Vichy.

"When does the invasion begin, Bill?"

Donovan, who hadn't stopped pacing, replied almost absently.

"Right now, it's looking around the 16th of the month, but that could easily change. Weather, last-minute information… you know all of the variables that can come up."

"When do you leave?"

"In an hour. I'll land in Gibraltar sometime tomorrow. So, needless to say, I will probably be out of pocket and very difficult to reach for a few days. It's also vitally important that no one knows where I am. It would be too easy to figure out where we're going to strike if people know where I am off to."

Parker, who always marveled at the pace at which Donovan worked, said, "Of course. Mum's the word. Who else knows where you will be?"

"No one. Not even the President. If you absolutely need to get a hold of me, have someone get in touch with Eisenhower himself."

Parker nodded and said, "I doubt that anything will come up that will require your attention." After a pause, he continued: "I'll try to check in on Ruth while you're gone."

Ruth was Donovan's wife, who was, unfortunately, used to his long hours, unpredictable schedule, and secretive meetings.

Donovan smiled and said, "Thanks, George," and with that, moved from pacing in front of him to making his way to the door.

As he opened it, he turned around and said, "How are things going with Dr. Conway?"

Parker replied, "I'll be checking in on him tomorrow. He should be here a few days from now."

Donovan responded with a quick, "Good. We'll need him. He could impact so many different areas of the war for us."

Before George could respond, Wild Bill was out the door.

# CHAPTER 6

John Cullen, a rookie Coast Guard "sand pounder," was patrolling the beach on Amagansett. He was the low man on the totem pole, so that meant he had the midnight shift - every single night. 5'11 and a bit thin for his height, Cullen had thick reddish-brown hair and a round face that made him look even younger than he was. He really didn't even need to shave. Like most 21-year-old young men, he had enlisted immediately following the Japanese attack on Pearl Harbor almost a year ago.

He was mostly just looking forward to finishing his shift. Despite his desire to be done, his stride on the beach was always purposeful and reflective of a well-trained guardsman. Cullen's route covered six miles in total - 3 miles down the beach on Amagansett and 3 miles back to the Coast Guard station. But tonight, his stride was more cautious, simply because he couldn't see more than a couple of feet in front of him, so thick was the fog rolling into the shoreline. "No way am I going to be done early with this fog," he said to himself. He had his goals that he would always set just to keep things interesting. For example, he always wanted to be at the one-mile mark less than 13 minutes into his patrol.

His mind had drifted a bit during his patrol, as it always did. After all, there really wasn't anything happening tonight. Again. Aside from coming upon the occasional young couples parked along the beach necking or some fishermen coming in late from the sea, nothing ever happened out here. Sure, most of the residents obeyed the rules and did blackouts, just in case, but his tours almost always ended as they had begun: uneventfully.

Tonight, however, would be different.

On this particular shift, he found himself daydreaming. "Or," he pondered, "Night dreaming?" Just to keep things interesting, he was weighing his odds of meeting the girl of his dreams. He didn't have a steady girlfriend, but that could change each time he went home. "You never know when that special girl will come along," he reminded himself. Plus, with so many guys overseas, he figured that the odds would eventually catch up to him.

Cullen, raised less than 100 miles from where he now walked, changed topics with himself, and began to think about his plans for the upcoming weekend. He'd go home as he did most weekends so he could do laundry and have his mom's home-cooked meals. He'd hang out with the few friends that were still in New York. Most of his buddies had shipped out to somewhere. They had all been scattered around the world. Cullen was one of the lucky ones. He enlisted in the Coast Guard and, of all the places that he could have been shipped to, landed in his own backyard. Not a bad deal.

His mates were decent guys. If they weren't allowed to leave the base, they would spend their time reading the newspapers and listening to the radio. One of the programs that he never missed was at 7:00 PM on Sunday nights. The Jack Benny program was one of the most listened-to shows in the country.

Cullen loved the banter between Phil Harris and Benny. Some of the other shows that he and his buddies listened to were "Charlie McCarthy," and "Fibber McGee and Molly." For more serious shows, they tuned into "The Whistler" or "The Shadow." Radio was the primary form of entertainment for the guardsmen and the shows helped them not to get too bored for too long.

As Cullen kept walking, he realized that tonight felt different. Between the fog and the time of night, mixed in with the extreme quiet, Cullen was a bit spooked. He and his fellow guardsmen didn't carry weapons on their patrols. There had never been a need to do so. He was a little more than two miles into his route when he thought that he heard something.

He checked his watch. He was clearly behind schedule. But again, the fog coming in off the sea was really thick tonight. He was caught in that unusual place where he couldn't see at all in the dark, but the flashlight provided little more than a glare.

He stopped to listen. Nothing. As he started to walk again, he thought he heard another noise. This time, he was sure. It came from somewhere in front of him. Was it a voice? He stopped and tried to focus only on the sound. It wasn't a voice. It was voices.

CHAPTER 7

Parker was tired. He thought about heading home, but he looked at the latest pile of information that Peg had dropped on him. The reports coming in from around the world were constant because activities around the globe from the last few months were constant. Most of the information dealt with the decisive battle for a small island in the Pacific named Midway. The Americans had gambled big and won big, sinking 4 Japanese aircraft carriers. Parker read something that wouldn't come out for years: The U.S. had cracked the Japanese code for communication, and we knew that the Japanese were targeting Midway. That one piece of information made all the difference. The shrewd planning of Admiral Nimitz and his men was on display as well. The Japanese had no idea that American aircraft carriers were less than 200 miles from them; they had assumed that the carriers were all at or close to Pearl Harbor. The trap was set, and the Americans, with a whole lot of courage and even more Providence, defeated the Japanese and changed the entire trajectory of the Pacific war.

America desperately needed that victory. George actually smiled as he read through the report. All of this was classified information that was on a need-to-know basis. And very few people needed to know. He couldn't discuss any of this with anyone, including his wife.

Europe, however, was a different story. The U.S. was trying to get its footing across the pond, and there was more chaos over there than anything else right now. They needed one leader - one guy who was tagged with all of it, one owner. Egos were not helping, and there were several to go around. Churchill wasn't shy about anything. Nor was his General Montgomery. Patton was always going to be a problem. De Gaulle was no picnic, even if he wasn't even in power.

The only man for the job appeared to be Eisenhower, but he was unproven. His background was mostly in supplies, logistics, and planning, and those three qualities would be critical in this war. At least he had his ego in check, and whoever could get anything done over there would need to figure out how to make the orchestra perform. As he thought through it, he could see the wisdom in choosing Ike, but time would tell.

Even though it was well past midnight, he decided to read one more report from Europe. Unlike the Pacific Theatre, the Americans were behind when it came to intelligence gathering in Europe. So, at this point, the Yanks were quite dependent on their cousins when it came to Intel.

The file that he had picked up was called "Operation Anthropoid," and he was quite interested in it because it was the code name for a mission that had been planned in England for several months and had been executed a few months prior. The plan itself had the full support of Edvard Benes, the former head of the Czech government. He was forced to flee his country to England when the Nazis invaded in 1939. Eager to show the Nazis that the Czechs were not finished (and to tell the rest of Europe that Benes himself wasn't finished), Benes, being pushed by Stewart Menzies, the head of England's MI6, came up with the idea of assassinating Reinhold Heydrich, one of **the** highest-ranking Nazis in the Third Reich who had been handpicked by Hitler himself to oversee all of Czechoslovakia. In the last several months, Heydrich had turned the country into a manufacturing machine for weapons, artillery, and ammunition.

Known as "The Butcher of Prague," Heydrich had also systematically eliminated much of the Czech resistance, mostly through executions. If there was even just one suspicion raised about one's support of the Czech underground, it was common for the SS to show up at one's door, force the adults outside, and shoot them on sight. No questions. No trials. So ruthless and unpredictable were his raids on homes to find and kill informers and spies the result was that the Czech underground had been all but shut down. No Czech citizen knew who he or she could trust, so people kept to themselves rather than risk being executed. Heydrich was the epitome of ruthless and cruel. Even Hitler called him "The man with the iron heart." The man with two nicknames had earned them both.

As evil as Heydrich was in hunting down and executing Czech resistance members, there was a whole other level of evil that he was responsible for. Reinhold Heydrich was one of the key architects of the plan to exterminate Jews. He had chaired a conference just outside of Berlin in a city called Wannsee. The Wannsee Conference took place almost a year ago in January. The attendees of the conference represented the leaders of the various departments in the Third Reich. Its purpose was to come to an agreement on what to do with the Jews in German-occupied Europe.

The Final Solution, as it came to be called, was to deport as many Jews as possible from German-occupied soil and route them to Poland and other countries. Those who were able-bodied might end up in factories that produced weapons, tanks, airplanes, and ships, or parts for all of those things. The weaker would be shipped to a very different sort of factory: a death factory, commonly referred to as concentration camps. People of all ages would be "exterminated." The existence of these camps was not widely known, but the Roosevelt administration knew about them. It was a source of immense frustration - disbelief, really - to Donovan and Parker and many others that no one was doing anything about them.

Conversely, delighted with his plan, Hitler rewarded Heydrich by naming him to rule over all of Czechoslovakia and turn it into the manufacturing machine that it had become in a few short months. The country was a critical component of Germany's war efforts. It manufactured several weapons, machinery, and ammunition.

Parker had seen pictures of Heydrich. He was a tall, thin man with cold, piercing blue eyes and a square jaw with a large, long nose that didn't seem to belong on his face. With his perfectly combed blond hair, he was the poster boy for the Aryan race. Through a combination of shrewd rewards and many more reprisals for the Czechs who worked in the munitions factories, he had the country's production humming with efficiency and output. And he had the country completely in fear. Thus, there is a need for Benes, under increasing pressure from the Allies, to act.

The mission was planned over 8 months, and it morphed to take on more objectives. The Allies wanted to see the Czechs do something, as Menzies said, "More than placing violets on the grave of the Unknown Soldier." When the planning was completed, it was agreed that the Czechs would send nine exiled Czech military personnel from England to their home country with several different missions. Only three of the nine would be tasked with assassinating Heydrich.

The nine men had parachuted into three different cities, all of which were off course from their original targets. The three men who were assigned to Operation Anthropoid were Joseph Gabcik, Jan Kubis, and Josef Valcik. The three made their way to Prague and met with their underground comrades. When the leaders of the Czech underground were told of the mission, they begged their new friends not to go through with it. They knew Heydrich and the ultimate price that the entire country would pay if the assailants even attempted to do something. The three men were unmoved. They had their orders. And so, they began to plan.

They studied Heydrich's movements and daily routine and kicked around several ideas for killing him. Ultimately, they decided to take him out in broad daylight as he was being driven to his office at Prague Castle. They knew that on pleasant days, the Butcher of Prague rode in the back seat of one of a fleet of armor-plated Mercedes Cabriolet B convertibles and that he had only his driver with him. And the top was almost always down.

On May 27th, the assassins acted. Their plan was to wait along a street that was on Heydrich's daily route. The street itself had a right-angle curve after it crossed the train tracks, which meant that the car had to come to almost a complete stop before it could make its turn. Valcik would be near the street, about 100 kilometers ahead of Gabcik and Kubis. Valcik would signal when he saw the Mercedes, step back casually onto the sidewalk, and not do anything else unless needed.

At 10:15 AM, the men were in position along the street, waiting. At exactly 10:30 AM, after what seemed like an eternity, Valcik finally signaled to his two comrades that the car was in sight. Thirty seconds later, Gabcik saw the dark green Mercedes come into view. He began to drop his long overcoat that had been concealing his weapon and waited for the car to come to a virtual stop. He saw Heydrich sitting in the back seat, reading a document of some kind. Gabcik whipped out his Sten submachine gun.

Here, Parker paused and shook his head. He could have predicted what came next. The Sten was a mass-produced, cheap gun made in a factory outside of London that was known to jam.

A lot. The Brits had relied on the Thompson submachine gun or the "Tommy Gun" from the U.S. as their main weapon of choice. However, that changed when America got into the war.

The Thompson factories just couldn't keep up with the demand and, after Dunkirk, the English started contracting with The Royal Small Arms Factory in Enfield. Thus, the birth of the Sten was an acronym for the two designers named Shepard and Turbin, who developed the gun, and Enfield, where it was made.

Being that the mission was planned in England, it would follow that they had English weapons, reasoned Parker.

"Those poor guys," he mumbled.

Sure enough, the Sten had jammed, and Gabcik froze as Heydrich saw him.

In what would prove to be a fatal mistake, the Nazi ordered his driver to stop, stood up in the car, and began to remove his Luger pistol from its holster to shoot Gabcik. It was then that Kubis appeared, tossing an anti-tank grenade at the car. His aim was off. The grenade rolled up to the right rear tire and exploded, spreading shrapnel everywhere and seriously wounding Heydrich. His driver got out of the car and gave chase but realized after a minute that he had better go back and tend to his boss.

A nationwide manhunt began immediately to find the assassins.

Parker yawned a bit and looked at his watch. "I need to get home," he told himself. He cheated and counted how many additional pages there were to read. There were only five more pages left, so he pressed on. He was expecting to hear about the assailants being caught or some action to shut down the country while the manhunt was on.

His gasp was audible. He was wrong on both fronts.

Heydrich had survived the attack and lived another week. The report was not definitive but speculated that he eventually died from ensuing infections.

There was a state funeral with all the trimmings, and the turnout in Berlin numbered in the thousands.

Privately, Hitler was furious about Heydrich's assassination. He was also angry that Heydrich had allowed himself to be in such a vulnerable position. An open car with no security as he rode through the streets of Prague, always at the same time of day. How could his friend have been so foolish? And so arrogant?

The three assassins were eventually turned in by traitors in the underground. Chased all over Prague, they eventually found themselves trapped in the bowels of a church. With hundreds of German soldiers closing in on them and being down to one bullet each, they committed suicide.

As bad as this was to read, none of it shocked Parker. The gasp had come from what followed.

In retaliation for Heydrich's assassination, the Nazis arrested 13,000 people within the country. Many were tortured and sent to concentration camps, including Kubis' girlfriend.

But that wasn't enough. The worst was still to come.

The town of Lidice was chosen by the Nazis because they believed that the city had contributed to Heydrich's death by collaborating with the assassins. It hadn't. The nine men who parachuted into the country came nowhere close to Lidice.

On June 9th, close to 200 men in the town - and any boy over the age of 15- were lined up against a wall and shot by the Nazis.

There were reports that 65 women were also shot and killed. The children were shipped off to concentration camps.

Once the executions were completed, the Nazis burned the entire city to the ground.

There was not one adult citizen of the city that survived. All were killed or sent to concentration camps.

If that wasn't bad enough, a few weeks later, the same horror that took place in Lidice would be repeated in a town called Lezaky, which Parker had never heard of.

This time, all of the men and women were rounded up and shot.

Almost all of the children were sent to a concentration camp, where they were gassed.

George Parker, a long-time cop who had seen his share of death over the years, was frozen. Numb and shocked. He couldn't think. He couldn't process. He couldn't speak. Finally, after several minutes, he managed one question: "What kind of animals are we dealing with over there?"

He would not even bother to go home. After reading that report, he wouldn't be able to sleep anyway.

# CHAPTER 8

Coast Guardsman Cullen shined his flashlight - the only thing that he carried that could even be thought of as a weapon - in the direction of the sound that he heard.

Within seconds, he was standing face to face with a man who seemed to come out of nowhere. Behind this stranger, he could make out the silhouette of another man. And behind the second man, two more men had stopped in their tracks.

Cullen shone the flashlight into the first man's face.

"Who are you?" asked Cullen. Quite honestly, Cullen was a bit surprised. He was certainly not expecting to come upon anyone at this hour. The man looked at him, equally surprised. It took him a second to recover.

He said, "We're fishermen from Southampton, and we ran aground here."

"What's your name? Probed Cullen

"George Davis," came his reply, a little too quickly.

Before Cullen could ask him for some identification, the second man stepped closer and said something to Davis in what sounded like a foreign language.

"German?" said Cullen to himself.

Davis, responding in perfect English to the other man, said, "Shut up, you fool. Everything is all right. Go back to the boys and stay with them."

Cullen subconsciously reached to his hip for his gun, which wasn't there. As the man turned back to look at Cullen, whom he couldn't see because of the flashlight, Cullen said, "Why don't you come with me to my station?"

Davis said rather calmly, "Now, wait a minute. You don't know what this is about." Cullen kept his light in Davis's eyes.

Davis asked him a strange question: "Do you have parents?"

Cullen, backing up slightly: "Yes."

Davis: "Would they mourn you if you were dead?" Cullen didn't answer.

After a moment of awkward silence, Davis spoke again: "I don't want to have to kill you."

More silence, both men processing the situation.

Davis again, now moving toward Cullen: "Here! Take this."

He had reached into his pocket for his wallet. Cullen took another step back. Davis kept coming and handed him several bills, paused, and then gave him more.

"Here's $300. Forget about this."

Cullen, not knowing where the other three men had gone, weighed his options. He had no weapon. There were at least four men and only one of him. He was two miles from the base. He decided to look cooperative, stuffing the money into his pants pocket.

He and Davis turned from one another and went their separate ways. Cullen tried to walk calmly and not look back. When he felt safe enough to run, he did so. He would say later that he made it back to the station in record time, fog and all.

He went right to his superior officer, Boatswain's Mate Second Class Duey Williams, and told him what happened. He also showed him the $300, which turned out to be $260. The stranger on the beach either couldn't count properly or had purposely shortchanged him.

Williams' immediate reaction was, "Oh, boy, this is big!"

He wasted no time. He called the station commander, and within minutes, they were organizing a group of guardsmen to go back out and search for the strange men.

Williams made sure each guardsman had a 30-caliber rifle as they went back out.

Within an hour they were joined by 20 Army soldiers who helped them look for any clues as to the foreigners' whereabouts.

What finally helped them came much too late. It was the eventual clearing of the fog. Not until almost 7:15 AM did they find some buried material. They dug up explosives, maps, and even a bagful of money. But the four men were nowhere to be found.

# CHAPTER 9

After encountering Guardsman Cullen, George Dasch, and the other three men raced back (as fast as they could in the fog) to where they had buried the stash.

They quickly dug up the bag of money and threw more of it into Dasch's sack.

Then, they again tried to make the area look as normal as possible.

They had to move fast.

Dasch's confrontation with the young coastguardsman was unexpected. He was caught completely off guard. Who would have thought that, at that hour and in that fog, anyone would even bother being on the beach?

His handling of the situation wasn't exactly a confidence booster for the other men.

To his surprise, Burger attempted to smooth things over. "Couldn't be helped," he told Quirin and Heinck.

Quirin said, "I came here to help my country win the war. We should have killed that sailor."

Heinck merely grunted. Burger couldn't tell if Heinck's grunt was one of agreement with his comment or Quirin's.

Dasch, recovering quickly, said, "If we had killed that kid, we'd have the entire American Navy looking for us. I paid him enough money to keep his mouth shut. It was the best decision based on the circumstances."

He said it in a way that sounded like he was trying to convince himself as much as the others.

They had changed their clothes again and were well on their way to the Amagansett train station. Dasch had regained his composure and was doing a stellar job of having them navigate the side streets, moving in and out of the shadows.

There was a 6:59 AM train into New York City that they needed to be on.

They got to the train station about 20 minutes before departure. Dasch bought the tickets and four copies of the New York Times.

The train was crowded, and the men had no problem mixing in with the other passengers. They settled in for the long commute into the city, each sitting separately from one another.

Dasch looked inside a pocket of his coat and pulled out a men's handkerchief. It looked ordinary enough, but it was vital to their mission. On it, written in invisible ink, were the names of two key contacts in the area who would help them as necessary. About an hour and a half later, they got off in Manhattan.

He took the men to breakfast and waited for Macy's to open so he could buy American-style clothes for his compatriots and walk around the city.

When it came time to find a hotel, Quirin and Heinck registered at the Martinique, and Dasch and Burger settled in at the Governor Clinton Hotel, a few blocks away.

Dasch chose this hotel for its history: George Clinton was the first Governor of New York, and he also served as Vice President of the United States under Thomas Jefferson and James Madison. It also didn't hurt that the hotel itself rivaled any other dwelling in the city in terms of service and ambiance. George John Dasch, the former waiter in New York, was now staying in one of the premier hotels in the city and being served his extravagant meals by people who were finally waiting on him.

# CHAPTER 10

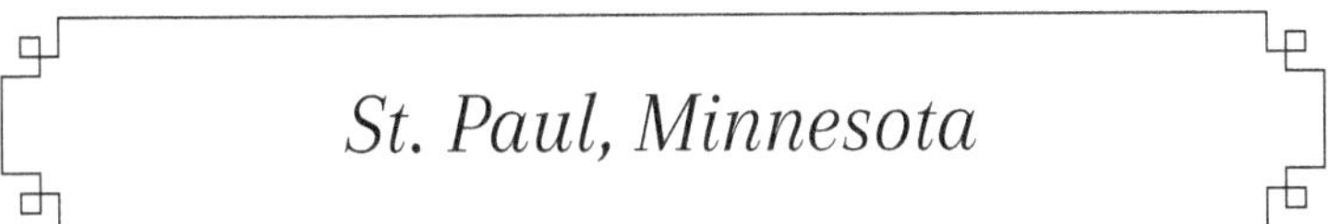

## St. Paul, Minnesota

Frank Sweeney was having a wonderful time. The 24-year-old former Army Air Force pilot had spent the last couple of days with Leigh Conway and her father, Edwin, seeing some of the sights in and around the Twin Cities. Edwin, always protective of his daughter, had managed to strike a nice balance of giving the young couple some time by themselves and not appearing to be their chaperone.

They were sitting at the Lexington Restaurant, located on the corner of Grand Avenue and Lexington Parkway in St. Paul. The restaurant was large, with dark paneled walls and soft, thick rugs throughout. There were several private rooms that were almost always full during the lunch and dinner hours. It was quickly becoming a popular destination for the mayor and other public officials to cut deals and be seen. The "Lex" was one of the many haunts several years ago when Prohibition was the law. Ten or twelve years ago, it wouldn't have been uncommon to see Dillinger or the Barkers dining there, often with the politicians.

As they sat waiting for their food to arrive- Frank was pushing the walleye, which is a freshwater fish that is considered a delicacy in Minnesota - Edwin turned to Frank and said, "Thank you again for getting us out of Germany, lad. I can't tell you how grateful we are. I assume that Mr. Parker pulled some strings, because Jimmy insisted on signing up to serve in your army immediately."

Jimmy was Edwin's son and Leigh's brother. He had been held by the Germans at the Nazi's aeronautical laboratory in Germany as insurance to make sure that Edwin, one of the foremost aeronautical engineers in the world, gave everything that he had to the Nazis' secret jet engine airplane program. Leigh had accompanied her father to Germany and taught school there while he worked in the lab. Edwin was a widower, having lost his wife Hannah a few years earlier when they had lived in Ireland.

Unbeknownst to the Conways, Jimmy would be assigned stateside during the entire war, courtesy of Wild Bill Donovan. They couldn't risk having him re-captured by the Germans.

"I'm very proud and thankful that Jimmy wanted to serve in helping us defeat the Nazis and the Japanese. We will need every able-bodied guy that we can find," said Frank.

Leigh shivered. "I still can't believe that we made it out of Germany alive. The odds were not in our favor."

"You can say that again," Frank replied rather quietly. "So many things had to come together at just the right time. Let's be honest. I was sort of thrown into this thing, and the clear priority was getting the information about what you were working on back to the powers that be. The escape plan was more of a "We'll cross that bridge when we get to it." They were all silent for a minute.

Then Frank said, "Only God could have orchestrated all of it to get us all back here safely."

Both Conways nodded at that, sort of a "You can say that again," nod. Edwin spoke again: "You know, lad, one thing that I have been working on in my spiritual life is to give thanks, particularly when God answers our prayers. We all tend to be great about having a lot of prayer requests, but I, for one, am not always as good about offering prayers of thanksgiving for Him answering our prayers. And He certainly answered all of them. The fact that we all got out safely is a true miracle."

"Yes, Dad, that is so true!" agreed Leigh. "And let's not forget Hans and Esther and Esther's parents getting out as well. With Esther's parents being so involved with sneaking so many Jewish people out of the country safely, I can't imagine what the Nazis would have done to them."

Hans Ungrodt was a German double agent pretending to work for the Nazis when in fact, he reported to MI6, Britain's international spy organization. He and Frank had stumbled upon one another in Germany and quickly decided to work together. Esther was soon to be Hans' fiancé, and her parents, Peter and Winnie, had helped dozens of Jewish families escape Germany, mainly into Switzerland. They were remarkably brave and dedicated people.

Leigh continued: "What haunts me are the people that are still there, stuck with no way out."

"The network is still in place, Leigh," said Frank. "I saw firsthand the precautions that they all took. They were incredibly careful and borderline paranoid, which was definitely wise. I think they'll be OK. After all, they were extremely compartmentalized, so the left hand didn't really know what the right was doing. They took every precaution imaginable. It might take them longer to get more people out, but I would bet that it will only be a temporary setback."

They all reflected on that for a minute.

Edwin, hoping to lighten the mood, asked Frank, "Have you had a chance to talk to Hans since we made it here?"

"Briefly," replied Frank. "Hans will be joining us when you and I fly to Washington in a few days. They are in Milwaukee now with Esther's relatives, probably seeing the sights there like we are doing here."

Leigh nodded and said, "Maybe I could take a train to Milwaukee at some point to see Esther and catch up. After all, you two will be gone soon." Her eyes moistened at the thought, which made Frank's throat tighten a bit.

Edwin came to the rescue again and said, "Well, that's not for a few days yet. Let's enjoy our time here and now. Frank, I'd love to talk to your dad about his business. It sounds exciting."

Frank, thankful for the change of subject, jumped in and said, "Oh, Dr. Conway, he could regale you for days with stories. He's been in law enforcement for most of his life, and he certainly has some remarkable experiences. Some are quite serious, some are heartbreaking, and some are downright hilarious. He doesn't really talk all that much about it, though, probably because he has never wanted to worry my mom about all of it.

But if you get some time with him alone, I'm sure he'd enjoy telling you about it. I'm a little biased, but my father is truly a remarkable man. He is proud to be an American, and he is also proud of his Irish heritage."

Edwin smiled and nodded once more. "I would love to sit down and talk to him about all of it. To build a business from nothing to what it appears to be today is a story worth hearing. In the meantime, tell us a little more about St. Paul. I'm particularly interested in its history."

As the waitress brought the food to the table, Frank thought about Edwin's question and said, "Well, let's see…"

"There are a couple of stories that might interest you. When you think of St. Paul, you really have to start with the Mississippi River. Everything was centered around the river. And after that, railroads were big, too. Both still are dominant even today, for the most part."

Frank paused and looked at Leigh, who smiled at him.

"Do you know what the first name of the city was? No, of course, you don't," said Frank, answering his own question.

"I'll tell you how St. Paul came to be. It's kind of a neat story. Most people just assume that Minneapolis is the capital of Minnesota because it's so much bigger. But about 120 years ago, Fort Snelling was built. It's located a couple of miles south from here, where the Mississippi and Minnesota rivers come together."

Edwin nodded, and Leigh was just so happy to be with him that Frank probably could have blubbered on about anything, and she would've enjoyed it.

Frank stole another glance at her. "Man, I can't believe that

I'm actually here with her. She is so beautiful," he said to himself. 5'6 with titian hair and large, expressive, almost almond-colored eyes, 23-year-old Leigh Conway was, in a word, stunning.

Yet she didn't see herself that way, and that was one of her many attributes that Frank was drawn to.

He was brought back to earth by Edwin, who prompted him with a clearing of his throat and a, "So, Fort Snelling?"

"Huh?" "Er, I mean, pardon?"

"Yes, lad, you were talking about Fort Snelling?"

"Yes. Fort Snelling. Right." Frank collected himself and then continued.

"So, anyway, Fort Snelling was established to protect the area from hostile enemies. It sits well above the river, so anyone wanting to attack would be hard-pressed to climb the bluffs to get there. The fort was also there to really establish dominance in the fur trading business up and down the river. And it did that for quite some time. By the 1840's the area had become the main hub for the fur trading business. Now, enter a Frenchman named Pierre Parrant. Parrant was a former fur trader turned bootlegger."

"Bootlegger?" asked Leigh.

"Yeah, you know, people that make and move liquor illegally. In this case, it was mostly whiskey. It was big back then, and it was REALLY big here for about thirteen years in the 1920s through 1933. Making and selling most liquor was illegal in the U.S. during that period of time. That is, up until nine years ago when the U.S. Congress discontinued Prohibition. More on that another time."

"I think I may have read about that a little bit several years ago," said Leigh.

"Yeah, it was a big deal all over the country. St. Paul became absolutely infested with criminals and gangsters, which, ironically, really helped my dad's business."

"I'll have to ask your father about that," said Edwin. "One thing that I can tell you for certain: I can't see Ireland ever banning alcohol, although they do ban the sale of it on Good Friday."

That brought a chuckle from Frank and Leigh.

"Dad would love to tell you about those days," Frank replied. "He has a lot of stories about all of that. Anyway, this Pierre

Parrant guy was supplying all of the whiskey to the soldiers at Fort Snelling, and the officers saw the effects of all of this and shut him down. Parrant was a stubborn guy, a French Canadian, so he moved a few miles upriver, pretty close to where we are now, but closer to the river. Parrant's nickname was "Pig's Eye" and" -

Leigh, shaking her head for a moment in bewilderment: "Wait, Frank, did you say, "Pig's Eye?"

"Yep, I sure did. "Pig's Eye." Frank took a French fry and began to munch on it. "I guess he was blind in one eye, and he looked a little different. So, Pig's Eye."

That got a laugh out of Edwin and Leigh.

"Meanwhile, the whole area around here became known as Pig's Eye. People would actually use it as a city address back in the day. A lot of French people came to settle in this area, mostly due to Parrant's notoriety. Then along comes a French priest named Father Gaultier."

Frank continued: "Gaultier was aghast when he heard what the area was called, and he made it his mission to change the name from "Pig's Eye" to "St. Paul."

He picked up another French fry, took a quick bite, and continued.

"Supposedly, he referred to Saul's conversion in the New Testament, and he said the same thing would take place here. Hence the name "St. Paul." A few years later, Minnesota became a state, and St. Paul was named the capital city."

"Wow! I had no idea about any of this!" exclaimed Leigh.

"As long as we are talking about names, what kind of a name is Minnesota?" asked Leigh. "What I mean to say is, how did it get its name?"

"It's an Indian word," said Frank. "It means "The land of **sky-blue waters.**"

He went on, "We have so many lakes here. Minnesota is known as "The land of 10,000 lakes," but we actually have closer to 15,000 lakes in the state. There are more lakes in Minnesota than in any of the other 47 states. Anyway, several of the states in the Midwest were named by the Indians. Wisconsin, where Hans and Esther are, neighbors us. The St. Croix River separates Minnesota and Wisconsin. Wisconsin means "A river runs through a red place" or something like that. People think that it refers to the Wisconsin Dells, which is full of red-colored sandstone rock."

"That sounds beautiful," said Leigh. "Would these Wisconsin Dells be on the way to Milwaukee?"

"They would indeed," replied Frank.

He noticed that Edwin was really enjoying the walleye, and that Leigh was eating some french-fries and not touching her walleye sandwich.

"You don't like the walleye?" he asked.

"I am about to try it," she replied. "You know how the Irish are with potatoes!"

Frank laughed. "Good point," he said.

"Keep going, lad." Edwin from the cheap seats.

Frank went on: "Michigan is east of Wisconsin, and it's another one of our states. "Michigan" means "Big Lake" or "Big Water." Lake Michigan is huge, but Lake Superior is even larger. Both are part of the state of Michigan. Go to northern Minnesota, where you will find the shores of Lake Superior. It's so large - I think it's something like 32,000 square miles, and its maximum depth is over 1,300 feet- that it borders Michigan, Minnesota, Wisconsin, and Canada. The Indian name for it is "Gitche Gumee," which means "Huge Water.""

"We have much to learn about the United States," said Edwin.

"That's for sure," agreed Leigh.

"All in good time," said Frank. "We can start with this lunch.

I'm glad that you picked the walleye. You won't regret it."

Leigh laughed. "Well, seeing how you raved about it, I didn't think we had much of a choice!"

The Lexington was primarily known for its steak, but the walleye was a close second.

They chatted a little more about what else that they planned to do in the next week or so, before Edwin and Frank would have to leave for Washington, D.C. Now that they were officially an item, Frank and Leigh were realizing how precious time was, especially in this crazy and chaotic time of war. They wanted to make every minute count.

# CHAPTER 11

# Berlin

The second most powerful man in all of Germany was not in a good place. At least mentally. Physically, he was in a great place - one of his most favorite locations. The 5'10-inch officer with a stout body, full face, and pronounced jaw with short, thick brown hair sat in his plush office surrounded by some of the finest art in the world. The fact that every piece of it was pilfered was a detail that few knew and even fewer cared about. And the collection in the office - his collection, as he would remind anyone who asked - was a small fraction of what he had stored and hidden all over occupied Europe. It was all his now. Most of the original owners were Jews who were either no longer alive or wouldn't be for long. The luckier ones were working in Nazi-run factories, producing armor and ammunition to support the evil party that took everything from them. This irony was not lost on Hermann Göring.

For a man who was known for his expensive taste in everything that he possessed, Göring paid for nothing. His extensive wine collection was also made up of stolen bottles. Most of the ornate furniture in his office and his homes -he had more than one of those, too - were all stolen from the wealthy Jewish people whose assets were seized over the years.

Of all of the beautiful art in his office, his eye usually found its way to two different and distinct framed photographs. He preferred the second one over the first. The first photo was of him with the Fuhrer after Germany's successful conquest of France two years ago. Hitler gave

Göring the unique title of Reichsmarschall, which meant that he now had seniority over every other officer in the Fatherland's military. It was a proud moment, to be sure, and it positioned Göring above all of his rivals, known and unknown, with Goebbels and Himmler being the two most critical. His relationship with both men was always challenging. Trust was not a word that one could use to define Göring's relationship with anyone save the Fuhrer.

Now his eyes made his way to his most prized possession, which - surprise! - he hadn't paid for, either. The Carin II, a 27.5-meter yacht that was gifted to him by a group of car manufacturers was truly spectacular. It didn't hurt that Göring had made sure that these men all profited well during the rise of the Nazi party.

The Carin II was named after his first wife, who had died in 1931 after a long illness. His second wife, Emmy, a nationally recognized actress, didn't seem to mind the ship's name. Emmy was a star - far more popular than Hitler's constant companion, Eva Braun. And much better looking, Göring observed to himself. The Carin II had hosted Mussolini in 1937, shortly after it was berthed. It hosted the Fuhrer himself the following year. Göring loved to be at sea with it, often taking it from Hamburg up the Elbe River to the North Sea, then all the way up Germany's western coast to the island of Sylt, about 235 kilometers away.

He stared at the ship longingly, knowing that it would be a while before he could sail with her again. The Carin II was in storage, well hidden in Berlin, and he knew that he would not be out with her again until after the war. The war. His mind quickly came back to the present.

The events of the past week were enough to drive any man crazy. Of course, he was not just any man. And that one fact was why he immediately came to the only conclusion that he could. He knew what had to be done.

Oh sure, he had been through the rage, the fury, and the sheer incredulousness in trying to grasp the level of Colonel Robert von Greim's foul-ups. Von Greim, a wannabe competitor of Göring's, was a distant second to him in terms of power and influence in the Luftwaffe, Germany's Air Force. Because of von Greim's incompetence, the greatest aviation engineer on the continent was no longer helping Göring's Luftwaffe. As a matter of fact, Edwin Conway, one of the two main engineers who were working to develop the first jet fighter for war, had escaped the country on von Greim's watch.

He allowed himself to brood a little more. That fool von Greim had ruined everything! While it was true that the jet itself wouldn't have been ready for at least another couple of years, just having it as an additional option would have made a huge difference in the war. All of the monies spent and all of the time that Göring himself had invested in getting the program this far was now in real jeopardy.

He reflected on his own boasting about no foreign air force ever being able to penetrate Germany's air defense systems, that bombing Germany would be impossible. In a speech he had given less than a year ago, he had declared: "No enemy bomber can reach the Ruhr. If one reaches the Ruhr, my name is not Göring. You may call me Meyer."

That was met with wild applause and a few chuckles. After all, they were laughing at – um, with - the second most powerful man in all of Germany. And he had made that claim in part because he knew of the jet engine's capabilities. The jet would fly 2 or 3 times the speed of the single prop fighters that the Allies had. It would be no contest in the battle for the skies over Europe.

Britain's defeat would be imminent, as would America's soon after. But that had all changed now.

Being the Fuhrer's right-hand man (and, in his own mind, Hitler's obvious successor), Göring knew that Germany's network of spies was vast. No one was surprised by the reach of Germany's intelligence throughout Europe. What people would be surprised about would be the number of spies that had been sent to the United States over the years. And even though this debacle was less than a week old, Göring already knew where Edwin Conway had escaped to, thanks to agents who reported to the man that he was about to call.

Von Greim's incompetence quickly morphed into Göring's problem. Edwin Conway needed to be stopped. Allowing the Allies access to Conway's vast knowledge and understanding of the jet engine could seriously damage the Fatherland's chances to win the war. The way that America was mass producing planes, tanks, and even ships, Göring was convinced that, with the U.S.'s superior production capacity, the jet engine could be in production relatively quickly. And that just wasn't something that The Fatherland could risk.

The answer was obvious: If Germany couldn't have Conway working for her, then no one would. Conway had to be eliminated. But it would have to happen in such a way that wouldn't tip the Americans off to Germany's extensive spy network in the U.S. He decided to get the one man on the phone who could make something happen quickly. Hermann Göring was a man of action, and this was a mess that needed to be cleaned up quickly.

He pressed the button on his phone and barked at his secretary, who heard him more from his office than over the speaker: "Get Canaris on the phone!"

# CHAPTER 12

Like most of the German hierarchy, Admiral Wilhelm Canaris was tired. "Exhausted" would be a more accurate description. He sat in his expansive office on a particularly cold and dreary German day. The outcome of the war in Europe was anything but certain. And Operation Barbarossa, Germany's invasion of The Soviet Union, was not going well. The Axis powers had committed an astounding 3.8 million soldiers and 600,000 motor vehicles, tanks, and other weaponry to the war with the Soviets, more than any other war in history. The war certainly started well, but slowly began to falter. It reached the "Uh oh" point when the Nazis failed in their effort to take Moscow. The Russian weather had been an ally to the Soviets. Blizzards stalled the Germans' advancement into the capital city, allowing the Soviets to regroup. German tanks and other vehicles were literally stuck in the snow and mud, becoming sitting ducks for the Soviet troops. The weather was so cold that the German planes couldn't fly to provide any kind of support or protection. With the failure to take Moscow, the entire battle for the Soviet Union was very much in doubt.

It was also a horrible war, as wars go. Both sides were ruthless and inhumane in their methods, efforts, and policies. Hitler himself had communicated a "take no prisoners" directive, and that included Soviet civilians and not just Russian military personnel.

Canaris hated to even think about it, so bad were the stories coming from the sensitive reports that he was privy to. And with the Allies getting ready for an invasion of their own somewhere - where was still a mystery to Canaris and the German military - he knew that his country and the other Axis members would be spread too thin to fight on more than one front.

"This is a different war than the one I fought in," he muttered to himself.

During the Great War, he had worked extensively to sabotage different French entities in and around Morocco. After his success there, he and a few other German agents snuck into the U.S. He had a hand in the plan to plant bombs - successfully - at Black Tom Island in New York Harbor. The manmade island, very close to the Statue of Liberty, was home to over 2,000,000 pounds of small armaments and ammunition, including 100,000 pounds of TNT. On July 30, 1916, German-planted bombs blew up the munitions. The initial explosion was the equivalent of an earthquake measuring 5.5 on the Richter scale, and it was felt as far away as Maryland. Most of the windows in lower Manhattan were blown out, as were the stained-glass windows in St. Patrick's Cathedral. Even windows as far as Philadelphia had exploded. Four were killed and dozens injured. The spies also planted other bombs in various arms factories around the northeastern U.S.

Canaris, a complicated man, stood all of 5'3. His height - or lack thereof - had probably hurt him in his career, he surmised. But then again, only one man had been chosen to be the head of the Abwehr, Germany's Military Intelligence organization. And that man was him. He stared into the mirror on his wall and wondered where the years had gone. He was a career Navy man with a strong background in espionage and building spy networks. And he was loyal to his country.

But not so loyal to his Fuhrer. Like most of the German people, Canaris had been excited about Hitler's rise to power. He hated Communism and wanted to see Germany return to its glorious days of old through the Socialist plans that their new leader had. But once Hitler invaded Czechoslovakia, the good Admiral began to have second thoughts.

Those second thoughts evolved to downright opposition after the atrocities that he saw firsthand when Hitler ordered the invasion of Poland in 1939. When he witnessed clergy being shot and a group of Jews locked in their synagogue as the building was set ablaze, he complained vehemently to Wilhelm Keitel, the Chief of Armed Forces for the Fatherland, who had Hitler's ear.

Keitel warned Canaris to drop the allegations since it was Hitler himself who ordered the atrocities in the first place. The irony here is that Canaris was the man who, years earlier, had come up with the idea of making German citizens who were of Jewish descent wear the Star of David on their coats whenever they went outside. Now, this same man was appalled at what his countrymen were doing to Polish Jews. Hence, this is the reason that Canaris was viewed as complicated.

Ever since Poland, Canaris vacillated between doing something to bring Hitler down and just going along with things. But increasingly, he couldn't stand by and just watch his country devolve into a land of ruthless, masochistic mass murderers. He had begun to quietly and selectively open up to a few very close and trusted friends. Somehow, they would need to determine how to remove the madman and avoid escalating a war that was already well on its way to getting completely out of control.

His thoughts were interrupted by the familiar knock on his door. He knew it was his secretary. "Excuse me, Admiral, but Herr Göring is on the phone."

Göring. Hitler's self-proclaimed right-hand man. Canaris had been a solid partner for Göring in the past. Two weeks ago, Canaris had sent eight men on their way to the U.S. in two different submarines on a secret mission to blow up bridges and munitions factories and to set off bombs in public places, among other things. Canaris' goal was to slow down the military manufacturing engine in the U.S. He also wanted to create havoc around the country and sow seeds of doubt among the American people. He wanted to get the American people to think thusly: "Germany hadn't done anything to the Americans, so why should we expend the lives of thousands of young men in Europe when the real enemy was the empire of Japan?"

Canaris had named the mission himself: Operation Pastorius. Francis Daniel Pastorius was the leader of the first German settlers who came to America in 1683. Pastorius established the city of Germantown, just outside of Philadelphia. Canaris, always enjoying a bit of irony, thought the name fit for the mission.

The Fatherland's reach into the U.S. was indeed significant, thanks to Canaris. At least it had been. But the network that had taken years to build had met with a serious defeat only two years earlier.

Fritz Duquesne, a German operative with a long and checkered past who had been sent into America years earlier, had been ordered by Canaris' organization to set up a spy ring in the mid-1930's. Duquesne was a veteran of the Great War over two decades ago and had fought for the Fatherland all across Europe. He escaped several military prisons over the years, once by dressing as a woman. The organization, which came to be known as The Duquesne Spy Ring, was a vast consortium of spies that had gathered in the northeast portion of the U.S. in the pre-war years. Their initial mission included getting jobs with airlines so they could report on the movement of American ships across the Atlantic, work in munitions factories so they could detail the types and numbers of weapons that were being developed, and report on the U.S.'s development of new war technology.

Eventually, if the Americans entered the war, sabotage was also on their to-do list.

Their biggest coup took place in 1937 when Canaris determined that his country needed the coveted and super-secret Norden e bombsight. The bombsight was designed and made in America and was a huge breakthrough technology for improving the accuracy of American bombs being dropped from the air. Canaris assigned Major Nicholas Ritter to determine how best to steal the plans for the bombsight.

Ritter was an excellent pick, for he spoke English fluently and had lived in the U.S. for 10 years as a textile manufacturer. Ritter understood not only the language but the culture. He quickly made plans to get to New York, where the bombsight was made. He recruited a machinist and draftsman named Herman Lang, who worked at the Carl L. Norden factory in New York City. The bombsight itself was complex, being made up of 2,000 individual, hand-crafted parts. Lang was in good company at the factory. Carl Norden was of Dutch descent, and most of the workers in the factory were German and Italian immigrants. Lang had an ingenious way of getting information on the bombsight. He would take some of the blueprints home at night by carefully stuffing them in his clothes. Once home, he would wait for his wife and daughter to fall asleep, and then he would get up and trace over the blueprints on a separate sheet of paper. The next day, he would get into work early and return the blueprints. As he left for the evening, he would take the next set of prints and do the same thing. This went on for several days until he had everything that he needed.

The next challenge was determining how Ritter was going to get the blueprints back to Germany. After ruminating on it for several days, he devised a clever plot to ensure that the plans would make their way to the Fatherland. He created a custom-made umbrella with a hollow stem. On January 9, 1938, Ritter slipped the blueprints into the stem, took a cab down to the docks, and walked aboard the steamship Reliance. The only potential glitch in the entire operation was the American guard at the dock, who took a real liking to the unique design of the umbrella and asked to look at it. After some pleasantries, Ritter bid the American goodbye and boarded the ship.

The Reliance was getting ready to launch for Bremen, a port city in Northwest Germany. Waiting for Ritter in Germany was his unsuspecting American wife and two children, who were anxious to see their father. Equally anxious to see Ritter was another group of people with much more sinister motivations. And that is how a secret, proprietary American technology that took years to perfect came into the hands of the enemy, thereby ensuring that the Germans would be on equal footing with the Allies when it came to dropping accurate bombs. Canaris and his brilliant plan were celebrated, and the little man gained a tremendous amount of political capital with Hitler and, therefore, the Nazi hierarchy.

Ritter's one mistake was his recruitment of a man named William Sebold, who was in fact a double agent and worked for Hoover's F.B.I. Thanks to Sebold, the entire ring was eventually brought down. 33 Germans were arrested in September of 1941. 19 pled guilty, and the rest opted for a trial. The trial concluded one week after Pearl Harbor. All were found guilty, including Lang. In January, they all received prison sentences that totaled over 300 years. But Ritter was long gone by then, having been reassigned by Canaris.

Hoover, ever the opportunist for some P.R., crowed to all who would listen that bringing the Duquesne Ring down was the largest apprehension of spies in U.S. history. That didn't sit well with Canaris, who wanted another opportunity to get even with Hoover and redeem whatever stains there were with his peers. Operation Pastorius would be the vehicle to ensure that both of those objectives would be met.

CHAPTER 13

As he looked out the window from his office near the top of the 1st National Bank building, Michael Sweeney allowed himself an actual smile, albeit a small one. A serious man who kept most of his emotions inside - that was the cop in him - Michael had much to smile about, or at least to be content with. He nursed a cup of coffee and took in his surroundings.

At 57, his 6'1 frame was still solid and toned. He absently stroked his gray mustache as he took in all that had happened in the past few weeks. His thick hair matched the color of his mustache, save for a little dark stretch at the top of his head. His steely blue eyes would almost twinkle when he did smile. At least that was what his wife Maggie told him when she encouraged him to let his hair down.

But make no mistake: Michael Sweeney didn't smile all that much. He wasn't a grouch or a pessimist. He was just more on the serious side. After all, his entire life had been spent protecting people and their most prized possessions. That kind of job didn't exactly land you on the Jack Benny show.

He loosened the top button on his suit coat and leaned against the corner window that looked northwest toward the capitol building. He had one of the few offices that afforded a panoramic view of the Twin Cities. He could see Minneapolis to the west and the mighty Mississippi to his east. Further up the river, he could also make out Holman Field, which was the main airport in and out of St. Paul. The airport was named after

Charles "Speed" Holman, a daredevil stunt pilot who was the first pilot hired by Northwest Airlines in 1926. Holman was killed in Omaha five years later while putting on yet another air show.

Further south of the airport were the Wabasha Street caves, where a whole lot of bootlegging used to take place. The caves housed the Castle Royal, a high-class restaurant and supper club during prohibition. Famous bands like the Dorsey brothers and other great talent like Cab Calloway and Harry James also performed there.

The caves were formed in part by the Mississippi itself, then expanded by man, who used it for everything from mining to growing and storing mushrooms. The restaurant shut down a year ago with the start of the war. "Too bad," thought Michael, "Good food and a lively place to go to."

The restaurant had attracted outlaws and politicians alike. The outlaws included John Dillinger, the Barker gang, and Alvin "Creepy" Karpis, who Michael knew personally. After all, Karpis used to get a free ride in a Sweeney Armored Car to and from the courthouse when he was on trial for the kidnappings of two of St. Paul's wealthiest people, William Hamm of Hamm's Beer fame and Edward Bremer, principal at Bremer Bank in St. Paul.

Karpis was the first person to be #1 on the F.B.I.'s most wanted list who was actually captured alive. The other three - Dillinger, Pretty Boy Floyd, and Baby Face Nelson - all died in shootouts with the Bureau and/or local police.

The caves ran dark and deep, and a couple of speakeasies could always be found in them during Prohibition.

"Those were certainly interesting days," thought Sweeney.

Virtually everywhere he looked from his office could conjure up memories of his days as a cop. Each decent-sized site came with a memory or story of some kind.

He snapped himself back to the present day and found himself trying to gauge how cold it would be when he left his office later in the day.

November in Minnesota was not normally a pleasant month. While September was great - really, just an extra month of summer - and the first half of October was beautiful - it seemed that people came from everywhere to enjoy the beautiful colored show that the leaves put on every year - November was the warning shot for what would eventually come.

Often dreary and overcast, the month conjured up images of dried-out leaves all over the ground, winds that could knock over little old ladies and kids alike, and cold and cloudy days that gave way to accelerated darkness. And then there was the "S" word: Snow. It was not uncommon to get dumped on in November and have it stay on the ground until April.

"Today, though, was actually quite nice. "Crisp" would be a good word," said Michael to himself. The sun was out, at least partially. There were still some stubborn leaves on the large maple tree across the street from the bank that had refused to yield to the inevitable.

After enjoying the view for another couple of minutes, he turned inward, literally and figuratively. He looked around his office and his eyes came to rest on a wall that was full of citations and photographs that covered his career.

There were five photographs that stood out, ones that, in those rare pensive moments, he would always find himself drawn to.

The first one had been taken almost 20 years ago. It was a picture of him and a few other men standing in front of the very bank that he now officed out of, the First National Bank, the largest bank in the state. A Sweeney Detective Bureau armored car was parked between the men and the bank itself. It was Sweeney Detective's first armored car. "We were all a lot younger then," he smiled to himself.

He harkened back to those early days trying to get funding from banks for the design and build of the armored car, lining up potential clients, talking to his fellow cop friends about being the escort service for criminals, interviewing former or current cops who he trusted to work security and private detective work. The list was endless, as were the days. And nights.

His wife Maggie was in favor of it. They had talked long and hard about Mike leaving the force, and Maggie had pointed out that he hadn't been happy in quite a while in his work. The politics and corruption were just too much. She encouraged him to make a go of this new idea. Knowing that he had her support made all the difference in the world to him.

His eyes found their way to the next four photographs that always seemed to be in his line of sight in these reflective moments.

The second photo that tended to catch his eye was of James J. Hill, the railroad magnate and philanthropist who was known as "The Empire

Builder." Hill, born in Canada, made his fortune in St. Paul, primarily through buying and building railroads and routes.

He and Michael had become friends through Michael's police work. Hill saw the Irishman in action and found Sweeney to be everything that his reputation had been: honest, forthright, and incorruptible.

These qualities were critical to Hill, for he had a very unique problem: he had too much money sitting in too few banks. Hill needed someone whom he could trust to transport his money between banks and elsewhere. He called Michael one day and explained his dilemma to him, and then asked him to take on the responsibility of managing his money transportation needs.

Michael agreed to do the job on the side. Incredibly, the way that most money was transferred back then was using plainclothes cops who would carry suitcases full of money with them on streetcars or buses. As he took on the significant responsibility of moving Hill's capital, an idea began to form in his head about better ways to transport money and other important documents.

Out of this work for Mr. Hill came the birth of the Sweeney Detective Bureau. It was then that he and Maggie decided that he would leave the force and design the first armored car in America. Sweeney Detective eventually became three separate businesses: The armored car division, private security for individuals and businesses, and private detective work.

The next photo that he tended to park on was one that reminded him of how life can so quickly change, especially as a cop. This picture was of him with Frank Frazer, a patrolman with whom he had been close friends over 30 years ago. They had grown up together on the force. Fraser loved patrolling. He had passed up several promotions so he could stay on the street, close to the action. On what would be his last shift, he was chasing a guy down Market Street in St. Paul.

The man had escaped from Stillwater Prison. The fugitive jumped on a streetcar on the corner of Market and 4th Street, and Fraser leaped on right behind him. The perpetrator turned and shot Fraser twice. Fraser and another cop still managed to subdue the guy and take him into custody, but Fraser was bleeding badly.

He hung on for two days before dying in the hospital, leaving a wife and young daughter.

Michael was one of the pall bearers at the funeral. He could still hear the absolute wailing of Fraser's wife during the service. It would be one of many police funerals that he would attend over the years. He had quietly seen to it that Fraser's daughter had her school covered all the way through college.

The picture that he normally saved for last was of his son, Jack. Jack had been a cop in the city and rose to a detective faster than anyone on the force. The picture was of the two of them the day that Jack made detective. Jack was in his dress blues, as was Michael. The photographer took the picture just as Michael was beaming as the two shook hands.

"He was such a fine young man," Michael said to himself. "Lord, I miss my boy."

As he did whenever he stopped to look at the photograph, his throat tightened, and he had to fight back the inevitable tears. It had been ten years since Jack died in the line of duty, but it might just as well have been yesterday, so fresh were the wounds. Yes, he died a hero, saving many lives that day at the bank when he interrupted a robbery in progress. But he still died. And Michael and Maggie missed him every single day.

They would often cry themselves to sleep in the first few years. Eventually, they began to talk about Jack. Not long conversations. Maybe a mention of his name. Or an old photograph. The anniversary of his death was always difficult. And his birthday. And, of course, the holidays. He and Maggie could talk about him without one of them breaking down anymore. At least much of the time.

He felt like he was somehow betraying Jack if he looked at the other photos and not his.

There was one last picture that he had on the wall with the others. This one also made him smile. It was of Michael with his partner on the force, George Parker. They were best friends. Even though the two men hadn't seen much of each other in recent years, there was a permanent bond that formed between two guys who did stakeouts together or covered each other as one of them rushed a guy who was trying to kill them. Michael Sweeney had George Parker's back, and that road went both ways. Michael was a few years older than George and was even an inch or two taller.

Both had married well. In Michael's case, he was engaged to a young woman named Bridget McLaughlin when he met one Maggie Flynn from

Dubuque, Iowa, and that was that. Michael and Maggie fell in love and were quickly married. Since then, they had raised a family, started a very successful business, and much to their mutual chagrin, had become quite well known in the Twin Cities. Michael occasionally wondered about what became of Bridget. She was gracious when Michael broke off the engagement. They hadn't even set a date at that point. Someone said that she had married a doctor and lived over in Minneapolis.

He was so grateful that he met Maggie when he did. They were hopelessly in love, even after all of these years. Maggie understood the price of being a cop's wife. It actually got worse after Michael left the force to start the Detective Bureau. But she never complained. She knew in her heart that Michael's priority was his family and that the best way to love her husband was to let him be what he was meant to be: a cop turned entrepreneur who had a passion for protecting people and their assets.

Maggie loved to cook, but keeping the rest of the large home clean was left to someone else. With Michael being gone so much, there weren't enough hours in the day to effectively manage all of it and keep it all clean, all the while watching over four rambunctious kids.

They had had a few women come through over the years, and the last one was somewhat new but very good. Michael, a stickler for order, would run his finger along the sides of the dining room table on occasion just to check if the new woman - Betty Fischer- Michael often couldn't recall her last name - was as thorough as Maggie claimed that she was.

So far, Betty hadn't let them down. And she was also a very good cook, helping Maggie with many of the meals each week. A tall woman with short, dark hair, Betty tended to tower over Maggie and the girls. She was friendly and seemed to enjoy the Sweeneys. The Sweeney women were always friendly and accommodating with anyone who came into their home to help. It was obvious to any visitor that Michael and Maggie had raised their children to be polite and respectful to everyone.

Michael made a mental note to compliment Maggie on her good hire.

His thoughts turned back to his former partner. He and George Parker had certainly covered a lot of ground together. How they had solved some of those cases in St. Paul was always well noted in the newspapers.

Most of the cases just required a lot of hard work and follow-up. The Twin Sleuths, as they were called, worked cases differently. They would take large pieces of paper and write out the case, complete with pictures of the victim and also the suspects. They would canvas neighborhoods and "gum shoe" it, calling in favors from tipsters or street thugs that they had put behind bars on other occasions. They'd done a lot of good for the city and brought some peace of mind to the families of the victims. And that was enough for him.

But again, Michael got tired of all the corruption. It was one thing to watch hardened criminals act corruptly. One sort of expected that, and Michael's job was to find the bad guys and put them away. But when the corruption inside of the department matched - or, in some cases, exceeded - what was out on the street, **that** was just too much for Mike and his partner to tolerate.

Too many cops were on the take and paid to look the other way. And it wasn't just the patrolmen. It went all the way to the top. In fact, the men in leadership were actually the worst. Whoever sat in the Chief's chair set the tone and direction for the entire department. It had started with John O'Connor, the infamous Chief of Police in St. Paul, who made far more money from bribes and payoffs than he did from his Chief's salary. The O'Connor Layover System, as it was known, allowed criminals - and some big named ones to boot - to live in St. Paul hassle free, as long as they did their crimes across the river in Minneapolis.

Dillinger, Baby Face Nelson, Ma Barker and her boys, the aforementioned Creepy Alvin Karpis, even Al Capone himself had spent time in St. Paul, all under the protective care of the St. Paul Police Department.

This went on for decades.

Michael hated the system. It encouraged - and rewarded - corruption at every level of the department. Heck, even many of the patrolmen, seeing how the game was played, would shake down store owners for free products, free meals, a cut of their profits, anything - in exchange for doing what they had sworn an oath to do.

He had seen the writing on the wall and got out well in advance of it getting worse. Which it did. As rumors of a repeal of Prohibition began to swirl in the early 1930s, the gangsters had to look for ways to "diversify." Enter bank robberies and kidnappings.

By 1932, thanks to the O'Connor system, a staggering 20% of all bank robberies in the entire country took place in Minnesota. Sweeney Detective Bureau was one of the few companies who benefited from all of this crime. Sweeney's armored cars were in high demand. They were basically tanks on wheels, and they rolled 24/7.

The citizens of St. Paul were growing weary of playing host to the infamous. Then, the rules were broken.

Things came to a head in June of 1933 when William Hamm, the wealthy heir to and President of Theodore Hamm's Beer and Brewing Company in St. Paul, was kidnapped. In St. Paul.

The timing couldn't have been better. Prohibition spawned a massive growth in crime, and the Sweeney Detective Bureau was right there to help the cops move the bad guys from jail to courts and vice versa and to move monies between banks.

The end of Prohibition in '33 put a huge hole in the criminal element's pocketbook. As bad as bank robberies had already become, they got even worse.

And kidnapping became a lot more popular as well. By then Michael had a full fleet of trucks, and Sweeney's trucks made even more runs from bank to bank. And they still had time to take the same criminals to the same jails and courts.

Michael's design called for inch-thick concrete slabs to slide into the doors and bottoms of the cars.

He also had specially made thick glass that could take a few rounds from a Tommy gun. The trucks only got 1 mile to the gallon, but no one was too worried about that.

As the years progressed, Sweeney Detective Bureau became a trusted name all over the state. Michael even had an office in Duluth to service the banks up there. The suite of armored cars and trucks was on the go every day of the week, trying to keep up with all the demand. Plus, Michael's armored cars were the first on the market and the only ones available for several years. Having this kind of head start gave the company the opportunity to establish longer agreements and deeper relationships so that when competition finally did arrive, most of the city was committed to the Irishman and his trucks.

The other two businesses—the private detective division and the protective security entity—were natural add-ons to the armored car business. Even Michael himself used to do some of the detective and security work, occasionally moonlighting as a security guard at one of the banks or handling a sensitive assignment that needed discretion.

He had tried to get Parker to go in with him as a partner, but George, being younger with younger children, just couldn't take the risk. Plus, he wanted to see just how far he could go with the F.B.I.

And he had gone far. Parker, now with the O.S.S., had come to town a few weeks earlier to brief Michael on why he had needed Frank's services for a very special assignment over in Germany. George hadn't had to do that. He could've just grabbed Frank, who had been assigned to an Army Air Force base in England.

But friendship trumped everything else, and he had come to St. Paul to let Michael know face-to-face what he was about to get Frank into. That's just how their friendship operated, even in war. And George and his family were there for Frank and Maggie when Jack was killed.

Michael had seen firsthand how wonderful people can be in a time of tragedy. But life gets back to normal for everyone else. Not so much for the grieving family. Yet there was George, calling daily for months after Jack's funeral. He had made sure to be available to Michael no matter what the hour. Michael would never forget that.

Just as he and Maggie had begun some semblance of recovery, so had the kids.

Much of the small recovery was due to Frank's safe, if temporary, return from Germany and the emergence of one Leigh Conway, the daughter of Dr. Edwin Conway, who would soon be working for the Allies.

Leigh and Frank were an item. Anyone could see that there was a special relationship that was being formed between the handsome, athletic (and now former) Army Air Force pilot who had risked his life for his country in what amounted to a suicide mission, and the beautiful titian haired schoolteacher with the wonderful Irish accent who was already beginning to fall in love with her new country.

They had met in Germany under extremely difficult circumstances, but their bond was immediate and growing deeper by the day. George told Michael that he could see it quite plainly in the two days of their debriefing sessions in Switzerland and London. And Frank privately told him as much.

"Well," Michael had told George, "At least one good thing has come out of this crazy war."

He would be seeing George again, and sooner than he thought.

# CHAPTER 14

Admiral Canaris picked up his phone and gave Göring a rather neutral greeting. After some light pleasantries, Göring came to the point.

"Admiral, I need your help to resolve a somewhat delicate situation."

Canaris, feigning ignorance: "Oh? Well, of course, Herr Göring. You know that I am always willing to help you."

"Thank you, Admiral. One of my incompetent underlings has managed to completely foul up a sensitive program that had huge potential to help us win the war through air superiority." "Yes, I am familiar with that initiative," said a guarded Canaris.

"And, of course, you know what happened recently with Dr. Conway?"

"Very unfortunate." Again, Canaris, ever the spymaster, not giving Göring anything.

"Yes. "Unfortunate" would be one word, Admiral. I can think of several others that would be more reflective of the severity of this situation, but "unfortunate" will do for now."

Silence. Canaris was going to make him state clearly what needed to be said.

"Admiral, if Dr. Conway's work should fall into the hands of the Allies, that would be, shall we say, more than "unfortunate." (You need to take care of this for me).

"Yes, that certainly would be, Herr Göring, particularly for your underling that allowed it to happen in the first place. Perhaps he can be given no other job other than to correct this situation." (Me? Why me? It's your mess.)

"I'd like you to activate whatever resources you have to put this "unfortunate" incident to rest." (Get in the game. Do I need to order you?)

"I would be happy to partner with you in any way that I can, Herr Göring." (If you're dragging me into this, I'm taking you with me.)

"Look, Admiral, I know that you have men who have recently landed in America. Or are about to. And I know that they have been trained in espionage, sabotage, and assassinations. I also know for a fact that Dr. Conway is in America right now. We've traced him from London, where he met with English and American intelligence, and the Americans won the debate about where he could add the most value."

Canaris made him sweat for almost a full minute. Just as Göring was about to ask if he was still on the line, Canaris said, "Yes, we can re-purpose those assets that are now in the country. I can deploy them to get rid of the problem."

"Thank you, Admiral. Please make sure that your people understand that, under no circumstances will Edwin Conway be allowed to live. I can send you pictures of him. He also has a son and a daughter that"-

"Yes, Herr Göring, we are aware of his family situation. His son, who von Greim had held as a hostage so Conway would work on the project, has already volunteered in the American Army, which means that he will be in training for the next several weeks, at a minimum. We also don't know which base he will be on. Regardless, we have very few assets anywhere near the many bases that the American military is utilizing." "And the daughter?" asked Göring.

"She and her father are currently in a city in the upper middle part of the country, a state called Minnesota. They are both currently staying with the family of the young man who was sent in to get them out of the country. Our sources tell us that the Americans are taking things slowly with Dr. Conway. They want him to see their country and get comfortable with it, so he will feel good about giving the Americans all the critical information that he had built up when he was here."

Göring was impressed that Canaris already had a lot of information on the Conways. And maybe a little relieved?

Then: "Could we try to kidnap her, Admiral?"

"Frankly, that would not be my first choice. This particular family that she is staying with is well respected and well known in that region of the country. Also, the father is a former police detective who now runs his own detective agency. So, I would bet that he has excellent security. Our best option is to take out Dr. Conway, preferably in a way that makes it look like an accident."

"And why should we do it in such a way that makes it look like an accident, Admiral?"

Canaris, doing the classic eye roll, followed by the head shake, was clearly frustrated and doing a poor job of hiding it: "Because, Herr Göring, we have assets in the country that are currently undetected and, in most cases, not even suspected. We'd like to keep it that way."

Göring, having a "head slap" moment, is left speechless for a minute as he tries to cover for his obvious stupidity for asking such a question.

"Well, of course, Admiral," he sputtered. "That is obvious. I was wondering if you were saying that an accident would be quicker and require less planning. Speed is of the essence here. It would be bad enough to allow Conway to give the Allies all this incredibly sensitive information. What would be worse would be having Conway himself actually working on the technology. That would accelerate the project dramatically. So, regardless of how it's done, it must be done quickly."

Canaris, now squeezing the bridge of his nose with both fingers, followed by another look at the ceiling with a simultaneous head shake, said wearily: "Yes, Herr Göring, that is an interesting point. I will make sure that our people understand the urgency of this situation." More silence.

Then Göring: "Thank you, Admiral. Please keep me informed." (The problem has now been handed to you by me. Now take care of it.)

Canaris: "Herr Göring, before you go, according to the Fuhrer's rigorous procedures in such cases as this, the Fuhrer has made it quite clear that we need a written affidavit with explicit instructions from you. I'm sure that you agree that we need to follow the Fuhrer's protocol." (Oh no, you don't, you fat fuzzball. You're not pinning this on me. Your fingerprints need to be on this one.)

Göring, feigning temporary amnesia: "Oh, yes, of course. I didn't realize that these rules applied to even the two of us. If you insist, I'll have something hand-delivered to you by tomorrow."

(Really? You're really going to play that card? I'll remember this!)

Canaris: "Thank you, Herr Göring. This is a significant departure from the original mission that these men were recruited for. Upon receipt of your letter, I will commence immediately." (I'm not lifting a finger until I have something in writing from you.)

Cold silence for a moment.

Göring, coldly: "Thank you, Admiral." (Now I'll REALLY remember this.)

Canaris: "I appreciate you bringing this problem to me. My staff and I are always available to help in - what did you call it? Oh, yes - a delicate situation like this." (This is your mess. We'll try to bail you out of it, but if it doesn't work, I have a little document from you that is my insurance policy.)

With that, the conversation ended. Both men claimed victory for themselves.

# CHAPTER 15

George Dasch stared out the window of his suite on the 17th floor of the Governor Clinton Hotel. He looked down on 31st Street and saw the hustle and bustle that he had come to know when he had lived in the city years before. He had enjoyed his years in New York. The sheer volume of people was remarkable, regardless of the time of day or night, for that matter. There was an energy here that one didn't find anywhere else.

But it had a different feel now. Clearly, the war had changed things, even in New York. There was less hustle and bustle and fewer horns honking. But still, it was the most vibrant city that he had ever been to.

He looked away from the window and caught his reflection in the mirror next to the door. He saw his receding hairline. It seemed like every time he looked in the mirror, it had moved backward from the previous spot. His face was getting even more gaunt. Dasch's eyes looked like two small marbles that were stuck deep into the recesses of the moon. He sighed in disgust.

Looking around their large suite, he reminded himself that things could always be worse. The furnishings were all elegant and classy. Even the glasses in the room were made of fine crystal. This definitely beat Germany. He liked America. Sure, working as a waiter in the city was no picnic, but he had done all right for himself.

They were into their second full day, which meant that the other four men on the other sub would be going to shore tonight, somewhere off the coast of Jacksonville.

Dasch knew a few more details about the assignments than the other men did. Still, much of the mission had been compartmentalized. This thought made him look over at his suitemate, Ernst Peter Burger, whom everyone called Peter. Burger sat in a soft chair studying some maps. He was average in almost every way. He had a plain, serious face. Medium height, medium build. Quiet, but when he spoke, he didn't mince words. A very serious, introspective man. He rarely smiled. As a matter of fact, Dasch couldn't remember him ever smiling.

He had purposely picked Burger as his roommate because he knew of Burger's past. Peter Burger was not exactly the ideal German spy. Yes, he had spent time in America, so his English was better than most. He had even served in the National Guard here. But when the Depression hit, he migrated back to Germany and joined the Nazi Party, working his way up to being an assistant to the Chief of the Nazi Storm Troopers. No small task, that.

But he made the mistake of criticizing the Gestapo - in writing, no less - and that landed him in a Nazi concentration camp for close to 18 months. The Nazis even harassed his wife when he was trying to survive in the camp. Then, for reasons that no one understood, shortly after serving his time, Burger was recruited by the Abwehr, Germany's intelligence organization, for secret missions. Dasch had picked up on comments from Burger during their training that made his commitment to the mission come into question. Nothing blatant. Just a tone, perhaps?

It was time to tell him.

Earlier in the day, Burger had noticed that Dasch was acting strangely as they finished their room service breakfast. He had decided to not ask Dasch, figuring that Dasch would let him know later what was eating at him. Now, Burger took a break from his map reading, looked up to see Dasch staring into the mirror, and finally asked what the matter was. Dasch paused, looked at Burger for a moment in the mirror, and said, "I'm going to tell you something, and if you don't agree with me, we will fight it out right here and now, and one of us will go out that window." With that, Dasch turned squarely to face Burger, setting his feet and striking a defensive pose.

Burger stared at him for a minute, gathered himself, and said, "Go on."

Dasch waited a few seconds and said, "I've decided that I have no intention of going through with this mission. In fact, I plan on calling the F.B.I. and telling them that I want to meet with J. Edgar Hoover in two days in Washington, where I will divulge all our plans. We will all die here if we go ahead with this. If I give us up, I expect that I will be treated as a national hero of sorts here."

Burger said nothing for several moments.

Then: "What about Quirin and Heinck? Do they know about this?"

Dasch, still wary, shook his head. "I arranged for them to get rooms over at the Martinique for a couple of reasons. First, it's always best to split up and spread our risk. Our superiors obviously liked that idea. But second, it also allows for me to get to Washington without them seeing me leave the hotel."

Burger, as usual, remained silent, waiting for Dasch to continue.

But Dasch was waiting to gauge a response from Burger and said nothing. Finally, Burger gestured for him to go on.

Dasch said, "Look, I'm taking a huge risk here. I am telling you that I am not going through with this mission. I am going to Washington to meet with J. Edgar Hoover. Do you know who he"-

"Of course, I know who he is," whispered Burger, growing agitated.

"All right," said Dasch, beginning to whisper himself, which made no sense when one thought about it. "Look, if you're with me on this, we can be heroes here in America. I have no plans to go back to Germany. I think Hitler will lose this war, and Germany will be doomed."

Burger stared at the floor, thinking. Then he asked again about the other two men.

Dasch didn't hesitate.

"Quirin and Heinck are Nazis through and through. They will finish this assignment. And if they knew that we were even considering ruining things, they would remember their orders and complete the mission. But they would kill us first." He let that last part sink in.

"And don't forget about the other four members who are due to land tonight. Kerling is another Nazi. He will complete this mission or die trying. He would not hesitate to kill either one of us."

The two men stayed silent for several seconds, Burger digesting Dasch's comments and Dasch trying to gauge how Burger would react.

The silence was finally broken by Dasch, who looked directly into Burger's eyes and said, "Peter, this is your only chance to pull out of this thing and still spare your life."

More silence. Burger, still quiet, now staring at the floor.

Dasch was wise enough to not say anything more and let him think through all of it. After all, this was a major departure from the group's plan and the direct orders of the Fatherland.

After a full minute, Burger looked up at Dasch - or through him - for what seemed like an eternity and then started to nod slowly. He finally spoke and said, "On that, we can agree."

And for the first time, George Dasch thought he saw Peter Burger emit a small smile.

CHAPTER 16



It was after midnight when Commander Joachim Deecke ordered his sub, 300 yards offshore, to surface. Deecke, all 30 years of age, had 10 years of service in Germany's navy but barely two years as a lieutenant of his own ship. He would be commander of this vessel for about 11 more months, although he didn't know it yet. At the end of October of the following year, the sub would be lying on the bottom of the North Atlantic, having been sunk by a GAU-8 torpedo from an American Avenger. Deecke and all 50 of his crew would perish.

Similar to the exchange that occurred off the coast of Long Island two nights earlier, Deecke quickly wished the four men good luck and hurried them off of his vessel. He needed to get back to Brest, France, as quickly as possible to get resupplied for his next mission.

The four spies emerged out of the water and made their way to shore. Edward Kerling, the clear and appointed leader of the group, led the other three to a cluster of palm trees a few yards up the beach. Thanks to a nearly full moon, they could see the silhouette of the 220-foot U-584 submarine gently swaying in the warm waters of the southern Atlantic.

Unlike their comrades to the north, they didn't bother wearing

German military uniforms. They had landed on Ponte Vedra Beach, about 18 miles southeast of downtown Jacksonville, in their body-length swimsuits. Florida's east coast was somewhat warm most nights, but the November air had a bit of a bite to it on this particular evening. They didn't have the cover of fog, but the town of Ponte Vedra was so small that there was no one around for several miles.

The moonlight provided a path to help them find their way along the beach. Kerling was struck by the sheer beauty of the setting. But that thought quickly left him as he motioned his men closer to the line of palm trees. They immediately began digging holes to bury their weapons, explosives, and extra cash. No one said a word as they worked quietly, attacking the sand as fast as they could with the small shovels that were put in the raft before they came ashore. Within 10 minutes, the two German sailors that had followed them in the second raft carrying the supplies saluted them and hurried to get back to the submarine and its crew, who were impatiently waiting to get out of American waters.

Kerling, 33, was a strapping man with movie star looks. 6 feet tall and a solid frame of 190 pounds, one would be hard-pressed to find any fat on him. He had deep-set blue eyes and a chiseled jaw that was square and strong. His brown hair had grown out a bit, but it did nothing to make him look…what? Softer. He was a soldier, to be sure, and the perfect example of Hitler's dream of an Aryan race.

He was a no-nonsense soldier who, one way or another, was going to be faithful to his mission. From the very beginning weeks before in Germany, Kerling's intensity stood out among all the men that were selected for this assignment. While he was the assigned leader of the team, each man would have looked to him to lead them even if he hadn't been so designated.

He had a unique background and was well-suited for the mission. He had lived in the U.S. for several years and had held several jobs, from meat packer to chauffeur. He even married a German immigrant while in the country. Kerling had also worked in several states while in America and knew his way around the country. He knew the highways and railways, and his English was flawless.

As comfortable as he was in America, he had also returned to Germany several times in the last few years, the last being about six months ago.

That was when he met Lieutenant Kappe, who recruited him for this daring assignment.

Besides his leadership and commitment to the Nazi cause, Kappe saw a ruthless killer and soldier who would follow orders. He also knew Kerling to be an excellent marksman who could think on his feet and improvise when necessary. The others in his group were capable but would still benefit from Kerling's leadership and example. They were too raw to question Kerling's decision-making and would do as they were told.

The other three men had lived in Chicago for several years. Hermann Neubauer was a cook at the Palmer House Hotel and later worked at the Bismarck Hotel in the Second City. He fled America in 1940 and went to Germany to help the Fatherland fight the war.

Neubauer's partner, Peter Thiel, had lived not far from the Palmer House since his parents brought him to America as a 5-year-old. Thiel was now all of 22. While Neubauer had purposefully returned to Germany to help the cause, Thiel had run away from America and happened to land in Germany. He had gotten in trouble with a girl, fled to Mexico, and eventually found his way to Berlin. Both men were so fluent in English that they immediately caught the eye - or maybe the ear - of Kappe.

Herbert Haupt was the fourth man in the group. Another German born young man who became a U.S. citizen at the age of 10, he was a year older than Thiel. Through a series of poor decisions and bad timing, he found himself in Germany at the outbreak of the war and viewed the mission as a way to fulfill his duty to Germany.

Haupt would do what he was told, but Kerling knew that he would have to keep his eye on him just to be safe. The difference between Kerling and the other men was that the three men on this mission were part-time Americans, but when push came to shove, their German heritage would trump any semblance of American loyalty. On the other hand, there was no debate or hesitation when it came to Kerling. He was a Nazi. Nothing more, nothing less. While the others viewed the mission as an order that needed to be followed, he was actually looking forward to fulfilling his duty, no matter the cost.

The four men continued hacking away at the ground, which was initially soft sand. About two feet down, they hit a harder texture. They dug for another foot or so and then began burying their weapons, explosives, and part of their money. They marked the area well, putting some heavy rocks of unique shapes directly over the treasure.

In addition to keeping a good portion of the money - it would come in handy for where they were headed and what they had to do - Kerling took a special handkerchief that had been given to him by Lieutenant Kappe as he was boarding the submarine in France. George Dasch had received an identical handkerchief. To the naked eye, it appeared to be what it was supposed to look like - a beige men's hanky.

However, written on it in invisible ink were the names and vital information for a couple of key contacts that could, if needed, serve as their accomplices in America. These people had the means and wherewithal to help Kerling and his men succeed in their assignment. And they were just as committed to the mission as the men who came ashore. Kerling had a good idea of the identity of at least one of the people. He would make contact as soon as he felt safe to do so. In the meantime, they had to get off the beach and move.

# CHAPTER 17

Helmut "Del" Leiner sat in the living room of his small apartment in Queens. One thing about living in Queens: you just got used to the noise. Whether it was cars or trains, people were always doing something. It got to the point that if there wasn't some sort of noise, people became almost uncomfortable.

Small in stature with a thick head of sandy brown hair and a light mustache to match, Leiner had the sort of face that was unremarkable and, therefore, hard to remember. On top of this, he kept a low profile, which made it easy for him to move in and around New York society with ease. His brains more than made up for his lack of brawn. Not only did Leiner work for the Abwehr, he was a quiet but strong player in the Third Reich. 33 years old, he was a supporter of the German American Bund, the pro-Nazi organization with chapters around the U.S.

Leiner was even awarded the Golden Insignia, a prestigious award given to people who were considered pioneers of the Nazi Party. He reported directly to Walter Kappe. In addition to his healthy compensation from Kappe, he worked as a gardener. But not just anywhere. Del Leiner was the main gardener for two different U.S. Congressmen. He reported regularly back to Germany any pertinent information that he could glean. It was amazing what he learned as a result of just "being around."

Leiner was trained by Kappe in Germany well before the war was even a possibility, and he was deeply embedded in American society, having lived here for 13 years. So far, he had had no close calls with the U.S. authorities. As a matter of fact, both

Congressmen and their families loved him and thought he did an excellent job maintaining the grounds on their properties. He always received an invite to their Christmas parties and even was invited to their 4th of July get-togethers, since much of the tables and inside surroundings were decorated with many of the flowers and plants that he maintained for them.

He would be one of the least suspicious people on anyone's list when it came to possible spies. It's not that Leiner hated America; he just loved Germany. He had an intense loyalty to his native country and to the man who ran it. And this love trumped everything else. After all, the Fatherland was in a war, and Germany must stop at nothing to win it, even if that meant that innocents would be sacrificed. He viewed his role as being on the front lines of the battle, but just in a different theater and with a different enemy. He would attack the head of the snake so that the U.S. would have fewer resources in which to fight the war. There was no limit to what he would or could do. He would take his orders from Kappe directly and Hitler indirectly, and he would follow through on every single one of them. No matter what the cost.

As he sat reading the New York Times, as was his habit, he checked the want ads for any hidden communique from the Fatherland. If there was an ad for a gardener role with a P.O. Box that started and ended with the number 4, he knew that he had to get in touch with Kappe. They had a meeting place in the most public of places: the New York subway. The two men lived only three stops apart from one another. If they did meet, it was always on the same train and at the same time: the 8:00 AM train into the city on the day after the ad was placed.

Most people on that train would be reading the newspaper on the way in. The two men would have a simple message scribbled on one of the inside pages. He and Leiner would exchange information this way. Whenever possible, the messages would be coded. Lately he had noticed, that Kappe had gotten lazier. He wasn't sure if that was because the messages were getting more complex or if he just felt like the risk was so low. Either way, Leiner preferred the simpler approach. He just had to make sure that the exchange of the papers went flawlessly and that both men walked out of the station with their newspapers firmly in hand.

As he perused the paper, his eyes came to rest on the ad: "Wanted: A proven gardener to care for assorted plants and 3 small gardens of green beans and tomatoes. Send information to box 424 in Brooklyn." He would meet Kappe the next morning.

# CHAPTER 18

Leiner jumped on the train, made his way to his normal car, found his regular seat, and settled in. It being a Sunday morning, the train had extra seats available. Two stops later, Walter Kappe walked into his car and found a seat next to Leiner. Both pretended to read the paper. Seeing as the car was only half full, they were able to speak quietly and not attract a lot of attention.

Kappe was the first to speak. "Everything going all right?"

Leiner, perusing the sports page, merely grunted and said, "The Florida team is **en route** to Cincinnati. I will leave soon to meet up with them. The New York team is here as well."

"That's good. Because our orders have changed."

Leiner stiffened, then quickly recovered. "What do you mean, 'Our orders have changed?'"

Kappe, turning the page of the newspaper and casually looking around the car to see if anyone was watching them: "We have a change in plans, and it is coming right from the top."

Leiner, clearly irritated because this was a change that he had not been expecting: "That's just great. What now?"

Kappe, now growing irritated himself: "My dear friend, may I remind you that you take orders from me? So, get a hold of yourself."

Leiner said nothing.

Kappe again: "The New York team will stay on task. Their orders will not change. I want to see some action out of them. They need to start looking at how to blow up the targets that we have established for them. I want their priority to be the ALCOA plant so that we can drastically slow down America's mass production for their war efforts. We are going to need Kerling and Thiel pulled from their operation. Neubauer and Haupt will continue as is. Let them get to Chicago as planned, but only for a couple of days. I don't want to spook them too badly. Then have them come here. Dasch can take them in temporarily as part of his team."

Leiner nodded and waited for Kappe to continue. He didn't. Leiner glanced at Kappe expectantly. Kappe was lost in thought, still pretending to read the paper. The nice thing was that the New York Times Sunday edition was thick and had a lot of ads, which gave credence to Kappe and Leiner taking their time getting through the news.

Finally, Kappe spoke again: "I will call Kerling myself and talk to him directly. This is a risk, but it must be done. Time is of the essence. Apologies to you, Herr Leiner, but having Kerling hear it from me directly will eliminate any miscommunication. I will tell him to get to St. Paul immediately. We have an assassination target there that requires our immediate attention. All the information on our target is right here in the paper, and I will hand it to you in a minute. I have a copy in my apartment. We have some assets in and around St. Paul that we can also utilize to help us. Again, this information is in the papers that I am handing you. Please familiarize yourself with this information in the unlikely event that Kerling and Thiel fail in this assignment. Also, to be clear, this entire mission is under your responsibility. I will make the contact with Kerling, but I will make it clear to him that he will be reporting to you for this temporary role."

Leiner, listening intently but appearing to be studying a Marshall Field's ad, said, "This must be a very important mission. And a very important target. Not only is it a last-minute change, but we are willing to use all eight men if necessary to take out this one individual."

Kappe merely nodded ever so slightly.

Leiner, clearly intrigued, wanted desperately to grab the papers out of his compatriot's hands and look at what could be so urgent. But he remained disciplined in the moment. He would look only when he knew it was safe to do so. Still, he couldn't help asking: "When you say, "from the top," who does that mean? Certainly not the Fuehrer?"

Kappe was weighing how much to say. The more Leiner knew, the more vulnerable he could be if he was caught. On the other hand, Leiner wasn't an idiot. For a plan that had been in the works for months to be changed at the last minute… well, that would clearly indicate to even a novice that something big must be happening. He opted to tell him. After all, he would need to gain Leiner's trust over time, and Leiner had given Kappe no reason to not trust him.

"This comes from Canaris, at the request of Göring himself."

Leiner stiffened again. And swallowed. Then, like any good self-serving Nazi, he saw the opportunity in this for him. If he could make this mission successful, there is no telling where he could go within the Party. On the other hand, if it failed…

Kappe, reading his mind, turned to him and said, "You will likely never have an opportunity like this again, Herr Leiner. I suggest that you make the most of it."

# CHAPTER 19

Across town, George Dasch was getting frustrated. Even downright angry. He had spent the day so far trying to get someone - anyone - at the local office of the F.B.I. to take him seriously. After having yet another agent hang up on him, he threw the phone down in frustration.

Burger was out with Quirin and Heinck, taking in an early matinee movie called "Casablanca." Apparently, it had gotten rave reviews in last night's newspaper, according to Burger. Dasch wanted Burger to occupy the other two men's time while he got things set up with the F.B.I. As far as Quirin and Heinck were concerned, Dasch couldn't have cared less about their whereabouts as long as they stayed out of his way. Burger agreed with Dasch's idea - demand, really - that nothing be said to the other two men about Dasch's and Burger's plans.

After he composed himself, he ordered some room service. The best steak on the menu, a baked potato with butter and sour cream, and a double order of asparagus. It was well before dinner time, but he didn't care. "O.P.M." was now in play for Dasch: Other People's Money.

After finishing the meal, he decided to give up on the local F.B.I. office. He picked up the phone and asked the operator to dial F.B.I. headquarters in Washington, D.C.

After a couple of minutes, he was connected to the FBI. His experience was not a lot different than how he was treated by the New York office. He was passed around to several people.

Finally, in exasperation, he said to the agent, "What's his name?" that he would be in D.C. the next day and that he fully expected to meet with J. Edgar himself, and that the name of his mission was "Operation Pastorius." Dasch even demanded that the guy write all of this down. He ended the conversation with, "I expect that you will want to honor me as a national hero." He wasn't sure if the agent was sincere when he heard the guy say to him, "Yeah, OK, Sir, we'll get a man right on that." With that, he heard the now all-too-familiar "click."

Burger came back to the room 30 minutes later.

"I am leaving for Washington on a train that departs in an hour," announced Dasch.

"These people are not showing me the respect that I deserve over the phone. I will be in Hoover's office tomorrow afternoon. In case of an emergency, I will stay at the Mayflower Hotel, which is only a few minutes from the F.B.I. headquarters. Don't try to contact me unless it is absolutely necessary."

"They probably get a lot of these kinds of phone calls, so it's hard for them to know who is real and who is not," Burger rationalized.

"Well, they'll know that I'm real after a five-minute conversation," replied Dasch.

"Just make sure that you mention me in all of this, that I am fully cooperating, and that I am in total agreement with telling them everything," said Burger.

"Don't worry, I will make sure that we share the credit for this," said Dasch. "Your job here is to stall Quirin and Heinck so that they don't get suspicious of what we're up to."

"I can do that, but get back here as soon as you can."

Before Dasch could reply to that, Burger kept going. "Another thing I've been thinking: Make sure that the feds don't let the other six men in our group know that you and I did what we did here. I think it's best if that is kept between the F.B.I. and us. No good can come from that if that information would get out."

"That's a very good idea," replied Dasch. "I will include that in our list of demands."

"One more thing," added Burger. "I need the names of the local spies here who are supposed to help us. I have to make it look like I am in the know, especially if you get delayed down there and they contact me."

"Valid," thought Dasch.

"OK, their names are Leiner and Krepper. Here are their phone numbers. Leiner lives in New York. Somewhere close to the city. All I know about Krepper is that he lives in New Jersey, also close to the city. I would guess around Newark, but I can't say for certain. But that information must stay between us, Peter. No one else can know about that. These two names are higher up in the party, I think. We will bring more value and have more leverage if we reveal these names to Hoover at the appropriate time."

Burger merely nodded.

After a moment of silence, he said to Dasch, "If you had been unwilling to reveal those names to me, it would have given me second thoughts about trusting you. So, I'm glad that you did."

Dasch looked up at him from his dinner and simply said, "We are partners in this."

With that, he got up from the table and said, "I am going to throw a couple of things in my suitcase and be on my way." Burger, quite serious, said, "Say hello to Hoover for me."

C H A P T E R   2 0

All four men had made it to Cincinnati. They all checked into the Gibson Hotel. Kerling and Thiel would share one room, and Neubauer and Haupt would be in a separate room on a couple of floors below. Kerling told them to meet in the restaurant downstairs at 7:00 PM that evening for dinner. In the meantime, Thiel had decided to stretch his legs and go for a stroll. As Kerling was organizing his clothes for the next day's train for New York, the phone rang. He wasn't expecting a call this quickly. Nevertheless, he answered it and was surprised to hear Kappe's voice on the other end.

Kappe opened the conversation.

"You appear to be on schedule."

"Yes," replied Kerling. "There have been no surprises. We had no problem getting to the beach under the cover of darkness and were undetected. The beach was completely deserted. All the trains ran on time as well. Thiel and I leave for New York tomorrow as planned. I expect to arrive at approximately-"

"You will forget New York. At least you and Thiel will."

"Oh? And why is that?"

"There's been a change. Something else requires your immediate attention. And your skills."

"What about Neubauer and Haupt?"

"They will go to Chicago as planned, and then head to New York to be a part of Dasch's team until you get there with them. They will still focus on their original objectives." Silence. Kerling was processing.

Finally: "So tell me, Herr Kappe, what could be so urgent that would require such a change in plans?"

It was Kappe's turn to be silent for a minute. He, too, was processing.

He came to the same conclusion that he had when telling Leiner. Kerling needed to know everything. This was not an ideal way to operate, but given the stakes, he had no choice. There was no time for speaking in codes or drop box exchanges of information. He would just have to run the risk that the plan had so far gone as flawlessly as Kerling and Leiner had indicated. Still, he needed some semblance of assurance.

"Tell me, were you followed at all from the train station to your hotel?"

"No. I am sure of that."

"Did anyone look suspicious to you when you checked in?"

Kerling, letting out a rather large sigh, said in a tired voice, "No. No, Herr Kappe, you trained me well. No one looked suspicious when we were checking in."

"And did you hear any odd clicking noises on the phone when you picked it up?"

Kerling, now annoyed: "You are going to hear a clicking noise in a minute if you don't tell me what's going on."

Kappe, taking the bait: "Now see here, Kerling. You report to

Leiner, who reports to me. You will not speak to me in that"- "Look, Kappe, I'm tired. I've been at sea for 17 days and have just traveled all night on a train to get here. I am responsible for three young men - kids who mostly have no real experience in anything but are expected to do things that most men would agree are unheard of for people with so little experience. Now you're telling me that my assignment is changing. Just tell me what's going on."

Kappe was equally irritated in his own right but decided to remain focused on the task at hand.

He swallowed a bit, took a deep breath, and started in: "All right, here's what is happening: Last week, we had perhaps the world's foremost aeronautical engineer escape from the Fatherland. He and his family are Irish, not German. We have tracked him to St. Paul. His son and daughter came with him, but the son has already enlisted in the American military and is in training somewhere in the U.S. The daughter is with him in St. Paul. We are quite confident that the Americans are giving them a few days to adjust to their new country, and then the father will be put on a plane to Washington for a full and complete debriefing with the American military. Here, he will likely give them everything - every detail- about our secret project." That drew a gasp from Kerling.

Kappe went on: "If he makes it to D.C., he will likely be untouchable."

Kerling, listening intently, said, "Yes, Washington would certainly be a lot more complicated."

Kappe continued. "They will want to use his knowledge and gain all that he had been working on for The Fatherland. He was assigned to a top-secret project for the Luftwaffe that was sanctioned by the Fuhrer himself. Now, all those years of research and development that he had done could be handed over to the Americans. We cannot allow this to happen. Worse, not only would he give them the information, but he would spearhead all the efforts to get this technology into the war. And believe me, we would not want our enemies to have this technology and use it against us."

Kerling nodded, realized how silly it was to do so, and said, "I understand."

After a moment of silence between the two men, Kerling asked, "Does this man have a name?"

"All of the information on him and his daughter will be waiting for you when you arrive in St. Paul. It will be in an envelope that will be delivered to you once you check into the Commodore Hotel. The hotel is a seven-minute cab ride from the St. Paul Train Depot. Get on the first train that you can and take Thiel with you. Send Neubauer and Haupt to Chicago and have them lay low for a couple of days. Further instructions will be sent to them about getting to New York."

Kerling asked the ultimate question: "What exactly am I supposed to do with this man?"

Kappe didn't hesitate. "He is to be eliminated immediately by any means possible. We would prefer it to look like an accident. We don't want the Americans to know that we have a presence in their country just yet. They will know soon enough when we start blowing up their bridges and munitions factories, and Jewish-owned retail stores and poisoning their water supply. We won't care at that point, but them thinking this man was murdered may tip them off to our larger plans."

Kappe paused, letting all this sink in.

"Again, do your best to make it look like an accident, but if you can't, then take him out in any way that you can. He MUST die so that he can take all his secrets to the grave with him and not give them to the Americans. Clearly, we must get this done while he is in St. Paul. If he gets on that plane to Washington, we will likely not have another chance at him."

Kerling gave a deep sigh and said as much to himself as to Kappe, "I really need to think about this. I've been to St. Paul once, but it was several years ago, and I was just passing through. I really need to think how…"

Kappe broke in, saying, "Yes, of course. You have the whole train ride to come up with a plan. You'll report to Leiner and keep him up to date on your plans. Leiner must bless whatever actions you take before you take them. We need to maintain discipline of command in this process."

Kerling said nothing, so Kappe continued.

"Likewise, only when you are completely sure that he is dead should you notify Leiner. Then, get out of St. Paul immediately. You should probably go back through Cincinnati before heading to New York. Less conspicuous that way. I'll have Leiner there to meet you. The three of you can then make your way to New York. Once you're back there, we will commence with the original plans with all eight of you. But remember, you only have a few days to eliminate the target. We expect that he will be whisked away to D.C. shortly."

"All right," replied Kerling. "Your orders are quite clear, but in good German discipline, I will repeat them: There is a target in St. Paul who must be eliminated. I am to take the next train to St. Paul and stay at the Commodore Hotel, where there will be an envelope delivered to me. The envelope will have all the information on the target and his daughter. The father is to be eliminated at all costs, but I am to try to make it look like an accident if possible. We cannot and will not actually kill him without Leiner's go-ahead. Likewise, I should confirm with Leiner that the target has been eliminated only when I am absolutely positive that the man is, in fact, dead. Once the mission is complete, Thiel and I will head back to Cincinnati, where we will meet up with Leiner. From there, we will all head to New York. In New York, we will meet up with the others. From there, the original mission will continue. Neubauer and Haupt are to go to Chicago as planned and make their way to New York in a couple of days upon getting their instructions from you. For however long I am out of New York, Neubauer and Haupt will report to Dasch."

"Yes, thank you, Kerling. That is an excellent summary. Let me add that the daughter is not of importance to us unless she can be leveraged as needed to complete your mission."

Kerling, still pondering, said, "I would prefer that we leave the daughter out of this, but if we must, we will use her to accomplish the mission. Holding her hostage only invites trouble and complicates any sort of escape for us."

Kappe, getting nervous about being on the phone so long, wrapped it up.

"All right, we are clear on the next steps. It was good that you summarized. I doubt that I can convey to you the importance of this mission, Herr Kerling. You must successfully complete this assignment. And you must do it quickly. There is no higher priority than this operation."

Then, quietly but with urgency, Kappe said, "The entire war may depend on it."

"I assure you that I will find a way," said Kerling.

"Good luck. The Fatherland is counting on you. And remember, you were equipped with cyanide pills for a reason." Before Kerling could reply, Kappe hung up.

Kerling immediately left the hotel, walked a couple of blocks, and found a stranger to ask where the nearest gun shop could be found.

# CHAPTER 21

Frank and Leigh were sitting on the bluffs of St. Paul off Prospect Boulevard, taking full advantage of the unusually warm November day.

"We better enjoy this kind of a day while we can. We don't hardly get any of these in November," observed Frank.

They were overlooking the eastern bank of the Mississippi and looking directly west upon downtown St. Paul. Betty had made a picnic lunch for them, and they were sitting on a plaid blanket, ready to investigate what was in the baskets. It was a chance for some time alone. Leigh's dad was going to stick around the Sweeney's home and talk with Michael for a while.

The young couple could see Harriet Island quite easily, as well as the many different shops along Concord Avenue and Wabasha Street. Across the river was the St. Paul Cathedral, and to the right of that, by several blocks, stood Minnesota's state capitol building, an impressive structure of its own. Between the Cathedral and the Capitol was the tallest building in the city by far, the 1st National Bank of St. Paul. All three buildings were displayed prominently against the bright blue, cloudless sky.

"So that's where your dad works," said Leigh. "The bank looks impressive, even from here. You can see the "1st" sign so easily."

"Yes, you certainly can," replied Frank. "The sign itself is 50 feet tall, and they say that it can be seen from as far away as 75 miles from the air at night and around 20 miles away on the ground. The neon technology was installed in it about 6 years ago."

"Wow," said Leigh. "That's amazing!"

"Yep. Dad's office is up on the 20ᵗʰ floor," said Frank. "He's got a beautiful view of everything from up there. The building itself is pretty amazing. It was the first structure to actually connect to another building. See that skyway? It's on the 17ᵗʰ floor of 1ˢᵗ National, and it connects to the 16ᵗʰ floor of Merchants Bank. That was completed eleven years ago. Sure comes in handy in the wintertime."

"Would it be all right to go there sometime?"

"Of course! My dad would love to show you around."

Both were silent for a moment, and both were comfortable in that silence.

"And the lobby at the bank… that's where Jack…?" her voice trailed off.

"Yes," said Frank quietly. "That's where it happened. He thwarted a bank robbery, and no civilians were hurt. Died a hero, but he still died. There isn't a day that goes by that I don't think of him."

Leigh took his hand in hers. "I am so sorry, Frank. He must've been a remarkable man."

"He was. He really was. I often wonder what he would be doing now. He would probably have his own precinct by now, married with a few kids. He was an amazing leader. Everyone just looked to him to show them the way."

Leigh gently moved the conversation in a slightly different direction. "Your sisters have been so kind to me. And your mom is wonderful, too. I realize that we are throwing a lot at them right now, what with my dad and me being here."

Frank looked at her and said, "You have no idea how good this has been for my family. Meeting you and your dad has really helped the family finally move on a bit from Jack's death. We may never fully get over it, but you have reminded everyone that there are still some wonderful things to pour your life into and to let the past own you is no way to live. I will always be grateful to you for that, Leigh," he said quietly.

Once more, a little silence.

Leigh leaned her head on his shoulder for a moment. And Frank loved it.

"We sure have been thrown into the war in a hurry, haven't we?" she asked.

"You can say that again. Two months ago, I was training as a pilot in England, and you were teaching children in Germany. Since that time, we've blown up an airfield, destroyed a state-of-the-art factory, thwarted a technology that could have ensured a German victory in Europe, and escaped from the Nazis by riding in a couple of caskets all night."

"You forgot the part where we trekked through part of Germany and Switzerland, only to be confronted right before we were going to get on a train to Lucerne," said Leigh, still resting on his shoulder.

"I also killed men. I've never done that before," said Frank, ever so quietly.

"You did what you had to do, Frank. You had no choice."

Frank reflected on the confrontation with the two Gestapo agents. And he concluded, as he had the previous 100 times, that Leigh was right. He had absolutely no choice. They were evil men, intent on harming Esther's parents. And Leigh. They would have tortured and killed him, Frank reminded himself, and the Conways would still be stuck in Germany.

He glanced over at her. A tear ran down Leigh's cheek.

Frank gently wiped it away and gave her his handkerchief.

She pulled her knees up to her chest and rested her arms on them, staring across the Mississippi.

"It's just so strange to think about what we have already seen. Death. Persecution of the Jewish people. Propaganda. Seeing what would normally be decent people be forced to conform to an agenda that has been thrust upon them with the threat of prison or worse. And evil. Pure evil. Reckless evil. We've seen that up close and even experienced it firsthand."

"Yes," he said. "We have seen it and lived among it, to be sure."

They both sat quietly, lost in their own thoughts.

"Amazing how comfortable we are together, even in silence," said Frank. "I guess being watched and followed and having your lives threatened will do that."

Leigh smiled at him. "I fancy you may be right about that." "How about a movie tonight?" he asked.

"What's showing?"

"The Talk of the Town." "It stars Cary Grant and Jean Arthur."

Leigh thought for a moment.

"The only movies we saw in Germany were propaganda films. If I had to see that madman's face and listen to one more of his speeches, I wouldn't know what I'd do. Anything would be better than listening to him and his minions. I know who Cary Grant and Clark Gable are. And let's see… Crosby and Hope, of course. And Erroll Flynn. A fine Irishman, I might add, as is Crosby. Did you know that Bob Hope was actually born in England?"

"No, I didn't. And Errol Flynn is from Australia."

"He may be from Australia, but he is of Irish descent. Flynn, Frank! Flynn! You better not let your mom know about you doubting the heritage of someone named Flynn!"

"Duly noted. However, my dear Miss Conway, I couldn't help but notice that the only Hollywood stars that you can name happen to all be male."

"Well, that may be true, but I'm sure that you can enlighten me on Jean Arthur and Barbara Stanwyck and a host of other female starlets."

Frank didn't really have a good comeback to that one, so he opted to transition it by mentioning his sisters. "Evvie and Kathryn love Cary Grant."

"Let's invite them along!" said Leigh. "Maybe we should invite my dad and your parents as well."

"We could do that," said he.

"That would be nice, Frank. Don't you think?" Leigh looked at him with innocent earnestness.

"Sure. Why not?"

He looked across the river and saw the huge Ford plant, figured that they were probably ramping up to make… what? Tanks? Jeeps? That brought him back to the moment at hand, wondering when he would see Leigh again.

"Tomorrow, I'll take you to see the Como Zoo."

"Where's that?" asked Leigh.

"It's in St. Paul, a few miles north of here. It's a great place to see a lot of animals. A lot of them are native to Minnesota. Kind of a funny story. It was started 45 years ago, all because someone gifted the mayor of St. Paul three deer, and he had nowhere to put them. There was a large park called Como Park, so that's how the Zoo portion started. They carved out a bunch of acres from the park and developed the zoo. All because the mayor wanted to keep a few deer."

"You're kidding," said Leigh.

"Nope. Do you have deer in Ireland?"

"Of course, we have deer in Ireland, silly," teased Leigh.

He smiled at her and said, "How was I supposed to know? I was only there for a very short time."

Leigh smiled back at him and said, "Maybe someday I can bring you back for a visit."

"I'd like that," he replied. "Maybe we could explore around County Cork. Dad says that that's where my grandparents came from."

They sat in silence for a couple of minutes.

Then Frank casually said: "Your dad will be flying back to D.C. soon. The whole military leadership is probably going to want to talk to him. And I'll be who-knows-where. But the nice thing about working for the O.S.S. is that my assignments shouldn't be for months at a time. They'll likely be sort of in and out jobs, or jobs that require me to be doing a lot of research in Washington, vetting enemies, and stuff like that. I'm hoping I'll be able to get back here somewhat regularly."

Leigh looked at him sideways and said, "Are you just trying to make me feel better? Frank, this is a major worldwide war. You can't possibly know what will be required of you." He shrugged and then changed the subject.

"Let's see what Betty cooked up for us. Looks like chicken sandwiches. And some Old Dutch potato chips! Wow! Now I know that I'm home! These are made right here in the Twin Cities! They used to be made in St. Paul, where the company was started, but a few years ago, they betrayed us and moved across the river to Minneapolis." He snuck a chip out of the bag and took a bite. "These are so good! What I would've given for a few of these when I was over in Europe!"

Frank looked around the basket and saw a plate full of homemade chocolate chip cookies, which were his favorite. He wondered if Betty's recipe would be as good as his mom's. He passed a sandwich to Leigh, along with a bottle of Pepsi.

"What a funny name, Pepsi," she observed.

Frank was momentarily surprised by her comment but then realized that so much of everything here was brand new to her.

"Kind of an interesting story about Pepsi. Sort of what many of us in our country would call "The Great American Success Story." He went on: "There was a pharmacist in North Carolina.

That's a state in the southeastern part of the U.S."-

"Do you mean North Carolina, one of the original thirteen colonies of the United States and the first colony to vote for independence? The one that was one of eleven states to secede from the union because they actually believed that slavery should remain legal?"

Frank was about to interject but was too slow for her. "Hmmm… wasn't that the state where the famous pirate Blackbeard was killed by British troops off its Outer Banks? The one that, in 1903, hosted the first manned flight of an airplane when the Wright brothers took off from a site near Kitty Hawk? The one whose capitol is Raleigh? That North Carolina?"

Frank looked at her in awe, part of an Old Dutch falling out of his mouth. Leigh was sporting a rather impish smile.

"Oh, OK, Miss Smarty Pants. I forgot that you are a teacher and that you studied the U.S. extensively."

That brought a giggle of delight from the beautiful girl whom he had completely fallen for. She quickly composed herself, looked at the young man with the sky-blue eyes, and said, "Oh by all means, Captain Sweeney, please regale me further with the history of Pepsi Cola."

"All right, all right. That's enough of that, Miss Conway." Now it was Frank's turn to grin. They continued to smile at one another, then Leigh said, "Well?"

"Well, what?"

"Aren't you going to finish your story about Pepsi?"

"Why? So you can make fun of me?"

"I would never make fun of you, Captain!"

"That's "former Captain." I don't even know what I am these days."

"Hmmm. Let's see… how about "Daring Spy?""

"Not funny."

"No? You don't like that one? What about "International Man of Mystery?"

"Not even close," replied Frank.

"Well, what then?" asked Leigh.

Frank's turn. "How about "I can't believe we made it out of Germany without any support or plan" Guy?"

"That could work," said Leigh.

# CHAPTER 22

Kerling gathered the other three men in his room.

"Forget having dinner together. Order room service instead. And order it early. It's best that the four of us aren't seen together in public at this point."

The other three men looked at each other and nodded.

He then proceeded to tell them of the change in plans. Neubauer and Haupt, both from Chicago, looked relieved that they were still heading home for a couple of days.

Thiel looked a bit lost but recovered quickly and bluntly asked why the plans had changed.

"There is a very high-value target in St. Paul that needs to be addressed," is how Kerling framed it. "I don't have a lot of details beyond that. I'm sure that more information will be forthcoming."

Thiel pressed on: "What sort of high-value target could be in St. Paul? They don't have any major munitions facilities. Is it the Ford plant up there? Have they switched production to make tanks or jeeps or something?"

"You are thinking too narrowly, Thiel. A high-value target doesn't always mean a building or bridge. It can also mean an individual."

Thiel, simultaneously running his mouth in conjunction with his brain:

"So, they are pulling us off our mission to take a person out. It must be someone very important. Is Roosevelt going to be in St. Paul?"

Kerling rolled his eyes.

"No, it's not Roosevelt. It is someone who escaped from Germany who had something to do with airplanes. He apparently could be quite useful to the Americans if he is permitted to live."

Neubauer merely said, "Huh." He was anxious to get back to Chicago to see his family for a few days. Neubauer had deep ties in Chicago, having worked as a chef in a couple of the more high-profile hotels there.

Haupt, the youngest member of the team, was also anxious to get home to see his parents.

His only comment to Kerling and Thiel was, "Good luck."

What he really meant to say was, "Sure glad it's not me."

Kerling, feeling like he was losing the battle of the mind with all three of these men, silently stared at one face for a few seconds before moving to the next one.

Finally, he spoke, a little too loudly. "Let me remind you that you are soldiers of the Third Reich. You were sent here on a mission that has now changed. Welcome to war! Change is constant, and the soldier who stays alive comes to learn in a hurry that change is his friend."

He paused, letting that sink in.

Then he continued: "Things have gone perfectly since we left France. Think about it: we arrived in Florida on schedule, with not even one bullet fired at us over the course of the 18-day voyage; we met no resistance whatsoever as we came up to the beach; our trains left on time, and we arrived here in Cincinnati even a few minutes early."

He paused once again, looking at each man, making sure that they were all engaged.

"We have taken every precaution. We even came to Cincinnati first because there was a chance that the Americans would naturally be watching the routes up and down the East Coast, even though they have no idea of our mission or that we are even in the country."

He could see that he was getting through to them and that they were beginning to focus and remember their training.

"I remind you that we were all sent here to blow up bridges, hydroelectric plants, munition buildings, armament factories, and the like. And while we are at it, shops that are owned and operated by Jews. Not to mention what we are going to do to the water supply. We spent over three weeks doing nothing but training for these actions. We are to create havoc and chaos everywhere that we can. The overall mission hasn't changed! Thiel and I have a detour that will only take a couple of days to complete. So, you two get to Chicago and stay there like we discussed, for the time that we discussed. And keep your mouths shut about all of this. Do you understand?"

"Yes, Sir!" Neubauer and Haupt fairly shouted back.

"There's a train heading to Chicago at 6:45 PM tonight. It makes a few stops, and it will get you into Chicago tomorrow morning. Be on it. Stay in Chicago for a couple of days and then get to New York. I will make sure that someone meets you at the train station in New York. Wire me your train information for New York when you get it. Thiel and I will be at the Commodore Hotel in St. Paul. I'm staying under the name of Kelley. We will take a different route to get up to St. Paul. We'll take a bus to Indianapolis that leaves at 7:00 PM tonight and then catch an overnight train to St. Paul. Assuming that you get to New York before Thiel and I arrive, you'll take your orders from Dasch until I take back command."

All three of the other men looked a bit sheepish but wisely opted not to say anything else.

"That's all. And remember, keep your mouths shut about all of this."

With that, Kerling got up from the table and began to pack. Thiel quickly followed his lead, and Neubauer and Haupt were out the door in a flash, thankful to still be heading to Chicago for a couple of days.

# CHAPTER 23

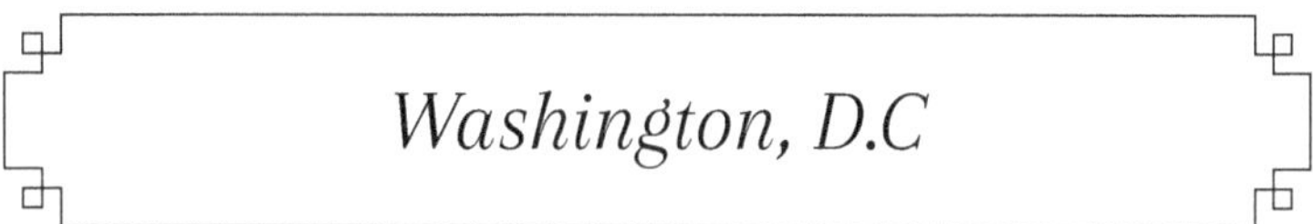



The Mayflower Hotel, boasting "The second greatest address in Washington, D.C.," was situated on Connecticut Avenue, a mere 15-minute walk from 1600 Pennsylvania Avenue.

George John Dasch sat in the lobby of the magnificent structure, having enjoyed a wonderful night and exquisite breakfast on The Fatherland's dime. Or Reichsmark.

Dasch was waiting for some agent from the F.B.I. to meet with him. He had gotten into town late last night and decided to wait until the next day to meet with the Bureau's brass. The day started with more phone calls to the main office, and he ran into the same problem: No one would take him seriously. Finally, he got someone who committed to come over there "in the next hour or two" to talk to him. He hadn't realized that he had been passed around within what the F.B.I. called its "Nut Desk."

"I'm going to be a national hero for this, and here I sit, waiting for someone to come and pick me up," he fumed. "What kind of an outfit is Hoover running, anyway? Canaris would never run his organization like this."

Finally, a man in a dark suit, a white shirt, and a black tie walked into the lobby. He slowly took off his sunglasses, looked around, and caught Dasch's eye.

"Must be him," they both thought simultaneously. The agent came over, introduced himself as Agent James Hessler, and shook Dasch's hand.

Hessler, 5'8 and bow-legged, was built like a brick wall. He was in his mid-30s and had been with the Bureau since he finished college. He was an All-Star running back in St. Paul at Humboldt High School on the west side of the city. His jet-black hair and green eyes set him apart from most other men. He was half Syrian and half German, which was an interesting combination. There was virtually no body fat on the guy. He would make a lousy undercover cop because of his looks. He just tended to stand out, which is why he worked mostly as an investigator. The fact that he could run like the wind likely played a factor in being selected for this particular assignment with Dasch. No one was going to outrun Agent Jim Hessler.

"Mind if I sit down?" asked Hessler.

"Actually, yes, I do," said Dasch, looking around the lobby as he spoke. "What I have to tell you needs to be done in the privacy of a conference room at your headquarters, not in a public place like this where I can be observed."

Hessler looked at him more closely, just to see if the guy was drunk. Or nuts.

Dasch looked right at him, his eyes never moving off of Hessler's.

"Look, Mr. Dish…"

"Dasch! It's Dasch! D-A-S-C-H! What is the matter with you people? After what I have to tell you today, you'll want to give me the highest medal that you can find."

Hessler, wondering why it always seemed to be him who drew the short straw, finally relented, and said, "OK, Mr. DASCH. Let's go. I have a car waiting outside."

With that, they walked out of the Mayflower. It would be a short visit for Dasch, without a doubt, the nicest place that he had ever stayed.

"Did you enjoy staying at the Mayflower?" asked Hessler.

"Yes, it was very nice. I am staying at the Clinton Hotel in New York, and that is also excellent," replied Dasch. "But I think the Mayflower is nicer."

"I wouldn't get too used to it," said Hessler under his breath.

# CHAPTER 24

Edwin Conway sat in Michael Sweeney's home office, enjoying his pipe with some American-made tobacco that Michael had obliged him.

"The American tobacco seems to be milder, and what's the right word? Sweeter?" asked Edwin.

"Yes, I would say that is correct on both counts," replied Michael. "I once had a friend send me some tobacco from London, and I found it to be a bit strong for my liking."

"Well, this is definitely an easier smoke," agreed Edwin. "Thank you."

"My pleasure."

Edwin shifted in his chair. "I meant "Thank you" for a whole lot more than the tobacco, my good man," said Conway.

Now it was Michael's turn to shift a bit. He was uncomfortable with compliments or recognition. He could only muster a nod and smile. He got up and put some more logs on the fire that he had started an hour before in the large fireplace. The fire came to life and set a warm, relaxed mood in the room.

Edwin continued, "Please tell me about your business. Frank told us a few things, but it sounds like an amazing story."

Michael sat back down in his chair. As he leaned back, he said, "I'm truly a blessed man. My parents were as Irish as they come. Sweeney, of course, and my mother's maiden name was O'Shea. They were from the County Cork area."

"Ah, County Cork. I know it well," said Edwin. "A beautiful part of our country. Some of the friendliest people that you would ever want to meet. They're especially known for their hospitality."

Michael smiled. "I sure would love to get there sometime. Maggie wants to go as well. Maybe after the war."

He continued, "My parents came to this country with nothing and managed to scrimp and save so they could put a down payment on 40 acres about 20 minutes from here. The town is now called South St. Paul. Anyway, they farmed. Corn and soybean mostly, and they eventually had some cows for dairy as well. They were simple people with hearts of gold. And they loved America, having come here right in the middle of the Potato Famine in the old country. They taught us about faith, family, and farming, and they lived it, too. Great people. Most of my siblings are still in the area. We're a close-knit family."

"A fine Irish clan," said Edwin.

Michael smiled and nodded.

"Anyway, after doing some real estate, I decided to become a cop. Believe me, there weren't a lot of choices back then for men of Irish descent. As a matter of fact, it hasn't really gotten all that much better in the ensuing years."

"And why is that, Michael? Edwin asked.

"Prejudice, I guess," he shrugged.

"We sometimes get stereotyped in our nation. The Italians are either restauranteurs or gangsters. The Mexicans are primarily thought of as gifted laborers. Very family-centric. The Germans are engineers. Clinical and a bit harsh, probably due to the sound of the German language itself. They always sound like they're angry with someone or something. And our black citizens. Well, that's a topic of major embarrassment and shame in our country. They are a long way from being treated as they should be."

They were silent for a moment, lost in thought. Then Michael said, "I almost forgot! The Irish typically are cops or firefighters. Of course, it's not all true, but those are the stereotypes."

"I believe I broke that stereotype," said Edwin.

Michael laughed. "You sure did! An Irish aeronautical engineer? That's sort of like an English chef, isn't it?"

"About as useless as a glass eye in a keyhole," said Edwin.

They both chuckled at that. Both were puffing on their pipes and enjoying the moment.

"Please continue," said Edwin. "I really want to understand the process of how you got to where you are today."

Michael looked up at the ceiling again, trying to figure out what to cover next.

He then just started talking, taking Dr. Conway and himself down memory lane.

"I walked a beat for several years. Oh, sorry. That means I was a patrolman. We were assigned a route in the city, so we got very familiar with the people and the surroundings. My beat was the Rondo neighborhood, and our home here is located right in the middle of what was my old beat. Relationships were formed, and people got used to seeing me around and vice versa. So that went well, and I was fortunate to have some good partners along the way. We solved some cases, and then I was offered a detective role. The patrolmen are feet on the street and are there to first try to prevent crime. The detectives typically show up after the crime has been committed, and their job is to solve the crime and catch those responsible. Not unlike things in Ireland, no doubt."

Conway nodded and motioned for his new friend to continue.

"Anyway, I guess they thought I might be good at detective work, so they moved me into a detective role. That's when I partnered up with George Parker, and we became the best of friends. We solved a lot of cases together. Some were real who-done-its**, and a few were actually kind of funny** when we looked back on them. Anyway, I did that for a few years and eventually I became the chief of detectives for the St. Paul Police Department."

Edwin was listening to every word, clearly intrigued by it all.

"There was a lot of corruption going on within the department. Cops would be on the take…"

"Excuse me, Michael. On the take?"

"Yes. Taking bribes, doing unethical things."

"Oh, dear me," said Edwin.

"It was pretty bad," replied Michael. "And it went all the way to the top of the organization. That means to my boss. He was as crooked as they come. His name was John O'Connor, and he implemented the "O'Connor Layover System."

"The O'Connor Layover System?" asked Edwin. "And what would that be, exactly?"

"Basically, he went to all of the gangsters and said, "You can live in St. Paul, and we will leave you alone. We won't arrest you or harass you or come after you. But you do your crimes in Minneapolis or any other city or town. Keep the crime out of St. Paul. And you pay me and my cronies a fee every time you come into town."

"This is outrageous!" cried Edwin. "And he's an Irishman to boot!"

Michael had a sad smile on his face. "Yes, he certainly was."

He continued: "Anyway, the gangsters would all meet at the Hotel Savoy, which is just a few miles from here. It was run by another Irishman by the name of William "Reddy" Griffin. They would pay Griffin the bribes, and that money would go to Chief O'Connor and other city figures. That is, once Griffin got his cut of it. That worked until Griffin died. Then, the same process took place at the Green Lantern, a bar in downtown St. Paul. They would pay the owner the money. His name was Dapper Dan Hogan, and he was a kind of Irish Godfather. Hogan knew everyone, and everyone knew Hogan. He made a lot of money from this arrangement, as did Chief O'Connor and the other politicians in the city."

Edwin, fascinated by all of this, asked, "When was a stop put to all of this?"

"Well, for Dapper Dan, it ended when a car bomb went off with him sitting in the front seat. That was maybe 14 years ago. They never arrested anyone for that job. Everyone is fairly certain that it was his number two guy, Dutch Sawyer. Sawyer felt that Dapper Dan had not been generous enough with him, and he was sore about the fact that Hogan had never paid him back after Sawyer had paid the $25,000 bail for Hogan when he had been arrested a few years earlier. I talked to George about this, and he told me that the F.B.I. files show that Hogan had $50,000 stashed in a safety deposit box. After Hogan had died, his widow went to get the money out of the box, and it was already gone. Sawyer was the only person other than Hogan who had a key to the box."

"Remarkable!" exclaimed Conway.

"Yes. Sawyer took over the operation after Hogan was murdered, and he ran it until things finally got cleaned up several years later."

"And how did things finally get cleaned up, Michael? I can't imagine it was very easy, that?" asked Edwin.

"It didn't really end until about five or six years ago. You have to understand that, because of this system, St. Paul became a magnet for criminals from all over the country. Some of these people you have probably never heard of, but they are household names in America. People like Al Capone, John Dillinger-"

"I've heard of those men," interjected Edwin.

"And a host of other ones," continued Michael.

"To make a long story short, one of the local newspaper owners - a guy named Kahn- hired a guy out of Chicago who came up here and placed listening devices in the police department itself. The guy from Chicago was actually the nephew of Elliott Ness, who took down Capone. He and his men were called "The Untouchables" because they couldn't be bribed or compromised. All the information was recorded on record albums. The authorities finally had the evidence that they needed."

"So, O'Connor went to jail?" asked Edwin.

"No, no. He had retired many years before the reforms took place. He got off scot-free. I think John died in 1924 or so. But many cops and public officials were prosecuted. Some went to jail, and others were fired."

Michael paused to light his pipe again. He waited until it got going, then continued.

"Maybe the most corrupt Chief of Police of them all was a guy named Tom Brown, or "Big Tom Brown," as he was known by," said Michael.

Michael, seeing that Edwin's pipe had to be re-lit, offered a book of matches with the Sweeney insignia on them. Edwin smiled in gratitude and made a show of putting the matchbook in his pocket, much to Michael's amusement. Michael went on:

"Brown was a large man, as you might have guessed. He was not from here. Somewhere back east. I want to say, West Virginia. Anyway, he took a cut of the ransom money from a couple of high-profile kidnappings in St. Paul. The first one was in June of 1933, and it involved the kidnapping of William Hamm Jr., of Hamm's Beer fame. The second was six months later. The same group kidnapped Edward Bremer, from the Bremer Bank family. Hamm and Bremer were two big names in St. Paul. The ransom paid for Hamm was $100,000, and the amount for Bremer was twice that. Brown also killed at least one witness who had a lot of evidence against him regarding the kidnappings and taking a cut of the ransom money. Shot him in cold blood in an alley. No witnesses, so he claimed it was in self-defense. No one could prove anything different, even though everyone knew that he shot the guy and planted a gun on him. He also tipped off the criminals as to when the cops were going to raid their homes. Magically, the cops would always just miss the criminals by a few minutes."

Edwin Conway shivered. "Horrible. Just horrible. I'm glad that you were able to leave when you did, Michael."

"Yes, I am as well, that's for sure. You see Edwin, much of this came about because of Prohibition here in the U.S. It was the law of the land from 1920 until 1933. As a matter of fact, it was the Volstead Act that made most alcohol illegal."

Michael paused as he thought back to those days.

"The author of the bill was Congressman Volstead, who was actually a congressman from Minnesota. Grew up in the southwestern part of the state. Granite Falls, I believe. A good man with good intentions, I'm sure. Anyway, people wanted their booze, and they were going to do whatever they had to in order to get it. Of course, that opened the door for all of the illegal activity. The gangsters made millions as a result. But once Prohibition ended, their revenue stream dried up overnight. That's when they turned to bank robberies and kidnappings."

Conway, drawing from his pipe, said, "That must've been great for your business!"

Michael chuckled and said, "It sure was. You need to understand that, because of the O'Connor system, St. Paul became a magnet for every gangster and up-and-coming gangster around. For example, did you know that just ten years ago, in 1932, over 20% of all bank robberies in the entire United States took place here in Minnesota? 20%!"

"Simply remarkable," lamented Edwin. "I certainly feel safe here now, and I have seen no evidence of crime here at all in my short stay."

Michael nodded and said, "Oh, trust me. We don't have a perfect city. Crime will always be part of our lives because we are all imperfect creatures who have this issue in each of our lives called "sin.""

Edwin nodded in violent agreement. "I am a member of that club."

"As am I, unfortunately," replied Michael.

He continued, "The current Chief of Police is a man by the name of Clint Hackert. Clint is an old friend, and he was one of the reformers. He is a good and decent man. He and a few other gentlemen have really worked hard to clean things up over there. Clint runs a clean ship. The other thing that changed is that the Police Chief isn't appointed by the mayor anymore. It's a committee of public servants who make the appointment, thereby lessening the chances of political payback."

Edwin again: "The engineer in me finds this all fascinating. It sounds like a lot of progress has been made to fix a very broken system."

Michael nodded again and said, "It was a long time in coming."

"Michael," said Edwin, "Let's get back to my original question: How did you actually start Sweeney Detective Bureau?"

"Ah, yes. Sorry. I got so entrenched with the last few years that I forgot to explain to you how we got started. Do you see the picture over there on the wall?" The gentleman in the picture to the right of the window?"

Edwin turned around. "Yes, I see it. He looks rather well to do."

"That is a man by the name of James J. Hill. He was a Canadian who moved here in the latter part of the last century and got into the railroad business. He eventually bought several railroads and, just as importantly, railroad routes. His nickname was "The Empire Builder." "As fate would have it, we would run into one another when I was a cop. I used to moonlight at 1st National Bank as a security guard, so I would see him quite often. We developed a friendship, and he eventually approached me about moving his money from bank to bank. You see, Edwin, back in the day, the only way that money was moved from bank to bank was to hire plain-clothed cops, who would ride the street cars or buses with suitcases full of money. You can imagine the problems with that sort of a process."

Edwin looked incredulously at his friend, leaned back, and eventually said, "Well, I suppose there really wasn't any other way, was there?"

Michael shrugged and asked, "How did they do it in Ireland?"

It was Edwin's turn to laugh. "I have no idea. Nor would I have any reason to even contemplate that!"

That brought Michael a chuckle, and he continued with his story.

"Anyway, I took the job on the side, and that got me thinking about alternatives and safer ways to move money. That's when I designed the first armored car in America. The business just started taking off, and as mentioned, Prohibition really helped to accelerate the entire operation."

"What an amazing story," said Edwin earnestly. "I am quite happy for you."

"As you know, Edwin, any sort of "success" comes at a price. There were a lot of sleepless nights and not a lot of days off. But God works all things together for good, right? The department's corruption was completely out of hand, and I just didn't want to be associated with it. Have you ever heard that Irish saying, "Lie down with dogs and…""

"You'll rise with fleas," finished Edwin, smiling again.

"Ha!" shouted Michael, "I forgot who my audience was! I shouldn't be surprised that you would know that one." He genuinely liked this fellow Irishman.

He continued: "Plus, the business had grown to the point where I really needed to run it full-time. There just weren't enough hours in the day to do both. I was blessed because my beautiful bride was very supportive and understanding. We have been great partners in this whole venture."

Michael stood to stretch and poke the fire again. He motioned for Edwin to stay seated.

"By the time Prohibition had ended, the business was very diversified. There are three segments to it today: The armored car side, private detective work, and security, both personal and corporate."

"Michael, my friend, you are a blessed man."

"You'll get no argument from me on that," said Michael.

The two men were having a wonderful time together. The war had brought them together for at least a little while. Their children would bring them together permanently. And the next few days would cement their friendship forever.

# CHAPTER 25

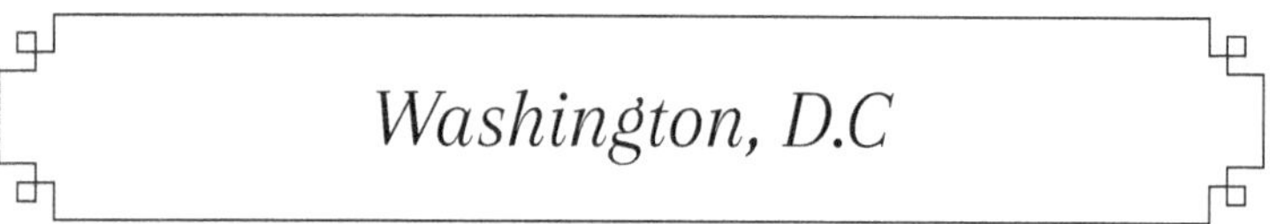

## *Washington, D.C*

F.B.I. Deputy Director D.M. Ladd sat in his office in Washington, D.C. Ladd, known as "Mickey" to his friends, was a bit puzzled. He re-read the report that had made its way to his desk.

At the outbreak of the war in Europe in 1939, Ladd's boss, a man with the last name of Hoover, had assigned him to hunt down and find every Nazi in the U.S. Reading between the lines, the assignment actually meant to hunt, find, and spy on every Nazi in the country.

There were more than a few.

D.C. was the last stop of many for Ladd. After coming to the city from North Dakota, he worked in his father's office. His father was the U.S. Senator from North Dakota. From there, Mickey operated one of the subway cars that ran from the city to the capitol building. He did that mostly in the late afternoons. The mornings were spent in law school. He finished law school in 1928 and joined the Bureau almost immediately upon passing the bar. As with almost all FBI agents, he moved around. A lot. He and his wife started in Butte, Montana. From there he went to New Orleans, followed by D.C., Chicago, and finally back to D.C.

He and his wife had no children. He loved the Bureau, and he respected his boss. Didn't always agree with him, but he did respect him. Being the son of a senator hadn't hurt him. He learned the politics of the Bureau and managed to make it to his current role while not burning any bridges along the way.

6'2 and 220 pounds, he looked more like a linebacker than he did an FBI agent. "Must've been all of that corn and beef on the farm in North Dakota," he'd tell anyone who asked about his size.

When it came to his job, he always erred on the side of caution. He would pursue every report or accusation when it came to hunting Nazis on U.S. soil. Or at least he would have someone else do it.

The Bureau had all but finished milking the success of blowing up the Duquesne Ring last year. That truly was a huge victory. For the country, for the F.B.I., and for Hoover himself, and not necessarily in that order. He was never shy about taking credit, all within the auspices of promoting his organization.

They needed to be every bit as diligent today as they were before, which explained why he was re-reading a report from Agent James Hessler. He decided to call Hessler's boss and have him come to his office.

Within two minutes, Special Agent Dave Bouquet was waiting outside Ladd's office. Carolyn Joanis, Ladd's secretary, ushered him in and showed Bouquet to a seat across from Mickey.

Bouquet, who oversaw a number of the Washington D.C.-based agents, reported directly to Ladd. 6'2 with short dark hair and a lean athletic frame, he was as practical and logical an agent as the Bureau had. His dry sense of humor and his ability to imitate Hoover provided a lot of laughs in the Bureau, but only with a very select and trusted - read: SMALL - group of friends. He and Ladd were tight and had spent a good many hours together outside of work. He managed his relationship with his boss well. He knew when to kid around and when to be serious.

When Ladd was upset, Bouquet wisely gave him his space. At the end of the day, Bouquet was a highly decorated agent dedicated to the Bureau and the men who reported to him. And to the guy that he reported to.

After some light pleasantries, Ladd asked him about Hessler's report on one George John Dasch.

"Well, Assistant Director, it goes like this: This guy claims that he and three other Germans were dropped off the coast of Long Island, very close to the Hamptons, three nights ago. Their mission is called "Operation Pastorius," and they were sent here to, in his words, "infiltrate and disrupt the war effort." Bouquet looked once more at Hessler's notes and then looked up and said, "He said that he wouldn't give any more details than that until he spoke with Hoover. But we all know Hess and his ability to get more information out of a suspect."

Ladd, showing no reaction, said, "Go on."

Bouquet looked again at his notes, then continued: "There was another submarine that was due to drop off four other men two nights ago. This one was supposed to land off the coast of Jacksonville. They have similar orders, but Dasch isn't giving specifics. Hess got the sense that he didn't know but didn't want to tell us that. When you think about it, it might make sense to keep the two operations separate in case one of the groups was caught. Both teams are due to meet in New York in the next few days. The team from Florida was taking trains to Cincinnati just to avoid a more direct route up the coast. Two of the four men are going from Cincinnati to Chicago for a couple of days. Apparently, they don't want to all be seen together, so they are splitting up. Seems they believe that we are watching the eastern seaboard more closely than we actually are."

Ladd asked Bouquet his opinion of all of it.

Bouquet paused for a minute to collect his thoughts.

"To be honest, everybody thinks he's just another nut. We've had so many of these in the last few months. He had been passed around from agent to agent. He claims that he called our New York office, and several agents hung up on him."

"Anything else?" asked Ladd.

"Just one last thing: He came here, stayed at the Mayflower, and is insisting on meeting with Director Hoover. He told Hessler that he won't talk to anyone but the Director."

"Dave," said Ladd, "You've told me what everyone else thinks. But you haven't told me what *you* think."

Bouquet sat back for a moment and collected his thoughts.

"I don't know, Mickey… he very well could be a nut. But what is he doing staying at the Mayflower? You have to have some money to do that. Plus, who would give those kinds of details? I mean, a sub off Long Island and another one off of Jacksonville, plus trains and itineraries? His English is apparently excellent. Claims to have lived here for several years before going back to Germany right before the war. And Hess says that he is very sure of himself, to the point of being arrogant."

Ladd sighed. His inner battle had already begun.

"Don't waste your time. Enough agents have talked to him. They've all reached the same conclusion. Besides, this has got to be the tenth story like this from somebody this month. Same song, different verse."

"But what if they're wrong? They're all overworked as it is right now, so they probably are not taking all of these situations as seriously as they should."

"Look, you have more than enough to do as it is. You can't even keep up with everything Hoover has thrown at you right now, and there is no end in sight. Don't forget, you also have to search for Japanese spies and sympathizers as well."

"But if this is the one that you choose not to pursue, and the story ends up checking out, you are going to have an entire **omelet** on your face and a lot of explaining to do. Plus, it will make your boss look bad and the Bureau, too."

He made up his mind: "Dave, bring him up here. I'll take a few minutes with him. I want you to stay while I talk to him. We'll do this together."

"Yes, sir," was Agent Bouquet's reply.

"So much for dinner," he said to himself.

# CHAPTER 26

# St. Paul

Michael and Edwin were still talking when there was a knock on the door. Not waiting for a reply, in came Maggie with Betty.

"We thought you could use some tea, Dr. Conway," beamed Maggie. "You'll have to forgive him, but Michael is more partial to coffee. Must have been all those nights on patrol way back when…"

"I would love some tea, Maggie. And please, please call me Edwin."

Betty tended to the tea for Edwin, and he gave her a smile and nod of thanks. He took a quick sip and said, "Delicious!" which won him a smile of gratitude from both women.

"I'm glad that you like it, Dr. Conway. I'll come back in a few minutes to check and see if you need anything else. Perhaps some biscuits?" asked Betty.

Conway smiled again. "Very impressive, Betty. Yes, we mostly call them biscuits, but you call them cookies."

The woman blushed a bit. "I'll bring a few in for you gentlemen to sample a little later, then."

"Thank you, Betty," said Michael.

"And you. What's your name again?"

Maggie laughed and said, "Oh, Michael, you are as bad as all of the Irishmen in all of St. Paul itself."

They shared a knowing smile. There was no doubt in Edwin's mind as he witnessed this little exchange, that the love between these two was deeply grounded.

With that, the women exited, with Maggie smiling all the way back to the kitchen.

"She's quite a woman, Michael."

"Yes, she is. She would have to be to put up with someone like me for all these years. Speaking of that, your wife sounds like she was an amazing woman."

Edwin smiled. It was a wistful smile. Michael could see the sadness in Edwin's eyes, just for a moment.

"She was. Ours was like your situation. I was gone a lot, lecturing and consulting all over Europe for many years. We had about five years when the kids were old enough so that Hannah could travel with me occasionally and meet some of the people that I had told her about for so long. Those were special times. She loved to travel with me, and I loved bringing her and showing her off."

Edwin stared out the window for a moment, momentarily lost in thought as he thought of his beloved wife and helpmate.

"You know that you have someone special when they will sacrifice so much of themselves for you and the family. She never put herself first in anything, though she surely could have."

"I'm so sorry, Edwin. What a loss for you."

"Thank you, old boy. There's not a day that goes by that I don't think of her."

He paused for a moment and said, "Now that my children are grown, there are times when I just long to be with her again. The wonderful thing is that I know that I will see her again soon." Michael nodded in agreement. "I am so thankful for our common faith because we believe exactly as you do."

"Michael, by chance, have you ever heard of a German Pastor named Dietrich Bonhoeffer?"

"Yes, as a matter of fact, I have!" Said Michael excitedly. "How do you know of him?"

He's very well known in Germany. Five years ago, he wrote a book called…"

"The Cost of Discipleship!" finished Michael.

"You know of this book?" asked Edwin, clearly surprised.

"Know of it?" Replied Michael. "I own it!"

He walked over to his bookshelf and picked it right out and showed Edwin.

"Oh, Michael!" He exclaimed, "This is one of my favorite books. I can't believe that you have it! Leigh and I would go to hear him preach when he was anywhere near us in Augsburg. He had quite a following in Germany until they silenced him."

"Where is he now?"

Edwin shifted in his chair and whispered, "He works for the Abwehr, Germany's intelligence organization. But it is just a front for him. It allows him to travel in Europe and he continues to preach and teach, among other things. And he is secretly helping to smuggle Jews out of Germany. He is no more a Nazi than you or I."

They were interrupted by a knock on the front door.

Michael started, "Can someone"-

"I'll get it!" yelled Kathryn.

They sipped their coffee and tea as Kathryn yelled again that she would get the door.

"She has a boyfriend who is from Costa Rica, and we expect that they will be engaged shortly," explained Michael.

"That's wonderful news!" exclaimed Edwin.

"Yes. Kathryn is our adventurer. Her soon-to-be fiancé is a psychiatrist. It's likely that she will end up with him down there rather than him starting over up here. The funny thing is, she's more Irish than all of us. Maybe more Irish than even you, Edwin!"

That brought a laugh from Dr. Conway.

"She must be expecting a package or something," said Michael.

They could hear the whole conversation at the door.

Kathryn, expectedly: "Oh, hello, Mr. Fischer! Anything for me today?"

The mailman replied, "Yes, Miss Kathryn, I believe there is a letter for you here somewhere. But the reason that I rang the doorbell is because there is a certified letter for your father that he needs to sign for."

"Sure, sure," said Kathryn. "Come on in. My Dad is in his study to the right. Just go right in. You said something about a letter for me?"

After a moment, Fischer said, "Yes, here it is."

Kathryn said a quick "Thank you," and was racing upstairs to read her letter.

There was a short knock on the door to the study, and Michael welcomed Erik Fischer into the room.

"Edwin, this is our mailman, Erik Fischer. Erik is married to Betty, who served the tea a few minutes ago."

Fischer, 38 and just a little on the pudgy side, walked over to shake Edwin's hand.

"It's a pleasure to meet you, Mr. Conway."

"The pleasure is all mine," said Edwin.

"Betty told me a little about you. You're from Ireland? Are you going to live here, or are you just visiting?"

"Just visiting. But I have to say that I'm falling in love with Minnesota."

Erik smiled and said, "You may change your opinion in a month or so."

Conway smiled at that and said, "Well, then it's good that I won't be here that long, my good man. I'll be leaving here in a few days."

"Oh? Well, that's too bad. But at least you will get out of here before the nasty weather starts. I hope you're going somewhere warm."

Edwin started to reply, but Michael interrupted and said, "Erik, you mentioned a letter that I needed to sign for?"

"It's right here, sir."

He brought the letter to Michael, who signed it and gave it back to him.

Michael then said, "Thanks, Erik. I really appreciate you being so conscientious about getting us our mail every day, and especially you taking the time to hand deliver these kinds of time sensitive letters."

"No problem, Mr. Sweeney."

Then to Edwin: "Nice to meet you, Mr. Conway."

"The pleasure was all mine, Erik."

"Always nice to see you again, Mr. Sweeney."

"Thanks, Erik. Take care of yourself."

And with that, Erik exited, leaving Edwin and Michael to themselves again.

"Sorry about him calling you "Mr." instead of "Doctor," said Michael. Edwin just shrugged him off and smiled.

"Come on, Edwin. Let's go for a stroll around the neighborhood. Maggie insists that I do something active each day, and the best thing to do is to walk around the block a couple of times."

"Sounds good to me," said Edwin. "I could use the exercise as well."

With that, they were out the door and strolling down Hague Avenue in no time.

# CHAPTER 27

## *That Same Day in Washington, D.C*

Dasch felt like he was finally getting some respect. Special Agent Bouquet had come and gotten him and was escorting him up to the Assistant Director's office.

They got off the elevator and walked up to Carolyn Joanis.

"Hi again, Care," said Dave. "He's expecting us."

"Not a problem, Special Agent Bouquet," she said. "Please go right in."

Dasch hesitated, taking it all in. The F.B.I. is intimidating to anyone. It was finally dawning on Dasch that he was about to have an audience with some of the most powerful men in the country.

Bouquet had paused at Ladd's door, turned around, and gestured for Dasch to enter.

Dasch picked up the pace and entered Ladd's office, continuing to take it all in.

Bouquet, coming right to the point, said, "Assistant Director, this is Mr. Dish"-

"Dasch!"

Bouquet, with a bit of a smirk on his face, said, "Dasch."

Ladd, wasting no time, motioned for Dasch to sit down at his conference table.

"So, Special Agent Bouquet says that you have a few things that you want to tell us."

Dasch, relishing the moment but still a bit in awe, said, "Where is Director Hoover? I thought that I was quite clear that I wanted to talk to Mr. Hoover," his voice cracking as he said it.

Ladd said nothing and stared straight through him.

Then: "Mr. Hoover is out of the country at the moment. I can assure you that he has given me full authority to speak for him whenever he is out of the country or unavailable to communicate with."

Dasch, still believing that he was in control, said, "I guess this will have to work."

Looking at Ladd and not paying any mind to Bouquet, Dasch proceeded to outline his terms. He only got one sentence out when he was cut off by Ladd.

"Look Mr. Di"-

Bouquet leaned over and loudly whispered to Ladd: "I think it's Dasch."

"Are you sure?" whispered back Ladd.

"Pretty sure. Just remember the Morse Code three dots and a
…"

"Dasch," finished Ladd.

"Now you have it!" beamed Bouquet.

Dasch's eyes dart back and forth between the two men, watching in a combination of horror and disbelief.

Ladd gave Bouquet an exaggerated thumbs up and turned back to their visitor and said, "Dasch." "Mr. Dasch, the Bureau doesn't negotiate in these situations. If you have something for us, then you better tell me now. If it checks out, you will be given consideration. So, you have my terms. Now make up your mind. I am a busy man."

Dasch, taken aback by the lack of respect he was being shown, could only muster a "You will be giving me a medal after you understand what I have to tell you."

"I'll be the judge of that," replied Ladd, clearly communicating the lack of impression that his guest was making on him.

Dasch, looking to save face, said, "All right, I'll tell you what I know, but I am also telling you that I want consideration after I tell you all of this. I fully expect to walk out of here a free man and, further, be offered a very good job somewhere in your government, maybe even with you at the F.B.I."

Ladd repeated, "If it checks out, you will be given consideration. You have managed to get a meeting with Director Hoover's right-hand man, which, I assure you, is no small task. I'm not going to ask you again."

Dasch began to lay out the entire plan for him, starting with the training in Germany, the trip from Brest, how they avoided the Allied fleet in the Atlantic, the confrontation with the Coast Guard sailor when they landed, his attempt to bribe the guardsman, telling him that he was giving him $300, but when he later checked, he saw that it was actually $260. He also told Ladd about the other sub that landed off the coast of Ponte Vedra Beach in Florida and that they would be making their way to Cincinnati, with two of the team members going onto Chicago.

Ladd glanced at Bouquet, who gave him a shoulder shrug.

Ladd, looking to dot every i and cross every t, asked Bouquet to call the Coast Guard in Long Island to see if Dasch's story could be corroborated. Bouquet left the room and went out to make the call.

Dasch shook his head, smirked, and kept talking. Ladd asked him about his work history, how long he had been in America, and how he was chosen for such a mission.

Dasch, never shy when it came to stretching his qualifications, bragged about how he had been handpicked by the Nazis and was the designated leader of his team.

Ladd was really listening, and the more Dasch talked, the more concerned he became. Sure, one could ignore Dasch's exaggerations about his own abilities, but the story itself had too many specifics and particulars to ignore.

Dasch was still going strong when Bouquet opened the door.

"Excuse me, Assistant Director, but could I speak to you out here for a minute?"

Ladd looked at Dasch and said, "Please wait here. I'll be right back."

Outside of his office, Bouquet looked ashen. "We've got a problem."

Ladd, rather glumly, afraid that he already knew the answer: "And what would that be?"

"His story checks out. At least the part about landing on Long Island. Amagansett, to be specific. I spoke with …"

Bouquet, looking at his notes, finally said, "Boatswain's Mate Second Class Duey Williams. He's the guy in charge up there. He said his rookie guardsman, a kid by the name of Cullen, came running back to the H.Q. the other night, and he looked like he had seen a ghost. Told Williams the whole story about a guy trying to bribe him. Said the guy told him that he was giving him $300, but when he got back to Williams and his outfit, he counted the money, and it was actually $260."

Now it was Ladd's turn to go pale.

# CHAPTER 28

As he and Special Agent Bouquet stood outside his office and out of earshot of Dasch, D.M. Ladd was trying to slow his brain down to think.

He couldn't resist the first words that came out of his mouth.

"I want the names of every agent in New York who hung up on this guy. And that goes for our office here as well."

Bouquet, smart enough to know not to say anything, just nodded.

Ladd again, still upset but at least starting to breathe:

"You need to get in here with me so we have two sets of ears listening to all of this. Get a recording device in here. Better yet, we need to move the conversation into the conference room down the hall. I want Dasch to know that the mood is changing here. The conference room is a bit more intimidating and formal. We are going to start all over with Dasch and make him report the whole story. He's probably missed some things, so making him repeat it might spark some other memories or provoke more questions from us."

Bouquet nodded again, still not willing to say something that might set Ladd off.

"Notify our people in Cincinnati and Chicago. Tell them that we may have something brewing here. Use Jon Eickstead and Bo Kemper in Chicago. I can't remember the best men in Cincinnati right now. Tell them that we will get some names to them shortly."

"I know a guy there," said Bouquet. "He's very good and very discreet. I would think that Cincinnati will be more of a short-term surveillance whereas Chicago will be a pickup."

"Good, Dave," said Ladd. "You're dead on. Cincinnati will be a surveillance job and Chicago will potentially be pickups."

"I'll make those calls right now and have a recorder brought into the conference room in a couple of minutes."

Ladd was still distracted and trying to compartmentalize all this new information.

After another minute, he told Bouquet, "We will get the names from Dasch when we go back in to talk to him. With the exception of Eickstead and Kemper and your contact in Cincinnati, don't say a word to anyone else about this. No one. We need to hear the whole thing before we decide on our next move."

Then, more to himself than to Bouquet: "The Director is unreachable for the next few days. He'll be back in the office four days from now. If we have to, we'll move without him, and I will have to brief him when he gets back."

Bouquet merely said, "That sounds like a good plan," and went to ask Carolyn for a recording device.

Ladd, regaining control now, had a clear head. He told Carolyn to get his friend George Parker on the phone and to get some food for the conference room.

Agent Hessler, who officed down the hall, walked into the waiting area.

"Jim!" called out Ladd.

"Sir?"

"Nice work on this thing with Dasch. Please escort him to the conference room and sit with him until I come back in. I need to take a call here and I should be back in there within 10 minutes or so."

"Yes, sir. If you're OK with it, I can continue to talk to him and subtly see if I can get any more out of him."

Ladd merely nodded, his mind starting to race again.

Hessler walked into Ladd's office and told Dasch to follow him.

Dasch and Hessler made their way out of the room, Dasch with a self-satisfied smirk on his face, clearly knowing that he had kicked the beehive.

Carolyn Joanis called her good friend - and sister-in-law- Peg MacFarlane. Peg answered on the first ring, as was her practice.

"Hi, Peg, Carolyn here."

"Carolyn! How good to hear from you!"

"We miss you over here. The office has never been the same since you and Mr. Parker moved over to O.S.S."

Peg laughed and said, "Out of the fire and into the frying pan! It's the same pace over here as it was at the Bureau. Although I do have to say that the atmosphere over here is a lot less formal, which I enjoy."

It was Carolyn's turn to laugh now. "Some people think that the "F" in "F.B.I." actually stands for "formal," so I don't see that changing here anytime soon."

"I suppose you're trying to get a hold of Mr. Parker?" asked Peg.

Carolyn lowered her voice a bit. "Yes, and apparently, it's pretty important. My guy here is looking a bit upset, and it sounds urgent."

Peg said, "OK. My guy is out for at least another hour or so, maybe two. But I will tell him to call your guy as soon as he gets back in."

"Thanks, Peg. Looking forward to seeing you at Thanksgiving."

"Same here, Care. It'll be good to get the clan together, even though we'll be missing a few people. I'm glad that Congress finally cleared up the confusion around the date with their proclamation last year. We were fine for seventy-five years until FDR had to try to change it."

She was referring to the President's directive in 1939 to move Thanksgiving up a week in order to appease businesses and allow for more shopping days for Christmas, thus increasing the economy. The results showed no overall impact on businesses, just a more spread-out shopping season. Thus, Congress decided in December of 1941 to declare that the 4th Thursday of November would forever be Thanksgiving.

Carolyn signed off and walked into Ladd's office.

"I just got off the phone with Peg McFarland. Mr. Parker is out of the office right now but should be back within an hour or two. I told her to have him call you immediately upon his return."

"Thanks, Carolyn. If he calls back and I am in the middle of the meeting with our guest, please come in and interrupt me. I need to talk to Mr. Parker as soon as possible. Also, it looks like a late night for me. Would you please call my wife and let her know that I won't be home in time for dinner?"

"Yes, sir."

With that, Ladd signed a couple of memos, re-read Agent Hessler's report, and made his way to the conference room for the next session with Dasch.

# CHAPTER 29

Neubauer and Haupt left the Gibson at 6:00 PM. They took separate cabs to the train station, which took all of 15 minutes. They got into two separate lines, and each purchased a first-class berth for the trip to Chicago. Both had requested berths in the same car. That took all of 10 minutes. The walk to the train took about 7 minutes. They were on board and settled in their respective berths about 13 minutes before the planned 6:45 PM departure.

Kerling and Thiel came out of the hotel a few minutes later. All four men had accidentally arrived in the lobby around the same time. They tried to keep any conversation with Haupt and Neubauer to a minimum. Kerling actually separated the two groups after a couple of minutes. He and Thiel left the hotel about 10 minutes after Neubauer and Haupt. They followed the same discipline, taking separate cabs and standing in separate lines at the bus station.

Kerling had found a bus and train combination that took them to St. Paul via Indianapolis. He was trying to avoid Chicago just in case things went wrong. The risk was too great to have all four of them in the same city, even for a short amount of time. They had been lucky in Cincinnati. He didn't want to press his luck any more than he already had.

The whole trip would take about 16 hours, door to door. That meant that he and Thiel would be in St. Paul around 11:00 AM the next day, give or take.

The 3 ½ hour bus trip to Indianapolis was, in a word, boring. The only good thing about it was that the bus was less than half full. Thiel was sitting somewhere way in the back. Kerling chose a seat toward the front, sitting on the aisle in order to discourage anyone from sitting next to him. It worked. He used the ride to continue to plan the attack on Edwin Conway. He had to do all of the thinking. Thiel was just too inexperienced. And cocky. Those two qualities made for a deadly combination. Literally.

Toward the back of the bus, Thiel sat by himself and chomped on a steak sandwich with some french fries that he took with him from the Gibson. Once he finished the sandwich, he would try to get some sleep. It wouldn't take long. He knew that Kerling would be doing all of the planning. Kerling wanted it that way, and he had no problem with that. Kerling was quite clear with him: all he had to do was follow orders.

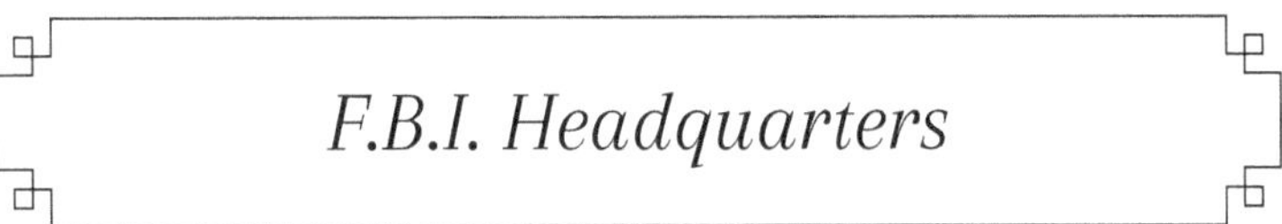

# *F.B.I. Headquarters*

It was past normal hours at the Bureau, but the three of them were still at it. They sat in a conference room not far from Ladd's office. The cherry wood table had the F.B.I.'s insignia carved into it, perfectly placed in the middle of the table. The table itself was designed for no more than twelve people. Twelve high-back leather chairs were placed around the table. There was a pitcher of water with fine crystal glasses, along with a stainless-steel coffee pot and four cups and saucers perfectly surrounding it. Pastrami, turkey, and ham and cheese sandwiches sat on the table, along with a few bags of potato chips and several bottles of Pepsi. Two ice containers with fancy ice tongs were there as well, along with several pieces of chocolate cake and - what else? Apple pie, of course. Carolyn had it all organized.

In one corner of the room was the American flag. The opposite corner held the F.B.I. flag.

Likewise, there were two pictures that were hung on two different walls in the room. One was of F.D.R. The larger one was more strategically placed and had a light from the ceiling trained on it. It was a picture of J. Edgar Hoover.

The private room was reserved for only the top personnel in the Bureau. The walls were paneled with dark wood, similar to the cherry wood from the conference table.

The mood in this room was decidedly different from Ladd's office. The conversation there had been somewhat informal and a bit unguarded.

Where there was once skepticism, there was now belief. And concern. And a sense of urgency.

The tone had changed from a listening session to one of interrogation. Whether Dasch picked up on that remained to be seen. He was too busy talking.

D.M. Ladd and Special Agent Bouquet continued to listen to George J. Dasch tell the whole story to them. They interrupted him with more questions.

"How long has this mission been in the works?" Ladd asked.

"Operation Pastorius has been in development for several months. We did an intense three-week training outside of Berlin at a place called Quentz Lake. There were several more of us being trained there, but they decided to go with just two groups of four. We were the best of the group, so they chose us. And they picked me to lead the mission," he said, for roughly the fifth time.

"Yeah, we got that part," said Bouquet.

"What is the significance of the name "Pastorius?" Dasch rolled his eyes at that one.

"Clearly, you don't know your history, Agent Bouquet. Oh, excuse me: Special Agent Bouquet. Let me educate you. Francis Pastorius was born in Germany and was asked by a group of merchants to form a settlement in America. This would happen in the late 1600s. He ended up purchasing 15,000 acres in Pennsylvania, in an area that is now called Germantown. He earned his law degree from a school in Nuremberg before he settled in America. He became the town's leader and even drafted the first known protest against slavery in America. He was, without question, an outstanding German. Perhaps this is the reason that Admiral Canaris chose this name for our mission." Bouquet continued with his own question:

"Whose idea was this?"

"Do you mean, whose idea was it to do this mission?"

"Yes. Whose idea was it to send the eight of you into America? That is, in addition to you, of course." Bouquet couldn't resist that last zinger.

Dasch didn't even pick up on it.

"We take our orders from Walter Kappe, who might be an

American citizen. Regardless, he has spent twelve years over here. He reports to Canaris, whom I'm sure you have heard of."

"Spell it."

"What? Kappe?"

"Yes. Kappe."

Dasch, dismissively: "K-A-P-P-E."

Ladd, now: "You mentioned that there were more than just the eight of you that were in training. Where were the others assigned to go?"

"As far as I know, they flunked the course. So, there was never any talk as to where they might be assigned."

"Tell us again what sort of training they put you through at Quentz Lake."

"All right, I will repeat it for you. Weapons of all kinds: handguns, machine guns, knife work, improvised weapons, and sniper training. We spent a lot of time on demolitions. Anything that could disrupt the military efforts and impact the morale of the American people. We were sent in to scare the American people and put doubts in their minds as to why we wanted to fight in Europe when the Japanese were the real enemy."

Ladd, again: "Targets."

Dasch: "What?"

Ladd: "Targets. What were your targets?"

Dasch took a drag from his cigarette, blew the smoke into a circle, and looked coldly at his two interrogators.

"I wonder how the American people would react if this information ever got out? How would civilians feel about their water supply being cut off? Or better yet, poisoned? The **list** of targets we have is extensive. Niagara Falls for the hydroelectrical grid. Specific bridges that are critical to transporting weapons and ammunition. For example, the Hell Gate Bridge is right in New York. Do you know that that bridge is over 1,000 feet long and over 100 feet wide? It is the - how do you say it? The pinch point for all rail travel in and around New York and the whole northeastern portion of the country." Dasch paused, knowing that he had their attention.

"Or maybe the ALCOA factories where more weapons and ammunition are manufactured. What do you suppose blowing up a couple of aluminum factories would do to the war effort? Of course, I'm sure that you know that in order to make aluminum, you have to have cryolite. And almost all of America's cryolite comes from Greenland, of all places. And the largest plant that gets the cryolite is just outside of Philadelphia. Blowing up that plant would shut down all of your capabilities to make the aluminum needed to produce more weapons and ammunition. You see, gentlemen, the Abwehr has done its homework."

Neither Ladd nor Bouquet said a word.

Dasch continued, feeling as though he was educating the two men, which he clearly was.

"Now, let's make it more personal. How about some Jewish-owned retail stores? It would be nothing to plant bombs in their elevators or display areas, timed to go off right at the busiest times of shopping. The holidays are just around the corner, right? What about targeting some dams, so that entire neighborhoods would be flooded and swept away, with families still in them? Or planting some bombs in some of the subway stations or train stations in New York and other major cities? And all of this taking place randomly. Even simultaneously! All with no rhyme or reason. We would be unstoppable because you would have no idea where and when we would strike next. And don't tell me that you would be able to figure it out because each of us in this room knows that that would not be possible."

Ladd just stared at Dasch, not showing the sheer panic that he was feeling inside. He looked at Bouquet, who was undoubtedly trying to hide the same thoughts. They both knew that Dasch was right; this was the unthinkable, something their country and their Bureau could not possibly anticipate, plan for, or prevent. Check. Mate.

No one said anything for a full two minutes. Dasch continued to alternately stare at them and blow more smoke toward the ceiling.

"How were you funded?" Bouquet again.

"We were given an enormous amount of American cash. Here, let me show you."

Dasch took his briefcase off of a nearby chair and opened it.

Bouquet couldn't hide his surprise. "Holy mackerel!" he exclaimed. He began thumbing through the wads of bills. "There must be …"

"About $84,000, with more hidden back on Long Island and the hotel room. Unless the Coast Guard found the stash that we buried on the beach," Dasch said, rather nonchalantly.

Ladd and Bouquet exchanged glances. If there had ever been any doubt about Dasch's story before, there was none now. A guy like him wouldn't just be walking around with that kind of money. As they were getting to know him, they had already concluded that there was no way that he was even capable of making that kind of money on his own.

Ladd moved his chair uncomfortably close to Dasch. "Where are the other men that are a part of this mission?" Dasch, feeling the turn of the mood in the room:

"You should know that Burger - the man with me at the Clinton Hotel - is completely supportive of me being here. He just looked at this mission as a way to get back to America. Much like I have. So, I want a little of the recognition that will be awarded to me to go to him as well."

Bouquet rolled his **eyes,** but Ladd told him to knock it off without saying a word. Bouquet just shook his head in disbelief.

"The others. Where are the others?" pressed Ladd.

"They split up," replied Dasch. "The other two men under my command are at a different hotel, about four blocks from the Clinton."

"Name?" asked Bouquet.

"What?"

"The name. What is the name of the hotel where the other two men are staying?"

"The Martinique. It's nice, but not as nice as the Clinton. You see, when you're the leader, it's appropriate for"-

"What are their names? The other men with you?"

"Well, Burger is with me at the Clinton. The other two men are Heinck and Quirin, but their new identities will have different names, and I can't remember what they are at the moment." That goes for Burger also, by the way."

"What's your name? The one you used at the hotel?"

"George Davis. I have a passport here with that name on it."

Bouquet took the passport from Dasch and examined it. His glance at Ladd told his boss that the passport looked to be totally legitimate, and it would pass at any customs counter in the country.

Ladd said nothing but was privately in awe with all of it - the plan itself, how they got into the country, the targets, the amount of cash, the authenticity of their I.D.s, their cover story very well planned down to the smallest detail. Canaris was certainly a worthy foe.

"What about the men who landed off of Jacksonville?" Bouquet pushed.

Dasch shook his head in a condescending way to Bouquet and returned the eye roll.

"They were to land off of Ponte Vedra, about 20 miles south of Jacksonville. They were to take a bus to Jacksonville and then get on a couple of trains. They were instructed not to come directly to New York. I already told you that a couple of them are from Chicago, so the plan called for them to avoid the east coast trains that went directly up the coast, just in case any U.S. government or military agencies were looking for someone like us. They were to rendezvous in Cincinnati for a day, then the two from Chicago would head from Cincinnati to Chicago. The remaining two would stay in Cincinnati for a couple of days before making their way to New York. All eight of us were to meet in the city within a few days of arriving on land so that we could begin to plan and implement the different attacks. You'll find maps of all of the targets in my hotel room in New York. I believe Kerling would have the maps for his targets as well."

"Names?"

"Neubauer, Haupt, Thiel, and Kerling. Kerling heads up that team. All of the men will also have fake names and passports, but I don't recall what names they are using."

"What's Kerling's first name?"

"Edward. He might have a wife in New York. I thought I heard him say something like that once during our training. Each of these men speaks excellent English. Most have lived in the U.S. for several years. A couple might even be U.S. citizens."

Bouquet was writing the information down as fast as Dasch was talking.

Dasch again: "Neubauer and Haupt should be able to be found in Chicago. Haupt grew up there. He's a kid, really. Maybe 22 or so. Neubauer is older. He's around 33, give or take. He's been in America since 1931, I believe. Like I said, the plan was for them to lay low in their parents' homes for a couple of days and then make their way to New York, where we would have both teams come together for our first meeting."

Ladd now: "So, you said Kerling and Thiel were to stay in Cincinnati and come to New York separately."

"That's right."

"And that's just to make sure that you aren't all on one train together? Sort of like spreading your risk?"

Dasch nodded. "Exactly."

There was a minute of silence. Dasch, still not getting it, yawned and said, "Gentlemen, I think that I've had enough for today. Can someone take me back to the hotel? I need to sleep." Bouquet moved in but was waved off by Ladd.

"Yes, I agree with you, Mr. Dasch. We will pick you up tomorrow morning and bring you back here for more discussion. Agent Hessler will escort you back to the Mayflower. But I assure you that you will not be free to leave the hotel on your own. And don't use any of the phones while you are staying there. I will clear my calendar for tomorrow and meet up with you at 9:00 AM back in this same room."

"Please try to have some breakfast brought in for me, Mr. Ladd."

"That will all be arranged. I will see you tomorrow morning." Dasch nodded and moved to the door.

"Special Agent Bouquet: A word, please," said Ladd.

Dasch walked out and found Agent Hessler and another agent waiting for him.

Ladd turned to Bouquet and said, "Have four men assigned to him. One is at the backdoor of the Mayflower, another is in the lobby, and a couple are outside in a car. He is not to be let out of our sight. There's a lot more to glean from him, so we won't alienate him just yet."

"I'll take care of it," replied Bouquet.

"And tell our New York office that I want a call with them in an hour. We need to get them all the information that we have on the three men from Dasch's group. I want these guys put under surveillance immediately, with the goal being to arrest them in the next 24 hours. The same goes for our Chicago and Cincinnati offices. Let's get these men rounded up before they can act and before they suspect something."

"I'm on it," said Bouquet.

"One more thing, Dave," said Ladd.

"You give Hessler as many agents as he needs to watch Dasch overnight. I said four off the top of my head. But if you think you need to do that two or three times, just do it. You have all my support on this. Just to be clear: under no circumstances is he to make any phone calls until or unless we have the other seven men in custody. Have his phone removed from his room. And he cannot leave the hotel at any time without at least two agents with him."

Bouquet's nod and brief smile indicated a little bit of relief. He would take every man that he could find at this point.

# CHAPTER 31

George Parker had gotten back to his office later than planned. Peg MacFarland was not around, but her light was still on at her desk, which meant that she was still in the building.

Parker had settled back at his desk and started reading more reports. He was just digesting an update from the Pacific Theater when Peg entered and knocked.

She didn't stop all the way in as she said, "D.M. Ladd is on the line for you. Says it's important. Carolyn called earlier while you were gone. There should be a note on your desk telling you to call him."

Parker looked at her and gave the nod. They were beginning to communicate very effectively with little or no words, which was the ultimate example of trust and partnership.

Ladd and Parker went back a long way at the Bureau. They both rose through the ranks at the same pace and during the same years. Parker would likely have Ladd's job by now if he had decided to stay at the F.B.I.

But Parker was tired of all the politics and the grandstanding. Besides, he loved and respected Wild Bill Donovan. He only respected J. Edgar Hoover, and that respect was out of duty rather than devotion.

However, Parker's respect for Ladd was genuine, as was his affection for him. Ladd, in turn, felt the same way about Parker. As the rivalry between their bosses heated up, the two right-hand men quietly made a pact to share as much with each other as they could and to always keep the lines of communication open between the two of them.

Within a few seconds, his phone rang.

"D.M. Ladd! Good to hear from you, Mickey!" exclaimed George. "Mickey" is what all of Ladd's close friends called him.

"Mr. Parker! Hey, I don't even know what to call you these days. What kind of a title did they pin on you over there?"

Parker, chuckling, said, "I honestly don't know. I don't even know if I have any business cards yet."

After a few more minutes of small talk, Ladd decided to dive in.

"George, I'm going to tell you something that is really top secret at this point."

Parker was about to make a smart comment but thought better of it.

"All right, Mick. You certainly have my attention."

"We have firsthand knowledge of two German u boats that landed off of our east coast and dispatched two groups of four men. One of them landed off of Long Island the other night. And the other one landed off of the coast of Ponte Vedra, Florida, a couple of nights later."

"Where is Ponte, Ponte what?" asked George.

"Ponte Vedra," replied Ladd. "It's around 20 miles south of Jacksonville. Nothing is there, apparently."

All Parker could do was a low, "Holy Cow," kind of whistle.

"I know," said Ladd. "I know."

"Do you know where they are? Have you captured any of them yet? What were they sent here to do?" Parker's questions were clipped and drove right to the point.

"I can tell you all about that when I see you. Can you come right over?" Asked Ladd.


"I'll be there in twenty minutes," replied Parker. "Have you told your boss yet?"

"Unreachable for the next few days."

"Huh," replied Parker. "Mine too."

Silence on the phone. Both were wondering if the other knew about the pending "Operation Torch" in North Africa, but neither man said anything else.

Then Ladd: "Looks like you and I got the starting nods for our respective teams."

"Batter up," said Parker. "See you in twenty."

# CHAPTER 32

Parker actually made it over to Ladd's office in 18 minutes.

This time, there were no pleasantries. They got right down to business. Ladd recapped everything that they had learned from Dasch, from where each of the seven remaining spies were to the money to the plans that Dasch had talked about, complete with targets, all of it.

The two friends began to talk strategy. What if none of the men talked? How would they get them to talk? How big was the actual network beyond these eight men? Where was the country most vulnerable to an attack? Some ideas were beginning to form in George's mind.

He began to think through the next steps.

"Look, Mickey, we have at least a couple of days before they are all supposed to rendezvous in New York. I wonder if it would be a good idea to say nothing about this to anyone other than those that will be directly involved in the arrests. No one needs to know that this Dasch guy squealed on the whole thing. This might be the best way for Canaris and his people to stop trying to place spies over here. This can be a huge win for the Bureau if we can make it look like we captured these guys through our own efforts and intelligence network. Look at it this way: He sends his people over here, and we capture them almost immediately. He concludes that we have some sort of impenetrable wall." "I like that," replied Ladd.

"J. Edgar will love it," said Parker. "He can have all the credit and make it look like these guys walked right into his trap. Further, it might convince Hitler that he has a mole over there that is feeding us incredibly sensitive information. Let them chase their tales for a while."

"Great point, George. Good thinking."

The men sat quietly for a moment. Then Ladd spoke again.

"How should we collect the other seven guys?"

"Well, let's see," said Parker. "We know where the three guys in New York are. And we know- at least we think we know - where the two guys from Chicago are or will be. Chances are they will want to see their parents and family, right? On the other hand, we have no idea where in Cincinnati the other two guys are. So, logic would say that we watch the guys in New York and see if they lead us to anyone else. And we probably should pick up the guys in Chicago right away and see if they know where the guys in Cincy are staying. In the meantime, since your boy Dish"-

"Dasch," chuckled Ladd.

"Yeah, that guy," said Parker. "Since Dasch is staying at the Mayflower and also at the Clinton in New York, maybe this

Kerling and his crew are at one of the posh hotels in Cincinnati. I really don't know any of the hotels there, but your guys who are local would know. Maybe start their search based on the quality of the hotel."

"That makes sense," said Ladd. "Meanwhile, we'll separate the two guys in Chicago and see who will spill anything to us. The usual stuff. Divide and conquer." Parker nodded at that.

"Let me know if I can help," he said to his friend.

"You've already helped," replied Ladd. "Thank you, George."

"Just promise to keep me in the loop if any other information comes to light. I would be more than happy to dive in here and try to help you. While this is clearly in the Bureau's purview because it's on American soil, there is a case to be made that we should be involved anyway since it involves intelligence and espionage."

"Fair enough," said Ladd.

Parker decided to say what they were both thinking.

He turned to his good friend and said, "We were very fortunate that this Dasch guy came to us. We never could have stopped what they were planning."

Ladd nodded and said, "Can you imagine the damage that they would have done? And I'm not just talking about the physical damage to the infrastructure. The damage to our nation's confidence and morale, the message of vulnerability that we would have to recognize and admit to …"

"Mickey, I think this is God's hand in our nation. There really is no other explanation for it. I believe that we are fighting a righteous battle for the freedom of mankind, but also for our collective faith as a country."

"I couldn't agree more, George. God has truly spared us by orchestrating Dasch's coming in here. We'll probably never know if he got spooked by that rookie Coast Guard kid or if his own conscience got to him, or if there was some other reason that he came forward. I'm just grateful that this will spare untold thousands of lives, if not more. But let's not celebrate too quickly. Now we need to round these guys up."

That brought another nod from Parker.

Ladd again: "By the way, you never did tell me what your title is over there?"

George, with a bit of a smile on his face: "To be perfectly honest with you, I don't have one. At least, I don't know of one. Wild Bill is a pretty informal guy. The culture is one of teamwork and humility. We have no glory hounds over there. Donovan gives away any credit that comes his way. That's why people would run through a wall for him. He must've been a heck of a soldier."

Ladd smiled a sad smile of sorts.

"Sure, we have our fair share of strife and arguments," continued Parker, "But remember, we are in the building stages of this organization. It only started in July of last year, so we aren't even 18 months old yet. Plus, unlike you guys, the fewer the people who know about us and what we do, the better."

Ladd looked at his friend somewhat wistfully.

"That sure sounds refreshing," was all that he could and would say.

Parker smiled in a way that said, "I understand."

CHAPTER 33

One hour later that evening, F.B.I. Agents Fran Donaldson and Bill Weir were working on a counterfeiting case in Cincinnati with the Secret Service when the call came in from Bureau headquarters. Special Agent Dave Bouquet briefed them on their new case, which took priority over anything else that they had been working on.

He gave them a high-level summary of the case without divulging any sensitive information and emphasized the importance of apprehending the four men.

Donaldson and Weir were knocking on doors that evening, starting with the nicest hotels and working their way down. Their second visit was to the Gibson.

The night clerk wasn't much help.

"You should probably come back and talk to my counterpart who works here during the day. His name is Nick Mourouzis, and he has an excellent memory when it comes to guests."

Just when they were about to leave, the bellhop came up to Agent Weir and said, "I might be able to help you."

Weir, a lawyer by trade who came into the Bureau eight years earlier, asked the young man for his name.

"John Bonke. People just call me "Bonk."

"OK, Bonk, why do you think you can help us?"

147

"I'm sort of the doorman and baggage guy. I am really attentive to each of the guests because I work a lot on tips. There were four guys who left tonight within a few minutes of one another. It looked obvious to me that they all knew one another. They came down two at a time, talked for a couple of minutes in the lobby, and then one of them separated him and his partner from the other two. Then, like I said, they took different cabs. I heard them talking quietly to one another, though."

"This is good. Go on, Bonk," said Donaldson.

"Well, the first two guys, one of them was around my age, and the other was a bit older than that. The older guy was taller than the other fellow. As they got into their cabs, each of them told the driver to take them to the train station. One of them said to the other, "I'll see you in Chicago.""

"Very good, Bonk," said Weir. "What about the other two men?"

"They came out later and did the same thing," said Bonke. "Except they weren't going to Chicago."

"Were they possibly going to New York?" asked Donaldson.

"Nope. They were going to the bus station and heading to Indianapolis. The younger one asked, the older one about what time they got in… what did he call it? Oh, yeah, up north. What time do we get in up north?"

Donaldson and Weir looked at each other, a bit puzzled.

"Are you sure that's what he said? The younger guy?"

Bonke again: "Yeah. Heard him plain as day. And the older guy said the train arrives right around 11:00 AM."

"Wait a minute," said Weir. "You said "bus" before."

"I know. I know I did," said Bonke. "But they were going to the bus station here, taking a bus to Indianapolis, and then taking a train out of Indianapolis somewhere north. And the train would get in somewhere tomorrow at 11:00 AM. That's how I remember it. And I do remember because the younger of the two gave me a dollar, and the older guy gave me two bucks. Not bad, eh?"

Donaldson now: "So, Bonk, let me see if I got this right. The first two guys got into two different cabs. Both told their cabbies to take them to the train station. Right?"

"Yep."

"OK," continued Donaldson. "And then one of them said to the other, "I'll see you in Chicago?" "Yeah. That's right," said Bonk.

"OK. So far, so good," replied Donaldson.

"So now the other two **guys,** they also got separate cabs, and they each told their cabbie to take them to the bus station, right?" "Yep."

"OK, we're almost home now," said Donaldson. "But then the younger guy asked the older guy what time they arrive up north, and the older guy says, "The train arrives around 11:00 AM. Did I get this right?"

"Yeah. That's just what I told you."

Weir now: "And you're sure about the whole conversation? You couldn't have misunderstood any of this?"

Bonke, looking at Weir like he had four eyes: "Look, I'm telling you, I live and die based on my tips. I am extremely attentive in these situations because if I'm not, that's the difference between eating a hot dog and eating a steak when I get off."

Bonke looked at them both and said, "I don't work for free, if you catch my drift."

Donaldson and Weir looked at each other, and Donaldson looked in his pocket and said, "All I have is a 5 spot." Bonke snatched it, tipped his cap, and then looked at Weir.

Weir gave him a "You gotta be kidding me" look. He looked back at his partner, who shrugged at him and gave him the index finger circling, which is the "Let's go, cough it up" sign.

Weir, shaking his head, reached into his pocket for another Lincoln and handed it over.

Donaldson said, "I'm going to get our sketch artist down here right now. And I'm going to get this Nick Mourouzis guy to come in right now as well."

He stepped inside to call Special Agent Bouquet with an update.

Bouquet, still at the office, was surprised and a bit puzzled about the bus station information. He thanked Donaldson and told him to call again with any more pertinent information that they could glean from Bonke and Mourouzis.

His next call was to the train station in Cincinnati, checking on what time the next train was headed to Chicago, and what time it got in. He gave the gal on the line the names of Haupt and Neubauer and asked if they had purchased tickets for Chicago. She didn't have either name on her passenger list.

"They're using aliases," he said to himself. He asked for a list of all the passengers who were on the train to Chicago. There were thirty-two names. Of the thirty-two, twenty-six were male.

Of the twenty-six males, twenty had not purchased another ticket out of Chicago.

"At least we got it down to twenty," he thought.

His next call was to Jon Eickstead, his fellow Special Agent in Chicago. "Eick," as he was known, was another former athlete who played football at Indiana University. He and his wife Teresa had settled in Evanston.

"Dave, you know I love talking to you, but do you have any idea what time it is?" said a groggy Eickstead. He was a morning person, up at the crack of dawn, which meant that he tried to get to bed at an early hour.

"Sorry, Eick, but this is really important. I mean, REALLY important."

He explained the situation, not telling everything, but Eickstead, nobody's fool, quickly put things together.

"Man, Dave this is huge," is all that he could manage. After all, the guy was awakened out of a dead sleep.

Bouquet gave him the train information but told him that they had no pictures of the two men that they would be looking for.

"By the time we get a reasonable sketch to you, they'll be in the city someplace. We are betting that they will go see their parents, maybe even stay with them," said Bouquet.

"But on the other hand, they will be flush with cash, so who knows? In any case, sooner or later, they will want to see their families."

"Yeah, probably," replied Eickstead. After a few seconds of silence, Eickstead, who was one of the sharpest agents in the entire Bureau, had come up with a plan.

"Look, here's what I'm going to do: I'll put a total of four men at the station. They'll be instructed to follow the best two candidates who come off the train. We know that these guys are relatively young. Maybe by the time they arrive, we'll have exact information on their ages. And some sort of description. Anyway, I'll take Haupt's home and stake it out. I'll have a few of my men backing me up. Same deal with Neubauer."

Eickstead was phenomenal with names. He could easily ask Bouquet about any member of his family by name.

Bouquet couldn't help it. He asked, "Eick, I mentioned these guys by name once to you, and that was easily ten minutes ago. And I woke you out of a sound sleep."

"What? Did I get a name wrong?" asked Eickstead.

"No, no," said Bouquet. "All I know is that I had to look down at my notes to tell you his name."

"Which one? Haupt or Neubauer?" asked Eickstead.

"Oh, never mind," replied Bouquet.

"Look, Dave, it's not going to help me anyway because you said that they were traveling by aliases."

"Just forget it," was all Bouquet could come back with.

"Let me know when you find them. Get them into custody quietly, and I'll let you know the next steps. And Eick, be careful. We don't know if their families are part of this or not."

"Roger that," said Eickstead.

Just as they were about to end the call, Eickstead said, "Hey Dave, your brother, Greg, is he still in real estate appraisal in Minneapolis?"

"Ah, man," said Bouquet, "Now you're just showing off."

With that, he hung up as Eickstead started to ask about Bouquet's friend Tim, who owned a couple of duplexes in Minneapolis.

# CHAPTER 34

Neubauer and Haupt would arrive in Chicago on the same train, but no one would have ever known it. They had separate berths in the same car. When they were still about an hour from arriving in Chicago, Haupt checked to make sure that no one was around, then snuck into Neubauer's berth.

Neubauer had been dozing with a book in his hands.

"Are you awake?" asked Haupt.

"I am now," answered Neubauer. "What do you want? We shouldn't be seen together."

"Don't worry. I made sure that no one saw me come in here. Most people are sound asleep right now."

"So, what do you want?" repeated Neubauer.

Haupt, 22, was the youngest of the eight saboteurs who had snuck into America. He was also an American citizen, having been officially naturalized about twelve years ago. He stood close to 6 feet tall. He had thick dark hair and deep-set greenish-blue eyes.

While he had a fiancé in Chicago before he left the country, he was known to be a womanizer. He used to tell his friends that "Women are like buses. There's another one coming every fifteen minutes."

He also had a big mouth and was a big talker.

"I wanted you to know that I have decided to spend today and tonight with my parents. I miss my family, and I thought that one night with them wouldn't hurt. I also want to see my girlfriend, who I left behind. That is, if she would still even talk to me. I left before the war and wanted to see the world. I should've told her that I was going, but I didn't. Anyway, if you need to get a hold of me, my father's name is Hans, and they live at 2224 Fremont."

"What's your girlfriend's name?"

"Gerda. Gerda Melind. We were actually engaged."

"That's pretty bad, Herbert. To leave her like that with no explanation."

"I'm not sure you are one to talk, Hermann. Aren't you divorced yourself?"

Neubauer paused, stared at this young, arrogant punk, and then continued.

"Your address - that's not all that far from where I used to live," he said. "I was on Belmont Avenue, and my family still lives there. But I am going to do the opposite. I am going to stay in a hotel - probably the Sheraton Plaza - and then visit my family while still maintaining my residence at the hotel. If I'm not at the Plaza, look for me at the Hilton on Michigan Avenue."

"We probably won't be here more than a few days," said Haupt. "I wonder if they are going to eventually send me back here anyway. I used to work at an optical factory in West Garland Park that made parts for the Norden bombsight. I figure the Fatherland would want access to the latest generation of that thing, and that I could steal all the blueprints for it, or a parts list or something like that."

"We'll know our orders soon enough," replied Neubauer. "Just remember, if anything goes wrong and you get arrested, don't say a word to anyone about anything. They might work you over or make you all sorts of promises but don't listen to them. Too much is riding on this mission to have it fail because someone opened their mouth."

"I would never say anything, Hermann. That was made abundantly clear to all of us in our training."

"Good," replied Neubauer. "When we come into the station, don't just walk off this car. Go to the middle of the train, where all the coach seats are, and get off there. I will go down to the back of the train and exit there. Call me at the Sheraton Plaza when you get settled. Now let me try to get a little sleep in the time that we have before we arrive."

Haupt nodded and said goodbye. He opened the door, saw that no one was in the aisle, and snuck back to his berth. They would not see each other for several days after that.

# CHAPTER 35

The Sweeneys and the Conways decided to go out for breakfast. Maggie was thankful for the break, as was Betty, who stayed behind for some housecleaning.

Michael had a favorite hole-in-the-wall place on West Seventh Street. It had only been around for three years, but it was good food. They served breakfast at any time of the day or night, so he figured he'd give the Conways a real taste of St. Paul. Literally.

Mickey's Diner had grown to become a popular place for people from all walks of life. The diner was open 24 hours a day, so it did attract some of the riff-raff after midnight.

The restaurant's owner was Mickey Crimmons, another fine Irishman. He had a partner as well, but Mickey was the face **and** the name of the business. He was also a client of the Sweeney Detective Bureau. Michael had a man stationed in the diner on the midnight shift most nights for all to see. Normally a restaurant was an easy target for a thief or burglar, especially later at night. However, the presence of a Sweeney Security man was a great motivation for a troublemaker to commit a crime in some other establishment. As a matter of fact, there hadn't been one incident in the diner since Mickey hired Michael's company.

Mickey was at the restaurant almost every day, and his relationship with Michael was more than that of a customer and provider. They had forged a friendship. The friendship translated to a guaranteed large table for the group, which was rare at Mickey's since they didn't take reservations.

The restaurant itself was designed as a very large train car, complete with ten enormous windows that allowed for a very open atmosphere. It was 50 feet long and 10 feet wide, with bright yellow exteriors and red trim.

Mickey spared no expense when it came to signage. There could be no confusion when it came to the name - "Mickey's Diner" was displayed with neon lights so bright that you could probably play a major league baseball game there at midnight - and the décor on the inside was simple and clean with more bright colors. The long counter boasted many red-topped stools for the single eaters, with tables surrounding the counter. "Good food made fast" was the description that the locals had come up with, and it fit.

In addition to their breakfasts, Mickey's was known for excellent burgers and shakes, among other things. It was a place that one could go to, knowing that you would get a quick, decent meal at a fair price. Can't ask for more than that.

As the group of eight got settled, Michael went over to the counter and thanked Mickey personally for keeping a table open for him.

"Not a problem, Mike," he said, barely looking up. He was busy with the breakfast crowd, so Michael let him get back to work. "Sure appreciate the security that your people provide."

He made his way back to the table, which was in the very back of the restaurant, where there was a lively discussion about Christmas in Minnesota. By sheer habit, Michael made it a point to sit against the wall so he could see everything around him. Even when he and Maggie went to dinner, the two of them never even discussed who was sitting where. It was always decided by what seat gave the best view to the largest part of the restaurant.

Michael would just never sit with his back to a crowd.

"Oh, it's just so beautiful," gushed Maggie. "Rice Park, which is only a few blocks from us, is decorated beautifully with wreaths and countless Christmas trees. There are usually two or three bonfires going on at once, so people can stay warm. On most days leading up to Christmas, there is singing and caroling, usually with a small orchestra of sorts that will play as well. It is such a festive time here."

"It sounds wonderful," said Edwin.

"Having lived in Germany these last few years, we are so looking forward to a real Christmas in America, where we can truly celebrate our Savior's birth," said Leigh.

"Listening to you, Leigh, is a good reminder to all of us here who have the freedom to never take it for granted," said Evvie.

"And to fight for it, when necessary," added Kathryn.

Everyone nodded at that, and as the conversation continued, Maggie leaned into Michael and whispered, "I love this girl!" Michael smiled and winked at his wife in agreement.

"Evelyn, what's this I hear about you and a Navy sailor?" asked Edwin.

Evvie's eyes lit up and said, "It's all true, Dr. Conway. His name is Dick Myler, and he is somewhere in the Pacific right now. He is on an escort ship that travels with the Destroyers." "Myler. Myler," mused Edwin. "That sounds Irish." "It certainly is!" said Evvie.

Edwin beamed with delight but then got dramatically serious.

"But Kathryn is going to "break the mold," as they say, right, Kathryn?"

Kathryn laughed and said, "I always was the risk-taker in the family!"

"Costa Rica?" asked Leigh. "That sounds so beautiful!"

"Nothing is official just yet, but…her voice trailed off as she blushed a bit.

Frank, never one to miss an opportunity to give his sisters the needle, said, "Why Kathryn, is it warm in here? Your face is so red!"

That brought a laugh from everyone, and Kathryn, someone that rarely if ever lost a debate, replied, "You know, Frank, there is a saying… how does it go? Something about glass houses and throwing stones?"

Another big laugh followed, and it was Frank's turn to blush, to which Kathryn, knowing that she had her brother on the ropes, came back with an exaggerated show of concern.

"Why, Frank, are you warm? Your face seems to be so red!"

There was more raucous laughter, followed by Frank lifting his hands in surrender.

Just then, the waitress came up to the table to take their orders.

"Boy, am I glad to see you!" said Frank, which was met with even more laughter.

# CHAPTER 36

Herbert Haupt had kept his head down as he exited the train, but he couldn't help but smile. He was excited to be back in Chicago. He wouldn't allow himself to call it "home" anymore. He had a mission that he was charged with completing. Still, it would be good to see his parents. And hopefully, Gerda.

Haupt knew that he himself was the problem in their relationship. For whatever reason, he always over promised and under delivered. He talked big. When the boys in school made fun of him because of his accent, he would boast to them that they would be subject to him someday when the Germans took over the country.

"What a foolish thing to say," he chided himself. Just as quickly, he thought, "But it was true." All of those boys would be answering to the Fatherland. Some might already be doing so since a number of them had undoubtedly been drafted or volunteered after Pearl Harbor.

He stopped at a newsstand to pick up a paper, casually looking around to see if anyone had followed him off the train. So far, so good. He decided to take a cab to his parent's place. "Why not?" he reasoned. After all, he certainly had the money for it. He had enough to buy a couple of cars if he wanted to. Wait until his father sees the dough that he has on him. Plus, his clothes were brand new. His parents and family would be impressed when they saw him.

If anyone was looking for him, they'd be looking for someone who looked, well, like a German spy. He looked as American as anyone in the station, he told himself.

The cab got him to his parents' house - his childhood home - in about twenty minutes. He was excited as he got out of the taxi. He tipped the driver two bucks, grabbed his suitcase, walked up the sidewalk, and wondered if he should knock. He decided that he had better.

He decided on a bold knock, not a passive, "don't mean to disturb you" couple of taps.

In less than a minute, the door opened, and he was staring at his mother, who, when she saw him, could only open her mouth and stare back.

Herbert laughed at that and simply said, "Hello, Mother!"

She recovered quickly, shrieked, and gave him a huge hug. She called to her husband, who came to the door, smiled broadly, and vigorously shook his son's hand. They ushered him into the house and shut the door.

Across the street, in a dark sedan, sat Eickstead with his F.B.I.

pal Bill Flatley. Flatley, who had helped start Newsweek Magazine nine years earlier, was recruited by Eickstead five years ago. They worked together a lot and knew how each other thought. Eickstead wasn't afraid to get in one's face, and he didn't always wait until someone asked his opinion. His 6'3 frame only added to the intimidation factor that people felt when they were up against him. One always knew where they stood with Jon Eickstead.

Flatley, three inches shorter than Eick, usually had a smile on his face when meeting people. He brought a nice balance to his boss with a healthy dose of diplomacy. They made an excellent team. But Flatley, for all his tact, was by no means a pushover. He got what he wanted. He just took a different path to get there.

"They don't know anything about what he's up to," said Flatley.

"Yeah. You can't fake that sort of surprise," agreed Eickstead. "How do you want to play this?" asked Bill.

"Let's give them a few minutes. We have backup in the alley behind their house in case he decides to leave. I want to see if anyone else comes to the house, now that our boy is in there."

In the two hours that they were waiting, Eickstead got to a payphone on the corner and called Bouquet with the update.

Bouquet, clearly relieved that his friend had the situation under control, asked Eick when he was going to move in.

"Probably in the next ten minutes or so," said Eickstead. "No one has come to the home since the kid got here. And judging by his parents' reaction, they had no idea that he was coming. So, we'll go in and take him down to our office and book him."

"Eick, get as much information out of him as you can. We need to put the pieces together. Also, have your other guys picked up"-

"Hermann Neubauer?" replied Eickstead.

He could visually picture the eye roll that was coming from the other end of the phone.

"No. At least I haven't heard from them yet."

"All right. Give me a call when you hear something."

"Will do, Dave."

He clicked off, turned around and went into a coffee shop and grabbed a couple of cups, walked back to the car, and handed Flatley one of them.

"So, what did Bouquet say?" asked Flatley.

"Just wanted an update. Told him we would be moving in shortly."

Flatley merely nodded and kept watching the house.

"Let's finish these and then get the guys in the back ready," said Eickstead.

"Roger that," replied Flatley.

# CHAPTER 37

The Sweeneys and the Conways made it back to the house, where chores were divvied up. Leigh had volunteered to dust and sweep the floors, while Kathryn and Evvie took the sheets and did laundry. Maggie took a break while Betty, who had been there all morning, said goodbye and headed home. The Sweeneys did a fair amount of entertaining, even though they were homebodies at heart. Michael knew and had met a lot of people over the years, and entertaining guests was just something that came with the job. He and Edwin decided to go into his study for another discussion about the war. Michael wanted to learn more about Edwin's work on the jet engine, among other things. Michael offered him another tobacco patch for his pipe, and soon, the two men were engaged in a deep discussion about the world's events.

Frank, meanwhile, was looking for something to keep him occupied, so he decided to follow Leigh into the kitchen and pretend to help with the dusting and cleaning.

Leigh could see that it was a half-hearted effort at best.

"Well, I can see that someone hasn't had to do much of this before."

"What?" Frank asked. "Do you have a problem with my dusting style?"

"You call that dusting?" said Leigh. "Frank, you actually have to make sure that the rag makes contact with the surface that you are allegedly dusting."

"What are you talking about?" said Frank. "I'm an excellent duster."

"Is that a word?" asked Leigh.

"How should I know? You're the teacher, not me."

That brought a smile to her lips.

"You know, Mister, you have a lot to learn."

"Oh yeah?"

"Yes. Ladies, don't say, "Yeah.""

"Oh yeah?" repeated Frank.

"Yes."

"Really?"

"Yes," she nodded firmly.

"Well, whaddaya know," said Frank.

"Whaddaya? Whaddaya?" repeated Leigh.

"Yeah. Whaddaya know?" he said again. "Ugh!" Shrieked Leigh. "You are hopeless!" "Oh yeah?" he said.

"Yeah!" said she. Then she stopped and threw her hand to her mouth with eyes wide open.

"Gotcha!" shouted Frank, right before he had a rag hit him in his face.

# CHAPTER 38

Their train had arrived into St. Paul almost a half hour early. They had separate first class berths and each of the men got sufficient sleep once the train left Indianapolis.

Despite the speed at which they would have to act, Kerling opted to not be seen with Thiel, at least for the time being. If all went well, they would need to be out of the city and on their way to New York in a day or two anyway. Besides, Kappe had taught them that people would remember more details about two people working in tandem than they would one individual.

Leiner had reserved two rooms for them at the Commodore Hotel. The names that were used matched the false names on their passports: Edward Kelly and Walter Thompson.

They took the short cab rides to the hotel, walked into the lobby separately, and checked in. They ended up being on the same floor, a few rooms apart.

Kerling had formed a couple of ideas on the train ride up to St. Paul, and he would share them with Thiel as soon as they each got settled into their rooms.

Leiner had set him up in a two-room suite in the hotel. He was on the fourth floor, with a set of windows facing the St. Paul Cathedral.

As he looked out at the massive structure, Kerling felt nothing. Not a religious man by any stretch, he merely said, "Now there's some irony."

As he was unpacking in the bedroom of the suite, he thought he heard a noise by the door in the other room.

As he entered the main room, his eyes went to the door and then what was on the floor in front of the door: an envelope.

He opened the door and looked down both sides of the hallway. He saw no one.

He picked up the envelope and sat down at the desk in the room to look at its contents. In the envelope were pictures of their Target, a physical description, the address of where he was staying, and a picture of his daughter. Kerling, a lady's man if there ever was one, was struck by the beauty of the Target's daughter.

"Focus on the mission," he reminded himself.

There was also a relatively brief, handwritten summary of who Edwin Conway was and what needed to be done. No reason for killing him was stated, but Kappe had already made that part clear. At the end of the summary, there was an order to immediately destroy the summary itself and any other information that was not critical to the mission. Last, he was told to rely on his handkerchief for key contact information. The invisible ink on the handkerchief could be activated through heat. He took the iron that room service had delivered to him, waited for it to warm up, and then gently ironed the handkerchief, being careful not to let the iron itself stay on the fabric. Three quick but firm runs over the handkerchief revealed the two names and phone numbers. Leiner. That was no surprise. The second name was one that he didn't recognize. This person had an "NJ" after the phone number. "New Jersey," he said to himself.

He had decided to try to accommodate his superiors' wishes by making the first attempt look like an accident. If the effort failed, then he would forego any further efforts to have it appear to be accidental. Frankly, he'd prefer the "accident route," but time was not on his side. Expectations were high back in the

Fatherland about destroying and crippling the U.S. war machine. Also, once Conway left St. Paul, he no doubt would be untouchable, probably locked away at some military base, surrounded by security seven days a week. So, there was pressure to move quickly.

The likelihood of the first effort being successful was reasonable. No one here suspected anything, so there would be no guards assigned to Conway. They would certainly have the element of surprise. The only reason the odds weren't higher was because he would employ Thiel to execute it.

If needed, he estimated that the odds of the second attempt were close to 100% because it would be Kerling himself who would be doing the work. But it would leave no doubt that Edwin Conway's demise was intentional.

Not knowing how long Conway would be in St. Paul, Kerling decided that they would, unfortunately, have to begin immediately.

# CHAPTER 39

Herbert Haupt had only been home a couple of hours, but he felt the old Herbert coming back. He found himself bragging to his parents about what he was really doing back in America and how he had been handpicked for a specific mission.

He gave his father close to half of the money that he had with him and told him to put it in a safe place. His mother's eyes grew big when she saw how much it was. And his father shook his hand even more vigorously this time around.

He told them to not say anything to anyone about him being home. He then inquired about Gerda. No one had been in touch with her for a few months. Haupt decided that he would pay her a visit.

He had put his luggage away in his room and was coming down the steps to tell his parents that he was going to go over and surprise Gerda when there was a knock on the door.

He was not going to answer any doors, but he found himself standing in the entryway.

He decided to open the door.

"Hermann Haupt?" asked the tall man standing in the doorway.

"He's not here. He hasn't been here for a couple of years," answered Hermann Haupt.

"Really?" said the man. "I didn't know that he had an identical twin."

Haupt stood there, not moving, unsure of what to say. He decided to slam the door in the man's face and run to the back of the house, which had a door that led to a small backyard with an alley behind it.

He heard the front door crash open and a voice yelling, "F.B.I.!" "F.B.I.!"

Eickstead was in the house and running toward the back. A man stepped out of one of the hallways. Eickstead didn't even break his stride as he reached out with his left hand and pushed the guy into a wall. The man hit his head on a picture frame made of glass. Stunned for a second, he gathered himself and moved forward again.

Flatley was right behind Eickstead and caught the man off of the bounce of the wall. He looked at him for a second and sent him back into the wall, where the man banged his head a second time. This time, he slowly slid to the floor and sat, laid out and seeing double. A woman screamed from somewhere. Eickstead still moving forward. Flatley saw a woman rushing past him toward the man who was passed out. Flatley looked at her for a second, seeing if she had any weapons on her. He stops and draws his gun, looking back and forth toward Eickstead and the woman with the crumpled man on the ground.

Haupt made it to the backdoor, where he was met by another F.B.I. agent who also screamed, "F.B.I.!" He stopped dead in his tracks. Then Eickstead, barreling out of the back door, pushed Haupt down the steps, ending in a face plant right into the cement.

"Oops," said Eickstead.

The ride to the Bureau's Chicago office was quiet. Haupt didn't say a word. Wouldn't answer any questions. Wouldn't even acknowledge a question. Eickstead had him locked up and called Bouquet in D.C.

"Nice work, Eick," said Bouquet.

"Dave, I gotta tell you, it never gets old," replied Eickstead.

Just then, D.M. Ladd walked in with George Parker. Bouquet announced them, and Eickstead said hello to both.

"Very good work, Eick," said Ladd.

"Thank you, sir. Several of my men are still at Haupt's house. We've taken his parents into custody and are searching every square inch of the home now."

"Haupt isn't cooperating?"

"Not a word, Sir. And I mean that literally. "Not." "One." "Word."

Parker nudged Ladd and said, "I've got an idea. Do you have a plane in Chicago?"

"Of course," answered Ladd. "What are you thinking?"

"Let me make a couple of phone calls. But I'd get that plane ready if I were you."

"OK. Let's get back together in 30 minutes."

To Eickstead: "Keep him in solitary for now. We'll call you back in an hour. In the meantime, warm up the plane."

# CHAPTER 40

The Commodore Hotel, located on Western Avenue in St. Paul, was one of the premier residential hotels in the Twin Cities. It had a wonderful red brick structure with even more red brick and unmatched art deco on the inside. It was home to celebrities like Sinclair Lewis and F. Scott Fitzgerald during the roaring 20's. Dillinger and Capone were also known to frequent the Commodore. It was high end and high class.

Kerling and Thiel met secretly in Kerling's two-room suite on the fourth floor. Kerling had ordered enough food for two but made sure that Thiel was in the other room when the food arrived.

As they sat there eating, Kerling began to outline his plan for Thiel to take out Edwin Conway. He showed Thiel pictures of Sweeney's home and showed him on a map how to walk from the hotel. Kerling estimated that it was only about a ten-minute walk from the Commodore. He then showed Thiel several pictures of Edwin Conway and his daughter. Thiel, less tactful than his leader, whistled when he saw the picture of Leigh.

"We're here to do a job, Thiel. Get your mind focused on only that," barked Kerling.

Thiel said nothing. He was getting tired of taking orders from someone that he considered his equal. He was getting tired, period. Kerling might be older and more experienced than he was, but he didn't think that Kerling would be able to teach him much. Plus, the amount of sleep that he had gotten since arriving in the U.S. was by no means excessive. He needed some uninterrupted rest.

Kerling continued to outline the plan. It had a lot of gaps, but he defended it to Thiel by reminding him that their superiors preferred making it look like an accident.

"That preference automatically limits our options," observed Thiel.

"You'll get no argument from me about that," admitted Kerling. "But orders are orders, and we as soldiers are to follow those orders."

They thought for a while in silence.

Then Thiel said, "I think your idea is the best one. I will begin tomorrow morning."

Kerling nodded a bit regretfully and said, "We don't have much of a choice here. As soon as Conway heads to Washington, D.C., he'll be untouchable. We either get this done here and now or it won't get done at all. I'd much rather take our time and plan this out thoroughly. But again, we have no time." He paused, then continued:

"Whatever this man Conway knows, it must be important. You think about the assignment that we had in coming here. It's hard to imagine anything bigger or more important to the Fatherland. Yet here we are with this last-minute, major change that is obviously more urgent than what we were sent here to do."

He stared at Thiel for a moment and said quietly, "We must not fail."

Thiel nodded.

Kerling again: "Remember, once you complete the assignment, don't allow yourself to be followed. Report back here right away. Have your bags packed before you leave on the assignment. We'll immediately get on the next train back to Cincinnati."

Another nod from Thiel.

"One more thing," said Kerling. "If you can get this done, I will recommend you for a double jump in rank." That got an eyebrow raise from Thiel.

"Thank you," he said. "I could use the money."

"Your success will also introduce you to a whole different layer of the military and the leadership," Kerling stated. "Your name will be circulated amongst the senior staff. Remember, this must be an extremely important mission. It is coming from the very top of the Abwehr."

# CHAPTER 41

Michael Sweeney sat at his desk in his home office. He had two phones on the desk. One was the family phone, and the other was only for Sweeney Detective.

His business number rang. He picked it up and gave his usual greeting: "Michael Sweeney."

"Hey partner," said the voice on the other end of the phone. "Got a problem and I need your advice on a couple of things."

"I'm all ears."

"Do you know much about the German P.O.W. camp down near New Ulm and Sleepy Eye?" asked Parker.

"Not a lot. I want to say that it's made up mostly of several German air officers and enlisted personnel and that it is located in a converted state park down there somewhere."

Parker said, "That's my understanding as well. Pretty lax security, but most of the Germans there are thankful to be out of the war."

"What's up, Georgie?"

"This is off the record, Mike."

"Of course. If you're uncomfortable telling me anything, then don't feel like you need to tell me."

"Look, Wild Bill is out of the country, and I need someone to bounce some ideas off of."

"Why do I get the feeling that this is going to be something that I really don't want to know about?" asked Sweeney.

"Oh believe me, you're really going to not like what I have to say."

Michael let out a long sigh. "OK, then, let's get on with it."

George, trying to keep it concise, started with, "Within the past several nights two German u boats have landed off of the eastern coast of the U.S."

"What?" Michael thundered. "How?" "Are you sure?"

"Yeah, I'm getting all of this from a buddy of mine at the Bureau. Turns out Hoover is out of the country as well, so I'm making my own decisions on this and so is he. He's a Minnesota guy, by the way. D.M. Ladd. Everyone calls him "Mickey.""

"I don't think I know him," said Michael.

"Anyway, this information is coming directly from him. Turns out there were four saboteurs on each sub. One landed somewhere off Long Island, and the other one landed about twenty miles south of Jacksonville, Florida. These guys were sent into the U.S. to blow up bridges, power plants, munition factories, Navy shipyards, poison the water supply, you name it."

Michael's mind raced as he listened. "Wouldn't be that hard to do, George. Believe me, I know. I've done some audits for the government the last year or so, and my report was quite blunt about our vulnerabilities."

"Yeah, you would know," replied Parker. "Anyway, one of the Germans decided to turn himself in. Demanded to see Hoover himself. Apparently, the Bureau thought he was just another nut, but my buddy Mickey decided to meet with him and get his own take on the situation. Turns out this guy was the real deal. The other three in this guy's crew are in New York and will get picked up shortly. They are already under surveillance. The other four who landed in Florida are a little more difficult."

Michael reached for a pen and began to jot some notes on a piece of Sweeney Detective Bureau stationery.

Parker continued: "Two of them just left Cincinnati and took a bus to Indianapolis, and from there, they were going to hop on a train for some other destination. We don't have any idea where they are now. The witness said he heard "up north." The other two went to Chicago, and one of those guys was just picked up this morning. They are trying to find the other guy."

"OK," said Michael. "Sounds like things are going smoothly so far."

"Not bad," said Parker. "But we need to get this guy in Chicago to talk, and so far, he won't say a word. As in literally, not one word."

"So, what are you thinking?" asked Michael.

"I'm thinking we fly him up to Minnesota today and put him in the P.O.W. camp. These are work camps, and these guys work on area farms to help get the crop in, maintain all of the equipment, that sort of thing."

"And then you plant someone in there with him to get him to talk."

"Exactly."

They both paused for a second, then both said in unison, "Hans."

"I've got his number here," said Michael.

"That's all right. I already have it."

"You're going to have to move fast. There's no telling what these guys are capable of and what sort of timeline that they are working on," observed Michael.

"My thoughts exactly," replied George.

"If you can get Hans here on a plane, I will pick him up and make sure that he gets down to New Ulm or wherever he has to be by tonight."

"Perfect," said George. "An old teammate of mine lives in Sleepy Eye, which is one of the towns that the P.O.W.s are sent off to. His farm might be one of the farms that are being worked by the P.O.W.s. I'm going to call him and get him to go along with all of this."

"Under the circumstances, this is a pretty decent plan, George," said Michael.

"I assume that you're OK with letting Frank in on this?"

"Of course. He is one of our agents, after all. But please tell him to keep it quiet."

"Will do. Have someone let me know right away about when Hans will land. Man, this is big. We need to stop this thing before it starts. Keep in touch, Georgie. And good luck!"

With that, the two men hung up, and each started to plan.

# CHAPTER 42

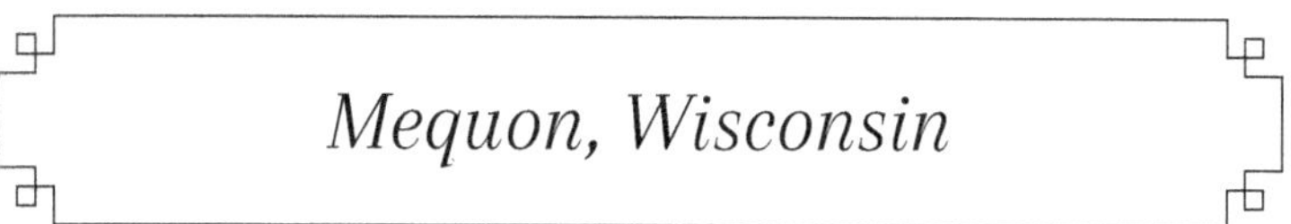

## Mequon, Wisconsin

Hans Ungrodt was having a wonderful holiday - that's what the Europeans called vacation - in Mequon, a suburb of Milwaukee. He was staying with some relatives, and his fiancé, Esther Stoffel, was with her parents and relatives from her side of the family. Hans and Esther became an item in Augsburg, Germany. Peter and Winnie, Esther's parents, were two of the leaders in the underground movement that hid and relocated Jewish people out of Germany to freedom.

Hans was what was known as a double agent. He appeared to be an Abwehr agent for the Germans, when in fact he worked for the British. He and Frank had crossed paths, having similar assignments in Augsburg.

It was Hans, a former rookie pilot with the German Luftwaffe, who flew Esther, Edwin, and Edwin's son Jimmy Conway out of Germany in the middle of the night. After the mission was completed, the Brits gave Hans a few days to relax and recover in the U.S.

He and Frank had worked so well together that their bosses had agreed to pair them together again should the need arise.

He was not short, but he would never be called tall, either. He had an average build, but wiry enough to be unusually strong for his size. His expressive, dark blue eyes were friendly but observant. They were somewhat hidden by his glasses, which gave him a professorial appearance. All of these features worked in his favor when it came to being a spy. In other words, he was a difficult man for anyone to describe.

Esther, an attractive brunette with a heart of gold, was three inches shorter than Hans but matched his extroverted personality. She was sitting across from him at the kitchen table, chewing on a pencil. They were in her aunt's home, planning their wedding.

The phone rang, and Esther got up to answer it. Hans was in the middle of looking at a short list of his relatives and adding up the numbers to determine how many guests would be at their wedding. He wasn't really paying attention to the conversation, but that changed when Esther said, "Hans, it's Mr. Parker."

That got him to sit up in a hurry. He looked at Esther, who shrugged and held out the phone for him.

"Hello, Mr. Parker."

Esther couldn't hear what Parker was saying, so she focused just on what Hans was saying back to him.

"Uh huh. I see. Where? When? Today? What time would - Now? Right now? Uh huh. Yes Sir. And my people know about - you will? All right. How long do you think - Uh huh. No, I understand. All right. Who will pick me - Well, at least I can say hello to them. OK then. Yes Sir. Thank you. I will greet them for you. Yes Sir. Goodbye."

"What was all that about?" asked Esther.

"They need me to do some work for them."

"Where?"

"In Minnesota of all places."

Esther looked at him. "Is it dangerous?"

"No, no, nothing like that. We're in America now, Esther. Not Germany."

He went over and hugged her. They held each other for a minute, and neither one said anything.

"How long will you"-

"I'm not sure. Probably a few days."

"OK."

With that, a car pulled into the driveway.

"Boy, he wasn't kidding," thought Hans.

# CHAPTER 43

George Parker called his old college teammate, Tarry "Belts" Boelter. Boelter was a shortstop at the University of Minnesota, and Parker was a catcher. Belts had spent many a night at the Parkers' home and appreciated all of the meals that Mrs. Parker had made for him and his Gophers teammates during their college playing days. After playing together for a couple of years in Class A ball for the Washington Senators' franchise, both young men decided to hang up their cleats and move on to professional life.

Tarry Boelter wasn't your typical German farmer. He actually taught at the local high school and coached the baseball team there as well. He'd come and help farm when he could, often getting up at 4:00 AM to complete as many chores as possible before heading off to school. Thankfully, he had the summers off so he could devote himself full-time to helping his dad on the farm.

After a few minutes of catching up, George got down to business with his old friend.

"Belts, aren't you involved in that P.O.W. camp down there?"

"Well, I guess, sure. You know my dad hasn't been feeling that well, so I've had to take over a lot of the work around the farm. And with all of the younger guys off fighting the war, the P.O.W.s really come in handy for us. For the most part, they work hard and don't cause any trouble. It also helps that so many people down here speak German."

"Good. Good! I need a favor."

"Sure, Georgie. Anything. What do you need?"

Without going into any details, George spoke in broad terms about what they needed to accomplish. Boelter, a true friend, could see that his buddy wasn't offering a lot of information, so he chose not to ask a lot of questions.

Within a few minutes, they had everything worked out.

# CHAPTER 44



*7:00 AM The Next Day
New Ulm, Minnesota*

Cottonwood River State Park was located in New Ulm, Minnesota. The park itself came to be because of the Works Project Administration. The W.P.A. was the brainchild of the Roosevelt administration, which desperately needed to do something during the peak years of the Great Depression. The W.P.A. partnered with state and local governments to create federally funded jobs around the country for public projects that helped build or rebuild the country's infrastructure.

Typically, the state or local authorities would provide the land, and the federal government would pay the salary of the workers. The result would be a new prison, a new school, new roads, or, in this case, a new park. Cottonwood River State Park boasted beautiful scenery and a wide variety of animals: white-tail deer, fox, coyotes, possums, raccoons, and even some minks.

Among other things, the W.P.A. workers constructed bunkhouses and a dining hall on the park grounds. They also worked on building a dam since the areas around the park tended to flood quite often.

New Ulm, located about 100 miles southwest of St. Paul, boasted a strong German population. Many of the churches would hold their services in German, and the German language was often the primary language spoken in homes. Many of the locals were second and third-generation Americans, having immigrated as early as the 1860s. Known primarily for agriculture, the city's most famous resident was the August Schell Brewing Company, a family-owned brewery that started in the 1800's.

But now New Ulm found itself with other famous inhabitants: German prisoners of war. They were housed within the aforementioned State Park in those same bunkhouses that were built by the W.P.A. workers a few years earlier.

There were nine other similar P.O.W. camps in Minnesota, and the number was growing. Most of the 160 prisoners at Cottonwood were from the German Luftwaffe, the Fatherland's Air Force. The majority of the inhabitants were bussed each day to Sleepy Eye, a town about 15 miles west of New Ulm. There, they worked at a large cannery. The other prisoners would be shipped off to work at local farms each day.

The working conditions were quite reasonable, and since most of the locals spoke German, the transition was relatively easy for the P.O.W.s.

Herbert Haupt, having just arrived at the camp the evening before, was shuffled off to a local farm that was owned by the Tarry Boelter family. Haupt would work there with three other prisoners.

Their assignment for the day was to clean all of the farm equipment that had been used during the harvest. This included changing the oil on each piece of machinery and getting all of the weeds and dirt out from in and around the engine block. They would also check the tires for air pressure and clean the barns where the machines would be stored. Without the four men helping, this would take Mr. Boelter at least a week to complete all of these tasks.

Haupt and the German fellow that he was assigned to at the farm began to talk in hushed tones in German, comparing notes as to how they ended up on the sidelines in the country that they had sworn to fight against on behalf of the Fatherland.

Haupt had confided to the other German how they had landed near Jacksonville a few nights earlier, two nights after a different submarine had landed in New York with another four-man crew.

"How'd you get caught?" asked his new German friend.

"I have no idea!" Haupt replied. "These F.B.I. guys just showed up at my parents' house in Chicago. I told them that I had nothing to say and that I wouldn't cooperate, that they were wasting their time with me. So, then they arrested me. Brought me to their office for more questions. I told them nothing. Next thing I know, I'm on a small plane to Minnesota. I land in St. Paul and am immediately brought down here."

"That's great that you gave them no information. That took some courage. You must be very good at what you do!" said the other man.

"At least there are a lot of German speaking citizens here, although I don't know how long I will be here for," said Haupt. "Why is that?" asked the other man.

"Because the charges are espionage and sabotage and something about harming America in a time of war."

"I'm in for the same thing, except I'm from Wisconsin," said the other man.

"We were working on subversive activities by using the local newspapers. There are quite a few Germans in Wisconsin, too," he said, leaning on the John Deere tractor.

They were both silent for a minute, then the other man spoke again.

"It's odd how you got caught. Someone must have slipped, or maybe some sort of communication was intercepted."

"We were pretty careful," said Haupt. "We were supposed to rendezvous in New York later this week. Maybe someone in New York slipped up."

"How many of you were in on this?"

"Eight in total, but a couple of the men from my group had their orders changed as soon as we made it to Cincinnati."

"Must be pretty important if they got their orders changed."

"Yes, definitely," replied Haupt. He looked around again to make sure that no one else could hear them speaking.

The other German kept putting a rag on the dirty engine cover on the tractor.

Haupt, lowering his voice even more, said, "We were sent here to blow up factories that produced weapons, vehicles, and ammunition for the war. We also had targets that included railroads, bridges, and even ships in the New York Harbor."

The other man stopped and looked at him. "That sounds a lot more exciting than writing propaganda in Milwaukee."

Haupt nodded, feeling a bit boastful.

"We were all handpicked, you know. And the training was intense. I could probably figure out a way to escape out of here. As a matter of fact,

I should do that. But not right away. I need to read about the security measures that they have here first. If you're interested, I'll take you with me when I break out of here." "You would do that?" asked the other man.

"Of course!" said Haupt. He looked around again before speaking.

"Our mission was to do anything we could to disrupt America's efforts to supply ammunition and weapons to the Allies. We were also to identify Jewish-owned businesses and bomb them as well. Most of this was to be focused on the eastern part of the country."

The other man, now moving toward the back of the tractor, nodded as if it all made perfect sense.

Haupt, almost absentmindedly, said, "You know, if I had figured out a way to escape from the airport in St. Paul, I could've helped the other two guys complete their mission."

The other man, still working on the tractor, asked, "St. Paul? What could be so important in St. Paul? Maybe blow up the Ford factory there? I heard they're producing jeeps and other army vehicles. That might justify a change in the mission."

Haupt, now feeling like the teacher and the other guy, the student, said, "Not "what." "But "who." "Who could be so important that the highest level of our military intelligence would change the mission at the last minute?"

The other man started rubbing slower and said nothing for a moment.

Then: "They didn't tell you who the target is? Is Roosevelt passing through the cities or something?"

Haupt laughed. "That's exactly what Thiel guessed. Roosevelt."

"Who's Thiel?"

He's one of the men sent to St. Paul. He's the junior man. Kerling is our leader. Smart, experienced soldier. I'll bet that he'll be moving up in the ranks if he can get this assignment completed."

"Kerling," said the other man. "Where have I heard that name? Is his first name Paul?"

"No, no," replied Haupt. "It's Edward. Not that his name matters. He's traveling under an alias. Edward Kelley." Now the real Haupt came out, the braggart and brash kid, really.

"We all have a few passports with different names and plenty of money to use when we need to. We get first-class berths on the trains and are staying in the best hotels, too. It's a great assignment from that perspective. Anyway, Kerling - I guess I should call him by his alias of "Kelley"- that's all of the training, you know. They teach you all of this when you're hand-picked to spy for the Fatherland. "Kelley" is a good-looking fellow, around 30 or so. He really knows what he's doing. He can blow up a building and wear different disguises, and his English is perfect, but his specialty is his marksmanship. He's a sniper and can easily take out a target that's a kilometer away."

"Well," said the other man, "I guess we'll know soon enough if his mission was completed or not. It must be a very important person that he will be trying to eliminate."

"Definitely," said Haupt. "All I know is that the target is a man who just got to America in the last few days. He had escaped from Germany with the help of a couple of spies. He is one of the most learned men when it comes to something to do with airplanes. He was working on some secret project in the Fatherland, and the orders were to kill him before he could give all this knowledge to the Americans. That's why this mission is so time sensitive."

Haupt didn't see the other man drop his towels. He didn't see the man's mouth drop open, either.

"Kelley" is really the perfect choice for the job," continued Haupt matter-of-factly. "His shooting when we were training was by far the best of anyone we had in the whole camp."

"I need some water," said Hans Ungrodt, as casually as he could. "I'll be right back."

"Bring me back some, would you?" asked Haupt.

"Sure," Hans said, not even bothering to turn around.

Tarry Boelter was spreading some feed for his chickens when one of the German workers approached him, calling to him while he was still a short distance away.

"Sir? Mr. Boelter?"

"Yes, young man. What can I do for you?"

"I need to use your phone. Right now."

Boelter stepped back, looked at the young man, and said, "I'm sorry, son. You should know the rules. The P.O.W.s are never allowed to use the phone or leave the farm."

"Yes, I am aware of all of that," replied Hans.

The Americans had purposely put Haupt and him on Boelter's farm. Tarry Boelter might be of German descent, but he was, first and foremost, an American patriot.

"Look, Mr. Boelter, I need to confide something to you. Normally I wouldn't share this with you. I am not even cleared to tell you this, but time is of the essence."

Hans casually glanced around before he continued.

"You need to understand that I am not a German P.O.W. I technically work for the British as a spy, but I am on loan to the

Americans and have a very important assignment. This is a matter of national security. I need to go into your house and use your phone. Now. You can even dial the number for me if you want, but I need to do this quickly. A man's life is at stake. Maybe even a whole family's. This might affect the outcome of the entire war. So, walk me into your house and make the call."

Boelter looked at him, expressionless. Processing.

Then: "I don't suppose you have any proof of this?"

"No, I don't. Most of these prisoners have no qualms about going through other men's things to see if there is something to steal or borrow. The risk is too great for me to carry anything that would identify me as anything but a German P.O.W."

Boelter looked at his shorter guest. The shorter man had glasses with dark blue eyes and a wiry frame. He was all business, and he appeared to be quite earnest in what he was saying.

"You sure don't look like a spy. But I guess that's the plan anyway, eh?"

Hans merely nodded.

"What's your name, son?" asked Boelter.

"Hans Ungrodt."

Who placed you down here on my farm?"

"A man named George Parker. I can't tell you anything else," said Hans.

"You don't need to, Hans. I just needed to make sure that you were the one George told me about. It all matches up with what George briefed me on."

"Good. Thank you," said Hans.

He looked up at the sky as he quietly told Boelter, "Look natural as we make our way toward your home. Make sure that your wife and children are not around when we make the call."

They began to make their way to the house and Hans, still not looking at Boelter, said, "Oh, and by the way, you cannot speak to anyone about this. No one, including your wife and children."

Boelter, a man of his word, looked back at him for a moment and then said, "Don't worry. George didn't tell me all of it, but I had a general idea what this was all about."

The two men walked to the back door of Boelter's two story home and entered the kitchen. The phone was on the wall and was the old-fashioned kind, with the cone shaped receiver. Hans gave Boelter the number to dial.

# *St. Paul*

Hans didn't even consider calling Parker first. He had to warn Edwin Conway. He called the Sweeneys' home and spoke to a woman named Betty. She said that the Conways had left a few minutes earlier and were on their way to shop downtown for a while and were then headed to Michael Sweeney's office.

"Is Frank there? Or is he with the Conways?" Hans was trying not to sound too excited, but it was difficult, even for a seasoned spy like him.

"No Sir, Frank left with them. He said that he wasn't going to allow them to try to get around the city without him."

"I see," said Hans.

"Can I take a message for them?" asked Betty.

"No, thank you. Can you give me Michael's phone number at work?"

"Certainly. His direct number is Capitol 4-8313."

There was a pause. Then Hans asked, "What does capitol 4 mean?"

"It's just easier to remember. The full phone number is 224-8313."

"Thank you," said Hans.

"Forgive me, Sir, but you don't sound like you are from here. Can I get your name?"

"I'm just a family friend. Thank you again." With that, Hans hung up the phone.

He immediately got an operator back on the phone and asked to be connected to the phone number that Betty had given him.

It took a few seconds, but Michael Sweeney answered on the first ring. "Michael, it's Hans."

"Hans? That was quick. Have you learned some"-

"They're after Dr. Conway! Conway is their target! Where is he?"

Michael looked at his watch. "They are either on a streetcar or are waiting for one. They should be downtown in approximately a half hour."

"OK," said Hans. "Please call Parker and let him know. Do you have a pen?"

"Yes," said Michael.

Hans could hear paper rustling.

"Go ahead."

"There are two men that are in St. Paul. I'm not sure where they are staying or how long they have been in town, but they probably just got in within the last day or two. This Haupt guy indicated that they have quite a bit of money and always stay at very nice hotels. I don't know if that will help you or not. Their names are Thiel and Kerling. Edward Kerling. Thiel is younger, and Kerling is around 30 and experienced. He's traveling under an alias. The name he is using is Edward Kelley. He's a sniper, among other talents. They were pulled off of their original mission at the last minute to get to St. Paul to eliminate Dr. Conway. Please call Parker and relay all of this to him. I am going to go back and try to get more information out of this guy. Can you send a car down here to come and get me? I need to get back to St. Paul so I can help with this."

"I will send a car for you immediately," said Michael. "I'll call George and brief him on what you've discovered."

Hans, in a quiet voice: "Michael, Leigh, and Frank are with Dr. Conway."

"I am aware of that, Hans."

Michael looked at his watch and said, "Maybe they haven't left the house"-

Hans interrupted and said, "They left the house a few minutes ago. I tried calling your home and talked to a woman who told me that they were going to spend the day in the city and then see you in your office."

Michael, now, thinking on the fly: "I will have men stationed at the streetcar a couple of blocks from here where they will probably be getting off. I'll have one of our armored cars there waiting as well. We can get them here very quickly and secure the building from the 15th floor and higher."

Silence. Then Hans said, "It sounds like you have thought of everything that you can possibly do for the moment." More silence as they both continued to think.

Hans finally said, "One more thing: The overall mission is to thwart the war effort on U.S. soil. He talked about blowing up bridges and munitions factories, among other things. But I should get back. I will try to see if I can get any more information out of this man."

"Descriptions would be good," replied Michael. "To be honest, I knew about the eight guys on the subs. George told me yesterday in confidence. But neither of us would have guessed that two of them were headed to St. Paul. The F.B.I. have sketches from Cincinnati that should be sent here, now that we know that they are in St. Paul."

Hans again: "I'll get anything else that I can out of him. I don't really care at this point if he knows who I am."

"I doubt that George or anyone back in Washington will want you to do that. Reveal your identity to him, I mean," replied Michael. "They'll want to keep all of this quiet so that they can try this method again at the P.O.W. camp when the next crisis occurs."

"Yes, Michael," replied Hans. "You are most assuredly right about that. I'll not let him know who I really am."

"I think that's the right call, Hans. I'll see you back here in under four hours."

Michael hung up and started to work the phones.

# CHAPTER 46

Edwin, Leigh, and Frank waited for the streetcar on Selby Avenue. The weather had reverted to classic early November temperatures in Minnesota: 30 degrees Fahrenheit, overcast and windy. As a result, the three were bundled up with hats and winter coats. Michael had insisted that Edwin borrow one of his long trench coats. Edwin obliged. He had also borrowed a winter hat from Michael to keep his head warm and ensure that he wouldn't lose all his body heat so quickly. Likewise, Leigh had borrowed a coat from Evvie, along with a matching scarf and gloves from Kathryn.

They were going downtown to see the sights in the morning and shop for clothes for Leigh. Washington, D.C., was a much milder climate, so Edwin figured that him buying a bunch of warm clothes in Minnesota didn't make a lot of sense. Once their shopping was completed, Frank would take them to see the Sweeney Detective Bureau, culminating in a lunch with Michael.

Selby was the next street north from Hague, where the Sweeneys lived. They had come out of the house, turned left and walked to the corner street, which was Milton. They walked north on Milton to Selby and waited for the streetcar to arrive. The walk took all of five minutes. It being rush hour, the line was going to be long, so they got there in plenty of time. The good news was that, with stops, they would be downtown in around twenty minutes.

"What a difference a day makes in the weather!" exclaimed Leigh.

"Welcome to Minnesota," Frank said, smiling. He then leaned into Leigh and whispered, "Better get used to it," and smiled. The smile on Leigh's face was downright mesmerizing to him.

As they waited on the platform, Frank began to fill in Edwin and Leigh on some of the things that they would see that morning. They heard the streetcar before they saw it. As it approached from the west, they all moved a step closer to where Frank thought that the car would stop. As the car got closer, he could feel the crowd behind them gently nudging them forward.

Frank really wanted the Conways to be able to sit during the ride to downtown. Leigh was standing between her two men, with her dad to her right. She had turned to ask Frank a question and had looked at him. Frank had turned to his left to see the mass of people behind him, pointing to Leigh about how there were way too many people with way too little room.

"Not a problem for us, though. The people behind us will just have to wait a few minutes for the next car to arrive. They run every ten minutes or so from this station."

The streetcar was now just beginning to slow in front of them.

"I saw this in Germany all the time," she said.

She turned and put her arm in her dad's arm and squeezed him to her. She was starting to lean in and tell him how happy she was that they were together. He had leaned to his left to listen to her, a smile on his face, when he suddenly and uncontrollably lurched forward, taking Leigh with him.

# CHAPTER 47

Thiel had made it to Hague Street by 6:45 AM. He was standing across the street, on the corner of Milton and Hague, smoking a cigarette and drinking hot coffee from a paper cup. He had a newspaper folded under one arm and would glance down at it every minute just to look the part of a businessman. He was dressed in an overcoat, had a hat pulled down low, and had dark sunglasses that hid a good portion of his face. The sunglasses allowed him to look almost sideways while appearing to be looking straight ahead, a neat trick that Kappe had taught them all during their training.

At 7:10 AM, he saw three people coming out of the Sweeney residence. He pretended to keep reading the paper, looking up to match the face with the picture that he had in his coat pocket. There was an older man and a young, athletic man sandwiched in the middle by a very attractive young female. They didn't appear to have a care in the world. He could hear laughter and knew that there was a conversation, but he couldn't make out the words. The younger man looked like he would be difficult to handle in a fight.

The older man was a bit shorter than his younger counterpart. For around the 50th time, Thiel looked at the picture just to be sure. There was no doubt that his target matched the picture. They were also coming out of the address that was identified, so that was further confirmation for him. He slowly followed them, stopping occasionally to look in store windows so as not to get too close too quickly.

When the three had made it to the small platform for the streetcar entrance, Thiel waited until there were several people behind them before he got on the platform. As the time drew closer to 7:30 AM, he began to inch his way closer, keeping his head down and his collar turned up. He had gotten rid of the coffee but held onto the newspaper. He would use it to hide his hands when the right moment came.

Thiel found himself surrounded by people who were not paying attention to anything around them. Most of the people were older men who had their faces buried in today's Pioneer Press newspaper. There were a few younger women who were checking themselves out with their compact make up kits.

"Probably married women whose husbands are in the war," thought Thiel.

He began to surreptitiously look around for his escape route. After a couple of minutes, he decided that it would be best for him to leave the exact way that he had come. Albeit his exit would be much faster than his entrance. He continued to inch his way into position. There was a large woman who was standing behind Conway and his daughter. And she was a force to be reckoned with. Thiel had tried to nudge his way in so he would be directly behind Conway, but she wasn't budging. She even looked at him as he tried one final time. Her positioning left a clear shot only for the right side of Conway.

There was still no one paying any attention to him, which would only help. These people were engrossed in a daily habit, and many of them had taken this same streetcar from this same station at this same time, day after day after day.

After a few minutes of staring at the newspaper, he heard the streetcar making its way toward the platform.

"Wait for the crowd to start to move forward. Then give him a solid push, enough to make sure that he goes over," Kerling had told him. "But don't take a running start at him or anything. That'll be too obvious and will get you caught."

He casually took another look around. A few of the women were chatting about their makeup, where their husbands were stationed, or how they were tired of the men at work who continued to flirt with them.

The streetcar was within sight and getting closer. He could see a white, middle-aged man in a uniform who was driving it. He was talking to another man who was standing next to him. The streetcar was now about one hundred feet from him.

"Wait," said Thiel to himself. "Wait." He took a quick look around. Still, no one was paying much attention. The women were starting to put their compacts back in their purses, and the men started to wrap up their papers.

The streetcar kept coming. 80 feet. 60 feet. 40 feet. He could hear the shrieking of the brakes.

At 20 feet he said to himself, "Now!"

He lurched forward, extended both arms, and pushed. He heard an "Ugh!" and turned around, walking briskly away from the platform with his head down, trying to disappear into the crowd that was waiting for the car to stop.

A woman screamed.

"Hey!" yelled a voice.

He broke away from the crowd, still walking at a clipped pace.

Brakes screeching in an ear-piercing way.

"Stop him! Stop that man!"

More screams.

He continued to move forward, not daring to look back.

"Grab him!"

Moving at a good pace, but not running.

"That! There! That! Stop! Him! Him!"

Now he heard a new noise. Movement of feet on wood.

More shouting.

He did what he shouldn't have done. He turned around to look. There was the young Sweeney man, leaping over the platform, landing perfectly and sprinting.

"Stop that guy!"

"Get out of the way! Out of the way! Out of the way!" Thiel took off, running for his life. Literally.

# CHAPTER 48

Leigh had locked her arm into her dad's and leaned in to tell him how happy she was and how thankful she was that they were out of Germany and together.

As he turned to look down at her and smile, he suddenly started to fall forward. Fast. His hat flew off in front of him, landing on the tracks. He was falling toward the oncoming streetcar and was inadvertently dragging his daughter with him.

Leigh's left arm was locked with Frank's, and Frank could feel her arm start to leave his. He instinctively tightened his grip on Leigh. She rocked forward but was able to plant her right foot and began to try to pull her Dad back toward her. She was losing him. Edwin was teetering, with the top half of his body ahead of his lower half.

"Dad!" screamed Leigh.

She yanked on him as hard as she could. At the same time, she could feel herself being yanked by Frank in a poor man's sort of chain.

Women were screaming. Men were starting to react and move toward them.

The brakes from the streetcar were screeching in a high-pitched wail.

Edwin seemed to be hanging in the air, arms flailing as the streetcar barreled toward him. While his feet were not on the tracks, his entire upper body was *over* the tracks.

He felt arms grabbing at him as he continued to teeter. More shouting and screaming.

"Grab him!"

"Help him!"

"Hold on!"

"Pull!"

All of this was done within mere seconds of feeling the push from behind. Time seemed to stop as he hung over the tracks, arms flailing like an acrobat about to fall off a wire.

Then, one final grab that felt like a bear hug, and he was being pulled back away from the tracks. His right hand hit the front of the streetcar as it tried to stop. It was a sharp pain, like someone smacking it with a two-by-four.

More bedlam.

"Is he OK?"

"What happened?"

Frank's training kicked in.

He checked on Edwin. "Are you OK?"

"Yes. My hand hurts a bit, but I am all right."

Leigh, clearly upset, was still shouting, "Dad! Dad! Dad! Are you all right? Are you hurt? What happened?"

"Pushed," was all that he could manage to say.

She put both hands to his face, cupping it for a moment and looking into his eyes.

She saw confusion. And a hint of actual fright, something that she had not seen in her father's eyes before.

Leigh spun around and put her back to him, spreading her arms wide. She looked around, wanting to protect him like a big brother stepping in to take on the bullies who were trying to hit his little brother.

Frank grabbed a man near Edwin. The man, surprised, didn't resist.

"It wasn't me!" he cried.

He looked at the next man and started toward him.

"Son, get a hold of yourself. Most of us take this train every day."

Frank again, still staring at the second man, shouts: "Listen, everyone!

"Did anyone see anything?"

Out of the crowd stepped a heavyset, middle-aged woman who said that she had seen a young man move closer to the platform.

"I thought he was rude, the way he was inching his way forward as the streetcar was getting closer. I can't swear that I saw him push anyone, but I know that he was very close to him and behind that poor man."

Frank's eyes looked out, away from the train. He saw a figure, head down with a long beige trench coat and a gray fedora hat with a black band in it, walking briskly on the other side of the street, away from the platform.

Frank lost him for a second because a truck had driven through the intersection, completely blocking his view.

Once the truck had cleared, the woman who had spoken up followed Frank's eyes and rested them for a second on the figure who was moving so quickly.

"That's him! That's the man! Hey! Stop! Stop him!"

Frank looked at Leigh, who was tending to her dad. She glanced back at Frank. There was a fierceness in her eyes as she looked at him, nodded, and said, "Go."

Frank began pushing through the crowd like a fullback taking on an entire defensive line on his own. He finally got through and around everyone and jumped the railing. He could hear more shouts behind him.

As he landed on the ground and started running, the lone figure turned around. His eyes met Frank's for a split second, and he began to run. He had a one-block head start.

"Don't lose him, don't lose him," Frank was saying to himself.

Totally focused on chasing the man now.

Heard a car honk and brakes screeching. Still not taking his eyes off him.

He had run right out into traffic on Selby Avenue. A car stopped three feet in front of him. From the other side of the street, another car swerved onto the sidewalk to avoid him, hitting a newsstand.

Newspapers flying in the air, along with some apples and oranges. More yells of shock and disbelief.

Some cussing from around him.

Another truck was coming up Milton onto Selby, trying to make a left-hand turn, followed by another truck.

Frank stopped in the intersection, not seeing the bad guy because of the trucks.

The second truck rear-ends the first one.

More chaos.

More yelling.

More cussing.

Horns blazing.

"Keep moving!" he yells to himself.

"Out of the way, out of the way!" he screams.

The first truck is stopped as he runs in front of it. He reaches the sidewalk and looks to his right.

The guy who had tried to kill Dr. Conway was not in sight.

Running down Milton now at full sprint, passing an alley on his left.

Quick glance down the alley.

Nothing.

Sprinting again.

Continuing down Milton until he is back on Hague Avenue. When he gets to Hague he stops and looks east toward his home.

Nothing.

He looks west on Hague.

Nothing.

He's lost him.

# CHAPTER 49

Hermann Neubauer was bored. He had been biding his time in Chicago while waiting to get to New York. He spent hours during the day checking out new movies. Over the course of the last couple of days, he had seen "The Pride of The Yankees," "The Man Who Came To Dinner," "The Magnificent Ambersons," "Casablanca," and "Saboteur." He enjoyed "Saboteur" so much that he saw it twice. The movie resonated with him. A Hitchcock thriller, it starred Bob Cummings as a munitions factory worker who is wrongly accused of sabotage. He stumbles upon a Nazi spy ring that has plans to destroy America. The movie made Neubauer wonder how far such an effort really extended beyond his eight-man effort. The Nazi Party certainly had deep roots around the U.S.

But people at his level weren't privy to what other efforts were taking place in other cities. It was very compartmentalized in that respect.

He had come to the U.S. in 1931 and made his living as a chef in Chicago. He had worked in the main restaurant at the elite Palmer House Hotel as well as the Bismarck Hotel on Randolph Avenue. Tall and lanky, Neubauer was a serious sort who smiled little and talked even less. The position as a chef was a good fit for his persona: task oriented with little meaningful conversation.

While living in Chicago, he met and married a local woman named Alma Wolfe. They lived there until 1940 when he decided to leave her (permanently, as it turned out) and go back to the Fatherland and fight for his native country. He went to New York and met with the German consulate. He received their almost immediate approval and then waited to get on a passenger ship to make the trek back to Germany.

Neubauer eventually embarked on the SS Exochorda. His friend and cohort Edward Kerling was also a passenger on that ship. They had decided to go back and fight together.

After arriving in Germany, Neubauer was quickly drafted into the Heer or the German Army. He was sent to the Russian Front, where he engaged in active battle. So active, in fact, that he took some shrapnel and had the scars to prove it. One was over his right eye, and the other was on his right leg. He was sent back to Germany to heal and was soon recruited by Kappe to train for Operation Pastorius.

He and Kerling were reunited for this assignment, and each of them had a younger partner. Kerling opted to take Thiel, who was a little more of a handful than was Haupt. While not as quiet as Neubauer, Haupt was adaptable and more compliant than the higher-strung and rebellious Thiel.

Upon arriving in Chicago, he opted for a room at the Sheraton Plaza. Once he was settled in, he decided he couldn't wait and jumped in a cab to make his way to his parents' home to surprise them. He walked down the alley and came in through the back entrance to the house at 933 W. Belmont, right in the city. It was a two-story row house, much like the kind that populated so many neighborhoods in Chicago. After they got over the surprise of seeing him, Neubauer confided to his parents and a couple of other relatives what he was doing, which was something that he would later come to regret.

As a precaution, he refused to stay with any of his family. Instead, he stayed at the Plaza, which was several blocks away. After all, like all the spies on the mission, he had over $4,000 in cash that was stored in a money belt that never left his person.

He was anxious to get to New York and begin the assignment. The train that he had booked was due to leave the following evening at 7:00 PM. With stops, it would take a little over 24 hours before he would arrive in the big city.

It was a very short stay in Chicago. He had said his goodbyes to his parents and a few close relatives. Neubauer didn't bother to look up his ex-wife. It never really occurred to him to do something like that.

He was in Union Station at 6:15 PM. About 100,000 people a day passed through the station, many of them U.S. soldiers and sailors. They were on their way to all different parts of the country, where they would either be in training or shipping out to the Pacific or Europe. Neubauer wanted no part of anyone in the military. Or anyone else, for that matter. He booked a berth in first class and had planned to spend the evening locked in his compartment.

# CHAPTER 50

## *Chicago, Illinois*

F.B.I. Special Agents Timothy "Bo" Kemper and Walter "Wally" Behrens had been parked across the street for quite some time and saw no activity. After a couple of hours, they decided to approach the Neubauer home. Due to limited resources, they had a hard time finding the right Neubauers. There were several Neubauers in the Chicago area, and, by process of elimination, they had finally concluded that they had the right house. Unfortunately for them, it had taken them almost two full days to arrive at said conclusion.

They looked like Mutt and Jeff and were actually known as such by their fellow agents in Chicago. Kemper was almost 6'4 and played tennis at Northwestern. Behrens was a former high school teacher and coach. Both were excellent at their jobs, although their individual styles couldn't be more different. Kemper refused to use his size to intimidate people. He was gregarious and personable. He had an unusually high voice for someone of his size. Behrens was more of your classic, by-the-book agent. They ham and egged it well together.

Neubauer's mother answered the door.

Kemper tipped his cap to her and asked if Hermann was around.

She hesitated and said, "No." Didn't volunteer anything. Just, "No."

Kemper asked if they could come in.

"Who are you?" she asked. Suspicious. Eyes began to dart back and forth between the two agents.

Kemper, still smiling, asked, "When do you think he'll be home? In the next half hour or so?" Now, her husband appears.

"What's all this about?"

Kemper steps past Mrs. Neubauer and into the house, extending his hand to the man. Kemper keeps the smile pasted on his face.

"You must be the man of the house! Very nice to meet you!" Neubauer Sr. hesitated a moment, then shook Kemper's hand.

Agent Behrens had followed Kemper into the home.

Kemper, with a big smile: "Mind if we sit down for a minute?" as he sat down in a chair that was covered by a brown blanket. Behrens sat in the matching chair opposite Kemper, which left only the couch for the Neubauers. "Who are you?" started Neubauer. "We demand"-

"Nothing. You demand nothing," said Behrens.

"Where is your son?"

"Our son?" Mrs. Neubauer now. "How should we…"

Behrens, quiet but menacing: "We know that he was here. We know that he arrived via submarine the other night. He landed off the coast of Ponte Vedra Beach, about twenty minutes south of Jacksonville, Florida. We know that he was traveling with three other men. We know that all four men took a train to Cincinnati and that your son and another man came here."

"Who are you?" repeated the elder Neubauer, still defiant.

They both flashed their badges, and that drew a gasp from Mrs. Neubauer.

"Nice Poker face," said Kemper to Behrens.

The Neubauers looked at each other, confused. Poker?

Behrens leaned forward: "So where is he?"

Kemper now leaned over to the couple in a "confiding" kind of way. "Ah, look, this might be the time for you to really consider your options. You see, aiding and abetting a saboteur is a very serious offense here in America."

Whispering now to them: "Especially" - he looked around and then back at them - "In times of war. I don't want to frighten you or anything, but people are put in the electric chair for this kind of thing. So, you may want to consider talking to my friend here, you know, before he gets angry."

Neubauer Sr. tried his best to look confident.

Just as he was about to say something about knowing his rights, Behrens leaped out of his chair and got in his face.

"Don't! Don't you dare say anything about your rights, Adolph."

Behrens was so close to his face that Neubauer could have easily deciphered what the Bureau man had had for lunch.

"You're going to jail. But only for a few days. Do you know why? Because you are going to get the chair. Your wife here is going to join you. And your son, too, assuming we don't kill him first. Unless you tell us right now where he is."

Neubauer was clearly rattled. Before he could speak, his wife blurted out where their son was. She gave them all of it, right down to the track number.

Kemper went to the door, opened it, and signaled to a couple of agents who were backing them up to come in.

Behrens kept an eye on the couple until the backups were in the room. He gave instructions to arrest the couple and bring them to the local F.B.I. office. He then pulled one of the men aside and told him to call the train station. He insisted that the train for New York be held until they got there. Under no circumstances was that train to leave Chicago.

He left without saying another word.

Kemper started to follow his partner out but stopped for a minute. He looked back at Mrs. Neubauer and said, "You did the right thing."

He looked at the end table that was next to the couch. He had noticed a photograph of a young man when they first came through the door.

"Is this Hermann?" he asked.

Mrs. Neubauer looked away. She slowly looked back at Kemper and gave a slight, resigned nod.

"Fine looking young man," he said as he took the photo out of the frame and slipped it into his coat pocket.

Behrens and Kemper jumped in the car and high-tailed it to Union Station.

# CHAPTER 51

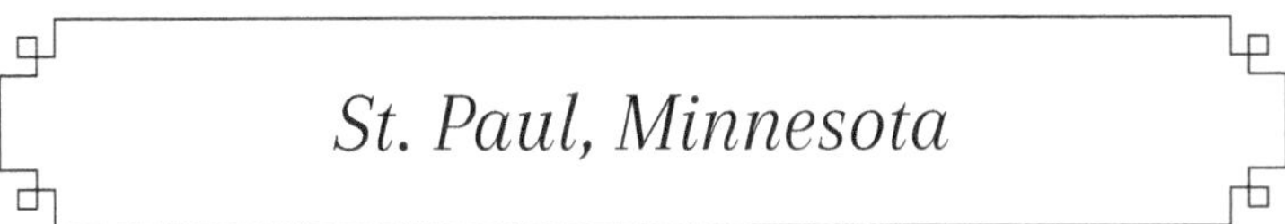

## St. Paul, Minnesota

Kerling played with the dial of the radio in his suite at the Commodore. He had packed his clothes and had his suitcase ready to go. He finally found a local news channel called WCCO, which was 830 on the dial. Cedric Adams, the local radio news host, was interviewing a reporter for the St. Paul Dispatch, the evening edition's newspaper. The reporter's name was Tony Kennedy, and he was filling Adams in on a developing story that began earlier in the day. It was about the attempted murder of a man who was waiting with a younger couple for a streetcar near the Selby and Milton intersection in St. Paul.

"What do we know about who tried to kill this man?" asked Adams, a popular host in the afternoon hours of the day.

Kennedy, a relatively new reporter for the Dispatch, was on his way to a stellar career. He had a nose for news and had a degree in Journalism from Marquette, which meant that he had both the pedigree and a good deal of natural ability.

"We got a general description from the witnesses of a young, well-dressed white male. He evidently had worked his way onto the platform to the point where he was directly behind the older gentleman. As the streetcar approached, he pushed the man, apparently intending the man to end up being struck by the approaching streetcar. He disappeared very quickly back into the crowd. The young man who was with the older gentleman who was pushed, gave chase but lost the suspect."

"Was the intended target hurt?" asked Adams.

"He apparently sustained a minor injury to his hand," replied Kennedy. "We did learn that the young woman who was with him was his daughter. She had an Irish accent."

"Maybe we can get them in here to talk to us," suggested Adams.

"That's the strange part about this story, Cedric," replied Kennedy. "They disappeared with the young man almost as quickly as the suspect."

Kerling listened until the end but didn't learn anything else. The big thing he learned was that Edwin Conway was still alive, and that needed to change.

# CHAPTER 52

They ended up meeting in Michael's office on the 20th floor of the 1st National Bank. Michael had two men posted in the lobby outside of his office. He also had two men on the first floor near the elevators and stairways.

George Parker got the call from Michael in the morning and was on a plane twenty minutes later. Michael, Edwin, Frank and Leigh were holed up in Michael's office. Hans showed up at noon and Parker was sitting with them by 2:00PM.

It was a somber meeting. They had moved into Michael's conference room. The shades had been drawn to prevent anyone from trying to shoot into the room.

Michael and Edwin were puffing on pipes. The others were drinking hot tea or coffee. Susie, Mike's sister who doubled as his secretary, had put out cookies and a plate of cheese and crackers to munch on.

George took the lead and asked them to walk him through what happened that morning. Frank, Leigh, and Edwin took turns and between the three of them, a thorough summary emerged of the day's events.

Once Frank realized the suspect was gone, he immediately came back for Leigh and Edwin. Frank got them back to the house and called his dad.

Michael broke into the conversation and said, "George, it was probably five minutes after hanging up with you that my phone rang, and Frank filled me in. I sent one of our armored cars over to the house and got them here in less than an hour. They've been up here ever since."

Parker nodded and then looked at Hans.

Hans talked about what he had gleaned from his time with Herbert Haupt. He told them that, based on Haupt's disclosure, the suspect that tried to kill Edwin was very probably Werner Thiel, and that the other man's name was Edward Kerling, with an alias of Kelley.

Parker also added more context around the overall mission of the eight Germans, and how everything that Dasch had told the F.B.I. was checking out.

"All right," said Michael. "We've got a lot of information here. What do we know? What sort of conclusions can we draw? I am asking these questions because we can't come up with any sort of a plan until we identify and agree on what we know."

There was almost a full minute of silence as each person assessed the situation from their own perspective.

Frank went first.

"We are assuming that this Dasch fellow is leveling with us. As Uncle George has said, so far, it appears that he hasn't led us astray. Plus, Hans' work in getting Haupt to open up has corroborated well with Dasch's information. It appears that Dasch doesn't know about the change in plans. Why? Because it must have happened after both subs had already left for our shores. It must've taken somewhere between two and three weeks for those U-boats to get to the eastern coast of our country. So, whoever is running this mission must've picked Kerling and gotten to him when he came ashore. After all, we've only been back from Germany for a few days. I would conclude, then, that this order to eliminate Dr. Conway is coming from the top of the Nazi regime. The fact that the order came down quickly and there was an immediate effort to drop everything and do it would tell me that. And to show you what a priority this is, the two men - Kerling and Thiel- were ordered to stop a mission that had obviously been planned for months- a major mission, mind you, making this priority number one."

"Makes sense," said Michael. "Well done, son."

"I'd rather not say this, but I feel like I have to," said Hans. All eyes turned to the young German.

"Please forgive me, Dr. Conway, but assuming Frank's assessment is correct, the Nazis rarely change their minds about these things."

"Your point, Hans?" asked George.

"That it is not a question of if they will try again, but when? And how?" said Hans.

"Which also likely means that they will continue until they are successful," thought Michael, not wanting to say it out loud. He glanced at Parker, who, by his look, told Michael that he was thinking the exact same thing.

After a moment, Leigh spoke.

"Hans is right. We need to assume that what happened today will happen again. Mr. Parker, you need to get my dad out of here and onto some sort of a military base in the U.S. where he can't be reached, where no one can get to him."

George sat silent, pondering everything that was said, whether verbally from the young people or non-verbally from his old partner.

Ironically, it was Edwin Conway who spoke next.

"Thank you, lassie," he said to Leigh. "You're always watching out for me. And you and Frank saved my life today." He turned to face her and took her hand in his.

"On the surface, your idea makes a lot of sense. But when you really think through it, it won't work."

"Why, Dad?" asked Leigh. "I don't understand."

It was Frank who put it together.

"Leigh, I think what your dad is trying to say is that you will **be** right back in the same boat that you were in before you got out of Germany. They will get to him through you. Or Jimmy, even though he's in the military. But probably you. They'll try to kidnap you or threaten to kill you if he doesn't come back and finish the project. They'll put a bounty on you or your dad, or both of you. Jimmy, too."

Edwin, quietly but firmly: "I will never allow that to ever happen again."

Leigh now, thinking out loud as she processed all of this: "What if we got word through to the Germans that Dad committed to not work on the jet engine? That no one would have access to his work until after the war?"

No one said anything, and after a few seconds, she just looked down at the conference table and said, "I know. Foolish idea."

Frank again: "Look, we have to do something. We can't just sit here and let the Nazis either make continual attempts on Dr. Conway's life or have them go after Leigh or Jimmy as leverage. And while no one is saying it, everyone is thinking it. As long as Dr. Conway is alive, they will continue to come after him, especially if the orders are coming from the top level of the Party over there."

Hans looked at each person in the room, slowly moving from one person to the next. He wanted to make sure everyone was listening to what he was going to say.

He was blunt.

"You all need to understand something here. The Nazis put no value on human life, especially when it comes to war. If they have to send someone here with absolutely no chance of survival, but their clear orders are to kill Dr. Conway, they will make such orders without hesitation."

He paused and looked around the room again.

Then: "And, unfortunately, they have scores of soldiers who not only will carry out those orders, but they will fight to be able to volunteer for the mission to begin with."

Hans' comments, while harsh, were a cold slap in the face that made everyone think in reality, as opposed to some sort of hopeful fantasy that the worst was now over.

Edwin again, with firm conviction and a quiet determination: "George, I want to be clear about a couple of things. First, I will always be incredibly grateful to you and Director Donovan - and, of course, to Frank and Hans - for getting us out of Germany. We had no hope until Frank showed up and figured out a way to allow us to escape. That is a debt that I doubt that I can ever repay."

Parker merely nodded, knowing that Dr. Conway was about to deliver a difficult message that he was not going to like.

Conway continued, "But, isolating me somewhere and leaving Leigh to always be looking over her shoulder is an unacceptable solution. The Nazis really have three options to choose from: Jimmy, Leigh, or me. For all we know, they have spies within your government who already know where Jimmy is. There has to be another option."

Next Hans spoke. "I apologize for what's the phrase that you use here about bad news?"

"Being the bearer of bad news," answered Michael, Frank, and George in unison.

"Yes, yes," said Hans. "I am sorry to be the bearer of bad news, but we also mustn't forget that the other six men are focused on the original mission, which was to blow this country up to " he paused, then the three Americans again said in unison, "kingdom come."

"Yes," said Hans. More quietly now: "To kingdom come."

George answered and said, "The F.B.I. has jurisdiction on the saboteurs and thwarting their plans. They've got almost every major east coast office engaged in this effort. I am running point on this situation. Dr. Conway is the O.S.S.'s responsibility, and I am his sponsor, if you will. My counterpart at the F.B.I. is in agreement with me taking the lead on this one."

Hans nodded. He once again felt that he had said what needed to be said.

More silence. More puffing on pipes and sipping tea.

After another minute, Frank slowly stood up and said, "I think I know a way out of this."

He turned to his father and said, "Dad, we are really going to need your help. You're going to have to call in some favors. You too, Uncle George."

Then to Edwin and Leigh: "You're going to have to trust me on this."

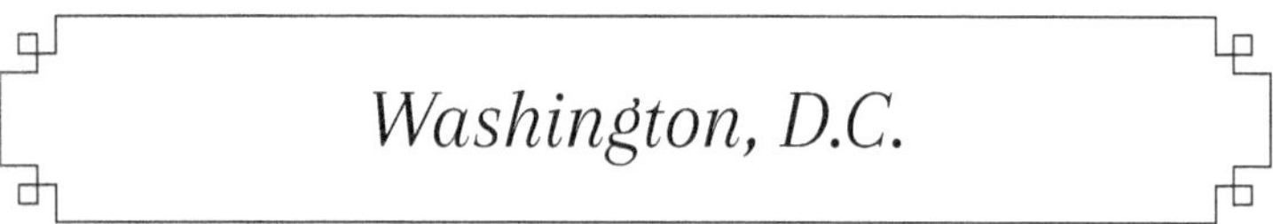

# CHAPTER 53

# Washington, D.C.

Ladd and Bouquet burst through the door of the conference room, startling Dasch.

"Well, good morning to you, too," said Dasch, looking at them over the newspaper.

Bouquet came right over, pushed Dasch to the point of him flailing his arms back in the chair in an effort to not fall completely backwards.

Dasch, stunned and more than a little afraid, shouted, "What are you doing?"

Ladd, stared at him, seething. "You lied to us."

"What? I lied to you? I most certainly did not!" sputtered Dasch.

Bouquet pushed him again. "You're lying about your lies."

Dasch clearly realized he was not in control now. "I have not lied to you! Tell me what you are talking about, and we can set the record straight. I have told you everything!"

"You didn't tell us about two of the men who landed in Jacksonville taking a detour to assassinate someone."

"What? What are you talking about? I don't know anything about any assassination. We had no such assignment."

The look in Dasch's eyes told them the truth: he knew nothing about this.

There was silence for a full minute. Then Dasch said, "Good. I can see that you believe me. Now, let's get back on track."

He looked at Bouquet and said, "Don't you ever push me again."

Bouquet came right back at him and pushed him again.

Dasch gathered himself and said, "That's enough. I know my rights! Perhaps I should hire an attorney."

Bouquet, still more angry than he had ever been: "That won't be happening, Dasch. Your days of high living are over. You are under arrest for espionage, sabotage, and planning to do egregious harm to the United States of America while the country is at war. You are a German citizen and German spy on American soil."

Dasch, clearly flabbergasted, could only sputter. He finally spit out a "This is outrageous! I came to you voluntarily!" sentence or two.

He got no reaction from either man.

He tried once more: "I know my rights!"

Ladd, not missing a beat: "Special Agent Bouquet here will not be reading you your rights."

Then, leaning down so that his face was only inches from Dasch's:

"Do you know why he won't be reading you your rights, Dasch? Because, you see, you have no rights. You are a spy and saboteur, an enemy of America. And contrary to what you may have dreamed, you will be treated as such. You better forget about the Mayflower Hotel. We have a cell downstairs with your name on it. And you better get used to it."

# CHAPTER 54

Thiel had disobeyed Kerling's order. He hadn't gone directly back to the Commodore. He ran instead to the St Paul Cathedral, which was down the block from the Commodore. A Mass was being said, and there were only about 40 people in the cavernous church. He snuck into a pew about 30 rows from the front and knelt down, only because everyone else seemed to be kneeling. He had no idea what was going on. He looked around at the people in the church, who seemed to know when to kneel when to sit, and when to stand. The priest - was that what he was called? - was speaking in a language that was not English and not German. Not only was Thiel not Catholic, but he'd rarely even been inside a church before. And he certainly had never been to a Catholic service said in Latin. While it would be a stretch to say that he was finding his rhythm with everything, he was at least going along and not looking too foolish. Of course, when he saw the altar boy ring the bells, that threw him for a bit of a loop. He was thinking that the boy was summoning someone up to the altar, so Thiel looked around but didn't see anyone moving. A couple of minutes later the boy rang the bell a second time. Thiel looked around again. "Someone's not paying attention," he said to himself.

After making sure that no one was watching him, he decided that the best option was to just not look up anymore. He noticed that many of the people had their heads bowed continually, so he opted for that.

After the mass, he walked out of a side door and took a taxi down Summit Avenue to St. Thomas College, where he spent the rest of the morning and early afternoon walking around campus. He found the library and decided to sit in there for a while.

After ditching his trench coat and hat there, he went to a department store and bought a different colored coat and hat. He also bought a sweater that had the St. Thomas insignia on it. The sweater made him look well, collegiate. He then decided to get a sandwich and coke at the soda fountain of the store. From there he grabbed another cab back to the Commodore, all the while keeping a lookout to make sure that no one was following him.

After being greeted by the doorman, he went up the elevator and walked directly to Kerling's suite, still looking behind him to make sure that he was alone.

He knocked the special knock - one tap, a pause, then two shorter taps - and Kerling's voice came through the door.

"Who is it?"

"It's me. Open up!" said Thiel in a loud whisper.

Kerling immediately opened the door. Thiel was looking down the hall again and a hand reached out and pulled him into the room with one yank. He gave a rather high-pitched gasp and stumbled into the room.

Thiel started to talk but he was met with Kerling's index finger to his mouth.

Kerling went over and turned on the radio. It took several seconds to warm up. Glenn Miller and his band were playing "Pennsylvania 6-5000."

Kerling turned up the volume a little louder than normal, turned, and stood only inches from Thiel.

"Where have you been?" he hissed. "What happened?"

"I think I got him," said Thiel. "I got up right behind him and pushed him into the streetcar, just like we planned. I pushed hard enough to make him fall forward into the streetcar but not hard enough to draw attention to me," he lied. "Of course, I couldn't wait around to be sure, but I gave him a firm push."

"No! No, you didn't "get him," spat Kerling. "While I've been sitting here wondering where in the world you could be, I found a local radio station that had a report on what happened. Conway has survived, although no one seems to know where he is at this point."

Thiel was stunned. He couldn't believe that it hadn't worked.

Kerling asked, "Was it at the streetcar station that we had discussed?"

"Yes!" said Thiel. "I thought it went off very well."

Based on Kerling's reaction, he decided that he had better come clean.

"I pushed him hard. I had to get out of there quickly. That Sweeney guy chased me."

"The father or the kid?"

"The kid. Although he's not much of a kid. He can run like the wind. I was just lucky that I had a head start on him. I was able to lose him. Just to be safe, I ducked into their Cathedral here and walked in on some sort of service going on. Did you know that they talk in some strange language in those places?"

That last comment was met with an eye roll from Kerling, who motioned for him to continue.

"Anyway, I stayed until it ended, then took a cab to the men's college around here. St. Thomas College, it's called. I figured a college campus is a pretty good hiding place. After killing a few hours there, I ditched my coat and hat, bought replacements, and got a cab back here. I'm certain that I wasn't followed."

Kerling stared at him for a while longer, then motioned for him to sit down.

Kerling began to pace. Thiel replayed the entire incident for him, but he didn't listen. Noise. Just noise.

After a couple of more minutes, Kerling woke up to the fact that Thiel was still talking and motioned for him to stop.

Thiel relented, then started to say something, and Kerling said, "Shut up."

Thiel stopped again and, this time, waited for Kerling to speak.

Kerling, with a low, quiet voice: "You need to get back to Cincinnati. I will stay here until I complete the mission. If I'm not there within three days, go on to New York. I'm going to write a name for you to contact there who is one of us. He will get you situated and can be trusted. In the meantime, get down to the train station and get back to Cincinnati. I don't care if you go back through Indianapolis or Chicago. Helmut Leiner will likely be in Cincinnati and staying at the Gibson. He is staying there under the name of "Helmut Landon." Go there and tell him what I have just told you. I'll either see you in Cincinnati within three days, or I will meet you in New York." Thiel nodded. Kerling was intense now, focused.

Thiel decided to keep his mouth shut and just listen. After all, it was clear that Kerling was not asking. He was ordering.

"Did you say that you already dumped your clothes that you wore on the mission?"

"Yes, I threw them into a trashcan on the campus."

"Good," said Kerling. "You were smart to go with the college man look."

Kerling continued, "Out of an abundance of caution, I will probably change hotels tonight. We can't take any sort of risk right now. If Leiner - or Landon - hasn't heard from me by the time you get to Cincinnati, that means that I am still working on finishing the job."

"Will you still get me that promotion?" asked Thiel.

Kerling could barely contain himself.

Thiel, immediately realizing that he had really overstepped, said, "Never mind."

Kerling took a minute to regain his composure. His face was still red, and he was trying not to spit out his words at the young fool.

"I suggest that you now focus on proving yourself in the coming assignments that we will have when we get to New York."

Thiel merely nodded and got out of the room as quickly as he could. He would spend the next several hours making his way to Cincinnati, replaying his actions over and over again in his mind.

# CHAPTER 55

## *Chicago*

Hermann Neubauer sat in his first-class berth, reading a novel and waiting for the train to move. He glanced at his watch. 7:10 PM. He rang the bell for the porter. In less than a minute, there was a knock on his door.

"Come in," said Neubauer.

The porter appeared and said, "Can I help you, Sir?"

"Why are we running late? We were supposed to leave ten minutes ago."

"I apologize for that, Sir. Apparently, some of the food was late getting out to the train. It should only be a few more minutes.

In the meantime, can I offer you a complimentary cocktail?"

"Just some wine. Red. Something light."

"Yes, Sir. I will be back in a minute with your glass of wine."

The wine came in five minutes, and now Neubauer was getting concerned.

After he finished the glass, he pushed the button for the porter again.

Within 30 seconds, there was another knock on his door.

"Come in."

As the door opened, Neubauer, without looking up, said, 'This is getting ridiculous. The weather is fine outside. I can't imagine it takes this long to bring some extra food on board this train."

"You know, you have a point there."

Neubauer noticed that something wasn't right. He looked up. He was not talking to the porter but to a rather large man in a dark blue suit with blond hair and a higher-than-average voice.

"Who are you?" This berth is occupied."

"Ah, that it is. But not for long. Do me a favor and stand up, and keep your hands where I can see them," said Agent Bo Kemper, who flashed his badge.

Neubauer complied, half in shock and half in amazement that he had been caught so soon.

He refused to say a word.

Kemper looked at him, smiled, and said, "Gotcha."

# CHAPTER 56

Clint Hackert, Chief of Police of St. Paul, sat in his office signing his name. Repeatedly. It seemed that most of his job now was signing something. Commendations, new hire approvals, promotions, the occasional termination, budget approvals, and capital improvements. The list was long.

Hackert was a cop's cop. He represented the new St. Paul Police Department, as evidenced by the fact that he was in his sixth year as Chief.

The position had been a revolving door before he came on board, and for good reason. The years - decades, really - of corruption within the police department had finally come to a stop when he took over. And that was by design, not by accident. Most of his predecessors had been on the take. So much so that in a span of six years, there had been ten - TEN! Chiefs of Police in St. Paul.

In addition to morally corrupt chiefs, there had been morally corrupt mayors. And commissioners. And cops. It was bad.

When his secretary came into his office telling him Michael Sweeney was on the phone, the Chief didn't hesitate.

Michael Sweeney was a big supporter of Hackert getting the Chief of Police position and had been a huge help to him as he transitioned into the role in his first year. There was a mutual respect between the two men. And Sweeney's detectives, mostly ex-cops themselves, had quietly helped Hackert's cops solve a number of crimes in the past few years.

"Put him right through," he told her.

Thirty seconds later, he was talking to his old friend.

"Michael, how've you been? Still helping my boys solve all kinds of crime?"

"Thanks for taking my call, Clint. I know how busy you are these days."

"Never too busy for a trusted friend. What can I do for you?"

"Clint, I'm going to need a favor from you."

# CHAPTER 57

Rice Park, located about a three wood and 8 iron from the shores of the great Mississippi, served as a main hub of downtown St. Paul. Calling it a park might be a bit generous, since the square lot of land is somewhere south of two full acres, with streets on every side that served as boundaries. The land itself was donated almost 100 years ago by Henry Rice, a local politician. For years it served only as a pasture for sheep to graze.

As the city progressed, development accelerated, to the point where the streets on the four sides of Rice Park were taken up by four large buildings.

On the northeast side of the park stood the beautiful St. Paul Hotel. On the hotel's left sat the St. Paul Library, itself an impressive structure that was built 35 years prior. Across the park from the hotel was The St. Paul Auditorium, which housed everything from plays and concerts to sporting events and conventions. And across the park from the library and next to the hotel was The St. Paul Federal Court House.

In one relatively small square, one had access to entertainment, food and lodging, education, and the Court system. The old joke used to be, "Go get educated at the library, walk over to watch a play, go back to the hotel for drinks, cause a ruckus, and be escorted over to the courthouse, all accomplished in one lap around the park."

Edwin Conway stood in an expansive office on the fifth floor in the Federal Courthouse. So large was the building that it also housed the St. Paul Post Office.

His room faced the park at an angle, and was directly across west 5th Street, which separated the courthouse from the hotel. In his temporary office - or cell, as he considered it to be- was a large mahogany desk and a comfortable leather chair that backed up against the window.

The building itself was forty years old and was designed by a gentleman named Willoughby Edbrooke, who was well known in the city for his work with large public buildings.

Edbrooke knew what he was doing, in part because many of his designs incorporated steep roofs, which allowed for gravity to do its work when it came to the inevitable large snowfalls that Minnesota is known for.

Many of the rooms were full of marble and mahogany finishes with high ceilings, giving the criminally accused something to ponder as they awaited their fates. Those included the likes of Alvin "Creepy" Karpis, members of Ma Barker's gang, and Evelyn Frechette, John Dillinger's girlfriend. Karpis, being captured alive, became quite familiar with the inside of the building.

One of Michael Sweeney's detectives told Edwin that Karpis and the other criminals were escorted to and from the courthouse with the compliments of the Sweeney Detective Bureau's armored cars. Edwin smiled at the thought and even felt a sense of pride.

Even though he and Michael were still getting to know each other, he admired the man and what he stood for. While it was clear that Mr. Sweeney was somewhat of a celebrity in local circles, it was also evident to Edwin that, like him, Michael wanted a quiet life out of the limelight. "He's pretty comfortable in his own shoes," Edwin noted. Should it happen, he could see Leigh being very happy as part of the Sweeney clan.

He looked back out the window at the hotel; then, his view expanded as he scanned the entire park. Beautiful. Bustling. He looked below to the street and saw four plain-clothes detectives - Mike's men - milling about at the entrance. They had their eyes constantly moving, watching who came in and out of the main entrance. He also knew that there were more men stationed at every entrance, on the stairwell and on every floor near the elevators, and finally, outside of his own suite. Mike had called it what? Oh yes. A "perimeter coverage" meant that there were a series of circles that started out wide and got smaller and smaller the closer anyone got to the Target. In this case, Edwin.

He moved to the desk that was provided in his suite. The aforementioned leather chair was made of a firm but comfortable leather. It was called a "high back," because when he sat in it, his entire back from his neck down leaned against the leather.

A cup of tea sat on his right, and he began to take small sips.

Despite everything going on, he was not nervous or frightened. He found himself at peace. If he was to die, at least he was right with the Lord. He knew where he was going. He would be reunited with Hannah, his beloved. Conversely, he wanted to see Leigh and Jimmy as adults, and enjoy their children - his grandchildren- if God would allow for it. He also wanted to be around to see the war end, assuming that the Allies would win it. The alternative would certainly change his perspective.

"Strange to be torn like that," he thought.

Edwin Conway was many things. He was a world-renowned aeronautical engineer. He was a wonderful father and had been a great husband to Hannah. But he was, first and foremost, a simple man of faith.

"What is that verse in Philippians? He closed his eyes and thought. He had memorized the entire book of Philippians a few years earlier, after he had lost Hannah. It had brought him great peace during those very challenging times.

He remembered it and began to recite it quietly to himself: "For to me, to live is Christ, and to die is gain. But if I am to live on in the flesh, this will mean fruitful labor for me; and I do not know which to choose. But I am hard-pressed from both directions, having the desire to depart and be with Christ for that is very much better; yet to remain on in the flesh is more necessary for your sake."

"Well, I have good company. At least Paul was torn as well," he mused. "And Paul wrote Philippians from prison. We have more in common than what I thought," he smiled as he looked around his "cell."

# CHAPTER 58

The St. Paul Hotel, the premier hotel in the city, was home to many famous people, from politicians to celebrities to yes, criminals. Offering 254 rooms in a luxurious, high-end setting, it was the place to stay for anybody who was somebody. Or trying to become somebody.

Charles Lindbergh, a proud Minnesotan, had a reception dinner held in his honor at the hotel after he landed safely back in the U.S. upon completing the first successful non-stop trip across the Atlantic; Leon Gleckman, known as "The Al Capone of St. Paul," had a suite at the hotel for several years where he conducted business. He wasn't alone. Another suite housed one Mike Malone, a U.S. Treasury agent who had infiltrated Capone's operation and whose sole role was to keep an eye on Gleckman and build a case against the gangster. And then there was a young, up-and-coming bandleader from North Dakota by the name of Lawrence Welk, whose band played at the hotel every Saturday evening.

Residing in room 634 was another potential "celebrity" of sorts: Edward Kelley, aka Edward Kerling, a German spy and soon-to-be assassin. Kerling was quite impressed with the hotel. The service was impeccable, and the food delicious. Each of the two nights that he had stayed there, he had come back to his two-room executive suite to find a handwritten note from the maid, a woman named Connie, who had come in to turn down the bed and leave a couple of pieces of chocolate on his nightstand. The note expressed Maid Connie's appreciation to Mr. Kelly for staying at the hotel. A nice touch. Unfortunately, unlike the other guests previously mentioned, his stay at the St. Paul Hotel would be a one-time-only event.

He had checked in two days earlier and immediately began to watch the room on the fifth floor, third from the corner of the courthouse. The inside information that he had received turned out to be very accurate. Edwin Conway, being an engineer, was nothing if not predictable. Kerling began to see that Conway had a routine. He also noted that Conway had not come out of the courthouse at all. Kerling had to hand it to the Americans: hiding someone in a courthouse certainly was creative, and one would doubt that short of an actual jail, was just about the safest place anyone like Conway could be.

As the German started to put his plan in place, he began to count how many men were assigned to protect his target, and it was a lot. All well-built, no-nonsense, well-disciplined men who never allowed themselves to be distracted. As he had planned from the beginning, this would not be an up-close kill. He knew that he would have no chance of escaping if he did it that way. No, this would need to be a headshot using a scoped rifle.

He had settled on a M1903 Springfield Rifle, the most accurate sniper rifle in the whole war. While it didn't have the thrust of his other option, the M1Garand, or the number of rounds in its chamber - the Garand had 8 rounds in its chamber compared to a five-round chamber in the Springfield - the M1903 was still the product of choice for most snipers. It was just a smooth squeeze and incredibly accurate. Besides, as Kerling had reasoned, he wouldn't need eight shots. He wouldn't have time for eight shots. He just needed one. Plus, so common was the M1903 that it would take even longer to identify where it came from, with the serial numbers filed off.

The books that he had checked out from the library across the park were stacked and served as a resting place on which to steady the rifle. The other factors that had to be considered - the distance, the wind, and the sunlight - were minimal in this case. Because the distance was less than 70 meters, any wind would be much less of an issue.

Given the fact that he would be taking his shot later in the day, there might be a slight glare at the point of shooting, but it should be manageable. The A1/Unertl scope would certainly help with that. The scope would help ensure accuracy up to 550 meters, give or take. The window that he would be shooting from was almost the perfect size for him to get the rifle to a spot that didn't protrude out the window far enough for a casual observer to even notice. "Yes," he thought, "This really is the perfect sniper's nest."

After a few practices, it took Kerling less than five minutes to get set up in the room. The rifle had been the only purchase that he had made during his short stay in Cincinnati. Immediately after talking to Kappe and finding out about the assignment, he went out and found a gun shop about three blocks from the Gibson Hotel. He passed himself off as a deer hunter, and the salesman was all too happy to make a sale on a very nice rifle. It barely fit diagonally into his large suitcase, and the scope was well hidden in the depths of a soft-sided briefcase. The A1 Unertl scope was a good one, and was standard issued to all snipers in the marines. He was fortunate in that the salesman had just gotten a used one in the previous week. Probably from a family who lost their son in the war, he reasoned.

Factoring everything, his final estimation still confirmed that the kill shot would be well less than 100 meters, which was well within the scope's - and the rifle's -specs.

Noise was another matter. He had picked a window of time around 3:00 PM, due to the traffic noise, which should help shield the shot. And there seemed to be a band of sorts in the park playing Christmas music the last couple of days, so that could help. Of course, he needed to get confirmation from Leiner that this was still a go. Leiner had made it clear to Kerling that he was not to take the shot without final confirmation from him. Leiner would call him right at 3:00 PM to give him the go-ahead. From there, the escape plan for Kerling had been mapped to the minute. If all went according to plan, he would be on a train within minutes of firing the fatal shot.

# CHAPTER 59

The Accomplice had the instructions and had coordinated with Edward Kelley, as he was known. Leiner had made sure that there was a healthy separation between all of the actors in this play so that if one was caught, that person couldn't sell out the others. The Accomplice walked through the role that was assigned again for the umpteenth time. There were a couple of variables that were beyond anyone's control, which wasn't unusual for this sort of an assignment. The variables related to the timing of all of it. One was how many minutes it would take "Kelley" to get out of the hotel, assuming that he could get out at all. The other was tied to how long the getaway vehicle would be either unnoticed or ignored by St. Paul's finest. The Accomplice actually admired how well the plan had been conceived. One had to give it to Leiner for an incredible plan. Very well laid out and, just as important, very well thought out beforehand, especially on such short notice.

That said, there was still risk. The Target had to be where he was supposed to be at the appointed time. There was about an 80% chance of that happening, given Conway's predictable habits. The Accomplice was told to wait until the cops came running over to the hotel from the Court building, to not race out of there, but to just drive normally. In other words, act innocently and don't draw any attention to yourself. Easier said than done. After all, this particular assignment differed from those in the past. This one really involved being more of a... what? Spy? Soldier? No matter. All parties were just going to do what they were told. Hopefully, this would be the first and last assignment that would involve this kind of exposure.

The likelihood of this mission coming to St. Paul - and thus to The Accomplice - was microscopically low. Still, it had gone well, at least to this point. After all, it was The Accomplice who had determined where the Target was being housed, and even found out the number of the suite, and had reported the information dutifully and promptly back to Leiner.

The Accomplice wondered how many others there were in America with similar assignments, or at least how many were available for such missions. Living in America could spoil a person, after all. How many would still give their lives for the Fatherland and the Fuhrer? Were there people in every large city? Were there farmers and union workers, and businessmen who were in similar situations that had been called upon for service? And of those called upon, how many would act? There was no way to know the answer to those questions, so compartmentalized was the network. But it was probably more than anyone knew or considered. Or maybe even hoped for.

Everyone had seen what Roosevelt had done last February on the West Coast with anyone of Japanese heritage. Over 120,000 Japanese were interned in 10 different camps around the country. Many of those people detained were U.S. citizens.

Why wasn't something like that done to people of German ancestry in America? Were there just too many? So many Americans of European descent now thought of themselves as Americans first. After all, there were generations of families who had been born and raised here. Regardless, the Accomplice had moved here and lived in America for almost 15 years now, having migrated in the second half of the 1920s.

The Fatherland was a chaotic mess back then with runaway inflation and no way to earn a sustainable living. Paranoia reigned because the ongoing sanctions and the punitive terms of the Treaty of Versailles had all but assured the German people that they would never control their own destiny again. That was a bitter pill for the populace to swallow. The treaty itself was punitive in nature, thus all but assuring that it would be broken one day.

The political scene was a mess as well, as several parties were trying to gain control of the country. Fractions were everywhere. The Accomplice left with many others and arrived in America in 1928. There were distant relatives in Minnesota, which certainly helped. The Italians and Irish were known to take in relatives who were complete strangers, and the Germans were no different in this regard. Family was family, after all. Learning English wasn't so bad since the family had studied English in school and at home.

There was a certain amount of respect and appreciation for the Accomplice's life in America. It was, after all, a country that had provided an opportunity. But when Leiner had called, there was no "asking" involved. It was a mandate with a veiled threat behind it.

The Accomplice was a bit insulted. There was no fear of Leiner. If the man had just been reasonable and had outlined the reason behind the demand, things would have gone much more smoothly. After all, while there was a real appreciation for America - The Accomplice held nothing against it until it had entered the war -Germany would always be "home." As Leiner had repeated numerous times, it's one thing to talk about such loyalties. But it's another to prove it. Here was a great opportunity to prove it.

Sitting and waiting now, glancing at the wristwatch for the third time in five minutes. It was 2:57 PM. Somewhere around 5 more minutes, give or take.

# CHAPTER 60

Edwin Conway sat at his desk in his suite at the courthouse with his back to the window. The chair was comfortable and large, allowing for only his head to be seen by anyone outside.

Conway conversed with George Parker, the only other person in the room who was visible to anyone staring into the window. "Well, George, I hope this works for your sake."

Parker paced. "Dr. Conway, let's hope it works for both of our sakes. We're taking a huge chance here."

Conway smiled. "Yes. WE are, although somehow, I feel that I am a bit more committed to this. You know, George, there's an old saying in Ireland that talks about the difference between being "involved" and being "committed." In a bacon and egg breakfast, the chicken is involved. But the pig is committed. I can't help but feel a little more committed than you are at this point."

George, trying to continue to be nonchalant for his audience, grunted an acknowledgment of agreement. He stared at the second phone that was in the suite. It sat on top of another table, out of view of the window. "Any minute now, that second phone line in the suite should ring," he thought, staring intently at it. Ten seconds later, it rang. "We're on," said Michael Sweeney. "Move!"

C H A P T E R   6 1

Kerling sat in his room, waiting. The gun was loaded, and books were stacked and aligned perfectly as a mount for the rifle. The window was opened just enough to maneuver the rifle and the scope as needed. He had sighted the scope in and was pointing it at the back of Edwin Conway's head. The shot was almost unfair. He had a clear view of the man's head. He had the scope centered on the middle of that same head. Traffic was busy and loud, and that same instrumental band sat in the middle of the park, playing a mixture of Christmas and church music. People were sipping coffee and hot chocolate and enjoying the scenery. Every year, the trees in Rice Park are decorated with tinsel and Christmas lights. The more noise and people around, the better the ensuing chaos and panic, which would allow him the optimal opportunity to disappear unobserved.

The phone rang as scheduled.

Setting the gun down carefully, he walked to the other side of the room to answer it. As rehearsed, he picked up the phone and said nothing.

"Update me." It was Leiner, right on time.

"The Target is right where he is supposed to be. I have a clear shot. Is my ride out of here ready?"

"Yes, your comrade is waiting as planned in the destination that we discussed. Do you have the medicine just in case?" Kerling snorted. Then, "Yes, I have the medicine here in my pocket if I get sick." He reached into his pocket and felt the cyanide pill.

Then, to Leiner: "If my comrade executes this properly, I won't be getting sick."

Leiner, sounding a bit nervous: "Let me be clear: You cannot be caught alive. There can be no ties back to who is behind this. None! Ever!"

Kerling, fairly spitting the words back: "Yes. You have been quite clear about that and I have planned every precaution for that not to happen." Silence.

Finally, Leiner again: "Get on a train to the second city that you came to upon entering the country. Stay at the same hotel. I will meet you here tomorrow to discuss the next steps."

Kerling tried to look out the window again at Conway. He stretched to see him still sitting in the chair.

Kerling: "Look, we need to talk about me getting out of the country. For all I know, Thiel has been captured. I haven't heard anything from Haupt. I don't know about Neubauer. If one of them has been captured and talked, there will be a nationwide manhunt on for me if there isn't already."

"Thiel is fine and is leaving shortly for the next city as planned. The men from Chicago should be on their way as well."

Leiner, trying to remain patient: "What's the matter with you? There is no such manhunt on right now. Your picture hasn't been in any of the papers. We have no evidence that anyone knows anything. Dasch and his crew are lying low where they are supposed to be. We have the original mission to think about once this is completed. Just stick to the plan, and things will work out."

Kerling, calm but forceful: "You better start working on a plan to get me back to the Fatherland. Kappe made no promises to me about that, but given the situation, I am not going to go to the electric chair over this."

Leiner, the strain clearly starting to show: "You let me worry about that. In the meantime, you have an order. I am hereby giving you formal authorization to execute that order."

Then, in a small but threatening voice: "And so help me, if you don't execute that order immediately, I will make sure you go right to the chair myself. Now do your duty and call me the minute you are free to confirm that it's done. Am I clear?" Kerling, in an equally firm and cold voice: "Yes, sir."

# CHAPTER 62

Kerling slammed the phone down with authority, staring at it.

Scott Price and John Malone, two of Sweeney Detectives' finest, heard and recorded every word of the conversation from the room next door to Kerling's.

They had bugged Kerling's phone the moment that he left the room to check out the books at the library.

After a couple of seconds, Kerling started back to the window. Suddenly, there was a knock on the door. Kerling froze. "Who in the world?" He instinctively reached into his pocket for his revolver.

"Who is it?" He asked, in as calm a voice as he could manage.

"Mr. Kelley, it's Connie, your maid. I have new towels for you."

Kerling breathed a sigh of relief. "Thank you, Connie. Please come back in 30 minutes."

"I'm sorry, Mr. Kelley. Normally I would be more than happy to do that, but my shift just ended at 3:00 PM and you are the last room to do. Would you like me to come back in 5 minutes?"

"Yes, that would be… Uh, No. No. That will not work. Please just leave them outside the door."

"I'm sorry, I can't do that, Mr. Kelley. That would get me fired." I could be in and out in less than 5 minutes if you could just let me in… ."

"NO!" Kerling fairly shouted. "Here, just hand them to me. I will open the door, and just hand them to me."

He opened the door partway to see an attractive petite woman with dirty blonde hair and bright blue eyes and a big smile.

"Can I bring these in and at least put them on the bed for you?" she asked.

"No, thank you. That will not be necessary. Wait here for a minute." He closed the door, composed himself, and went to the dresser and came back with what he hoped was a lazy smile and handed the woman two one dollar bills.

"Here, here. Hand me the towels, and I will take care of it."

"Well, sure, I can do that, Mr. Kelley. I'm sorry, but I will need the old towels before I can give you the new ones. You'd be amazed at how many towels we seem to lose around here, if you know what I mean."

Then, quickly: "Of course, I know that someone like you would never do such a thing. It's just that we have other guests who, well, let's just say that they seem to "misplace" a lot of our towels. And not just towels. Ashtrays, dishes from room service, and even the robes that we hang on the back of the bathroom door. Seems like everyone wants a souvenir from The St. Paul Hotel."

Kerling looked at her with a blank face for a moment, processing.

Finally: "Oh. Oh. Of course. Wait one more moment." He disappeared again, with the door closed. 30 seconds later he reopened the door and handed her all of the wet towels and wash cloths. Maid Connie gave him the new towels, and she stood there for a moment, and said, "Excuse me, Mr. Kelley, but are you all right?"

"What? Oh. Oh yes, I'm fine," he said. "I just need to get ready for an appointment, so if you'll excuse me. . ."

"Yes, Sir. Oh! Just one more thing: Can you please give me the ashtray from the room? I will swap you out a new one."

He went again back into the room and retrieved the cup and handed it to her.

Maid Connie: "I'm sorry about the rules, but this is what makes the St. Paul Hotel such a special place to stay. You see, we want to make sure that every guest receives the very best care, because we know that you have a choice where you stay when you come to town, and we want to make sure that you have an exceptional experience when you stay with us. And I would feel just awful if you had a less than satisfactory experience with us. Especially if I was responsible for that less than satisfying experience."

Kerling: "Thank you, Connie. Very kind. Very kind. Now, if you'll excuse me. . ."

"Yes, sir. Have a wonderful evening, sir. And someone will come back around 6:00 PM to turn down your bed for you.

Would that time be OK?"

"Yes. Yes. Thank you. Goodbye."

"Oh, and Mr. Kelley? Thank you so much for the wonderful tip. That was so kind of you."

"Yes, yes, Connie. You are most welcome. Goodbye."

With that, Kerling closed the door, took a deep breath, and focused back on the task at hand. He walked over to the window and thankfully saw that Conway was still sitting in his chair. He could make out another man standing in front of the desk, talking to Conway. The man who was doing all of the talking was gesturing to Conway and Conway was just sitting there, listening.

Kerling quickly changed into the uniform and, in less than a minute, was back at the window.

He quickly lined the shot back up. There was very little wind to consider. There was a slight glare due to the sun's position, but little had changed in the 5 minutes from when he last had the man sighted in. Music was still coming from the park. The small orchestra was playing a Christmas hymn. Silent Night.

"How appropriate," Kerling said to himself. "A song written by a German. It will certainly be a silent night for Dr. Conway."

The rifle was ready. The Target was lined up. Kerling zeroed in on the back of the head, blocking out all noises and distractions. He took a deep breath, started to exhale, and slowly squeezed the trigger.

The report was loud and was only partially drowned out by the sound of traffic and the music and normal buzz that came from Rice Park.

He waited for a second, but there was no doubt that it would be a direct hit. Conway's head burst, and blood exploded everywhere. His head shot forward and disappeared behind the large chair, his right arm sliding off the side of the chair. There could be no question that Edwin Conway would be of no help to the United States now.

Kerling, relieved that he had accomplished his mission, immediately moved into escape mode. Speed was of the essence now. He wiped the gun clean and removed the scope. He searched for the shell, which he had hoped would stay in the room with him. It had not. He would have no time to look for it outside. Kerling picked up the sack that he had packed in his suitcase and put the scope in it. He had already wiped down the room to eliminate any fingerprints. After the scope was safely and securely in the sack, he adjusted his uniform and carried only the sack and the gun to the door. The money that he had was stuffed into various compartments in his uniform and in his money belt.

Seeing no one in the hall, he quickly stepped out of room 634 for the last time. The gun was sent down the laundry chute, which was located just outside of his door. Then he made his way to the stairwell, where he walked down the six flights of stairs to the door with the large EXIT sign posted next to it. One more tug on the uniform, and then he opened the door. He didn't see as much as he heard: screaming and chaos. Horns honking. Sirens wailing. Cops yelling directions to people.

The mail truck was parked five feet from the door. His accomplice was sitting in it, anxiously waiting for him to come out. The mail truck blocked any view from the courthouse to the hotel and provided excellent coverage for Kerling, looking just like another mailman, to slide right in, undetected. They were on 5th Street and then made a quick right onto St. Peter Street, crossed over 4th Street, and came to Kellogg Avenue. They took a left on Kellogg and began to talk hurriedly. There was a dark suit with a black tie and fedora hat in the truck, and Kerling hurriedly began to change. They would be at the St. Paul Union Depot in five minutes.

# CHAPTER 63

George Parker was standing in front of the desk when the bullet hit. Worse than that, his suit was smattered with brain matter. Nothing can prepare a person for such a site. He hit the floor and pulled his revolver out, waiting for another shot. It didn't come.

"Shot fired!" He yelled. Immediately, the door burst open, and two of Sweeney Detective's finest came through, guns out and ready.

"Sniper fire!" shouted Parker. The two detectives, Pat O'Brien and Nick Flood, moved quickly out of the line of fire from the window. They looked down at the man on the ground. There was no doubt that the sniper had hit his mark. Flood crawled to the side of the window behind the desk and pulled the curtains closed. O'Brien, seeing that the damage was already done, positioned himself in the hallway, guarding against any further attack from inside the courthouse.

Within minutes, two St. Paul cops were moving down the hallway toward the suite. They looked young. "Rookies," said Flood to Parker. O'Brien and Flood stayed with the body while Parker moved into the hallway. He flashed his badge at the two cops and said, "Federal Officer." The two men stopped, both looking confused.

"This is a matter of national security, and this is, therefore, my crime scene," said Parker. More looks of confusion on the part of the cops. They were, in fact, rookies. This was typical of the department. Before any man took to patrolling the streets, they got their feet wet working in state and federal facilities, like the courthouse. It also gave them an opportunity to get to know the prosecutors, whom they would inevitably be working with when they graduated to the street.

"Uh, do you mind if we see your badge and credentials again?" asked the shorter of the two.

"Yes, I do mind," said Parker. Nonetheless, he produced both again for another glance, undoubtedly the first time that these guys had ever seen either one. As they were leaning in to look at the badge and creds, they both at the same instant noticed the mess that covered a good portion of Parker's shirt. Confusion turned to terror as they finally began to register what they were looking at. Flood and O'Brien looked at the scene, both registering the smallest of smiles at one another. The looks on the rookies' faces were something to behold.

"Go out and direct traffic for the ambulance that is coming." It clearly wasn't a request. It was an order. "And keep your eyes open for any suspicious characters hanging around the ambulance. Anybody that looks suspicious, you detain them and get their names and addresses and come find me. Make sure that the ambulance is backed up as close to the door as possible. Photographers are OK, but nothing closer than 30 feet. Got it? Ok, move!"

The two rookies didn't have to think twice. They wanted out of there in a hurry and moved quickly down the hallway.

Flood and O'Brien looked at each other and shook their heads.

O'Brien: "Were we that dumb when we started out?"

Flood: "You were."

Then, to each other: "Rookies."

They began to assess the scene. It was a single shot that was fired.

Within five minutes, a doctor arrived from somewhere within the courthouse. He called it as he saw it: They were all looking at a very dead body. Word quickly spread throughout the building that there was a corpse on the fifth floor of the courthouse.

Within minutes, there was an ambulance on the scene, with another doctor who pronounced the obvious: they were looking at a man who had been killed by a single shot to the head.

George left Flood and O'Brien in charge of getting the body into the ambulance and to the hospital as quickly as possible. He quickly made his way over to the hotel. No one was allowed on the 6th floor. The sniper's nest had already been identified and roped off by Price and Malone. Both men stood watch as Parker made his way into the room. Malone said, "Looks pretty clean in there. Wonder if he left any prints."

"Oh, I think we'll find some," said George. He reached into his briefcase and took out his fingerprint kit that he kept from his days with the F.B.I. After putting on the gloves, he went right over to the ashtray.

"Boys, anybody want to bet that we pick up some prints off of this ashtray?"

A couple of more cops came into the room to take George's statement. George flashed his credentials and didn't volunteer a lot, other than to say that the dead man was a foreign figure. He called Michael Sweeney and calmly said, "Shot fired. We have a dead body here. The police are already here, and more will be coming, so we need to get the body out of here as quickly as we can."

Michael said, "Ambulance is on its way and will be there in about three minutes."

True to his old partner's word, about three minutes later, an ambulance had pulled up behind the courthouse, and the body was loaded in and would be taken to St. Joseph's Hospital, less than five minutes from the courthouse.

Meanwhile, there was bedlam in the courthouse and Rice Park. The musicians didn't hear the shots, but reacted to what they saw in the crowd, which was a mass of humans running helter-skelter in every direction. Mothers had pulled their children in tight and made their way into the St. Paul Hotel, the St. Paul Library, and the St. Paul Auditorium for cover. Some ran into the courthouse as well. Other people were pointing at the courthouse, and some were pointing at the St. Paul Hotel.

# CHAPTER 64

Kerling talked first.

"I need to call Leiner but if for some reason I can't get him, tell him that Conway is definitely dead. I had a direct hit on the back of his head, and I saw the blood splatter all over the room. A lot of it hit the man that was standing across from his desk."

He could tell that his accomplice was confused, so he took a deep breath, then tried again: "OK, look. Conway was sitting at his desk with his back to me. I had a perfect shot at his head. The guy was standing across from Conway and his desk. When the shot hit Conway, his head exploded. Tell Leiner those words that Conway's head exploded, OK? The man is dead. I am 1,000 percent certain that the man is dead. There wasn't much left of the head, based on what I saw. Do you understand?"

The Accomplice nodded quickly and said, "Yes, I understand. His head exploded, and there was blood everywhere. He is dead."

Kerling replied, "Right. Better yet, send Leiner a telegram. Tell him that you found the bottle of wine that he asked about and it is, without a doubt, the right one. He is at the Gibson Hotel in Cincinnati. He's staying there under an alias. The name that he is using is"-

"Landon," said the accomplice. "I will do that."

"Right. Good!" said Kerling. He continued: "I assume that you were the one that scouted the courthouse and found out what room they had Conway in. All of the intelligence was excellent. Everything that I was told by Leiner was accurate, so excellent work on your part to get me all of that information."

"Thank you," said the Accomplice. "I took a lot of risks sneaking around and gathering information. I hope that no one remembers me doing any of that. I am down there somewhat frequently, anyway. But I'm glad that you found my information useful. I would appreciate you telling Leiner all of that."

"You can count on me doing that for you," replied Kerling, adjusting his tie as best as he could. He was already looking ahead for the Union Depot. "I couldn't have accomplished this without you. Our leaders in Berlin will be quite happy about this. I will do everything I can in my report to share the credit with you and recommend you for a medal."

The Accomplice, looking genuinely appreciative, said, "Thank you. That would mean a lot to me." Then: "Two more minutes and you will be there. Where are you headed?"

Kerling just looked straight ahead and said, "It's better that you don't know. I've been instructed not to tell anyone anything. It's better this way. If you somehow get caught, you won't have anything to tell because you won't know."

"I understand," came the reply. "I don't even know your real name. All I know is that your cover name is Kelley."

"Yes. The hotel people also only know me as Kelley, so they won't know how to trace me."

They pulled up to the train station and parked along the curb.

"I will dispose of the mailman outfit."

The Accomplice looked at Kerling one last time. "You now look like a normal, average businessman. There is a briefcase here for you as well, just to complete the businessman look. Do you have a few other false identifications? And the cash?"

Kerling nodded.

As he was getting ready to exit the truck, Kerling looked at the Accomplice one more time.

"Not only did you think of everything, but you also executed every part of the mission. I will duck into the men's room inside the depot for a minute and hide my other identifications. Once I emerge from the men's room, I will have another ID to show the conductor as I get on the train. It's all been arranged." The two looked at each other and then shook hands.

"Good luck," said the Accomplice.

"The same to you, my friend," said Kerling. "Today is a great victory for the Fatherland!"

With that, the man known to the Accomplice - and anyone who met him in the last four days - as Edward Kelley slipped into the crowd and was out of sight in seconds.

# CHAPTER 65

Michael Sweeney sat at his desk in the headquarters of Sweeney Detective Bureau. The office was located on the 20th floor of the 1st National Bank, just a few blocks from Rice Park. He called out to Susie and asked her to hold all of his calls for a while. Unusual for him to do so, but this was a very unusual moment in time. His sister was blessed with a memory that was borderline photographic. She somehow kept everyone's birthdays, anniversaries, and other memorable events in her mind, and she easily would memorize Michael's schedule for him each day.

"You have a call at 4:30 PM with the mayor's office and a dinner at 5:30 PM at the Lexington with Jon Althoff, the St. Paul Auditorium Chairman," she said, almost automatically.

For a moment, Michael was disappointed. Mayor Mark Gehan was doing a great job cleaning out the corruption in the city and the police department, which had been the key message of his campaign a few years ago. He had run against the incumbent Mayor, whom Michael knew. William Mahoney claimed that there was no crime epidemic in St. Paul and famously said, "If there are any gangsters here, it is because they have been invited here by the newspapers."

Mahoney was voted out of office and replaced with Gehan, who had said that he would make sure that the city "stopped the pussyfooting and indecision" regarding crime. Many groups finally got the voters organized and engaged when it came to the crime problem, resulting in a record

74% voter turnout for the mayoral election. Gehan had won by just 592 votes. His was a fragile majority, and Michael felt badly about having to reschedule the call. Especially since he might need the mayor's help in a day or two.

Plus, his good friend Althoff was buying dinner tonight, and wanted to discuss Sweeney Detective sponsoring an upcoming Automobile Convention at the Auditorium. A steak at the Lexington was the best in town. And a dinner with Jon Althoff was always a guaranteed fun evening.

That said, the decision to reschedule both events was not difficult. Michael called out to Susie again, asking her to reschedule the call with the mayor and to send his regrets to Mr. Althoff. "I'll be working late tonight, Suze. Please let Maggie know that I won't be home until much later tonight, and to not bother to wait up for me."

"Will do," she said, already picking up the phone.

"What would I do without her?" he asked himself.

He was in a pinch. The papers would be reporting the murder of an unnamed and mysterious individual at the St. Paul Federal Courthouse. The St. Paul Police Department personnel, some of whom were lifelong friends, were going to want some answers. Many of Mike's men were seen around the courthouse for several days leading up to the incident that took place a couple of hours earlier.

Sweeney Detective Bureau, a business with a stellar reputation and run by a man who had a stellar reputation himself, would be in the public eye and the center of some unwanted publicity. Michael knew that he would need to call in a few favors. Quite a few of them, actually. He would need to leverage George Parker's help, but George already knew that. Lastly, he needed some divine intervention. He'd already made the first call the other day to Chief of Police Clint Hackert, and Hackert had pledged his support. He would need to update the Chief now that things were in motion. Hopefully, Hackert would run interference for him with the department as well as with the newspapers.

# CHAPTER 66

Frank and Hans waited in the train station for Kerling to show up. They saw him walk casually into the station and make his way to the restroom. A minute later he emerged and moved quickly to the ticket counter. After Kerling collected his ticket, Hans went to the ticket counter while Frank watched Kerling walk several feet to a newsstand and coffee area.

Gary Nelson looked up from his ticket counter to see a young man staring at him. The man quickly flashed a Sweeney Detective Bureau badge at him that Nelson really couldn't see and asked him where Edward Kelley was headed. Nelson, who had transacted the ticket only a minute before, barely answered without even checking:

"His name's not Kelley. It's Keller. Chicago, on the Zephyr, leaves in 15 minutes. It's about 6 ½ hours to Chicago on the Zephyr. Fastest train that we have, and that is the fastest route in America right now. That'll get him into Chicago around 10:30 PM tonight, give or take. He'll change trains there and get on another train that leaves around 45 minutes later for Cincinnati. It'll be around three hours to Cincinnati. You guys the feds?" asked Nelson.

"No," said Hans. "What kind of ticket did he buy?"

Nelson now had to refer back to the receipt. After a few seconds, he said, "First class drawing room. Car number four, compartment two. I got him the same configuration for Cincinnati. Car four, compartment two."

"Did he say anything to you?" asked Hans.

"Nope. Just the usual hello and goodbye."

Hans said a quick thank you and walked away. He glanced back at Nelson, who was already helping another passenger, then got into another line to get a ticket to Cincinnati through Chicago. Once that was done, he walked back over to Frank for a quick chat. Hans gave him the train itinerary. They discussed the next steps.

Frank: "Hans, you can't let him out of your sight."

Hans: "I know, Frank. I've got the compartment directly across from him, so I can look out the peephole at him if I need to. He is most certainly headed to Cincinnati, but I will stay vigilant in tailing him. Remember, I've been trained in this game."

"Yes, I know. Sorry, Hans. We just have to see who else this guy can lead us to. It'd be great to take down the whole network, if there is one."

Hans looked at his friend and said, "We were in a much bigger jam when we were in Germany. There we were, the hunted. Now, we are on our home ground, and we are the hunter and Kerling is the hunted."

Frank nodded but reminded his friend, "All true. I like our odds better, but remember, this guy lived in the U.S. for years."

Hans gave him an "I forgot about that" look, and then realized that he himself had never been to Chicago. Or Cincinnati. Still looking confident, he shook Frank's hand and said, "I'll see you in a few days."

Frank nodded, said, "Be careful," and turned to walk behind one of the pillars. He pulled out a newspaper and watched Kerling - or Kelley -or Keller - walk out of the newsstand with a cup of coffee and a couple of newspapers, making his way to the train.

Outside the station, Frank met up with a couple of Sweeney Detective men who had been assigned to watch the mail truck.

"Did you get a good look at the driver? Can you identify him?'" asked Frank.

We had a hard time getting a good look without looking too obvious, said the taller of the two men. Short dark hair with a mustache."

"That's it?" asked Frank. That's all you got?"

"Afraid so. Between the hat that covered his head and ears and the dark sunglasses - "That's another detail. He wore sunglasses - anyway, that's all we could get."

"All right. Thanks, fellas."

# CHAPTER 67

Kerling got settled in his compartment. He hadn't slept much and was looking forward to the uninterrupted peace and quiet of the trip to Chicago. He had about 10 minutes before departure, so he got off to find a phone booth. He found a row of four against the wall. All four were occupied, but just as he approached, a young woman hung up and exited from one of the booths. She had seen him coming. Kerling nodded a quick "Thank you," and quickly settled into the booth. He put a nickel in the slot and waited for an operator to come on.

"This is the operator; how may I help you?" came the voice with a Midwest accent. "You" sounded more like "yooooo." "Funny people, these Minnesotans," he thought.

"I need to make a person-to-person call to Al Landon at the Gibson Hotel in Cincinnati, room 242. Here is the phone number."

Leiner answered on the first ring. "Hello?" he asked, rather apprehensively.

"Hello Cousin!" said the man on the other end of the phone.

"I am excited to see you tomorrow!"

Leiner immediately sounded more upbeat and said, "Not as anxious as I am to see you, James!"

Kerling: "I should be there as scheduled. And I am bringing the very finest bottle of wine for you as a gift. The store was exactly where you told me it would be, and I found the perfect bottle. The transaction for it was flawless, and no one can ever dispute that this is the exact bottle that you had asked me to get."

"Excellent!" cried Leiner. "My father will be so pleased. But are you quite sure that it is the right one and has the right date on it?"

Kerling, with no hesitation: "Oh, I am quite sure. I made sure to watch with my own eyes so that there would be no doubt that this is the right wine."

"Wonderful," replied Leiner, with a touch of relief in his voice.

"I will see you tomorrow, then."

"Yes, my dear cousin, you shall. We have much to celebrate!"

With that, Kerling was off the phone. The call itself lasted less than 30 seconds, and he was quite sure that he was safe. He made his way back to the train for some much-needed rest.

Leiner breathed a sigh of relief, followed by a short shriek of jubilation. And then he did a very quick, rather awkward…dance? Jig? Something. Only when he had confirmation from his contact in St. Paul would he allow himself to officially tell Kappe? But Kerling was so sure about it that he himself shouldn't have to wait. After all, Kerling had said that he saw Edwin Conway die with his own two eyes. How much more proof did one need than that? He decided to celebrate. With what? Well, Kerling did mention a bottle of special wine. Why not?

C H A P T E R   6 8

Frank made his way out of Union Station and found his car. From there, he went to St. Joseph's Hospital, the oldest hospital in the state. St. Joe's was just minutes from Rice Park. He took Fifth Street south to St. Peter Street and stopped for as long as he could before the drivers behind him started honking their horns. His quick assessment was that the scene was still chaotic. People were still mulling around the courthouse and the hotel, occasionally pointing upward to the window that was broken by the bullet. Frank could see their eyes move from the window at the courthouse to the hotel, trying to determine where the shot had been taken from. There were close to a dozen cop cars parked haphazardly everywhere, including on the sidewalks. He saw no evidence of the Sweeney Detective men anywhere near the park or the buildings that bordered the park. The ambulance was also gone. No coincidence, that.

He made a right turn onto St. Peter Street and drove west, crossing over Seventh Street and came to Exchange Street, where he made a left. The hospital was on his right. He parked right in front and began to make his way to the basement, where the temporary morgue was located. Dr. Herb Holman, a friend of his dad's, would be examining the body. Holman was the Ramsey County Medical Examiner and Coroner.

There were only a couple of reporters who were hanging out at the hospital, having chosen to follow the ambulance rather than stay and try to get something out of the cops at the courthouse. Frank managed to avoid them and took the stairs down to the basement.

The security was tight in the hospital, especially as he made his way down to the basement. The good news was that all of the men knew him and greeted him warmly. He hadn't seen any of these guys since he had enlisted in the Army Air Force almost a year ago. After a lot of back slaps and well wishes, he finally got to the morgue itself. The door to the morgue was guarded by two more Sweeney detectives, who greeted Frank, looked around, and opened the door to let him in.

There was Dr. Holman in his familiar spot doing some unfamiliar things.

"Well, the war hero returns!" he beamed. Even though he had on a mask, Frank could see the smile in his eyes.

"Hi Doctor Holman! It sure is good to see you again!" said Frank, not even bothering to shake hands, given the mess that was on the doctor's gloves and apron.

"I hope they're taking good care of you, young man," the good doctor continued.

"You won't hear me complaining," replied Frank. "No one knows how long the war will last, or if we can effectively fight two wars at the same time. I suppose we'll find out soon enough. I can tell you that the boys in Europe are committed to seeing this thing through. Hitler is nuts, and the Nazis are bent on world domination. We can't let that happen."

Doctor Holman, focusing on the task at hand, merely nodded and grunted his agreement.

Frank shifted to the reason that he had stopped in.

"How's it coming?"

"Making progress. We'll need at least a couple of more hours."

Frank nodded. "I'll let my dad know. He wanted me to check in with you and express our appreciation to you for dropping everything and helping."

Holman nodded again, but then took a break. "You know, Frank, I owe my life and career to your dad. When I was just getting started, I didn't really know anyone and hadn't done any autopsies, at least officially. I met your dad at church years ago when he was still a detective, and he took me under his wing. One night he was at a double homicide with his partner, George Parker, and he had one of the patrolmen call me and ask me to come over to the scene. It was over off of Summit Avenue, near St. Thomas College. Anyway, we're all in this beautiful living room with two dead bodies on the floor, and I am starting to do my work."

Holman paused and said, "Hand me that vice, will you, son?"

Frank, not really one to stare a lot at dead bodies, reached for the vice and silently handed it to Holman, choosing not to look at what he needed it for.

"Thanks, Frank. Anyway, your dad and George are looking for projection angles and have some witnesses lined up in another room to interview. They go into the other room to start a couple of the interviews, leaving me alone in the living room to do my work. I am primarily looking to confirm the cause of death and get at least an estimate on the time of death when the back door opens. The owner of the home walks in - he had come down the alley in back and walked in from the back yard - anyway, he steps into the living room, sees me leaning over his tenants' bodies, and pulls out a .45 and is ready to let me have it. Your Dad heard the squeak on the stairs and the back door opening and managed to shut the guy down before he did something really foolish. As far as I'm concerned, your dad saved my life that night. The other guy was going to shoot first and ask questions later. Thankfully your dad intervened in time."

Holman shuddered and tried to focus back on his work.

"Wow, Dad never told me that story," said Frank.

Holman, now engrossed again in his project: "Son, I can guarantee you that there are a whole lot more stories like what I just shared that your dad hasn't told you. Why do you think that in the rare times, he needs a favor, everyone he knows jumps in with both feet to help him? Do you have any idea how many lives your dad has saved or how many criminals he has put away?"

"I used to think I knew that answer, but I'm guessing that I really have no idea," answered Frank, now more than a little interested.

# CHAPTER 69

Erik Fischer was at the Post Office getting ready to head home. He had turned his mail vehicle back in for the day and said hello to a few of his fellow mailmen. There had been so much shouting and confusion already that day. Before getting ready to hit the streetcar, he opted to walk over to Rice Park and grab a hot dog from one of the vendors that inevitably could be found around there at this time of day.

There was still a buzz coming from around the park. The musicians had gone home, but the people who were in the park at the time of the shooting had come back after scattering upon hearing the gunshot. Many of them were standing in small groups with some St. Paul cops, who were conducting interviews. He sidled up to a young couple who had what looked to be about a three-month-old baby bundled up in a stroller.

"What's all the excitement about?" he asked.

The young man looked at him as if he was from another planet. "You don't know?" he asked.

"No. I just heard rumors like everyone else here."

The young woman now, butting in: "Well, you won't believe it. You just won't believe it! We can't believe it, and we were here! Isn't that right, Jerry? We saw the whole thing!"

The baby has stirred and is letting people know that he is awake.

"What? What did you see?"

The young woman talked right over her husband, the aforementioned Jerry, who shook his head as if to say, "Here we go again. Can't get a word in edge-wise."

The baby starts to crank up the volume.

She got closer to Fischer and said, somewhat conspiratorially, "Someone shot a guy with a rifle."

Fischer, looking surprised, started to say, "Where?"

"He was in the hotel."

"The guy who was shot?"

The woman, louder now, to make up for her son, who is not really all that interested in the conversation: "No. No. The shooter was in the hotel. He shot a guy who was in the courthouse!"

Fischer: "You're joking! Who in the world would do such a thing?"

Jerry, trying to re-join the conversation so that his wife would tend to the baby who was now in a full-frontal assault of the eardrums: "Well, this is only speculative at this point, but" - and that's all that he got out.

The wife, who miraculously had managed to ignore the screams from her little bundle of joy: "No one is really saying much, but a couple of the cops mentioned that the victim was someone foreign, and very important. But no one is saying anything more than that."

Fischer, fairly shouting now to keep up with the baby: "I hope the victim will be all right."

Both of the young parents: "Huh?"

Fischer, really raising the volume: "I said that I hope the victim will be all right."

Jerry: "Well, I wouldn't."

The wife again: "Oh, he's dead. No doubt about that. All of the cops are even saying that. The ambulance just left with the body. No sirens, and the fellows with the stretcher were just taking their own sweet time about it. The cops said that he died instantly and that he never had a chance."

Leaning into Fischer again: "There was a lot of blood. He got shot right in the head. I hear the walls in the room that he was in are a bit messy, if you catch my drift."

Fischer: "This is terrible. Just terrible."

The husband: "Come on, dear. Junior is getting hungry."

The wife: "Nice talking to you." Then to the husband: "Don't just stand there, Jerry, pick him up!" He needs his bottle!"

Fischer nodded to the wife, looked at Jerry, smiled the "Good luck with all that" smile that only men can understand, and made his way over to the streetcar.

# CHAPTER 70

Later that evening, Leiner was still celebrating in his room at the Gibson Hotel. There was a knock on his door.

Half in the bag, he barked, "Who is it?"

"Good evening, Mr. Landon, this is the bellboy. I have a telegram that just arrived for you."

Leiner was puzzled, then smiled broadly.

"Slide it under the door."

The bellboy quickly responded: "I'm sorry sir, but I need your signature that confirms that you received it."

Leiner hesitated. Then he half-staggered to the door, opened it, and looked at the freckle-faced kid holding the telegram.

"Got a pen?"

"Right here, sir!"

Leiner took the pen, scribbled his name - Landon - on the paper, and gave the kid a buck.

"Wow! Thank you, Mr. Landon!"

"Don't mention it, kid."

With that, he closed and locked the door, went over to the desk in his room, sat down, and tried to collect himself. He was hoping it was what he thought it was.

He tore open the envelope and read:

*Confirming the successful acquisition of your special wine. The shipment went perfectly. Congratulations on your success! I'm sure that the whole family will be thrilled to hear the news that the right wine has been acquired.*

*-E.F.*

*Sent at 6:00 PM Central Time from St. Paul, MN.*

*Western Union Office*

*12 Market Street*

*St. Paul, MN. 55101*

Leiner let out a sigh of relief, then tried to muffle a shout of exultation as he pumped his fists in victory. Confirmation had come. He would let Kappe know immediately, right after one more swig of wine.

# CHAPTER 71

The funeral service was very small and very private. It was held at The North Church near downtown St. Paul.

Because there was so much damage to the head, it was a closed casket ceremony. The only time that the casket was opened was for Michael and George to take one last look and make sure that everything was perfect. The two friends, standing next to the coffin, looked down at the body for a moment, patted it one last time, and then nodded to the funeral director to close the casket.

The rest of the attendees were about 30 feet away when the casket was opened for that brief minute.

Most people glanced at the body for those few seconds - it was hard not to - and watched the funeral director close the casket for a final time. The women all turned away once it was closed, holding back as best as they could from bursting into tears.

Betty, who had come to the church with the family, had only planned to stay for a few minutes. She had to get back to the Sweeneys so she could get the sandwiches and the rest of the food ready for the luncheon after the service. Her husband, Erik Fischer, the Sweeney's mailman, had stopped at the church to pay his respects and to take Betty back to the house to finish preparing the food.

"We'll see you back at the house, Betty," said Maggie. "Thank you for being so kind to make all of the sandwiches for the luncheon today."

Betty smiled and said, "It's my pleasure to do it."

Maggie turned to Betty's husband and said, "Erik, it was so nice of you to come as well."

Michael and Frank each shook his hand, and Maggie and the girls gave him a hug.

He smiled and nodded, and then he took Betty gently by the arm and they walked back outside to their car.

Michael, Frank, George, and Hans served as pallbearers, along with a couple of the funeral staff.

Sweeney detectives were located around the perimeter of the funeral parlor, with a few outside as well.

The Sweeney and Parker families sat together, just like in the old days. Maggie and the girls were all dressed in black with black veils hanging over their heads.

Leigh's brother Jimmy was still in training and had not even been notified of what happened.

Leigh held onto Frank's hand tightly throughout the service, with Frank whispering words of encouragement to her.

Pastor Steven Lee gave a great gospel-centered message about this not being our permanent home and that, no matter the cause or time, all of us would one day face death. He encouraged everyone to be prepared, for, as they had just witnessed, life is fleeting, and none of us know how long we have here.

The men ushered the casket into the hearse. From somewhere close, there were a couple of pops of flashbulbs. Michael gave the photographers "The Look," and the two photographers scattered. They would now have their pictures to complement the next day's headline about the murder of a mysterious man that the government wouldn't talk about.

The funeral procession slowly proceeded to Calvary Cemetery on Front Street, off Snelling Avenue in St. Paul. Michael's parents were buried there, and he had purchased several plots for his family there as well.

After the service at the cemetery, everyone came back to the Sweeney household. There were sandwiches, potato chips, brownies, and cookies ready to go. Betty had done an excellent job on very short notice.

As the afternoon began to wind down, Leigh felt a tug on her sleeve and turned around. It was Michael.

He hugged her and whispered something to her. She nodded and hugged him back.

# CHAPTER 72

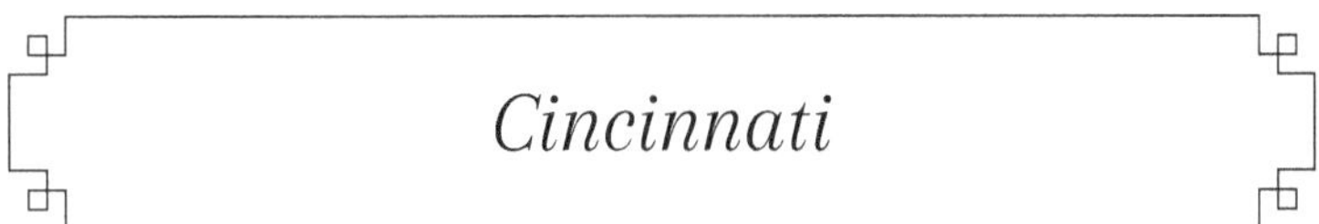

## *Cincinnati*

Leiner was…what? Relieved? Excited? Both.

He dialed the operator from his hotel room and asked to be connected to a number in New York City. After two rings, a voice came on the line.

"Hello?"

"Is this Mr. Kramer?" There was a pause.

Then: "You must have the wrong number."

Leiner: "I apologize."

Both parties hung up.

About 10 minutes later, Leiner's phone in his room rang.

"Yes?"

"Mr. Landon, this is the hotel operator. I have a call for you from New York. May I put it through?"

"Yes, please put it through."

After a few seconds: "Mr. Landon?"

"Yes, is that you, Mr. Kramer?"

"Yes, it is."

"Thank you for calling me. I have some wonderful news." Kramer/Kappe: "Oh? And what is that?"

Landon/Leiner: "As you know, I am expecting my cousin tonight, and he and his friend have both confirmed that he was able to find our favorite wine and that he is bringing it with him tonight!"

Kramer/Kappe: "But is he certain? Is he absolutely certain that it is the correct wine?"

Landon/Leiner: "Oh, definitely. He called me right after he found it, and I waited for his friend to confirm it. I have his friend's telegram here as well. There can be no doubt."

Kramer/Kappe, letting out a small squeal of delight: "Well, that is the best news, isn't it? Our family will be so thrilled that he was able to find it."

Landon/Leiner: "Yes, yes. It is wonderful news! The family will celebrate, as will you and I, when we see each other again."

Kramer/Kappe: "Will your cousin's friend be coming to visit as well?"

Landon/Leiner: "Yes, he stopped here and is now en route."

Another pause. "Excellent," said Kappe. "We are waiting on a couple of other friends who are supposed to be arriving soon from Chicago."

Leiner, reading his mind, said, "Although I haven't heard from them, I am sure that they will be there shortly. They were enjoying a few days with some relatives."

Kappe, still pondering, finally said, "Well, the main thing is that he not only found the right wine but acquired it. It will be good to get everyone together again. It has been way too long, and we have so much to catch up on. Do let me know the details about the wine when you get here."

"By all means, Mr. Kramer. We will see you very soon!"

With that, they hung up. Leiner finished his bottle, and 564 miles from Cincinnati, Kappe decided to open one for himself.

# CHAPTER 73

Kerling was well rested by the time the train pulled into Cincinnati. His private berth was comfortable, and the room service was excellent. He slept most of the way to Chicago, changed trains, picked up a Chicago Tribune paper from the porter, and returned to his berth. "So far, so good," he thought.

The Cincinnati Union Terminal opened only nine years earlier, and it was a state-of-the-art facility for train travelers. The city decided to consolidate six separate lines and have them all run into the new terminal. Business was booming these days, especially since the war had started.

Kerling had been impressed with it when he came from Florida only a few days ago. Once the train stopped in the terminal, he walked slowly through it, admiring the architecture along the way. He eventually made it to the taxis outside, hopped in a cab, and asked the driver to take him to the Gibson Hotel.

Kerling hadn't bothered to see if anyone was tailing him, partly because he believed that no one could be and partly because he just wasn't thinking. He was still reliving the last few moments in St. Paul and glad to have gotten out of there so quickly and smoothly. Honestly, the mission couldn't have gone better. He was onboard the train heading to Chicago in less than 15 minutes after firing the shot that had killed Edwin Conway.

Had Kerling turned around, he would have noticed a smaller, bespectacled man get in the cab right behind him and follow him to the hotel.

# CHAPTER 74

After the guests had left, Frank and Leigh decided to go for a walk together. It was one of those walks where neither person is really paying attention to where they are going, because they are so enamored with the person that they are with. What was supposed to be a ten-minute stroll ended up being almost a two-hour marathon.

They talked about everything, starting with the night that they met in Germany at a place called Burghoffs. Frank was taken completely off guard by Leigh's beauty. He remembers stammering when he tried to speak. And staring. For her part, Leigh was smitten as well, although she had a bit of a better grip on her emotions that evening.

They replayed their discovery of the treatment of the Jewish people living in Germany and meeting Esther's parents, who were part of a group of Germans who risked their lives daily in order to smuggle Jews out of the country; they even talked about the last night in Augsburg, including Frank rescuing her from two S.S. thugs who were searching for her.

She relived the memory of seeing her brother Jimmy for the first time in years, finding out that he was OK despite being held by the Nazis. And she talked about her dad.

"Frank, I love your country. I am so grateful to be here. I love your family. They have been so kind to me."

"What did you expect?" asked Frank. "We are Irish, you know."

She smiled at him and put her arm through his.

"Yes, you certainly are Irish. But I perhaps assumed that we would be safe here. And now we find out that we aren't. That the Nazis are here, too, and that they will stop at nothing to win this war. I would have thought that the ocean would have protected us."

Frank, casually looking around, said, "Yes, I thought we were safe here as well. I mean, think of it: of all of the places that they could have come, they come to St. Paul. The very ocean that you talked about protecting us was the same ocean that they used to get here."

They walked along in silence for a minute. It was a comfortable silence, each person thinking about the situation.

Finally, Frank spoke.

"Leigh, I'm probably going to have to leave soon. We have to find the people who are involved in this thing. We don't have a good feel for how big this is yet. We don't know what sort of network they have established here."

Leigh caught her breath, but then recovered quickly.

"I understand, Frank. But tell me, isn't this the role of the F.B.I. and not the O.S.S.?"

Frank sighed and then smiled faintly.

"I keep forgetting that you are - were - in the spy game, too." Leigh smiled back and waited for him to answer.

He continued, "The problem is that there are foreign spies on our soil. And that these guys have come over here in direct response to one of our O.S.S. operations. Luckily, Mr. Donovan and Mr. Hoover are both out of commission for several days.

That means their deputies are in charge. As I understand it, Uncle George has a very good working relationship with Hoover's number two man. They knew each other as field agents at the Bureau, and they trust each other. Plus, I think the F.B.I. man is looking for some help, which Uncle George can give him."

They finally looked up and saw that they were near the streetcar station where Edwin - and Leigh - had almost been killed, which brought back more memories.

"Any idea where the man who pushed us into the streetcar is?" asked Leigh.

"We have an idea. He is probably back in Cincinnati, or he is headed directly for New York. All eight saboteurs were supposed to rendezvous in New York. Haupt, the other guy that we sent to the German P.O.W. camp a couple of hours from here, is on his way to D.C. for further questioning. So right now, we have three men in New York that we have under surveillance, and one on his way to New York who we will be watching for. We have two - Haupt and Neubauer, both from Chicago - who are in custody. Dasch, the guy who spilled the beans to us, is in D.C. The only man unaccounted for is Kerling, and Hans is tracking him as we speak. We are sure that he will get to Cincinnati, make contact with at least one of the guys who is calling the shots, and then make his way to New York as well. So, all eight men are at least accounted for. That is, unless Kerling flew the coop somehow."

He paused, looked around for a minute, and then continued.

"Flew the coop?" asked Leigh.

"Yeah, you know, like chickens who escape out of their henhouse. They flew the coop."

"You Americans sure do talk funny."

"Be careful, there, young lady. You'll be an American in no time."

Leigh smiled at that.

"Well, I guess I better study up on the language." Then, in as masculine a voice as she could muster: "Right, buddy?"

For the first time in what seemed like ages, they both laughed.

# CHAPTER 75

Kerling had gotten settled into his room at the Gibson House Hotel. The hotel was one of the finest in the city. It was located on Main Street between 4th and 5th Avenue and housed many local and national celebrities. Known for its excellent food and outstanding service, the original hotel burned to the ground in 1912. Consequently, the newer version had several safety features when it came to preventing a fire, including a state-of-the-art fire and smoke detection system.

Kerling was looking forward to speaking with Leiner and giving him the blow-by-blow of the previous day's activities. He equated it to replaying an entire football game in one's mind and reciting all of it to an interested friend who would want to hear every detail.

After all, he had just pulled off an incredible feat. He (and, he supposed, Leiner) would be the toast of the Fatherland in a few days.

"Everyone will want to take credit for this," he lamented as he walked down the hall toward Leiner's room.

"Still, I should mention the local support that I received in St. Paul. Without that help, I never would've made it out of the city.

Yes, I should do that. It's the right thing to do."

He made it to room 615, gathered himself for a minute, and knocked on the door.

"Who is it?" called a voice from behind the door.

"It's your cousin."

"One minute."

It took a full minute before Leiner opened the door.

"Cousin, how good to see you!" Leiner said a little too loudly.

"Come in! Come in!"

Just as Kerling began to move into the room, they heard a voice yell, "FIRE! FIRE!"

They looked at each other, thoroughly confused for a moment, then the hotel's fire alarm went off. It was loud - so loud that they could barely hear one another. The people in the rooms on the floor came out and scattered like cockroaches exposed to light. They ran past the two men, some taking the steps and others, to the amazement of Leiner and Kerling, waited for the elevator.

An employee appeared with a megaphone. Clearly panicked, he yelled at everyone to not panic. That was helpful. He then yelled for everyone to drop everything and immediately walk to the nearest stairway and get out of the hotel as quickly as possible. Even then, some ignored the order and continued to wait for the elevator. This made the employee even more rattled. He came up to the small group at the elevator and raised the megaphone to tell them to take the stairs.

Leiner and Kerling looked at one another again, shrugged, and made their way to the stairs with the others. As the floor cleared out, a man emerged from another room down the hall. He was a little on the thin side and about average height. He allowed himself a brief smile as he made his way to room 615. Hans Ungrodt had more than enough time to plant two listening devices and search through Leiner's belongings. He found that Leiner had purchased two tickets to New York City on the 4:00 PM train, which was still a few hours away. He also saw the telegraph that had come from the Western Union. Whipping out a tiny camera, he photographed it and made a mental note to memorize it. He was in and out in less than three minutes.

CHAPTER 76

Michael and Frank made their way into downtown in Michael's 1942 DeSoto sedan.

"This sure beats the streetcar," said Frank.

They were both munching on chicken sandwiches that Betty Fischer had cooked up for them before they left the house.

"Don't make a mess in my car, son. With the shortages, there won't be any new cars made until after the war."

"Dad, forgive me, but you're going to have to educate me. Remember, I've been out of the country for a while." Michael began to explain the new reality to him.

"Because we were not prepared for a war on two fronts, let alone a war of any kind, all of the auto manufacturers were ordered by the government to stop making cars and to start making weapons. Tanks, airplanes, jeeps, army trucks, military ambulances, you name it. Production on almost all cars was stopped in February of this year. They made somewhere between 100,000 and 500,000 automobiles in those first two months, depending on who you believe. Everything else was converted to the war effort. To put that in perspective, the total number of cars manufactured in the U.S. last year was over 3 million."

"Wow," said Frank. "I had no idea…"

His dad nodded. "Only those citizens who are deemed "essential" are given consideration to get whatever is left."

267

"So, when did you get this car, Dad? She's the cat's meow!"

"I ordered it in December, right after Pearl Harbor, and I got it in January. I was one of the lucky ones. But it has to last us for who knows how long."

Frank thought about that for a minute.

"Boy, I bet an auto mechanic is going to be doing pretty well for himself for the next few years."

"Yes, son, I suppose so. If you can find one, that is. Remember, a lot of those men are fighting somewhere overseas, just like you have been."

They rode in silence for a few minutes.

"We have to win this thing, Dad. The alternative is too horrible to think about."

Michael took a minute to reflect on that before he responded.

"We'll win. Because we have to. To your point, the alternative would be so foreign to us. To not have our freedom and to come under the power and authority of a foreign ruler is just not something that Americans will ever accept. One only has to look at our history to come to that conclusion." Frank nodded in agreement.

Michael continued: "Lincoln said that if America fails, it will come as a result of a collapse from within. That is, we will get lazy and develop programs and policies that will incentivize people not to work. The government would end up becoming a sort of big handout to the masses. In a republic like we have, more government will never be the answer to the problem. It will be the problem."

Michael pulled up to the bank and parked along the curb. He greeted the Sweeney Detective Bureau cop who was guarding the bank with a "Good morning, Max!" and he and Frank hustled inside and got to the elevators. A minute later they were standing in the lobby of Sweeney Detective Bureau headquarters.

"Hi, Aunt Susie!" said Frank. His aunt had already been at work for almost an hour.

"Frank, it sure has been nice to have you back home, if only for a few days."

He gave her a hug and a peck on the cheek.

"Thanks. It's wonderful to be with everyone again."

"Oh, and Frank?"

"Yes?"

"You'd better not let that wonderful young woman go back to Ireland. At least not without you!"

Frank smiled and gave his aunt another hug.

"Yes, ma'am!"

They made their way into Michael's office. George Parker would be coming in momentarily, and the three of them would be getting a phone call from Hans, who no doubt had arrived in Cincinnati.

# CHAPTER 77

Leiner and Kerling settled back in Leiner's room at the hotel.

"I believe the Americans call that a "false alarm," said Leiner. "This hotel was destroyed by fire several years ago. As a result, they put in a very sophisticated fire and smoke alarm system."

"Yet someone still yelled, "Fire!" observed Kerling. "I heard it myself."

"True enough," replied Leiner. "In talking to one of the bellhops outside while we were waiting, he mentioned that there was probably a small grease fire in the kitchen or some such thing. Given the hotel's history, I suppose the slightest flame is enough to make everyone a bit uneasy."

They returned to the business at hand, and Kerling began walking his comrade through the entire "blow by blow" of how he had been able to kill Edwin Conway.

"After Thiel failed in his attempt at the streetcar platform, I had decided that there was no more time to waste. Our friend Mr. Kappe made that quite clear to me as well. Once I heard that they had put Conway in protective custody in the Federal Courthouse, I checked out of the Commodore Hotel and moved to the St. Paul Hotel, which had a direct view into the courthouse itself. Conway had a room that faced the hotel, so it all came together very quickly."

Kerling lit a cigarette, took a long puff, and then talked about the gun that he used.

"Picked it up only a couple of blocks from here. It was really the perfect gun for the job," he said. "It had come with an excellent scope that I needed to sight, but other than that, it was relatively straightforward."

"Excellent! Excellent!" said Leiner. "It was perfect German execution! We must take the time to write all of this up in a report for Kappe and his superiors."

"It really was a perfect shot," said Kerling. "I saw his head explode, and there was blood everywhere."

"Yes, yes!" cried Leiner. "The plan worked perfectly. It was brilliant! Expertly conceived."

Kerling, not wanting to be upstaged, said, "Yes. And even better executed."

Leiner, finally catching on, said, "Yes, of course. You carried your orders out perfectly. They must be toasting us in Berlin right now!"

"Our accomplice was critical in this mission and is deserving of some recognition as well," said Kerling.

"Certainly," replied Leiner. "I will recognize Agent Fischer's contributions to all of this. It was beyond fortuitous that we had an agent located in the same city as the target."

Kerling replied, "The good agent did mention to me specifically that it would mean a lot if we included in any report how we were helped in this mission by the agent on the ground."

Leiner merely nodded and said, "I will make sure to include all of it in my report. Who knows? We may need to activate Agent Fischer again sometime."

After a minute of silence, Kerling, ever the soldier, replied: "OK, we had success. We accomplished what was demanded of us."

Leiner, sensing more was coming, nodded and motioned for Kerling to continue.

"I've had some time to think since St. Paul. Now that I'm out of there and no one is looking for me, we now need to re-focus on why we came back to America to begin with."

Leiner, processing all of this, asked, "So you no longer want to get out of the country and return to Germany?"

It was Kerling's turn to nod. "At least not immediately. But soon."

Leiner looked relieved and said, "I was hoping that you would say that."

Kerling went on: "I would feel differently if the mission hadn't been successful. But I was in the train station less than ten minutes after I pulled the trigger. I'm sure that I wasn't followed here. No one has a picture of me. I used aliases. By the way, I assume Thiel is in New York?

"He's well on his way. Might even be there by now."

"All right," said Kerling. "I need to see at least part of the rest of this assignment through. But make no mistake: I expect a significant promotion as a result of the completion of this last mission. While you have no direct control over this, you at least have some influence. I expect your full support."

Leiner responded: "I will enthusiastically support you. I will push and influence in any way that I can." "Good," replied Kerling.

"However," said Leiner, "In exchange for my support, I need you to give me credit for the flawless planning that took place and the usage of our local contact in St. Paul. You see, Herr

Kerling, you are not the only one who wants a promotion."

"Fair enough," said Kerling. "I will support you as well."

"Excellent! Now that we have that out of the way let's return to the topic at hand."

Kerling again: "The teams have factories to destroy and ships to sink and bridges to blow up. I was thinking on the train here that we probably have to start with two large targets: the ALCOA factory in Pennsylvania and one of the major bridges that all of these defense manufacturers use to get their products to the naval docks. If we can attack the supply manufacturers and the transportation system here, we can effectively starve the Allies of ammunition and supplies. Think about it: we take away a significant portion of their munitions, and our submarines who own the Atlantic blow up the ships that are still able to carry what supplies they can still make."

Leiner: "I like that. Yes. That could very well work. After all, the whole operation is called "Pastorius," because that was the name of the man who led the first German settlement in America. And that happened to be in Pennsylvania. The ALCOA factory is in Pennsylvania. It could be what the Americans call "Poetic Justice."

"But," continued Leiner, "Don't forget that we also need to strike the Jewish-owned department stores. There are many of them in New York.

This was also an essential order from the Fatherland. We need to create dissension and impact the morale of the Americans."

Kerling, who was still thinking about how to attack the ALCOA factory and what he would need to successfully do it, absently said to Leiner, "While the morale objective is important, we need to first do the things that will directly impact America's ability to fight and influence the outcome of the war. The bridges and factories need to happen first. The morale - or lack of it - will be a natural consequence of plants and bridges being destroyed."

"Agreed," said Leiner. "I have managed to get many of the blueprints of the ALCOA factory as well as a couple of the bridges around New York City. There are dozens of factories to choose from after the ALCOA factory is destroyed."

Kerling: "Of course there are. But we will need to act fast, because security around the rest of the factories will immediately be tightened. I am thinking that we set bombs to go off simultaneously in two or three different places: ALCOA, a bridge, and maybe a government center of some kind."

Leiner nodded again. "We can discuss this on the train. Also, I would think that Dasch and his crew have had some time to think about all of this as well. Let's get something to eat. Our success has given me quite an appetite!"

Kerling put up a hand to stop him. "Look," he said. "I'll do the ALCOA job, but then I need to get out of the country, at least for a while. The F.B.I. is good. They'll eventually circulate pictures of me and do whatever they need to do to hunt me down. I am going to plan to leave the country once the bombs are planted at the chosen sites. I am not even going to wait around to see if they explode or not. After a few months, I will come back into the country and help whatever teams need me. But I need to get out of here for a while. My leaving would also minimize the chances of the entire team being caught."

Leiner said, rather nonchalantly, "That's between you and Kappe. We're going to need some reinforcements. They will either have to come via submarine again, or we find more local accomplices like we have in St. Paul and do things from within. Regardless of how they do it, it is clear that we need more resources if we are to make a difference in this war from here."

Kerling merely nodded in agreement. One of his concerns from the start of being assigned to Kappe's group was scalability. Could Kappe actually scale an organization, based on the needs and future needs of the war? Did he have the political pull within the Nazi ranks to get what he needed?

He replied to Leiner, "No doubt, Kappe's answer to these kinds of questions will be that the team will need to demonstrate that it can deliver on its objectives on this first mission in order to justify more resources and monies to continue to bring the war directly to the U.S."

Leiner agreed, saying, "Of course. So, we must deliver on the objectives of the mission."

He looked at his watch. "I still want to eat, but we better get packed for New York."

Three doors down from Leiner's room, Hans Ungrodt heard every word and was writing notes at a furious pace.

# CHAPTER 78

Michael, Frank, and George grabbed some coffee while they waited for Hans to call in.

As they waited, George decided to update them on the overall status of things as best he could.

"I've been keeping in touch with David Ladd, my counterpart at the F.B.I."

"We certainly caught a break with Hoover being out of town for a few days, eh Georgie?" asked Michael.

"Michael, you certainly know how to read the tea leaves," replied George.

Parker continued: "The overall plan remains in place. We are going to try to wait to get the remaining spies when they all meet in New York. They're going to pick up this Burger guy today. They're concerned about making him wait too long with no news from Dasch. They don't want him to get too antsy. The rest of the spies are either in New York already or are on their way. We obviously have Haupt. The F.B.I.'s office in Chicago picked Neubauer right off of the train as it was about to take off for New York. That leaves the guy who was with Kerling here. Thiel is his name. We think he's on his way to New York via Cincinnati. May be arriving in New York tonight or tomorrow morning. The F.B.I. will have people at the train station to pick him up."

Parker looked down at his notes again, then continued: The remaining two guys who are a part of Dasch's team are both under surveillance. Let's see here… Richard Quirin and Heinrich Heinck. They are at a hotel a couple of blocks from where Burger and Dasch were staying."

Frank said, "There's one more guy that you haven't mentioned, Uncle George."

Parker again: "Oh, and Kerling, of course. The goal is to make a clean sweep of everyone in New York. But that will be more Ladd's project than mine. Jurisdiction, you know. And politics. When Hoover gets back, he will want total credit for busting up this ring."

Michael spoke next: "While grabbing all of these guys is certainly critical, we have to continue to sell the story that Edwin is dead **and** that they accomplished this mission."

The phone rang before Frank could add his comments to the conversation.

"Yes, Susie," said Michael.

"Hans Ungrodt is calling in as scheduled."

"Thanks, Doozer." (Her lifelong nickname in the family). "Put him through, please."

A moment later, Hans' voice came through. The normal description would be that he came through loud and clear. But given the circumstances, a more accurate description would be that he came through "quiet and somber."

# CHAPTER 79

While George Dasch stewed in his makeshift cell at the F.B.I., David Ladd and Dave Bouquet flew to New York City. They went right to the Governor Clinton Hotel and quietly flashed their credentials to John Yesh, the hotel manager. He confirmed the room where Ernst "Peter" Burger was staying. Yesh knew him by his alias. All of it matched what Dasch had told them.

They asked Yesh to meet with them for a couple of minutes. He looked a bit confused but then quickly nodded and directed them to a room behind the lobby.

Ladd and Bouquet grilled him about Burger, no pun intended. When did he check in? Did he venture out of the hotel a lot? Did he get any visitors? Had he used the phone much? If so, did the hotel keep records of his calls? What was his temperament?

Yesh, a large, jovial man with a black mustache that matched his dark hair, prided himself on trying to meet every guest who stayed for more than one night. He didn't have all that much to offer.

He pulled a couple of records that indicated that his only phone calls were to the Martinique Hotel, which was a couple of blocks away. He had received no visitors, and ordered room service a lot. He did recall Burger leaving once or twice during the day for an hour or two. Once he came back with a couple of bags that had new clothes in them. The other time he came back empty handed, just as how he had left.

"Is there some problem here that I need to be aware of?" he asked.

"No, this is just a routine check," said Ladd. "We noticed that he was new in town, and we are just doing some routine follow-up. Nothing for you to be concerned about."

Yesh didn't believe that but was smart enough to not say anything.

At Bouquet's request, Yesh gave them a spare key. The three men made their way back to the front desk, where another man was now standing.

"Mr. Yesh, this is Agent Dale Holyer from our office in the city. He'll be hanging around here in the lobby for a few minutes while we go talk to the gentlemen in room 1705. Like I said, there is nothing to worry about, but Agent Holyer here is going to make sure that you don't get on the phone with anyone while we are gone. He and his partner will also be watching the lobby to see if anyone comes in looking for our friend upstairs."

Holyer, an older gentleman with graying hair, was one of the very few F.B.I. agents who was allowed to have a mustache, strictly because he occasionally did some undercover work for the Bureau. Besides, by his own admission, he would look strange without one.

He nodded to Yesh and said, "I'll just be right here watching. Let me know if you need anything. Oh yeah - do stay off the phone, huh?"

"Yes, of course I can do that, but I may need to answer incoming lines."

Holyer stared at him and shook his head. "No," he said.

Ladd and Bouquet walked back out of the front of the hotel to the street, where they had another four agents waiting in another car. Two agents got out and made their way to the back of the hotel to intercept Burger in case he tried to make a run for it. The other two stood by the car with overcoats on that covered their respective firearms.

Ladd and Bouquet took their time making their way to the two elevators, casually looking around the lobby for anyone suspicious. Seeing no one, they got to the elevators and waited until they could ride up alone.

The Governor Clinton Hotel always had young men operating each of the two elevators. Due to the war going on, these "young men" were kids that couldn't have been more than 15 years old. Bouquet slipped the kid a $5 bill and told him to beat it.

The guy looked at the bill, did a double take, and started to say something as he looked up into Bouquet's eyes. He immediately thought better of it and hustled away.

Once inside, Bouquet made sure that they were indeed on their way to the 17th floor. Yesh had told the men that room 1705 was a suite with two doors that were a few feet apart.

"Pretty nice hotel," said Bouquet.

"Adolph apparently spared no expense," agreed Ladd.

"I bet they're burning through the cash."

"Seeing Dasch's suitcase, it would appear that they have it to burn," replied Ladd.

"How do you want to play this?" asked Bouquet.

"I'll do the talking," said Ladd. "You just be your normal, charming self."

That brought a snort from Bouquet.

They saw the needle finally settle on "17" and walked out to the hallway. Not seeing any signs, they embarked to the right, which was the right choice. A maid's cleaning cart was at the end of the hall. No maid to go with the cart, though. She was probably cleaning one of the rooms.

They proceeded only about 20 feet or so and came upon room 1705 on their left. Ladd got up close and tried to listen for any noises. He did hear a couple of voices, followed by laughter. The radio. Burger was listening to a show. It sounded like "Fibber McGee and Molly," which was a long running comedy series about an Irish couple and their day-to-day foibles.

Ladd stepped back, nodded to Bouquet to get ready, took the key out, and quietly opened the door. Bouquet was right behind him, gun drawn.

C H A P T E R  8 0

Michael Sweeney had specially wired his phone into his intercom system, which operated as a speaker phone of sorts.

Hans spoke rather softly, and they asked him to speak up.

"I can't. I am only three rooms down from them. I can't take the risk that they will be walking by my room and hear me. And I don't want to go down to the lobby where they might see me. I don't want to give them any chance of seeing me more than once in different settings. As of right now, I am very confident that Kerling has not noticed me. Leiner certainly hasn't, either. Let's keep it that way."

"You're absolutely right, Hans," said Parker. "Try turning the radio on and have it face the door." "Hold on a minute," said Hans.

A few moments later, they heard a radio come on. Hans tuned into some sort of a music station. They were playing a Jimmy Dorsey tune.

Hans made it back to the phone and felt comfortable speaking a little louder.

"One of you may want to take some notes on this. What I am going to tell you has been recorded already, but you may want to have it written down somewhere so you can share it quickly with anyone else who could help."

The three men in St. Paul looked at one another. Frank quickly said, "I'll take the notes."

Hans, wasting no time, began.

"OK, here is what I know: I got into Cincinnati with no problem. As I said, I'm fairly certain that Kerling didn't see me. I pulled a fire alarm in the hotel to get everyone out of their rooms. While Kerling and Leiner were outside with everyone else I placed two listening devices in Leiner's room. I knew that they were going to meet there as soon as they got back into the hotel." "That was good work, Hans," commented Michael.

Hans kept on going, too excited to stop.

"They bragged to each other about the assassination of Dr. Conway. Leiner took credit for the logistics, and Kerling took credit for the kill. The good news is that they are both convinced that Dr. Conway is dead, and they have been celebrating. Also, they talked a lot about their next mission. They are going to be on a train later today, heading to New York. Leaves this afternoon at 4:00 PM. I don't remember the details, but you can have someone look it up. They'll probably be traveling under their assumed names of Kelley and Landon. Kerling might be

traveling under "Keller" rather than Kelley. I'm just not sure."

Hans took a breath and then started again. "When they get there, just make sure that no one loses them. I know that New York is a big city, and it's easy to get lost there. They have big plans. Leiner mentioned blowing up the ALCOA factory. I don't know what that is."

Parker again: "That's only the largest producer of aluminum in the country and probably the most important vendor to our country's war efforts."

That was followed by a low whistle from Michael and a "Wow!" from Frank.

Hans again: "Bridges and other munition facilities were mentioned. Shipyards. Government facilities. Kerling talked about doing more than one simultaneously because he thinks that once they hit ALCOA, security will tighten up really fast at the other sites. They also talked about blowing up Jewish-owned retail stores, where the public shops. That would create some real terror and turn the Americans against the Jewish people, much like Hitler did as he came to power. But Kerling said that those would have to wait until they did real damage to the actual war effort. Also, Kerling wants to leave the country as soon as the bombs are set at the ALCOA factory. Thinks by then the F.B.I. will have a dedicated effort to find him."

Hans paused to look at his notes, which he had written in German and had to translate into English.

It took him a few seconds, but then he continued: "Kerling told Leiner that they need to put a dent in the U.S.'s ability to produce ammunition and machinery for the war. By the way, Leiner mentioned that he already has blueprints of the ALCOA facility as well as some of the bridges in and near New York City. Maybe some shipyards, too. Now that I know what the ALCOA factory is, I can see that it would be a great target because the name of the operation - that's the other news here - is that the whole operation is called "Operation Pastorius." It's named after a man who led the first German settlement in America, and that was in Pennsylvania somewhere. The ALCOA factory is in -

"Pennsylvania," finished Parker.

There was silence on the other end of the phone. So much silence that Hans thought that they had been disconnected. He finally had to say, "Hello? Is anyone there?"

After another moment, Michael said, "Yes, Hans, we are still here. We are trying to process everything that you are telling us."

The translation to Hans was, "Not only would this be devastating to our country, but it wouldn't be that difficult to achieve these kinds of results."

Frank was still writing, shaking his head.

"They could really do this. And they only have eight men! Just think if they have more coming into the country!" Silence again.

Michael finally said, "It's a brilliant plan, men. You do see what they're doing, don't you? If they take out our infrastructure and distribution, it means that our military is sitting ducks all over the world. Our fighting men would be starved of ammunition, tanks, mortars, planes, ships, spare parts all of it. And meanwhile, the German navy still owns the Atlantic. Their subs would become even more dominant and wipe out whatever supply ships that we could even attempt to get across the ocean."

Hans was nodding, but of course, no one could see him.

"That's almost exactly what Leiner said. That is the essence of their plan."

Then Parker: "I need to get this information to Ladd at the F.B.I. He might have some of it already, but I doubt that he has all of it. He is in

New York right now, arresting Dasch's next in line. His name is Burger. They are trying to wait for the others to arrive in New York before they take any further action."

"The fact that they have access to the blueprints would indicate that they have someone or some people on the inside in some of these places," observed Frank.

"Good point, son," said Michael. "Some sort of partner, or someone that they are either bribing or blackmailing."

Now Hans: "Oh! That reminds me. I almost forgot. I have the name of the accomplice that Kerling utilized to get away in Minnesota. Their voices got a little quiet when they were talking about this part, so I couldn't hear this part very clearly. But I think they mentioned some guy named Fischer. I also found a telegram from him in Leiner's room when I was planting the listening devices. It was signed "E.F."

Michael froze. Erik Fischer. His mailman! Yes, it all fit. He would have access to a mail truck. And a uniform for Kerling to change into.

"I know who you are talking about," he told Hans.

Michael turned to Frank and George and said, "The guy is our mailman!"

"What?" said Frank.

Michael put his head in his hands.

"He saw Edwin. Met him at our house the other day. Betty's husband. Said hello and everything. Of course, I didn't say anything to him about who Edwin was. But he seemed to be very interested in Edwin. I remember he asked Edwin where he was going to after St. Paul. I had to step in and change the subject." "He was also at the funeral," said Parker.

Frank's hands had turned into balls of fists. As had his father's. Another voice entered the conversation.

"Hans, are you absolutely positive that they think I'm dead?" asked Edwin Conway.

# CHAPTER 81

The plan had gone off flawlessly. Dr. Herb Holman had finagled a body from the morgue that, with some work, would pass for Edwin Conway, especially from behind.

There was a lot of coordination and synchronization that had to take place in order to "sell" it to Kerling. Connie Parker, George's sister, played her part perfectly as "Maid Connie." Her job was to occupy Kerling long enough so that the corpse could be placed in Edwin's chair in the courthouse room where Edwin had stayed. Parker had a second, identical chair in a corner of the room that couldn't be seen from Kerling's perch. That second chair already had the corpse in it. Parker had dyed a rope the color of the chair. The rope was tied around the body, but at the lower part of the chair, where it couldn't be seen by Kerling from the angle that Kerling had. That was the only way to keep the body upright in the chair so Kerling could get his shot away. They had to make an exact duplicate of Conway's clothes and cut his hair exactly the same way that Edwin wore it, even down to the small bald spot that seemed to be growing by the day.

While "Maid Connie" was doing her act, Conway stepped away from the desk and changed into an ambulance driver uniform, including a hat, a fake mustache, and clear glasses. Parker slid the corpse, tied to the chair, behind the desk. All of this took less than 30 seconds. Michael and Dr. Holman coordinated the ambulance as well.

In all of the rush and panic in the moments after the shot, everyone would be looking at the body and not at the ambulance personnel. A couple of detectives from Michael's agency also were disguised as ambulance personnel and, with Conway driving, got the body out of there in a hurry.

About the only thing that didn't go as planned was identifying the driver of the mail truck that acted as an escape vehicle for Kerling. No one really got a good look at the accomplice, mainly due to how the sun was hitting the truck that day. The only description was "a white male with dark glasses and a mustache." Not terribly helpful.

Once the body had arrived at St. Joseph's Hospital, Edwin merely changed clothes but kept the disguise. The Sweeney detectives drove him to Michael's office in one of the armored cars. They came up the back elevator, so no one saw them. Edwin was staying in a small room off of Michael's main office. It had a bed and bathroom in it, along with a small desk and chair. A larger cushioned chair sat in the corner next to a standing lamp. Michael had kept the room for when the nights got too long to bother going home. The only way out of the room was through his office. There were two Sweeney guards posted in the lobby 24/7.

Aside from being a bit bored, Edwin was holding up well. Susie got him his meals from downstairs, and there was a police radio and a regular radio in the room to keep him busy. He was getting intrigued with some of the radio programs that were new to him. His favorites were fast becoming "The George Burns and Gracie Allen Show" and "The Whistler."

While Edwin was deeply grateful for the help and the protection, he was really getting tired of being a target. When Frank had laid out the plan for him, he readily agreed. Anything to keep Leigh safe. After all, she was as much a target as he was. Plus, he just wanted to get back to what he loved: aeronautical engineering.

About the only thing that had changed with him was an even greater sense of urgency to do whatever he could to defeat the Nazis and Japan. He realized that America would be his home for at least a while. Perhaps permanently, given Leigh's love for Frank.

He hadn't met anyone quite like the Americans that he had interacted with. Honest and forthright, loyal, and committed. Those were some of the words that came to mind.

"On the other hand, they're all Irish!" he told himself. "No wonder!"

David Ladd silently put the key into the door of Peter Burger's room. The key worked perfectly and any noise that came from the unlocking action was blocked out by the radio that was playing in the room.

Burger sat in a dark leather chair that faced the city. Ladd and Bouquet silently looked around the room for any weapons. And any other people. Seeing none, Ladd focused on Burger and the desk that he was sitting at while Bouquet silently began to make his way to the other room.

Burger chuckled as he listened to Fibber McGee and Molly on the radio.

His thoughts were interrupted by a voice behind him that rather quietly said, "F.B.I don't move."

Burger, keeping his eyes looking straight ahead, slowly raised his hands.

Bouquet moved quickly into the other room. After a few moments, he came out and said, "All clear."

Ladd cleared off the desk that Burger was sitting at, looked through the drawers while Bouquet kept an eye on their new prisoner, and then turned to Burger and told him to stand up.

Burger stood, all while keeping his hands in the air.

Ladd frisked him and found no weapons.

"You can sit back down," Ladd said.

"Thank you," replied Burger. "Can I assume that Dasch made contact with you?"

"I wouldn't be assuming anything right now if I were you," said Bouquet. "You're in a lot of trouble, Burger."

"Why don't we start with some introductions," said Burger, not looking very worried. "You know my name, and I would assume that you know all about me by now. But I don't know either one of you."

Ladd gave him the basics and turned the conversation back to Burger.

"We want to know what you're doing here."

"Surely Dasch covered all of this with you, did he not?"

"We'd like to hear it from you, Herr Burger." Bouquet, the "bad cop."

Burger, after a moment: "Oh, now I understand! Of course! You want to make sure that my story is consistent with what

Dasch told you. Do you mind if I smoke?"

"Yes, I do mind." Bouquet again. "Start talking."

Burger proceeded to tell them everything that Dasch had, with very little deviation from Dasch's version. In a two-hour interrogation, he covered when they landed, where they landed, the mission itself, the other four men who landed in Florida, the decision to have Dasch go to meet with Hoover, all of it.

"I am not a Nazi, gentlemen. Frankly, I don't really care for them. I was even imprisoned by them for a while a few years ago."

Ladd now: "Why? Why did you come here?"

"I told you: I wanted to come back to America."

"The other two men that are here with you…Are they at the Martinique Hotel?"

"Yes. You may want to be a little more careful with those two. They believe in the cause, so to speak."

"What are they doing over there?" Bouquet, inserting himself back into the conversation.

"Waiting on instructions from Dasch," said Burger. "They've been doing some shopping and going to some movies, just taking in the sights. They are expecting all four of us to get together for dinner tonight. You see, they know nothing about Dasch's and my plan to defect, if you will."

"Where are you supposed to meet them for dinner?" asked Ladd.

"Right here in this suite. We will order room service. They are supposed to come over at 7:00 PM."

"Will they be armed?"

"No," said Burger. "Our orders were quite clear about that. We are to not attract any attention to ourselves. No carrying unless we are on a sanctioned mission."

Bouquet jumped back in: "Who are your other contacts here in New York?"

"Two men named Leiner and Krepper. I don't know anything about them, though. I asked Dasch to give me their names as a test. He passed the test."

"Here's what's going to happen," said Ladd. "We will have access to any incoming phone calls that come in. If the phone rings, you wait until you get the go-ahead to answer it."

Burger merely nodded.

Ladd asked, "Do you have any questions?"

"Just one," said Burger. "Why do I get the feeling that you aren't going to treat us as heroes for telling you about all of this?"

Bouquet stepped in. "I don't know what world you are living in, but it certainly isn't one that we live in. If you tell us everything, and I mean everything, and you cooperate in getting us any other names that were involved in this, you might - just might - avoid the electric chair."

For the first time since they walked into his room over two hours ago, Burger felt a lot less smug.

# CHAPTER 83

have them come up to Michael's office. Both men showed up at noon. With Parker's permission, Michael got them up to speed and told them about Erik Fischer.

"We don't want the local cops involved in this, and we don't know the F.B.I. guys that are stationed here very well, so George here is letting us in on this thing. Interrogate Fischer. Find out what he knows and who he works for. Tap his phone at home. Take however many extra men that you will need on this, but do not let him out of your sight. As a matter of fact, put him in one of our safe houses and lock him in. Get every ounce of information that you can get out of him. We need to move quickly on this. Report back to me at the end of the day." "We're on it, boss," said O'Brien.

Flood nodded in agreement. The two men were Michael's most trusted detectives, and they were part of the entire plan to keep Edwin Conway alive.

After they left, George turned to Michael and said, "Those two guys are younger versions of us."

"But not as good-looking," replied Michael.

George and Frank chuckled.

"Where'd you find them?" asked George.

"Two ex-athletes from St. Paul. O'Brien went to Notre Dame, and Flood went to St. Thomas. Both went to St. Thomas Academy for High School, which is where the two of them met. They came knocking on my door one day. They were on the force here for a few years, both walking a beat and then graduating to detectives. They worked with Jack for a couple of years. After Jack is killed, they decide that they want a change. Flood has two kids, and another one is on the way. O'Brien has a couple of girls and is taking some law classes as well. They wanted more time with their families, and we try to make sure each of our employees can earn enough but also have time to help their kids grow up."

"You better be careful, Michael. I just might try to snatch them away from you and bring them over to the O.S.S."

Michael laughed. "Both guys are in their mid-30s, so they might have one more move in them. But you'll never get Flood. He's one of 12 kids and they all live here. His dad actually coaches golf at St. Thomas. You might have a shot at O'Brien, though. His wife is from the D.C. area."

"They seem like a couple of fine Irish fellows," said Edwin.

Frank had been waiting patiently for a chance to jump in and get things back on track. He saw his opening and decided to dive in.

"So, what do we do now?"

Michael caught George's eye for a moment, and both men smiled.

"Patience, lad," said Michael. "We are laying the trap. We'll get Fischer isolated and get some answers out of him."

"This is really a two-pronged effort," said Parker. "We are running things here, and Ladd and the F.B.I. are leading the effort in New York. They are waiting for Kerling and Leiner to arrive in New York. Hans is on the same train, no doubt, so we sort of have them surrounded, if you will. By the end of the day, they should have Burger and his two comrades in custody. It's all coming together, Frank."

"I just wish it would all come together a little more quickly," replied Frank. "We're running out of time here. The Germans aren't idiots. Their patience will run short very soon, given that they have spent so much time and effort - and money - to get these guys into the country to blow up buildings and bridges." "And to take out their number one target," added Michael.

"Exactly," agreed Frank.

"Not to worry, fellas," said George. "It will all be over in a couple of days. Just be thankful that you won't have to deal with all of the political fallout from all of this. People will be coming out of the woodwork to get their names associated with this effort."

"That's for you and your fed friends to figure out," replied Michael. "We're just your little old Midwestern hicks here who don't know anything about this spy stuff. Right, Frank?" "What exactly is a hick?" asked Edwin.

Frank merely smiled. Somehow, he wasn't as confident about all of this as his dad and uncle were.

# CHAPTER 84

The phone in Burger's room rang. He waited for Ladd to get to the extension, then answered. It was Dale Holyer in the lobby.

Ladd ordered Burger to hang up, which he did.

"The two subjects are on their way up. They are both wearing dark sweaters. One has a pair of tan slacks on, and the other is wearing black slacks. Both are around 6'0 feet, a bit on the thin side. Mid-thirties. Both have dark hair. I saw no weapons."

"Thanks, Dale," said Ladd. "Take the next elevator up to the room. Bring another guy with you."

"Yes, sir. I'll see you in a couple of minutes."

Ladd turned to Bouquet and said, "OK, we're on. They'll be up here and at the door in less than one minute."

About 45 seconds later, there was a knock on Burger's door. It was a single knock, a pause, then two knocks.

"They even have secret knocks," whispered Bouquet to Ladd.

Ladd looked at his watch. "Right on time."

Then to Burger: "Remember, open the door and step away so they can come in. We'll take it from there."

Burger nodded, unconsciously put his hands through his hair as if to look presentable and moved to the door.

"Who is it?' he asked.

"Let us in."

Recognizing Quirin's voice, he turned and nodded to Ladd and Bouquet and opened the door, then stepped back as planned.

Ladd stood in a closet to the right of the door and Bouquet positioned himself right behind the door as it swung open.

Quirin and Heinck walked into the suite and immediately looked forward at the beautiful view of the city.

"This is a much better hotel than where we are staying," said Quirin.

"Why did we have to stay in a cheaper place? It looks like you are treated like kings over here," said Heinck.

"And the view. We don't have a view like this," said Quirin.

"You may want to enjoy that view while you can. You won't have a view like this where you're going."

Both men turned around and saw Bouquet, who was walking toward them.

Heinck froze. Quirin, making a quick assessment of the situation, charged at Bouquet. Bouquet backed up, pulled his revolver out, and said, "Stop!"

Quirin kept coming. Ladd emerged from the closet and yelled, "F.B.I.! Stop, or I will shoot you here and now, and you will be dead before you hit the ground."

Heinck now woke up and his training kicked in. He grabbed a lamp to throw at Bouquet.

Of all people, it was Burger who yelled, "Stop! Stop! Stop!" Heinck had the lamp in his hand and had already reared back to throw it. He didn't stop to think that it was still plugged into the wall.

Now Quirin was the one to pause. Ladd's words were a dose of reality to the situation.

The door burst open, and Dale Holyer ran into the room, gun drawn. His backup, a guy named Clarke, was behind him, revolver out and pointed at Quirin's head.

"Get your hands in the air! All of you!" yelled Holyer.

"Now! Hands up now!" screamed Clarke.

Quirin and Heinck complied. Burger, off to the side, had already raised his hands before the command had ever come.

"What's all this about?" asked Quirin. "We just came to see our friend here."

Burger: "Forget it. They know all about us. That sailor on the beach must have really done some damage. Might have even followed us on the train."

Quirin and Heinck looked at each other, dejected. They began to talk in German.

"Knock it off," said Bouquet. He walked up to Heinck, stopped six inches from him, and bared his teeth, not at all in a kind way.

"A big part of me was hoping that you would throw that lamp at me. It would have given me all of the just cause that I would have needed to plug you."

Heinck snarled back at him and said, "Maybe we will have another opportunity to resolve this between us."

Bouquet stared right back at him and said, "Unfortunately for you, there will be no more opportunities for anything like that.

You're done."

With that, all three men were cuffed and taken downstairs to a waiting F.B.I. car.

Later, Bouquet said to Ladd, "What was all that malarkey that Burger was telling them about the sailor following them on the train?"

Ladd replied, "I made a concession to Dasch that none of the other six saboteurs would know that Dasch and Burger squealed to us. I promised Dasch that I would let Burger know this as well. They're all going to be on trial, and we can use this to our advantage. Maybe we'll tell the other six at some point and see if they will turn on one another. Or maybe we won't need it. It's a card that we have, and we can decide to play it or to throw it away."

"Smart play," said Bouquet.

# CHAPTER 85

Werner Thiel arrived in New York City without incident. He had played it smart and remembered his training. He used part of the trip to develop a plan to make it out of the New York terminal without being apprehended. Since no one had a picture of him, he liked his chances.

He had purposely searched out an older couple on the train and befriended them. They spent time in the club car eating and drinking and swapping stories. By the time they had gotten into the terminal, Thiel had insisted on helping them by carrying their luggage all the way out of the terminal.

While doing so, he managed to make it look like they were his grandparents, talking with them as they made it up the many steps to street level.

The couple was grateful for the help.

Thiel just smiled and made it seem like it was the most natural thing in the world.

If there was someone looking for him, that person would be looking for a young man travelling by himself with his eyes darting back and forth, suspiciously turning around, and looking everywhere.

Just to be safe, he ended up sharing a cab with the couple. He got out after a mile, after which they offered him money to help them, which he politely refused. Given how much money he was carrying, he couldn't help but chuckle to himself about their effort to tip him.

He found a payphone and dialed the number that Kerling had given him.

"Hello?" said a man's voice on the other end of the phone.

"I was told to call someone at this number," said Thiel.

After a pause, the other man asked, "Who told you to call this number?"

"A man who is my commanding officer."

"Where did you enter the country from?" the man probed.

"South of Jacksonville, Florida."

"How many other men were with you?"

"Three others, but I am by myself. My commanding officer will be here in a day or two, and he may have someone with him," replied Thiel.

"What are the initials of the man who leads your group?"

"E.K."

"And the man above him? What are his initials?"

Thiel had to think. "What was Leiner's first name again?" he asked himself.

"Ugh…I know his last name and I am trying to think of-" "No names!" barked the man on the other end of the phone.

"I know, I know," said Thiel. It took him another half a minute before he could get it.

"H.L.!" H.L.!" he cried.

Another pause.

"All right. Good," said the man.

They spoke only for another minute. The man gave Thiel the address to come to.

Thiel asked if it was an apartment or business.

He didn't answer the question directly.

All he said was, "You won't be able to miss it."

Thiel hung up and hailed another cab. He would be at the destination in about 40 minutes.

# CHAPTER 86

Detectives Flood and O'Brien watched Erik Fischer from across the street. He had left his home with the mail truck in front of it, and began walking the neighborhood, delivering mail. More often than not, he left the mail inside the door to each of the homes, or he pushed it through a small slab that had a metal cover on it. Once through the slab, the mail fell either onto the floor on the inside of the home or into a basket that people would have set up to catch the mail. Many of the ladies of the home appeared to know Fischer. He engaged with a number of them as he delivered their mail.

O'Brien drove the car right up to him. Flood hopped out, flashed his Sweeney Detective badge at him, and told him to get in the car.

Fischer, totally bewildered, asked, "What is this about? Can't you see I am delivering mail here?"

"That will have to wait," said Flood. "Now get in the car!"

Fischer started to run, but Flood caught him before Fischer had taken more than a few steps.

"I'm not going to tell you again," said Flood.

Fischer looked around, considered screaming, and then thought better of it.

He had no idea who these men were, but they didn't really give him any choice.

O'Brien drove with Flood in the back seat with Fischer.

"Let me see your badge. I just want to know who I am going to sue for kidnapping," said Fischer.

"Don't waste your time," said Flood.

He ignored Fischer's demand to see his badge.

O'Brien piped up from the front seat, "Look, this will go a lot better for you if you answer our questions without a lot of lip.

We'd hate to have to slip you a mickey."

Fischer, realizing that these guys were serious, softened his stance.

"I'm a mailman. I have no idea why you picked me up and what you want from me."

"Enjoy the ride, Erik. We'll be at our destination in a few minutes," said Flood. "We'll talk when we get there."

# CHAPTER 87

Werner Thiel was looking forward to making contact with the name that Kerling had given him. This was the name on Kerling's handkerchief that was written in invisible ink. He really had nowhere else to go, so he was very hopeful that this name panned out.

Thiel was tired. He had started to doze off in the cab. The stress of the last few days had really gotten to him. His first attempt at murder - he had to think about even the concept of that - had failed. Then he had to get out of town as quickly as possible, find his way back to Cincinnati, and hustle ahead to New York.

He was looking forward to a hot bath, some good food, and a comfortable bed.

No doubt it would be a brief stay before he would eventually meet up with Dasch and his team to begin the original mission.

The cab came to a stop.

"This is it," said the cab driver.

Thiel yawned, began to gather a couple of things in the backseat, and asked the cabbie how much he owed him.

He settled the fare and finally looked around to see where he actually was.

He had to do a double-take when he looked out to his left. The cab had stopped across the street from the destination. He pulled the piece of paper out of his pocket and checked the address again.

"This can't be right," he muttered.

Yes. This was the right address. But…?

He got out of the cab and grabbed his luggage out of the trunk. He looked one more time at the address, shrugged, and made his way up the curb to the address.

The man who came to the door proved to be more of a shock to him than the address itself.

All Thiel could manage was a "You've gotta be kidding me."

# CHAPTER 88

## *St. Paul*

Frank and Edwin were waiting in Michael's office when the phone rang. It was Flood and O'Brien. Frank told them to hold on while he went to find Michael and George.

His Aunt Susie was just packing up to leave the office for the evening.

"Have you seen my dad and Uncle George?"

"They went downstairs to get some coffee. I can call down to the coffee shop and have them paged," she answered.

"That would be swell. Thanks, Aunt Susie. Could you just tell them that Flood and O'Brien are on the phone?"

"Will do."

Frank went back into the conference room to talk to the two detectives.

"My dad and Mr. Parker are on their way back up here. Why don't we get started? We can get them caught up when they get here," said Frank.

"That's fine. Unfortunately, it will probably be a brief conversation anyway," said O'Brien.

"Why? What did you find out?" asked Edwin.

"We have Fischer isolated in another room here at the safe house right now," began Flood.

"It's a soundproof room with listening devices everywhere," added O'Brien.

"We've done everything to create an environment to get him to talk," he continued. "We fed him, got him whatever he wanted to drink, put him in a comfortable chair, and had the radio tuned to his favorite station. You name it, we've done it."

Just as Frank was about to ask another question, the door opened and in walked his dad with George Parker.

Flood and O'Brien repeated their conversation to the two older gentlemen.

"So? What do we know? What did you find out?" asked Parker.

There was a noticeable silence. Frank allowed himself a small smile as he pictured what was happening on the other end of the phone. O'Brien and Flood, friends since high school, were silently gesturing to each other about who had to tell the three men on the phone what they weren't going to want to hear.

"Well?" said Michael.

"Yeah. Um. Well …" stammered O'Brien.

More silence, followed by a huge sigh and some muttering.

Flood finally speaks up.

"Yeah. Um. Well…"

"Can one of you actually speak?" asked Michael.

"He swears that he had nothing to do with any of this, and we believe him," blurted O'Brien.

"What?" from all four of the men in Sweeney Detective's conference room.

His story checks out, boss," said Flood.

"Our guys never got a good look at who was driving the mail truck," offered O'Brien. "All they said was that the driver was bundled up from the cold, wore sunglasses, and looked like he had a mustache. Fischer has never had a mustache."

Flood jumped in next. "We can place him in Rice Park about 30 minutes after the shooting, but we can't place him there any sooner than that."

Parker: "How do you explain what Hans told us? Kerling and Leiner referenced him by name."

No response.

Michael now: "The telegram even had his initials on it: "E.F."

"Any chance that Hans might have gotten some of this wrong? Didn't he say that some of the conversation was hard to hear?" asked O'Brien.

"Anything's possible, but Hans is very thorough." Frank.

More silence.

Michael, summarizing: "So he denies all of it. I suppose you got nowhere with any more information about their network, their intentions going forward, all of that?"

"That's right, boss," said Flood. "He didn't know, and he claimed to have no idea about any of it."

Parker again: "Just how sure are you guys about him not having anything to do with this?"

There was another pause. Then: "I hate to say it, but we'd both put our badges on it," said O'Brien.

"We're obviously missing something here," said Frank. "We have Hans handing Fischer to us in a wrapped-up package. We need to go back over everything that he told us. He's probably on the train by now and is following Kerling and Leiner, and we have no way to contact him. We don't even know where he's staying when he gets there."

Michael spoke next. "Frank's right, we need to go back over everything. Let's all start over."

To Flood and O'Brien: "Don't let Fischer go just yet. Keep him there at the safe house. Have someone send a note to his family saying that he's doing some work to help some people out. Same with his post office superiors. Keep him there overnight and let him go at the end of day tomorrow. Get someone else over there to watch him. I want both of you to help us as we go back to the drawing board."

"He's married to Betty, remember?" said Frank. "She's probably worried sick."

"Ah, yeah. The funeral," said Michael. "I should've remembered that."

"Anyway, we'll jump on it right away, boss," said Flood.

# CHAPTER 89

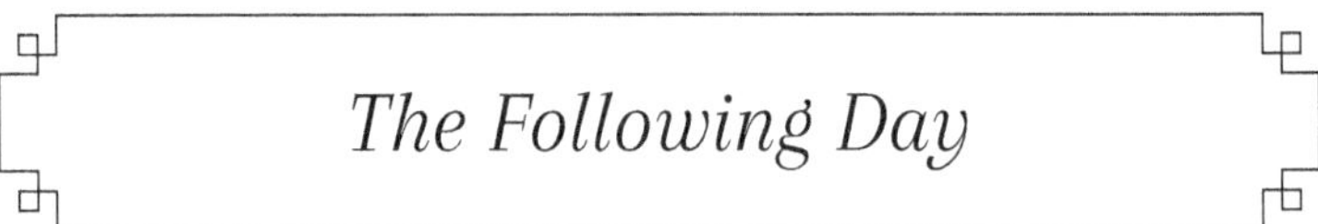

Carl Krepper was excited to see Kerling and Leiner. He had Thiel stay inside while he walked out to meet the two men on the doorstep of the building.

"That's quite a disguise," said Kerling to Leiner as they made their way from the taxi.

"No disguise," replied Leiner. "That's the real thing. He's a real pastor."

"You're joking,' said Kerling.

"No. No, I am not. Look at it this way: who in the world would be looking for a pastor when they are trying to find a spy?" Krepper came down the steps and greeted them.

Kerling didn't know what to say, so he said nothing.

Krepper looked at the two men, glanced around to make sure no one else was watching, then motioned for them to come inside.

Hans Ungrodt saw all of it and had to admire the Nazis' ingenuity. He had left his cab a block earlier and walked half a block toward the church, staying in the trees as he did so. Once he saw all three of the saboteurs, he made his way to a pay phone and asked the operator to call a number in St. Paul.

# CHAPTER 90

Just after hanging up with Flood and O'Brien, Frank, Michael and George looked at each other and started to talk about the obvious disconnect that they now had.

"Where in the world did this thing go off track?" asked George.

Michael was about to say something when the phone rang again.

It was Hans.

"Hans, where are you?" asked Parker.

"I'm actually in New Jersey," replied Hans. "We arrived a few minutes early and I've managed to follow Leiner and Kerling undetected."

"Excellent," said Michael.

Frank jumped in.

"Hans, we seem to be stumped back here. I took all of the notes from our conversation, and I have been re-reading them. You mentioned that the name of the accomplice that helped Kerling get away was Fischer, right?"

"Yes, that's correct, said Hans. "It also tied to the initials on the telegram that I saw in Leiner's room, remember?" "E.F." "OK, that's what I recall you said," replied Frank.

"Here's our problem," continued Frank. "Two of the detectives here - Flood and O'Brien - picked up this Erik Fischer guy and they are convinced that he didn't do it. He denied knowing anything about it, and they are convinced that he's telling them the truth."

Hans was thinking, so much so that Frank had to ask if he was still on the line.

"Yes, yes. I'm still here," he said.

"I don't know what to tell you. I heard what I heard, and I saw what I saw," said Hans.

Edwin now: "Didn't you say that the voices got a little lower when they were talking about their accomplice in St. Paul? So, for example, could it have been something like "Fresher" rather than "Fischer?"

More silence as Hans pondered that.

"I suppose it's possible," he said. "Maybe when you get the recording album that I made from the conversation, you can check it again."

"When will that be?" asked Parker.

"I don't know. I had it airmailed to you immediately while I was still in Cincinnati," he replied. "I had to do it that way because I didn't know how long it would be before I got back to St. Paul. Plus, I didn't want to run the risk of getting caught by some undercover Nazis with that in my possession." No one said anything for another minute.

It was Michael who broke the silence. "Regardless, we're starting all over back here," he said. "If you can get back here once the saboteurs are rounded up, we could use your help."

"Of course," said Hans.

"Hans, this is George again," said Parker. "I need the address where these guys are. I need to call my counterpart at the F.B.I. I promised him that this would be his arrest."

Hans gave the street address, and then said, "Can you arrange to get me a plane back to Minnesota once these men are in custody?"

"Consider it done," said Parker.

"You're not going to believe what this place is."

"What do you mean?" asked Parker.

"I'm telling you, you won't believe where they are staying," Hans persisted.

"Where are they?"

"The address I gave you is a church. St. John's Evangelical Lutheran Church in Newark."

"What?" the four men said in unison again.

"Yes. You heard me correctly," said Hans. "Their main contact is a local pastor, or at least he appears to be. He came outside to greet them, and he's dressed in the habit."

# CHAPTER 91

Pastor Carl Krepper had come to America in 1909. He became a citizen in 1922. Along the way he had gone to seminary. After moving to different churches, he settled at St. John's Evangelical Lutheran Church in Newark.

A short, stocky man with reddish brown hair, Krepper had moved back to the Fatherland in the mid 1930's but was assigned back to the U.S. before the war broke out. He knew Kappe and Leiner and was part of Kappe's training when he had moved back to Germany.

As he came out of the church, he looked upon his two comrades with a combination of joy and relief. He hadn't seen Leiner in several weeks, and he didn't know Kerling.

"Come in, my friends. You must be exhausted from your long trip. We have plenty of food and a couple of spare beds. I want to hear all about your adventures thus far!"

The three men made their way up the steps, and Thiel stuck his head out of the door, smiled, and nodded to them. He opened the door to them and quickly closed it when they were safely inside.

Kerling and Leiner got settled quickly as Thiel provided them with beer and a couple of sandwiches.

"Congratulations! Mission accomplished!" said Thiel.

"Is it in the papers?" asked Leiner.

"Yes. It was in the New York Times. Not a huge article, but it was there. It talked about an unidentified foreign man who had government ties being assassinated in a hotel in St. Paul. It said the cops and the government aren't talking at all and that the man must've been someone very important."

Kerling and Leiner looked at each other and smiled.

Krepper got into the act as well, bringing a bottle of champagne with four glasses.

"A great victory for the Fatherland!" he bellowed.

Kerling, still quite serious, looked at Krepper and Thiel, then at Leiner, and said, "All right. We'll have one drink, and Leiner and I will tell you the story, but after this, we will focus all discussions on the next mission and how we will need to plan how and where our first attack will take place. Where are Dasch and his crew?"

"We will make contact with them later tonight," said Krepper.

The next hour was spent listening to Kerling and Leiner ham and egg the play by play on the assassination of Edwin Conway. While Kerling remained serious, one could tell that he was taking great pleasure in describing in detail what he had to do in order to be successful. Leiner, never one to shy away from recognition, filled in the gaps by highlighting all of his planning and contact with their agent in St. Paul.

"I don't see how it could have gone any better," concluded Kerling. "I was on the train literally about 12 minutes after I fired the shot to kill Conway."

"I talked to Kappe," said Leiner. "He passed on the great news to Canaris, who told him that the leadership of the Party would be thrilled - and may I say, probably a bit relieved - with this result. There will be much celebrating in the Fatherland over this!" "Speaking of Kappe, he was called back to the Fatherland unexpectedly," said Krepper. "He sends his congratulations and also his regrets that he won't be here for the next phase of the mission."

"That's unfortunate," said Leiner. "I was hoping to speak to him directly about our successful mission."

"As was I," replied Kerling. Then to Leiner: "Perhaps we can call him together when he gets back to Berlin." "Gentlemen, a toast!" Krepper again.

"May all of the future missions of Operation Pastorius go as smoothly as this one!"

They all held their glasses up and yelled, "Prost!"

Upon hearing the German word for "cheers," Thiel looked at Krepper and said, "Hey, that reminds me. About your services here do you say them in that funny language that I heard in St. Paul?"

"Huh?" said Krepper.

Kerling just shook his head.

Outside the church, F.B.I. Assistant Director D.M. "Mickey" Ladd and Special Agent Dave Bouquet sat in a car, biding their time.

# CHAPTER 92

# St. Paul

Frank and Michael went home for the evening. As they rode in Michael's car, both sat silently, each processing and going over every detail that they could recall.

"I guess we should take some comfort in the fact that Edwin is safe, and that they are convinced that he's dead," said Michael. "That's the main thing."

"Do you think he'll be OK at your office?" asked Frank.

"It's been three nights or so. He's probably going a bit stir-crazy, but he'll be OK. I have men posted everywhere in the building and at least four guys within 25 feet of him at all times when I'm not there. There is only one way into and out of that spare office that he's in," answered Michael.

"It would certainly appear that we have managed to convince everyone that he's dead," agreed Frank.

"I know that you understand this more than anyone else," said Michael, "But I am not going to relax until we figure out this whole spy issue."

"Mom and the girls are going to really be sore at you for not telling them that Dr. Conway is alive."

Michael said nothing for a moment; then he became somewhat matter-of-fact. "Your mother will not like it, but she will understand. This isn't the first time that I haven't told her something critical about a particular case. Once she understands its gravity, she'll come around."

"I hate to even ask this, son, but you don't think Leigh has said anything to anyone?"

"Not a word, Dad. Not a word. She is fiercely protective of her father. There is no way that she would spill anything to anyone about it."

"Sorry, but I had to ask," said Michael.

"I understand," replied Frank. "It's important that we all feel comfortable asking those kinds of questions."

Michael pulled into the alley behind their home and then into the parking area in the backyard. He turned off the ignition, looked at his son, and quietly said, "She's a wonderful girl, Frank."

Frank looked at Michael, excited and bursting with enthusiasm.

"Isn't she swell, Dad?"

Michael chuckled, patted him on the knee, and said, "Yes, son, she is swell."

Frank, not just a little wistful, said, "I was kind of hoping we would be engaged by now."

"I understand," replied his dad. "I think you're wise for waiting, given the circumstances. But don't worry: when you're ready, we will have a wonderful wedding for you and Leigh. With her mom being gone and Leigh not having any sisters, I think your mother and sisters will fill in quite nicely."

"Thanks, Dad," said Frank. "You'll watch over her until I come back?"

"Of course. She'll stay with us at home until you come back. You just make sure you make it back." His voice cracked a bit when he said that.

Frank pulled on his dad's arm and said, "Don't worry. Nothing is going to stop me from coming home once this war is over."

In a very rare moment of vulnerability, Michael, thankful for the darkness in the car, said, "I've lost one son." His voice cracked again as he continued, "I couldn't take losing another one."

There was silence for a minute as he collected himself. He said in the darkness, "Son, your mom and I have prayed for you - for all of you kids - every single day. But I have prayed more for you since you left to go fight this war."

Frank, equally emotional, said, "I know, Dad. Please keep praying. My faith and trust is in the Lord, and I know that this is true of you as well. Of all of the many things that you have taught me, it has been to trust the

Lord in all things. Our family verse was the first piece of Scripture that I ever memorized. And it says that we are to trust in the Lord with all of our hearts and to not lean on our own understanding. And He promises that if we acknowledge Him in all things, He will be there to direct us. We can't ask for anything more than that."

Michael, now still emotional, smiled in the dark and said, "Proverbs 3:5-6. Yes, our family verse."

He patted his son on the arm and said, "Thanks, Frank. I guess I needed to be reminded of that."

"Iron sharpening iron, Dad."

Michael suggested that they take another minute to pray about finding the spy and for Edwin to remain safe.

They prayed together for ten minutes.

They had peace as they decided to go in and see their women.

# CHAPTER 93

Frank and Leigh went for a walk the following morning. She took his arm as they strolled around the neighborhood.

"My dad and I prayed together last night. It was an emotional time," said Frank, looking ahead.

"Your dad is such a good man, Frank. I not only like him, but I also admire him."

"He sure likes you, Miss Conway."

"Your whole family has been so kind to my dad and me. We could never repay you."

He stopped for a moment, turning to look at her.

"Look, I need to say a couple of things."

Leigh looked at him, wondering where this was going.

"OK," she replied.

Frank looked at her intently, realized that he was probably frightening her, and then smiled.

Her eyes never left his.

"I love you, Leigh. I knew it from the first time I laid eyes on you at Burghoffs in Augsburg. I couldn't tell you what I had to eat or drink there, but I could describe you perfectly, from how your hair was done to what you were wearing."

Leigh continued to look into his eyes, shyly smiling.

"I want to let you know that I will one day be back here to ask you to marry me. I've thought about it, and I don't think that it would be wise for me to ask you just yet. I will be called back into action here any day now. I think my Uncle George has stalled for me under the guise that we don't have the spy identified and in custody yet. Plus, we still need to get your dad out of here."

Frank looked at her to see if she was grasping everything that he was throwing at her.

"I want to do this the right way. Make no mistake: I am going to marry you. That is, if you'll have me. But I don't want to rush it like so many others have. I want to have a real wedding. I want it to be done right. For both of us."

He again looked at her. She was tearing up.

"Are you all right?" he asked. "I mean, if you'd rather, we could"-

"No. No, Frank," she said through her tears. "I will wait for you. I agree with everything that you've said. I have so much to learn about life here in America. I'd like to teach here and continue to get to know your family better."

Frank, with a huge sigh of relief: "OK! OK! Then we agree? Because my mom and dad want you to live with them. That is, if you are all right with that. And I'm sure that you can find a good teaching job somewhere in St. Paul. My dad knows a lot of people and he can get you introduced around town at some of the different schools."

"That would be great, Frank, but I want to be able to get a job on my own and not just because of your dad."

"Of course!" said Frank. "By all means, the principal will interview you, but Leigh, they will LOVE you!"

They hugged for a long moment. Here they were, standing on the sidewalk a couple of blocks from Frank's home.

"So, you don't mind waiting?" he asked.

"Of course, I'll wait," she said, her head buried in his chest. "It's the right thing to do, for all of the reasons that you have said."

"I'm so glad," said Frank. "Leigh Conway, I love you more than you can ever know."

She looked up at him with those beautiful brown eyes and said, "I love you too, Frank Sweeney."

# CHAPTER 94

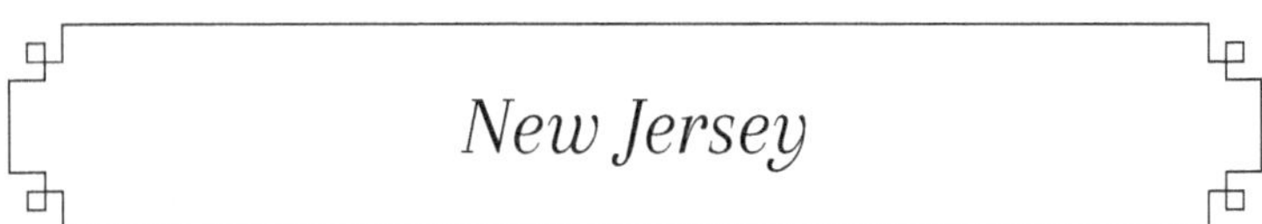

## *New Jersey*

The remaining saboteurs ate breakfast in the church's kitchen and began discussing their next missions.

"Dasch should have called last night," observed Leiner. "Where is he? I'm going to call the Governor Clinton Hotel and see if I can get a hold of him there."

He called the hotel and spoke with a John Yesh, the hotel manager. Leiner had to cover the phone in a moment of panic because he couldn't remember Dasch's alias.

Each of the men racked their brains. Thiel was no help. Kerling had heard the name once but couldn't recall it.

Krepper had been read in by Kappe and Leiner.

"Davis! George Davis!" whispered Krepper loudly.

"George Davis is the man that I am looking for. Is he still staying there?"

"Yes, our records show that he has not checked out as yet. Would you like me to ring his room?"

"Yes, please."

"It's my pleasure to do so. I will connect you."

The phone rang repeatedly, and no one answered.

"He's still there but must not be in his room," said Leiner.

Kerling spoke next.

"Why not try back in an hour and leave him a number to reach you?"

"I don't know," replied Leiner. "You both had two numbers on the handkerchiefs that were written in invisible ink: The Pastor's number here and my number. I'm hesitant to leave any more information at this point. I will give him until this afternoon."

Kerling shrugged. Before he could say anything else, the door to the kitchen burst open with four men screaming at them to get their hands up.

Kerling reacted first, bolting for the backdoor behind him.

Thiel froze, as did the Pastor. Leiner recovered quickly, saying, "What is this?" What's going on here?"

More yelling. He heard "F.B.I.," and he hung his head in submission. It was over.

Kerling had sprinted out of the room and down a hallway to a door that exited to a parking lot. He raced through the door and never broke stride. He saw some woods and made up his mind to get into those woods as quickly as possible.

"F.B.I.! Stop or I'll shoot!"

Kerling never looked back. The woods. All he could focus on was the woods.

More shouting. A shot rang out. Kerling flinched but kept going. Probably a warning shot. Feet on the pavement after him.

"Stop him! Grab him!"

He was now only 5 meters from the woods. He turned and looked back for a moment to see where his followers were. He had a good lead on them.

He turned back to look into the woods when a fist came out of nowhere and clocked him. He went immediately to the ground. Within seconds, he was on his stomach with his arms behind him. He felt the cold steel of the handcuffs being clicked onto his right wrist, followed by another click that married up his left wrist. Someone was telling him to get on his feet.

He heard another voice. He turned to look at the man who was speaking. He was a bit shorter than what he had pictured. And he spoke with a slight German accent. The man said, "This is the Nazi saboteur who killed Edwin Conway in St. Paul."

Kerling looked at the man and smiled. "Mission accomplished," he said.

# CHAPTER 95

## St. Paul

George Parker was back in Michael's office again, puffing on a pipe. He and Michael were wrapping up their conversation with Hans, who had called to brief them on the capture of the remaining saboteurs. Edwin had decided to lie down for a few minutes. All of the excitement of the past few days was catching up to him.

Hans relayed how he made sure that Kerling had heard Hans telling someone that Kerling had killed Edwin Conway.

"Great job, Hans," said Parker. "I have a plane waiting for you in Newark. I'll call Assistant Director Ladd and try to get things wrapped up. Get to the airport right away and come back here. The remaining item is the identity of the spy who coordinated with Kerling."

"Kerling isn't saying a word as to who helped him in St. Paul," replied Hans. "I even told him we knew it was Fischer, but he would give no indication at all as to whether or not I was right. He just sneered at me and refused to talk."

Parker looked at Michael, who was listening passively.

Parker sighed and said, "He's the Bureau's prisoner now. They'll have to figure out how to break him down."

"Where exactly are the other saboteurs?" asked Hans.

"Well, let's see," said Parker. "Dasch is in D.C. in a protective cell within F.B.I. headquarters. The rest of his team - Burger, Quirin, and

Heinck - are all in custody and on their way from New York to D.C. Haupt already left the P.O.W. camp here with an F.B.I. man and is in D.C. now. We never got anything else out of him. By the way, you did a great job on him, Hans. We never could have put all of this together without you getting him to spill the beans."

"Thank you, George, said Hans. "And that leaves the rest of them over here in New Jersey?"

"You forgot Neubauer, who the F.B.I. grabbed off the train in Chicago. He also should be in D.C. by now."

"Plus, Leiner and the pastor," added Michael.

Michael lit up his favorite pipe. "Imagine that. A pastor. These Nazis will stop at nothing."

"All right, Hans," said Parker, "Let's meet tomorrow at 9:00 AM here in Michael's office. Safe travels home. And sorry about the plane. It'll be a military plane with not exactly comfortable seating."

Hans chuckled and rang off.

Now it was just Parker and Sweeney. They had never bothered to introduce each other to people as a "former partner." They were partners forever. Hence Parker's willingness to share things with Michael that he would never share with anyone else.

"These are bad men, Georgie," said Michael.

"The worst," replied George, re-lighting his pipe.

"At least with the mobsters, you knew who you were dealing with," observed Michael. "There were rules, protocols that everyone adhered to. Everyone clearly understood who was good and who was bad. And you always kept the family members out of it. This is different."

"Mike, I'll never be able to get the reports that I've seen out of my head. The Nazis going into towns and killing all the men and boys, even the women and children. They have wiped out entire towns over there! Literally lined these people up against a wall and shot all of them. ALL OF THEM! And then there are the Jews. Frank saw firsthand what was going on over there with them. How can people be so evil? All in the name of one madman! I just can't get my mind around it."

Michael was leaning back in his high back chair, tapping his teeth with his pipe, listening to every word from his friend.

"When's the last time that you had a day off, Georgie?"

"I guess I can't remember when that was. I know I need it. I haven't seen Jane in two weeks. I've slept in the office and go to the Athletic Club to shower and put on a fresh suit every day. I miss her, and I know that she misses me."

Michael merely nodded, and his look told his partner to keep going.

"Donovan is great. A great man. Great to work for. Lets me run things the way I think they should be run. Almost never interferes or makes me do something that I don't agree with." "Sounds like a far cry from J. Edgar," offered Michael.

"And how, partner," replied George. "You watch, Mike. Hoover will be doing a huge P.R. effort on this whole thing with the saboteurs. He'll see the opportunity and seize on it. And he won't be wrong. He'll convince Roosevelt that we need to put this on the front page of every newspaper in the country and blast it all over the radio so that the Nazis won't try something like this again. That's how I sold Ladd on letting me get involved in this and help him. I told him that Donovan wouldn't want to take any credit for any of this, that the F.B.I. can get all of the

P.R. for it. The last thing that Wild Bill Donovan wants is for the O.S.S. to even be known out there."

"Let's be honest," said Michael, "It's the right thing to do. One can question Hoover's motivation, but it is still the right thing to do for the country."

"Yeah, I know," muttered Parker. "But that doesn't mean that I have to like it."

They were interrupted by Edwin Conway, who came into the room and took a seat.

"I started to lay down but smelled the pipes, boys. I have mine here but could use a little tobacco."

Michael smiled at that and tossed him a bag.

"As much as we don't want to, we've got to figure out a way to get you out of here, Edwin."

Conway nodded and said in his fine Irish brogue, "Tis time for me to get back in the game, lads."

# CHAPTER 96

Frank and Leigh were enjoying a moment alone in Michael's home office with the door closed. Michael, ever the early riser, had left at the crack of dawn to get downtown to his office. Evvie and Kathryn were helping Betty do some cleaning, and Maggie had left to drop off some food to an ailing friend.

"I know we're missing something," said Frank, "but I can't put my finger on it. It's just sitting there right below the surface."

Leigh pondered that for a while and said, "I guess we should just go back to the very beginning and start from there. Is Hans back from New Jersey?"

"Yeah, he got back late last night. He's at the Commodore Hotel. I'm leaving in a few minutes to meet up with him at my **dad's** office so that we can start tackling this thing together. Flood and O'Brien are already looking back on the case as well, interviewing more people around the St. Paul Hotel and the courthouse just to see if anything - or anyone - was missed. We're going to meet for lunch at my dad's office and compare notes. What are you doing today?"

Leigh lowered her voice and said, "I haven't seen my dad in a couple of days. Maybe I can meet you at your dad's office after I talk to him for a bit. I thought I'd bring him a fresh set of clothes."

She lowered her head a bit and talked more softly. "I suppose

Mr. Parker is going to want to move him pretty quickly now that all the saboteurs are accounted for. Which means that you'll be heading back, too."

Frank looked at her and saw tears forming in those big brown eyes.

"Leigh, I'm going to be honest with you. I don't want to go, either. I want to start a new life with you right here and now. But I am duty-bound to help win this war, and you know that that's what I have to do. And you will be asked to do your part in this thing as well, whether it's fundraising, rationing, or volunteering. Every American is called to duty."

She smiled and said, "But I'm not an American."

"Hmm. We'll have to take care of that," Frank replied with a smile back at her.

"Working for the O.S.S. will likely mean that I will be gone on missions, but those missions don't typically last for months or years on end. I will be flying back to Washington a lot, which means that I can sneak back here on occasion, if only for a long weekend once in a while. Believe me, we will have it better than the poor guy who is fighting on a beach somewhere in the

Pacific."

"And that is something to be thankful for, Frank," said Leigh. "But I also know that these missions that you will be on will be very dangerous in their own right."

Frank didn't know what to say to that. They sat in silence for a minute, holding hands.

Finally, Frank announced, "All right, I need to get going. I'll see you a little later today, then. Oh, and I don't want you traveling by yourself, so wait for me to call you here, and we'll figure out how to get you downtown."

"Yes sir!" said Leigh, with a half-hearted salute.

They hugged for a minute, and he kissed her.

"See you a little later today, Miss Conway."

"Likewise, Mr. Sweeney."

"Oh, and Miss Conway?"

"Yes, Mr. Sweeney?"

"I love you, Miss Conway."

"And I love you, Mr. Sweeney."

# CHAPTER 97

Flood and O'Brien had arrived at Rice Park to start working the St. Paul Hotel and the courthouse. Again. They decided to begin at the hotel and work their way down the list, starting with the hotel's general manager. They discovered nothing. The guy was extremely cooperative, but there was no new information to glean.

"Flooder, I have to tell you, this feels like a big waste of time," said O'Brien. "Tough case."

"Yep, couldn't agree more," replied Flood. "But who knows? Maybe we'll catch a break. It's happened before. Besides, this one has some serious implications regarding our country's safety. You know what the boss says: leave no stone unturned."

"All right, how about you take the kitchen and wait staff, and I'll take the maids?" suggested O'Brien.

"Fine by me, O.B.," replied Flood. "I'll meet you in the lobby in a couple of hours. We'll grab a bite then, and assuming that this is a dead end, we'll make our way over to the courthouse and spend the afternoon trying to kick something up over there."

O.B. again: "Maybe there are some people that the cops missed before. Or that some of our other guys missed. You know, maybe there were some employees who were off on the day we did our canvassing last time. Let's make sure we have the full list of employees from the General Manager."

"Almost forgot," said Flood. "He gave me two copies. Here's yours."

"Good. See you in a couple of hours."

# CHAPTER 98

As Frank sat in the streetcar on his way downtown, he spent some time silently praying. He prayed in thanksgiving that the saboteurs had all been caught and accounted for, and for the countless lives that had been saved as a result of this. He prayed with a grateful heart for The Lord interceding on Dr. Conway's behalf, sparing his future father-in-law, and for his plan to convince the Nazis that their mission had been accomplished. Next, he prayed for wisdom and focus, so that he could determine who this last spy was and where he was located.

Last, he prayed in thanksgiving for Leigh, the young woman who in a mere few weeks had captured his heart. He felt like he knew her so well already, given what they had already gone through together.

And yet he was realistic to admit that there was a great deal more that he didn't know about her than what he currently knew. "That's not a problem," he smiled to himself. "We'll have the rest of our lives to do that." That sent him down a whole different path, especially as he thought about having children together. "How many will she want to have? How many do I want to have? Wow! We have a lot to talk about!"

He was brought back to the real world when the streetcar stopped. About a dozen people got off, and another dozen got on. There was an older woman who had gotten on who had a couple of packages in each arm. Frank stood up and gave her his seat, and she smiled, appreciative of him. He nodded back, rather absently.

He glanced down and looked at her purse, something that he would not normally have even noticed. The purse was black leather, but it had gold initials embroidered into it. The stitching was done in such a way that it made it look like someone used elaborate calligraphy to stencil in the initials. He casually mentioned to the woman how eye-catching her purse was.

"Thank you," she said. "At least it'll never be mistaken for someone else's, so if someone took it, we would know that it wasn't by mistake."

He turned his head for a better look. "Is it "M.M." or "W.W"?" he asked.

"Oh, it's "M.M.," the older woman answered. "Although I probably should have them stich it up as "P.M." because, while my name is "Margaret," everyone calls me "Peggy." "So, my name is Margaret, "Peggy" Meehan," she said.

Frank again nodded and smiled politely.

"What's your name, young man?" she asked.

"Francis Michael Sweeney, but everyone calls me Frank," he said, tipping his cap to her.

"Sweeney. You look like the man who runs the armored cars all around town. His picture is in the paper a lot." "That's my dad," said Frank.

She waxed on about that for a few minutes, and they continued to chat until she got off at the next stop.

"Nice to meet you, Mrs. Meehan," said Frank as he helped her off of the streetcar.

"Please call me Peggy. All my friends call me Peggy. The only people who called me Margaret were the nuns at St. Joseph's Academy, and that was because I was always in trouble. Here, Frank, take one of my business cards. I work in a flower shop about a block from this stop. Great flowers for any occasion. You call me if you ever need any flowers for anyone."

She got off the streetcar, looked back at him and smiled, and was on her way. Frank waved one more goodbye.

As he sat back down, he got back to racking his brain about what he - what everyone - could have possibly missed in this whole thing.

As the streetcar started up again, he played it all through his mind one more time. Everything was fine until the push from Thiel on the platform at the streetcar station. No one had any inkling of anything being wrong up until that point. Hans' phone call from the P.O.W. camp that morning to his dad confirmed that Dr. Conway was a target - *the* target. He fixed his mind there for a bit. He was starting to think frame by frame, slowing everything down in his mind's eye.

How did Thiel know that they would be taking the streetcar that day, from that station? Or did he even know that? He could've just randomly followed the Conways and Frank that morning. But how did he know that the Conways were at his home, even staying at his home? Someone had to have communicated the whereabouts of the Conways to Thiel and Kerling. The obvious answer was the mailman, Erik Fischer. Yet Flood and O'Brien were sure - were downright positive- that Erik Fischer didn't know anything, even though the recording that Hans had made had mentioned Fischer by name. At least Hans thought that was what he had heard. The album recording had gotten to Michael's office yesterday. It didn't really help. The voices were a bit low. But the initials on the telegram did clearly point to Erik Fischer.

He reached into his pocket and pulled out the written record that his Aunt Susie had transcribed of the recording and began to read it again. He read every word very slowly.

"Since I have nothing else to go on, I need to assume that the answer is somewhere here in this record," he told himself.

"Think, Frank. Think!" he implored.

He read the record. He read it again. And again.

Margaret "Peggy" Meehan's business card fell out of his pocket.

"Huh. Must've been when I pulled out Aunt Susie's report," he said to himself. He glanced at it one more time as he put it back into his pocket.

Then, it began. It was like waking up in the middle of the night and staring outside, waiting for the sun to rise. But the sun never just suddenly appeared.

And that was true in this case with Frank. He began to slowly see some things.

He re-read the report again. Could it possibly be? Yes. It was possible. Maybe not probable. But possible.

He got off the streetcar about a block from the 1st National Bank. He was really processing now. He walked faster, still totally focused on what he had read in Hans' report. He began to jog, oblivious to anyone on the sidewalk or in the street.

"It actually makes sense," he said to himself.

His jog turned into a run. Still thinking. Processing.

"But how?" he asked.

Now he was in a full-blown sprint, through the revolving doors of the bank. Hans was leaning against a wall over by the elevators, waiting for him so they could go up to Michael's office together.

He raced across the lobby to Hans, out of breath.

Hans, with a newspaper in one hand and a cup of coffee in the other, looked up and saw Frank running full speed for him. He jumped at the sight.

Frank grabbed him. Hans spilled the coffee and dropped the newspaper.

Frank begins to shake him. Hans recoils. Frank, talking excitedly, pulls him into a small conference room, shuts the door, and asks him one question. Hans, listening, processing. Now Hans grabs Frank. Shakes him. They are now shaking each other, both talking excitedly.

They run out of the bank at full speed. No patience or time to wait for a cab. Frank leads and Hans follows as they run to a small office on Market Street. The address was 12 Market Street, about four blocks from where they stood. It is the Western Union telegram office.

CHAPTER 99

Leigh went looking for Evvie and Kathryn and found them finishing up the dishes in the kitchen with Betty.

Betty was washing down the table and counters while Evvie washed and Kathryn dried.

"I'm waiting for a call from Frank. I'm going to go down to your dad's office for a bit and maybe grab lunch with him. He didn't want me to go alone and said he would call me to tell me what the plan is in terms of getting me to the office. Do you want to go?"

"Oh, thank you, Leigh!" said Evvie. "I'd love to, but I promised a friend from high school that I would meet her for coffee just around the corner from here."

"And I can't either," answered Kathryn. "I have to meet Mom at the grocery store and help her get the groceries home. She was going from her friend's home to the store, and I told her that I would just meet her over there. I'm sorry, Leigh. That would've been so much fun!"

"Promise us that we will try to do this again. Maybe in the next day or two?" asked Evvie. "We could get Mom and make it a girls' day out."

"That sounds wonderful!" said Leigh. "Let's plan on it. After all, I have to get used to this American food!"

# CHAPTER 100

Frank and Hans got to the Western Union telegram office and found themselves behind two customers.

They looked at each other, seeing if the other man had a badge or anything that resembled a law enforcement officer.

Nothing.

They both eye-rolled and smacked their foreheads at the same time. It took almost ten more minutes before a clerk freed up to help them.

Callie Laine, an attractive young woman with long dark hair and striking brown eyes, smiled as the two men approached and asked, "How can I help you gentlemen today?"

Frank took the lead.

"This is going to sound a little strange, but please listen and work with us. We are trying to do research regarding a telegram that went out last week from this office. There was probably more than one. Here are the details."

Callie looked at the date and time and said, "Are you with the police?"

Frank, wanting to keep things honest, said, "We are not part of the local police department here. My dad runs a detective agency here, and we both work for a government agency that protects our nation."

"Do you have some identification?" she asked.

"We don't have any on us right now. Please trust me that this is a matter of critical importance to the safety of our country."

She looked at both of them, looked back down at the dates again, and said, "OK. How can I help?"

Hans breathed a sigh of relief as Frank pressed on.

"We need to know who specifically sent this telegram."

"Did you know that some detective was in here a few days ago asking one of my co-workers about this?" asked Callie.

"No," said Frank. "Who was it?"

"I don't know," she replied. "I was off that day, and my coworker couldn't find the file on this particular date."

"But you do remember it?"

"I remember the date, because I was working on that date."

"OK, great," said Frank. "Can you pull a record of the telegram that was sent on that date with the time listed below?" "Sure. Just give me a minute, please." She disappeared into a backroom.

"What do you think?" asked Hans.

"Feels right," said Frank.

"Yes. Yes, it does," agreed Hans.

"It has to be right," said Frank. "Otherwise, we're back at square one."

Callie Laine was back with a medium sized cardboard box in her hands. She placed the box on the counter and began sifting through the many telegrams that took place that day.

"Did you say morning or afternoon?" she asked.

"Afternoon," the two men replied.

A few seconds later, she had found the telegram in question.

"So, what do you want to know?"

"We know the initials on the telegram say "E.F." "We're trying to determine who actually sent it. Is there a signature or anything like that?"

Callie peered at the signature.

"It looks like an "E-something Fischer?"

"Is it Erik? Erik Fischer?" asked Frank.

She looked more closely, then pulled out a magnifying glass.

Nope. It's definitely not "Erik."

"Can you tell what it does say?" asked Hans.

"I think so, but let me just make sure," she said.

After another moment, she nodded once and said, "Yeah, it's not Erik. It's Elizabeth."

# CHAPTER 101

Frank was already running out the door. Callie Laine handed the sheet to Hans and said that she had a backup copy in the storage room. Hans sprinted out the door after his friend.

"Frank! Wait! Wait!"

Frank stopped for a second, waiting for Hans.

"What did you learn in there?" asked Hans.

"Hans, I'll explain later. Listen very carefully. Call my dad right now. Have him send a car to my house right away. Tell him that it's Betty. The spy is Betty, not Erik. Betty. The name "Betty" is short for Elizabeth. He'll understand. But get a car to my house immediately. Go back in and ask Callie to use her phone. Hurry!"

There was a cab sitting at the corner. Frank made it to the cab, dove in, and started to tell the driver to race to 928 Hague Avenue when he saw that there was no driver. He jumped over the seat and landed in the driver's seat and took off. He heard a guy yelling from the corner, but he paid no attention.

He made it to Seventh Avenue, drove up Grand Avenue which hit Ramsey Street, which was the steepest street in the city. He floored the accelerator and passed cars on the way up, and avoided cars that were carefully coming down Ramsey. It was a full orchestra of horns blasting away as he avoided every taker.

## CHAPTER 102

Evvie and Kathryn said goodbye to Leigh, and each went in opposite directions once they hit the sidewalk.

Just as they said goodbye, the phone rang.

She walked into Michael's office and saw that it was the regular family line that was ringing.

"Hello, this is the Sweeney residence."

"Leigh?"

"Yes, this is Leigh. Is that you, Mr. Sweeney?"

"Yes, it's me. Are you all right?"

"Me? Um. Yes. I'm fine. Is everything OK? Did something happen to Frank?"

"No, no, everything is fine here. Is my wife there?"

"Uh, no. She was going to bring some food to a friend who was sick. And then she was going to meet Kathryn at the grocery store, and they were going to bring some groceries home together."

"I see. What about Evvie? Is Evvie there?"

"No, I'm sorry, but she was meeting one of her friends for coffee."

Silence.

"I think Betty is probably still here. She was working in the kitchen a few minutes ago."

"Are you all right, Mr. Sweeney?"

"Yes, yes. Everyone is fine over here. Leigh, I wonder if you could do me a favor."

"Of course. How can I help you?"

"Where in the house are you right now?"

"I'm actually standing in your study. I hope it's OK that I came in here to answer the phone. I heard it ring, and once I saw that it was the regular family line, I thought it would be all right if I picked it up. You see, Frank was going to call me and make arrangements to have someone pick me up so I could come down and see"-

"Yes, Leigh, he mentioned that to me. And, of course, you should always feel comfortable answering the phone at home."

"Thank you, Mr. Sweeney."

"You're most welcome. So, back to that favor that I was going to ask you," said Michael.

"Yes, sir. What can I do?"

"Leigh, listen to me carefully. This is what I want you to do. Are you facing the street right now?"

"Um. Pardon me?"

"Are you facing the street now as you are talking to me?"

"Yes, yes, I am."

"Good. Good. That means that you are probably standing at the side of my desk, because you had to move around a bit to grab the phone. Is that correct? Just answer yes or no."

Leigh, a bit hesitant: "Ah, Yes."

"Good, Leigh. You are doing fine. Just fine. Now, I want you to continue to stand where you are. Don't turn around."

"Pardon me?"

"I said, don't turn around. Just trust me and do what I say. All right, Leigh?"

"Yes, all right."

"Great. Now, don't walk around to the front of my desk. Don't turn around and don't make any sudden moves. Just casually reach over and open the right drawer on my desk. Just open the right drawer. As you open the top drawer, you will see a revolver in that drawer. Look down casually. Do you see it?"

"Yes."

"Excellent. You are doing great, Leigh. The gun is loaded. It requires a firm grip and will feel heavy to you. That's because it *is* heavy. Now keep the phone in your left hand, and as casually as you can, take the gun out with your right hand and put your finger on the trigger." Silence.

"Leigh, are you there?"

"I'm here," she said.

"Hold it firmly," Michael repeated.

"I am," she replied.

"Now, Leigh, I need to tell you something, and I need you to prepare yourself for what I am about to say. I need you to remain calm and listen very carefully to me."

"All right, I will."

"OK, here we go," said Michael. "There is a very decent chance that when you turn around and face the door that leads to my study, that Betty will be standing there. She may have a weapon on her. If it's not a gun, it will be a knife from the kitchen. Do not engage her unless she first tries something on you. If she does, by all means, do not hesitate to shoot her. Can you do that?"

Leigh let out a small gasp.

"What? Are you - Why would sh -?"

Leigh stopped in her tracks. She slowly turned around.

There was Elizabeth, "Betty" Fischer, a few feet away from her, holding a knife in her hand, starting to approach Leigh.

Leigh raised the revolver up and pointed it right at her.

"You? You? How could you? How could you do such a thing?"

Michael now: "Leigh, listen to me. Are you listening to me?"

"Yes, I'm still here."

"Good. Very good. You are doing great! Frank is on his way. He apparently stole a cab and" -

"He what?"

"Yeah, I'm sure he'll tell you that story. So he should be there in a couple of minutes. I also have a carload of detectives who were a few miles away that should be there in a few minutes as well."

She heard a car screaming down the street toward the house, the horn continually honking. It was a yellow cab that had pulled up right onto the sidewalk and slid across the front lawn to a stop. Frank jumped out and raced up the steps, threw open the door, almost ran right past the study, and skidded to a halt, looking in as he slid by.

"Are you OK?" he asked Leigh.

Betty Fischer had not moved.

"I'm all right."

He approached Betty, who still had the knife in her hand.

To Leigh: "I'm going to take her knife. If she resists, shoot her."

He took the knife from her without incident.

"How could you do something like this?" asked Frank. It was more of a statement than it was a question. "My family treated you as one of our own. You worked here, cooked here, ate here…"

"My loyalty is to the Fatherland. I am a German and a member of the Third Reich first and forever."

"You helped kill Leigh's father. His blood is on your hands," said Frank, raising his voice.

"This is war!" she exclaimed, her face contorted in a rage of hate.

"I have my orders, and I carry them out. It was a mission that I didn't ask for. But as a soldier, I don't get to pick and choose. I do what is required of me. And I helped accomplish the mission that I was assigned to. Your country is trying to destroy my country. Do you expect me to do anything less?"

"Yes, I do!" Frank shouted. "I expect you to recognize that your so-called leader is a madman who started this war and has killed hundreds of thousands of people. No. Millions of people by now. He was unprovoked. He was warned. Yet he plunged your country into a war which you will not win. And you blindly follow him? What's the matter with you? You already live in the greatest country in the world! And now you want our country to live according to the laws of a diabolical, crazy, self-deceived evil idiot?"

"He is my Fuhrer!" She shouted back at him.

There was a pause as they both stared at each other.

Fischer again: "Tell me, *Agent* Sweeney, how many of my countrymen did you kill when you helped this girl and her father escape two weeks ago?"

Frank, getting angrier by the minute, said, "Apparently, one less than I should have."

She ignored that comment. Still spewing hate, she muttered, "By the way, my husband is completely innocent. The fool has become soft and is more of an American than he is a German. But he unknowingly provided me with an excellent cover. He knew nothing of any of this."

Frank looked at Leigh, who still had the gun trained on Betty Fischer. "Leigh," he said.

She didn't move, still focused only on Fischer.

"You were listening in on my conversation with Frank's dad from one of the other phones, weren't you? That's why you were standing behind me. You could tell by his tone that something wasn't right."

Fischer was expressionless. "When he asked where everyone else was in the house, I knew that someone had figured it out. I had to get out of here in a hurry. Taking you with me would have given me more leverage to get out of the country."

"And then what? Would you have killed me once I was of no value to you?"

Fischer didn't answer, which was an answer in itself.

There was more silence as they both stared at each other, neither one backing down.

Leigh spoke next. "So, it was you who was in the mail truck and took Kerling to the train station?"

"Of course, it was me. My husband and I are about the same height. He has several uniforms to wear. It was a colder day, so I had a natural disguise with the uniform, hat, and sunglasses. I applied a fake mustache. The mail truck was only gone for about 15 minutes in the middle of a very busy mail day. No one even noticed. It was easy. You both should know that a uniform helps people remember just that. They see the uniform and not so much the face. Didn't they teach you that in the O.S.S.?" Frank said nothing.

"Oh yes, I know a lot about you and your family, Frank. And you too, Leigh."

"It's a shame that you won't be able to share that information with anyone," said Frank. "But I'll give you some credit, Betty. Or should I call you Elizabeth? You are an excellent actress."

"No," she corrected him. "I am an excellent spy for the

Fatherland. They were fortunate to have me located here. There was no one else placed in this area to do this kind of work. You see, with me helping to accomplish this mission, my government will negotiate a swap of some kind. I'm quite sure that we have Americans that we are holding in Germany right now that your government will want back. I expect to be back in Germany within the next 30 days."

"Oh, I wouldn't be holding my breath on that if I were you," came a voice from the hallway.

"Uncle George!" exclaimed Frank.

"Nice work, both of you!" said Parker.

A few minutes later, the front door swung open and in rushed Michael Sweeney. He reached out to shake his son's hand, looked at Leigh, and gave her a hug.

"You did great!" he said.

"Thank you for walking me through everything on the phone. You stalled the situation long enough for Frank to get here. Although he probably wrecked some of your shrubs and flowers."

Michael turned to see a taxi in his front yard. "Looks like someone is missing their cab, too. Spring is a long way off," he said. "We'll all have recovered by then."

He looked at Betty Fischer, who, oddly, had a hard time looking back at him.

"I'll have to talk to Maggie about her hiring practices."

The other detectives arrived and put Fischer in handcuffs.

As she was about to be led away, Elizabeth "Betty" Fischer turned to Leigh, who was being held by Frank, and said, "I accomplished my mission. I don't regret it. But my condolences on your father's death."

Leigh looked at her and said nothing.

Michael said to a couple of his detectives, "Please, remove this person from my home. Oh, and get someone out here to get the taxi back to… Frank, where was it?"

Frank winced, remembering what he had just done. "Oh yeah. Ugh, right by the Western Union telegram place on 12 Market Street."

Parker now: "Take her to the local F.B.I. office. They are expecting her."

"And men?" said Michael. "This one is off the books, so let's keep it quiet."

The two detectives nodded and walked Fischer out through the back door.

# CHAPTER 103

"Let's head back down to the office to wrap all of this up," said Michael. I'll get Hans and Flood and O'Brien to meet us there."

He and Parker sat in front, and Frank and Leigh were in the comfortable back seat of Michael's Desoto.

It now officially felt - and looked - like winter. The streets in St. Paul had a light dusting of snow on them, as did the trees that lined those same streets. Michael parked along Robert Street. He and Parker got out, followed by Frank and Leigh. There was a lightness to the mood, a sense of relief. It didn't hurt that they could hear Christmas music coming from somewhere down the block.

Michael, sensing the moment, grabbed his partner by the arm and hurried him along to the door.

"We'll go on ahead and make sure that there's coffee and tea ready for everyone," he called back to Frank.

Parker, confused, said, "Wha...?" Then quickly recovered. "Yep, we'll take care of that. Want to make sure that the coffee is ready and that the tea is..."

"Hot," finished Michael.

"Yep, that tea has to be hot. Right now. We need to make sure that the tea is ready - er hot. Hot tea. There's nothing worse than cold tea."

They were gone in a flash.

Frank and Leigh looked around, smiled for a minute, and found themselves looking at their shoes.

Frank shuffled the snow around with his right foot. Leigh was moving her hair back behind her.

They both looked at each other right at the same moment. There were a couple of snowflakes on Leigh's hair, and just then, one settled on her nose.

She yelped and giggled, shooing it away. Her brown eyes sparkled as they met Frank's.

He could only smile at her, lost in her beauty.

"You are the most beautiful girl that I have ever seen in my life."

She smiled shyly and broke eye contact with him.

"What's the matter, Leigh?"

She buried her head in his chest, and he got to hold her.

"At this moment, there is absolutely nothing wrong," she said. "This moment is absolutely perfect, Frank. I wish we could freeze time right now and have this moment forever."

"I know," he said. "You said it perfectly. Much better than I ever could."

"I know that you will be leaving tomorrow," she said into his bomber jacket.

"That's true," he said. "How did you know?"

"I heard Mr. Parker talking on the phone, ordering a plane for tomorrow. And he said there would be a few people on it. Once he said that, I knew that he wasn't going alone. That probably means that Dad is going, too."

She looked up at him, smiling and trying to be brave.

"I don't suppose that you know that you're coming with us for part of the trip?"

"What?" Leigh was stunned, but in a happy way.

"Yep," said Frank. "I asked Uncle George, and he said that because of all that has happened, he made an executive decision. We're going to a research air base in Ohio. Uncle George is finished with taking any chances. Anyone who wants to debrief your dad is going to have to come to him. He'll be untouchable on that base. And he is going to have two rooms in his apartment on the base so that he can have a guest come and visit once in a while. You know anyone that might want to visit him occasionally, with me being gone and all?"

Leigh raised up on her toes and kissed him. They hugged, both not saying anything.

"Thank you, Frank."

"It's the least that I could do, Miss Conway. I want you to be happy."

"I am. I could never have thought that I could ever be this happy!"

"Leigh," Frank said quietly.

"Yes, Frank?"

He found himself looking at his shoes again.

It was her turn now. She took his chin in her hands and gently raised it so that his eyes would meet hers.

"Will you really wait for me? Are you sure?" He looked away again. "After all," he continued, "No one really knows how long this thing is going to drag on for, and"-

She put her finger to his lips, which made him stop.

"Mr. Sweeney, are you backing out?"

"What? What are you talking about? No! I'm not backing out!"

"Because if you are," said Leigh, "I'd like to know right now."

Frank looked at her, incredulous. "Leigh, what are you talking about?"

She began to smile. "Just wanted to be sure."

"You!" he exclaimed.

She was laughing now. "Why, Mr. Sweeney, I do believe that you're blushing!"

He held her close, looked her in the eyes, and softly said, "I love you, Leigh Conway."

"And I love you, Frank Sweeney."

They shared a kiss and held each other for a long moment.

Suddenly, Frank straightened up. "They're all waiting for us! We need to get up there!"

Leigh gasped. "Hurry!" she said. Then: "Stop! Lipstick!"

"You already have it on!" said Frank, taking her by the hand. "Come on. We have to"-

"No, Frank! You!"

"Me?"

"You! Lipstick! You have lipstick on you!"

"Me? How could I have…Oh! Yeah. Take my handkerchief. Hurry!"

# CHAPTER 104

Two minutes later, they tried not to burst through the doors, but did a poor job doing so.

Michael, George, Hans, Nick Flood, Pat O'Brien, and Edwin Conway were sitting in the conference room. As they came in, all of the men suddenly found themselves commenting about how good the coffee was, and what a beautiful view Michael's conference room had. Only Hans was looking at Frank, eyebrows arched and nodding his approval. Frank gave him the "knock it off" look, but Hans was having none of it.

And Leigh? It was her turn to blush.

Michael called the meeting to order and handed things over to George Parker.

"First, on behalf of the government of the United States, thank you for all that you have done to assist us on this mission. It was essential, and frankly, it took a tremendous amount of ingenuity to make it all happen."

He turned to Michael, shook his hand, and said, "Thank you, partner."

"Would do it again in a heartbeat, Georgie."

They both smiled. Then Michael said, "But let's not do it again. I don't think that I have too many of these missions left in me." That brought a laugh from the room.

George turned to Flood and O'Brien and asked for an update.

O'Brien started. "We all went back to the Western Union and had Callie Laine dig through her records. We found several more telegrams from Betty Fischer to Leiner and vice versa."

Flood joined in: "They were trying to speak in code, but it was obvious what they were attempting to do. Fischer told Leiner where to have them stay, got them the Sweeney's address, promised that she would have pictures of Dr. Conway, Leigh, Frank even of you, boss."

"It all happened right under our noses," observed Michael. "I need to pay more attention to what's going on in my own home."

"No one could have seen this coming, Dad," said Frank. "The odds of someone like that coming into our home are astronomical. What we don't know is whether her getting a job with us is coincidental or intentional."

George spoke up: "I think it was intentional. But the F.B.I. will grill her and see if they can get her to talk. That said, we'll probably never know for certain. I think it's worth warning other people of influence to double-check the hired help. If it makes you feel any better, this Leiner character was a gardener for a couple of U.S. Congressmen."

That brought about some surprised expressions and a couple of exclamations of "You're kidding!"

"This sort of thing could be more widespread than we realize," said Frank.

"What about her husband?" asked Hans.

"He's in the F.B.I.'s hands as well," replied Parker. "I tend to agree with Flooder and O.B. as far as their assessment of him. But the Bureau will have to figure that out."

"Frank figured it out," said Hans. "He asked me if I ever heard either Leiner or Kerling refer to Fischer in the masculine."

"We just all assumed that it was a "he," said Frank. "That was our mistake."

There was a knock on the door and Suzie stuck her head in and looked at Parker, giving him a quick nod with a smile.

Parker got up and said, "I'd like you all to meet someone who we all owe a tremendous debt of gratitude to."

He left the table, opened the door to the lobby, and motioned the guest to come in.

He was followed back into the conference room by a pretty, petite blond, five foot nothing with bright blue eyes and a shy smile on her face.

"Everyone, I'd like you to meet my little sister, Connie Parker. Or "Maid Connie," as she was known to our assassin." Everyone stood up and applauded upon her introduction.

"Take a bow, Joe," said her older brother.

"Joe?" asked Leigh.

"She's always been a tomboy," explained George. "One heck of a softball player."

Edwin Conway made a beeline for her and gave her a hug.

"Thank you for saving my life, young lady."

"It was my honor, sir," she said.

Everyone took their turn thanking Connie for her work in saving Dr. Conway's life.

"I have to tell you that Connie came up with all of the stall tactics on her own," said George. "There was just no way that she was going to allow Kerling to have a shot at Dr. Conway."

He turned to Connie and said, "All of this is classified, so no one may ever know what you did the other day. But the people in this room all know, and I hope that is enough for you. I am so proud of you, little sister!"

"We're all proud of you, Connie!" said Michael.

"Thank you all," she replied. "But I believe Dr. Conway had the toughest assignment of all of us. He had to sit still and truly trust the rest of the people who had a role in this to actually execute their duties. That's a lot of people to trust, Doctor!"

Edwin nodded and said, "If I can't trust my American friends by now, then there is something seriously wrong with me."

"It didn't hurt that all of us are Irish!" said Connie.

"Seriously, though, we are thankful that you came here to help our country defeat our common enemies," continued Connie. "Our freedom is at stake, and I know that we are all united in our efforts to maintain our liberty."

With that, Connie made her way out of the room. She would go back to her day job, teaching school. And no one would ever hear of her role that day.

# C H A P T E R   1 0 5

## *The Next Morning*

Edwin said his goodbyes to Hans, Flood and O'Brien. He was tired of staying in the small bedroom that was located off of Michael's office at the bank.

His new place of employment would be at Wright Field outside of Dayton, Ohio.

Michael had arranged for a police uniform to be brought to the office. Dr. Edwin Conway would leave Minnesota dressed as one of St. Paul's finest.

As he was getting ready to leave, he turned to his new friend and thanked him.

"Let's hope the next time that we see each other, it will be in a time of peace and gratitude for the defeat of America's enemies," he told Michael.

"I couldn't have said it better than that," agreed Michael. "And Edwin, I want you to know that we will treat Leigh as our own."

"Thank you, my friend. That gives me such peace to hear you say that."

He leaned in and said quietly, "The way things appear to be going, I suspect you and I will have a lot of time after the war to get to know one another even better."

Michael smiled at him and said, "Nothing would make me happier. Oh! I almost forgot!" He reached into his desk and brought out a small package.

'It's a pipe with a whole month's worth of tobacco for you."

Edwin looked at it, smiled broadly, and said, "Thank you, my friend. I look forward to the next time that we can enjoy our pipes together!"

The flight to Wright Field went quickly. There was no fanfare upon landing. Edwin would be working under an alias, which made sense. He was shown his quarters, and he would be quite busy in the weeks and months to come. The Americans were keen on learning more about jet propulsion, and Edwin Conway would be showing them the way. Other than a name change - he would be known as Dr. Edwin Chambers while he was at the base - it was the perfect scenario for him: a lab for research and a willing audience that he knew would use the technology for good.

Parker, Frank, and Leigh said their goodbyes.

Leigh had offered to stay with him on the base, much like they had done in Germany. Edwin would not hear of it.

"I am going to be so busy down here that I won't see you anyway. Besides, it's time for you to spread your wings. You have a wonderful family in St. Paul who loves you and wants you to stay. And there is a young man there who wants you to get to know his family better. This is the right thing for all of us, lassie."

"All right, Dad. You're right. I'll see you in a month, though, OK?"

"It's a date!" he said.

Parker, Frank, and Leigh landed later that evening at Holman Field in St. Paul. It had been a long day.

Frank and Parker would leave again the next morning. Hans had already headed back to Milwaukee for another day before he would meet them in D.C.

Back at the Sweeney residence, they sat in Michael's office. Michael and George were having a nightcap. Frank and Leigh opted for a couple of cups of hot cocoa.

Michael had a couple of copies of the St. Paul Pioneer Press, the local newspaper. The headlines were, "Nazi Saboteurs Caught." The subheadline read, "F.B.I. Thwarts Plan to Disrupt War Effort."

Parker glanced at the headlines and said, "Here comes the Bureau's P.R. machine."

Then: "I talked to Wild Bill."

"Is Director Donovan back in the country?" asked Frank.

"He is. The president wants to put the saboteurs on trial with a military tribunal and bypass the court system. He is adamant about doing it that way."

Michael, lighting his pipe, said, "He wants this done quickly to put the country at ease. He also wants to send a message to the Nazis about not trying this again."

"You belong in D.C., partner," said George. "You are reading the political winds very accurately." George had had enough of his pipe and put it out.

"The word back there is that Hoover is trying to convince Roosevelt to award him the Medal of Honor for breaking the case."

That brought a chuckle from everyone except Leigh, who looked a bit bewildered.

Frank said, "Don't worry, Leigh. He's not someone that you and I will ever have to think about working for."

"The saboteurs will be dead within a couple of months," said George. "Dasch and Burger might get a break and get life sentences, but the others will end up in the chair. Dasch expected to be treated like a hero, and truth be told, can you imagine the havoc that they could have wreaked if he hadn't spilled the beans?"

"There's no way that our country is prepared for that kind of sabotage," said Michael. "They would have had a lot of success before they would be caught."

"Hence the need to make examples of them," replied George.

No one said anything for a few moments, each thinking through what Parker had just said.

"Oh, one other interesting thing: No one can find this Kappe guy. He might already be back in Germany. And Leiner... there's been no consensus yet as to what to do with him."

Everyone just nodded and took it all in.

After a few moments of silence, Parker slapped his knees and said, "Well, I need to call it a night. We have a morning flight back to D.C."

"What time do you want me at the airport, Uncle George?" asked Frank.

"Wheels up at 9:00 AM, lad."

Everyone stood to say goodbye.

"Georgie, it was good to be with you again. Don't be a stranger. And take care of my boy."

"Roger that, partner."

The two men shook hands.

Leigh came up and hugged him. "Thank you, Mr. Parker. You gave my dad and me our lives back."

"It was Frank's plan that did it, not mine," he said. "But I sure am glad that it all worked out. I wouldn't even have bothered to fly back to D.C. if something had gone wrong. I would have been fired. Or worse."

He smiled at Leigh and said, "You'll like it here, Leigh. St. Paul, I mean. It's a great place to live. And the people are OK, too. But watch out for good-looking young men who work for the O.S.S."

Frank chuckled, shook his godfather's hand, and said, "I'll see you before 9:00 AM."

After Parker had left, Michael announced that he was going to bed. Maggie and the girls were fast asleep, so he reminded Frank and Leigh to be extra quiet.

"We're going up in a minute, Dad," said Frank.

"I suggest we leave here around 8:15 AM tomorrow morning, son. That should get you to the airport in plenty of time. Leigh, would you like to go with?" "Oh, would that be OK if I did?"

"Of course," replied Michael.

"Thank you, Mr. Sweeney. I'll be ready to go at 8:15 AM."

Frank and Leigh had a few minutes to themselves before going their separate ways to sleep.

They talked. They talked about the future. They shared their hopes, their dreams, and their fears. They talked about Leigh's mom, Hannah, who had passed away a few years earlier. And Frank's brother Jack.

And then they prayed together. For the war. For America. For Ireland. For the Allied leaders. They prayed for peace, and for protection. They prayed for greater faith in the days ahead. They even prayed about their relationship as a young couple.

Frank's parting the next day was difficult. Everyone got up for an early breakfast. Maggie and the girls fought back tears as they said their goodbyes. Frank told them that he was far safer in his role in the O.S.S.

than he would be storming a beach or engaging in battles thousands of feet in the air. They drew some solace from that, but not much. And truth be told, Frank wasn't altogether sure that he was all that much safer as he had purported. As a matter of fact, deep down, he knew that he wouldn't be.

At the airport, he shook hands with his dad, who told him to keep his head down. With that, Michael told Leigh that he would wait in the car for her.

Frank and Leigh walked to the hangar. It was a quick goodbye.

"I'll call you and write as often as I can," he told her.

"But where can I write to you?" asked Leigh.

"I'll get you an address once I get settled in D.C."

She fought back tears and was trying to be strong for him.

"I love you, Leigh Conway. Wait for me."

"I love you, Frank Sweeney. And I will wait for you."

They kissed one more time, and he held her for a long minute.

Then a voice called, "Time to go, Frank. Goodbye, Leigh." It was Parker.

She stepped away. She forced a smile and waved to George.

She looked at Frank once more and started to turn around.

He grabbed her, and they embraced one last time.

"Goodbye, Darling. I love you," he whispered.

"Please be careful, Frank. Promise me you will be careful."

"Of course, I will. I'll be thinking only of you."

With that, he turned around and walked to the plane, and she walked out of the hangar to Michael's car.

It was just Parker and Frank on the plane. His godfather waited until they were up in the air before he began to talk to Frank.

"We are invading North Africa in a few days. We are finally going on offense. I couldn't say anything before for obvious reasons. Eisenhower will oversee it. We'll get a full briefing when we land. There may be an assignment coming your way, but I won't know until I talk to Wild Bill. How's your French?" "Bonjour," said Frank.

"Buckle up, my boy."

# ACKNOWLEDGEMENTS

Part of the story for this book is true and based on historical facts. If any of said facts are inaccurate or proven to be wrong, that is the responsibility of the author and him alone.

The Nazis did park two submarines off Long Island and south of Jacksonville. But this occurred in June of 1942, not November. I moved the dates to coordinate with the ending of my first book, Operation Grab Bag.

All of the eight saboteurs were real, as were Leiner, Kappe, and Pastor Krepper. Krepper is worth reading more about. How a man of the cloth could embrace and support the Third Reich is a true head shaker. One won't have to dig too deep into his life to conclude that he and his theology were, shall we say, "messed up."

The eight saboteurs were caught within a few days of their arrival, thanks to Mr. Dasch, who, for reasons still unclear, went directly to the F.B.I. in Washington, D.C. As the book states, he was ignored by the Bureau in New York, and D.M. Ladd (another real character) did become his main contact in Washington. Dasch told many conflicting stories, and it is still difficult to ascertain what was real and what wasn't. But again, we will never know if he became afraid after running into Coast Guardsman Cullen or if his plan was to surrender all along. He certainly claimed the latter.

Regardless, he and Burger had their death penalties commuted and ended up receiving life sentences. The other six saboteurs were, in fact, executed by the electric chair within weeks of their arrests. Some reports claimed that Neubauer's and Haupt's parents were also initially sentenced to the chair, but their sentences were eventually commuted as well. F.D.R. wanted to show no mercy to any of these people and clearly wanted to send a strong message to anyone else who was considering such actions. That's why he insisted that it be a military trial and not a civilian one. Truman was responsible for commuting Dasch's and Burger's life sentences. They were deported after the war and returned to Germany with the express order to never again step foot into the U.S. While back in Germany; they were heckled and generally treated as traitors for the rest of their lives.

Helmut Leiner was charged with Treason, and the government was seeking the death penalty. He was found not guilty by a single judge based on a technicality. However, he was immediately rearrested and charged with trading with the enemy. He pled guilty and was sentenced to 18 years in prison.

Carl Krepper, the pastor, was convicted of lesser charges and served 12 years in prison. He died in obscurity many years later in a nursing home in Massachusetts.

Walter Kappe actually managed the mission from Germany and apparently did not come to the U.S. as part of the operation. There is limited information about him after the failure of Pastorius. His life before Pastorius is accurately portrayed in the book. He "fell in action at the front" in 1944.

Canaris ended up turning on Hitler and secretly worked to have him eliminated. He and Dietrich Bonhoeffer, the well-known pastor and theologian, were imprisoned together in the same concentration camp and hanged together on the same day in April of 1945, mere days before Hitler killed himself. Both men are definitely worth reading more about. Bonhoeffer's books are still used and quoted today in Christian circles. He truly was a remarkable man of faith.

To my personal horror, the stories about the massacres in Czechoslovakia were told accurately. Rheinhard Heinrich, the "Butcher of Prague," was, unfortunately, a very real monster who was deserving of his nickname.

J. Edgar Hoover did try to spin this story as "The F.B.I. always getting their man." According to some reports, he lobbied Roosevelt for The Medal of Honor and, at least initially, did not divulge the fact that Dasch had proactively surrendered to the F.B.I. Thankfully, his campaign to be given the M.O.H. failed. Awarding him said medal would have been an insult to those heroes who earned it through sacrificing their lives or putting their lives in peril in taking out the enemy and/or saving their fellow soldiers.

Regardless of Dasch's motive for turning himself in, there can be no argument that had the mission proceeded, there would have been massive damage to the infrastructure of the war effort.

The country and the F.BI. were woefully unprepared for any kind of attack on our soil. The Germans did have the blueprints and maps of several bridges, hydroelectric plants, and munitions factories in the northeast. The targets listed in the book were accurate. Had they been even remotely successful, it's not a stretch to think that the war could have had a different outcome. At a minimum, it almost certainly would have been extended. And it's a safe bet that Hitler would have continued to order more and more saboteurs into the country.

On a side note, one of Donovan's standard O.S.S. domestic training missions involved simulating attacks on many of these same targets. This included not telling anyone guarding the bridges and factories of said training missions. The O.S.S. found the efforts to protect these entities woefully inadequate and reported their findings to the various heads of the departments that were responsible for security. The response? The O.S.S. was "just showboating." Turf wars have been around for decades.

All of the stories related to St. Paul during the 1930s and 1940s are true. The crime, main characters, and history are accurate. In doing my research, I fell in love with Old St. Paul, so much so that most of the story ended up taking place there. There are just so many interesting facts and tidbits about the city that I could have written a whole book on them alone.

It's also true that Minnesota housed German P.O.W. camps, mostly made up of German airmen. All of the descriptions in the book are accurate as they relate to these camps.

The stories surrounding Michael Sweeney and the Sweeney Detective Bureau are also true. By all accounts, Michael Sweeney was a remarkable man. Understated, with his ego in check. And certainly not a man to mess with.

The main plot - that the Germans had two of the eight saboteurs try to assassinate Edwin Conway - is totally fictitious because Conway is a fictitious character, as are several of the Americans in the story.

Speaking of that, Connie Parker was a real person, although the actions she took in the book are not. She was a remarkable woman who is missed every single day. My description of her will never do her justice. She touched many lives, and she has left a wonderful legacy. We all love and miss you, Joe.

I am a student of W.W. II history and believe that there are so many stories that need to be told. There are too many heroes to count, from several different countries, mind you. My aim is to tell as many of these stories as possible so that the generations that come behind mine will remember, revere, and respect The Greatest Generation.

Ronald Reagan said, "Freedom is never more than one generation away from extinction." We all need to do our part. We are in a relay race of sorts, and someone completed their heat and passed the baton to us. May we be found faithful to not only have run the race but ensure that we are passing the baton on to another generation of freedom-loving, God-Honoring Americans. Another good reminder for those of us who live in the greatest country in the world: "To whom much is given, much is required." (Luke 12:48)

Last, one tangible way that the reader can help in this cause is to check out organizations like Honor Flights and The Wounded Warrior Project. Both entities do tangible work to help veterans from all of the wars of the past 80-plus years.

The proceeds from this book will go to both of these fine organizations. Thank you.

Read on for excerpts from my next book, in the Frank Sweeney series, tentatively titled, "Operation Torch."

# EXCERPT FROM "OPERATION TORCH"

CHAPTER 1

General George C. Marshall, 60 years old and a lifelong soldier, who also just happened to be the Army Armed Forces Chief of Staff, surveyed his audience. He had worked very hard over the last several months to convince Congress to extend The Selected Services Act, from one year to 2 ½ years. The original bill itself, which had passed just nine months earlier, was called the Burke-Wadsworth Act. It made men between the ages of 21 and 35 register to be drafted. It also called for these men to serve 12 months.

Marshall wanted - "desperately needed" would be more accurate - to extend the mandatory service to a minimum of two years.

Few people realized, and fewer people seemed to care, that the United States Army throughout most of the 1930's was the 19th largest Army in the world. Even countries like Portugal had larger armies than the U.S. There was no appetite on the part of Americans to participate in another war. And there certainly wasn't any money to make it happen. The Great Depression was still raging on. None of the "New Deal" efforts that President Roosevelt had implemented helped or made any significant difference to the U.S. economy, especially the unemployment rate, which averaged well over 15% for the entire decade.

Marshall, a career soldier and one of the most honest and straightforward men that the country would ever produce, made himself be totally apolitical. He was unapologetically blunt, when need be, even telling F.D.R. himself in plain language that the president was wrong on certain military issues.

He had to push the president to recognize that, beginning in October, these same men who had been drafted would exit, having done their one-year stint. There were even signs posted around military outlets that proclaimed, "OHIO," which stood for "Over the Hill In October."

The world was moving faster and faster toward another world war. Just two months earlier, Germany had invaded Russia. The world was watching the British getting pummeled in the London bombings; the Nazis had taken over France in mere weeks, and no one doubted that Hitler would continue to try to conquer any country that tried to stand in his way.

Churchill and the Brits were pressing their cousins to help them. F.D.R. had played it quite conservatively, helping here and there with some weaponry and a very limited number of pilots behind the scenes.

Marshall had seen the writing on the wall. He had to have Congress approve the 2 ½ year commitment. But he was facing an uphill battle. Many Americans had embraced isolationism. The politicians knew this and heard it from their own constituents when they were back in their home districts. The Senate would support the two years, seeing as though most of them weren't up for re-election in 1942. The problem was the House. The votes just weren't there.

Many democrats opposed the extension, and a good number of Republicans opposed it as well. Several Republicans just flat-out refused to vote for anything that Roosevelt wanted.

The dinner at the Army-Navy Club was critical to Marshall trying to garner the votes needed. The audience was forty Republican Congressmen.

After a dinner that included daiquiris and steak, Marshall rose to speak. He threw facts at the Congressmen. They listened politely. A discussion ensued.

The evening went on until 2:00 AM, when one of the Republicans said, "You make a strong case, but I will not go along with this. We will simultaneously support Mr. Roosevelt and sign our own death warrants politically."

Marshall showed a rare emotion that almost never came out: anger.

"So, you're going to let plain hatred of the personality dictate to you to do something that you recognize is very harmful to the interests of our country?"

That statement began to bring people around. Over the coming days, Marshall began to garner more support in the House.

On August 12, Sam Rayburn, the Speaker of the House, called the House into session, and so began an hours long marathon on the extension, including long speeches and debates. The galleries were full. Most of the attendees were service men and a good number of women that represented "Mothers for America," an organization that opposed the draft and certainly opposed an extension of said draft.

James Wadsworth, a Republican congressman from New York and the co-author of the original bill to impose a draft, worked the floor during the entire day, twisting arms and calling in favors from his fellow Republicans in an effort to harvest enough "yays." It was going to be an extremely close vote. After much debate and even more speeches, Speaker Rayburn called for a vote.

Majority Leader John McCormick pulled a last-minute rabbit out of the hat and got three of his fellow Democrats to change their votes from "abstain" to "Yay."

All of the votes were tallied on a piece of paper, and that paper was handed to Rayburn. Just before Rayburn was going to recite the final tallies, Andrew Somers, a New York Democrat, rose and stated that he was changing his vote from "Yay" to "Nay." This was permissible under house rules because the Speaker of the House had yet to formally announce the results.

Rayburn, knowing that with Somers' switch, the vote was now at 203-202 in favor of the extension, was now dealing with chaos on the floor. For reasons that could never be explained, he recognized the House Minority Deputy whip, Dewey Jackson Short, Congressman from Galena, Missouri. Short, in another head shaker, purportedly asked for a recapitulation - a recounting of the vote- and not for *reconsideration,* which would have opened the floor up for more discussion and allowed for members to change their votes.

Rayburn, who knew *all* of the House rules, immediately granted the recapitulation, which only meant that each member had to declare how they had originally voted, so that there could be certainty that the clerk had properly recorded each vote accurately. Recapitulation offered no room for anyone to change their vote.

Immediately upon a summary from the clerk that indeed the votes were accurate, Rayburn's gavel came swiftly down and he announced that the votes stood as recorded and therefore the bill had passed.

Now, there was total bedlam on the House floor, with cheers coming from the "Yays" and screams of a travesty coming from the "Nays." Rayburn quickly exited the House chambers. No one ever really could determine if Congressman Short had asked for "Recapitulation" or "Reconsideration." Regardless, there was no doubt as to which word Speaker Rayburn heard or, perhaps, chose to hear.

So, by a majority of 1 vote, America was able to keep the men who had been drafted nine months earlier in the respective services. And, thanks to the immediate implementation of the new draft, when Pearl Harbor was attacked less than four months later, General Marshall had about 1.5 million men under his command. This was still a far cry from what he would need to fight two different wars on two different continents with two different enemies.

C H A P T E R   2

General Dwight Eisenhower sat puffing on another cigarette. It was not quite noon, and he was already halfway through his second pack. He was not in the best of moods, but who could blame him? He was learning the art of politics, and he was not enjoying this particular lesson on this particular day in this particular part of the world.

The irony of using Gibraltar as his temporary home base was not lost on him. Gibraltar's history was long and legendary. Long fought over by the Brits and the Spanish, it had been in England's hands since the Treaty of Utrecht was signed in 1713. One of the reasons that there had been so many battles over this small area of the world is that whoever controlled Gibraltar controlled the entrance to and exit from the Mediterranean Sea and a whole lot of trade. And transportation lanes. At their narrowest point, the Straits of Gibraltar represented a 7.7 nautical mile separation between Europe and Africa. It was hard to overemphasize how strategic the area was as it related to this war.

His makeshift workplace was wanting but functional. He had taken over a reasonably sized home that had a couple of bedrooms, a small living room, and an even smaller kitchen. The larger of the two bedrooms was converted into an office. Mercifully, he had a fan that at least circulated some air in the stuffy, smoke-filled room. The walls were covered with maps and handwritten notes that Ike had made over the last couple of weeks. He had many strengths, not the least of which was his ability

359

to plan strategically. Logistics were key in any campaign, and no one understood this better - and had proven it - than Eisenhower. From here, he planned the Allies' first meaningful assault on the German army. His chief opponent was a sharp German General named Erwin Rommel. Known as the "Desert Fox," Rommel was extremely popular with his men, and many felt that he was Hitler's top General in this war.

Today was really the first day that he had time to process everything that had occurred over the last nine months. There was the Arcadia conference with the British in Washington, D.C. last winter, which kicked off a joint discussion around the Allies' first real offensive effort in the European theatre. It was a strategic session, and not without emotion. The Americans were trying to catch up to the Brits in terms of quickly learning the Germans' strategies, including their strengths, their military leadership, and where they were most vulnerable. The conference felt like the older brother trying to patiently coach his younger sibling on what he had already experienced on the field, with the younger brother wanting to forego the lesson and get into the game so he could experience it all for himself.

The U.S. contingency pushed for invading somewhere on the continent. That meant France, which had fallen two years earlier. The **Nazis** had control of the north and western portions of the country, and the Italians had a small portion of the southeast. The remaining unoccupied portion of the south, known as the zone libre, was occupied by the Vichy, the controversial French government. Ike knew that it was only a matter of time before this last bastion of French influence, no matter how weak and ineffective that it was, would officially "fall" to the Nazis.

At the same time, Stalin had been pushing Roosevelt and Churchill to establish a second front somewhere to put some real pressure on the Axis. Uncle Joe had his hands full holding off the Nazi efforts in Russia, and he was looking for some much-needed help. Thus, there was a need for some sort of offense, somewhere. Anywhere.

The Brits had politely but firmly disagreed with the Yanks on France and wanted the first offensive to begin in Northern Africa. Over many days of discussions, it became clear that North Africa would be the first place that the Allies took the war to the Axis.

Ike sighed. "That's how *we* got here. But how did *I* get here?" He shook his head and marveled at his meteoric rise. Less than three years ago, he was a Lieutenant Colonel, for goodness' sake. Even though he had never seen combat in the Great War, here he was. He could only imagine the second-guessing that went on when he was named as the supreme commander for this invasion. His biggest contribution in his career? He was a tank training commander. Stateside.

Yet, he knew that he had been handpicked for this role, and he knew that this was just the beginning. Only a few weeks earlier, General George Marshall had named Eisenhower supreme commander of the North Africa mission. Over the last several years, General Marshall had shepherded him, mentored him, and coached him. He owed the General a great deal. Ike knew that if the North Africa campaign went well, there was a reasonable - all right, likely - chance that he would be named Supreme Commander for the entire European theatre.

Most surprisingly, the Brits had agreed in full with Marshall's decision to name Eisenhower as supreme commander over this invasion. Of course, Churchill couldn't help but poke his nose into the planning. That was just his way. Ike was learning to manage him. And for all of the old man's bluster, there was no question about his commitment to defeating Hitler. For all of his meddling, Churchill supported Ike privately and in public.

About the only positive that Churchill had as the war began was that he was following the incredibly naïve and incompetent Neville Chamberlain. The English had rallied around Sir Winston, and his leadership and insistence on never surrendering and total victory resonated with the citizens, most of whom had developed a healthy hatred for the Nazis. After all, the bombings of London that took place were unprecedented in that they targeted the civilians of London and not the military.

Ike would need to do some self-talking to get through this initial mission. It was clear that he had been overruled by Churchill with regard to where to start the offensive. And that meant that the British military leadership had gone around him to plead their case directly to Sir Winston. And, worse than that, Churchill had then lobbied Roosevelt, who capitulated. By the time it got to Ike, the unanimous proposal was to start with an "easier" mission - was there such a thing? - And begin a more modest attack on North Africa. After taking Africa, the allies would make their way to Sicily and then Italy. From there, France would likely be the next target. And, if all of this worked, they would finally get a crack at entering Germany and taking the war directly to Hitler. A tall order, to be sure.

If he was honest with himself, Ike would admit that starting in North Africa was probably the most prudent decision. However, to add insult to injury, he was even challenged by his Combined Joint Chiefs of Staff as to *where* in North Africa they should attack. He favored three eastern landings, which allowed for Oran, Algiers, and Bône. Focusing on these three areas would allow for a relatively quick capture of Tunis. Plus, the rough waters in the Atlantic worried him, so he would rather not try to land in Morocco.

But the aforementioned Joint Chiefs brought up another point: Should neutral Spain enter the war and support the Axis, this would very likely result in the closing of the Straits of Gibraltar, effectively cutting off the Allied landing force and jeopardizing the strategic shipping lanes. Hence their "preference" for Morocco and not Bône.

Eisenhower weighed the options. Landing in Casablanca instead of Bône would also mean that it would take a lot more time to get the Allied troops to Tunis. This delay ensured that the Germans would have more time to enhance their positions in Tunisia and prepare a defense for the inevitable fight that would come there.

The last thought that was rolling around in his head was the need for a win - any win. Good news in Europe was hard to come by since they officially entered the war last December.

His thoughts drifted to his former boss, one General Douglas MacArthur. They didn't get along very well when Ike had served as the General's aide in the Philippines before the war. Ike had tried repeatedly to get MacArthur to prepare for an eventual invasion there, but MacArthur ignored him. Worse, Ike had become a convenient scapegoat for his boss. Once, when MacArthur, whose ego was unmatched, had proposed to the Philippine President that the Armed Forces of the country hold a huge parade to show their strength, President Quezon was incensed and insisted that Macarthur forego such a terrible idea. He wanted the troops to keep training. MacArthur, seeing how adamant (and angry) the President was, merely said, "It was Ike's idea." Ike had heard every word.

Although the public wasn't aware of this, it was no secret among those closely engaged in the war strategy that MacArthur and Roosevelt didn't like one another. F.D.R. called MacArthur "The most dangerous man in America." Not to be outdone, MacArthur told his aides that Roosevelt "Was incapable of telling the truth when a lie would suffice."

Between fighting the Japanese and trying to work with the President, "Dugout Doug," as some of his men had come to call him since he hurriedly left the Philippines, had his hands full over there. What good news had come from the war in the Pacific was mostly due to the Navy, and specifically the cunning and courage of Admiral Chester Nimitz. There were two victories that he had a major hand in.

Jimmy Doolittle had pulled off a miracle on April 18th, when he and 79 airmen took off from the U.S.S. Hornet and U.S.S. Enterprise aircraft carriers in the Pacific in bombers - bombers! Nothing like this had ever even been attempted before. They dropped their load on Tokyo and tried to hightail it to China. Most of the planes ran out of gas and had to crash land in China, well short of their targeted landing spots. One crew even had to land in Russia.

Regardless, Doolittle's Raiders struck fear in Japan and struck hope in America. The increase in morale in the U.S. could not be overstated. While the actual damage to Japan was somewhat minimal - 50 dead and 400 injured - it was a huge moral victory for the U.S. The daring plan told the American people that Japan was vulnerable and that good would indeed prevail over evil.

Doolittle's ruthless strike was followed up a couple of months later with a decisive naval and air victory at the Battle of Midway. The Japanese lost four aircraft carriers in that battle.

While victory was still far from assured in the Pacific theatre, no one could argue that real progress hadn't been made. Less than a year after Pearl Harbor, the Americans had the Japanese on the defensive.

Ike was thankful for the success of his counterparts over there. After all, America had to win two wars on two different fronts, and that would always be the mission. Privately, he was almost as grateful that he wasn't reporting to MacArthur any longer.

He knew that Europe needed a victory. Certainly, the troops needed a victory. Roosevelt needed a victory. Maybe the person who needed it more than anyone was Churchill. No matter how brilliant and how courageous their leader was, the London bombings were taking their toll on morale in England. While the Brits were angry and were willing to do whatever it took to stop the Jerrys, a successful offensive would restore their resolve and reassure them that victory was not only possible, but imminent.

He brought himself back to the task at hand. In the end, Eisenhower knew that he would need to go with the Joint Chiefs' recommendation. "Given everything, it's the right call," he told himself.

But that didn't make it any easier to stomach. Much like Lincoln, he would have to master his emotions and check his ego at the door. "It might be helpful if a few others would do the same," he said to no one in particular. But he also knew that that was not going to happen any time soon. Between Churchill, Roosevelt, and Stalin, all of the oxygen was always sucked out of the room. Add in the likes of Montgomery and Patton, and you had people downright suffocating left and right.

"Theoretically, I could have passed on this job," he mused. Then, after a couple of seconds: "No. There was no way that I could have done that. If there was someone better, they would have found him and given the job to him. I'm it. I'm in it all the way. We must succeed at any cost."

With that, he went back to planning the first major offensive of the war. And lit up yet another cigarette.